A DETECTIVE INSPECTC

HEAVY IS THE CROWN

JACK GATLAND

Published by Hooded Man Media.

First Edition: April 2022

PRAISE FOR JACK GATLAND

'This is one of those books that will keep you up past your bedtime, as each chapter lures you into reading just one more.'

'This book was excellent! A great plot which kept you guessing until the end.'

'Couldn't put it down, fast paced with twists and turns.'

'The story was captivating, good plot, twists you never saw and really likeable characters. Can't wait for the next one!'

'I got sucked into this book from the very first page, thoroughly enjoyed it, can't wait for the next one.'

'Totally addictive. Thoroughly recommend.'

'Moves at a fast pace and carries you along with it.'

'Just couldn't put this book down, from the first page to the last one it kept you wondering what would happen next.'

Also by Jack Gatland

DI DECLAN WALSH BOOKS

LETTER FROM THE DEAD

MURDER OF ANGELS

HUNTER HUNTED

WHISPER FOR THE REAPER

TO HUNT A MAGPIE

A RITUAL FOR THE DYING

KILLING THE MUSIC

A DINNER TO DIE FOR

BEHIND THE WIRE

HEAVY IS THE CROWN

STALKING THE RIPPER

A QUIVER OF SORROWS

MURDER BY MISTLETOE

BENEATH THE BODIES

ELLIE RECKLESS BOOKS

PAINT THE DEAD

STEAL THE GOLD

HUNT THE PREY

TOM MARLOWE BOOKS

SLEEPING SOLDIERS

TARGET LOCKED

COVERT ACTION

DAMIAN LUCAS BOOKS

THE LIONHEART CURSE

STANDALONE BOOKS

THE BOARDROOM

AS TONY LEE

DODGE & TWIST

For Mum, who inspired me to write.

For Tracy, who inspires me to write.

CONTENTS

PROLOGUE

Everyone remembered where they were the night Jeffrey Tsang, heir to the Tsang Clan gang of West London was abducted; what they'd find harder to explain was *why* they were there in the first place.

White City used to be a rundown area; even though the BBC Television Centre, and the multitude of B list celebrities that hung around it hadn't been that far away from the lower-class estates over the years, where to the south-east the narrow, dark streets of Shepherd's Bush were rife for attacks and violent muggings while to the north, Ladbroke Grove was a place that suffered from poverty and overcrowding, a postcode where it wasn't uncommon for eight-person households to squeeze into two-room apartments.

Even the term *apartment* felt too posh for the area; the more common *flats* used instead, as gangs with names like *Third Set, 12 Anti, 12 World, Ten Eleven* or the out of place *Mozart* would attack and often kill each other for seemingly no reason on a semi-regular basis.

But over recent years, and despite the violence and gang

culture that had continued to rise in the area, house prices had also rocketed, with high-end shops appearing in the newly developed *Westfield Shopping Centre*, and posh members clubs like *Soho House* taking over the now-closed BBC Television Centre, creating hotels and cool media locations, with rooftop swimming pools and exclusive bars and restaurants aimed at a richer clientele, a growing gentrification of the area that brought with it wealth, wine bars and a higher class of *criminal*.

Jeffrey Tsang had been one of those higher class criminals; a third-generation Triad prince, he was long connected to the *Wo Shing Wo* Triad through his long-dead father and two uncles, Benny and Kenny Tsang, the self-proclaimed overlords of West London and Soho. He was an ambitious young man with an idea to take these scattered gangs of local teenagers, mainly dissociated boys with box cutters in their pockets and a need for *scratch*, for cold hard cash, and make something *bigger*. He knew that Chinatown, and the constant battles his uncles had within it, weren't for him; There was no interest in working with his own family, such as they were, or getting involved in the growing, distasteful activities throughout the area, including illegal people trafficking—bad business for all when you got caught, or when a truckload of illegal immigrants died in the back—and had branched westwards.

He'd done well. He'd worked with some of the local kids, the more talented musicians and rappers among the scum he'd met, farming them out into the London club scene, getting their violent drill raps uploaded onto the internet, and therefore available to other teenagers out there; teens who wanted the same extravagant lifestyle, and who would come to Jeffrey Tsang and offer to do anything to get onto the ladder.

His plan was to legitimise himself, create a new persona as a media celebrity—all while keeping his criminal activities under the counter.

After all, it worked for South London.

He'd opened a nightclub in a small, upcoming area between White City and Hammersmith; *Tsang City*, a modest location, it'd once been his uncle's Karaoke bar, won from him in a game of chess on a cold, winter night. Now it played sick rap songs—always the latest tunes—and was a place to hold court while his army of ambitious teenagers kept him up to date.

He wanted to open another one in Soho, but he also knew doing this would gain the attention of the Wo Shing Wo, and the last thing he wanted was for them to decide they wanted a piece of his growing pie; some kind of very expensive tribute from him. Or worse, they took the whole damn thing from him, claiming someone had rigged the chess game, that he'd deliberately spiked his uncle Kenny's drink, making him easier to beat.

The fact this was exactly what Jeffrey had done was irrelevant. All was fair in love and war, and it was Kenny's fault, not Jeffrey's, if he fell for it. Kenny even started a rematch, hoping to win his club back, but Jeffrey had decided it was time for *that* match to end.

Violently.

Jeffrey had spent months creating a ready-made army of cannon fodder teenagers, all ready to die on their swords for a brick of cash, some weed, and some street cred. Jeffrey detested them *all,* but was damned if he was giving them away.

On the night in question, Jeffrey was in his usual booth, way back in the VIP section of the club, if you could be 'way back' in a club the size of a large corner store basement, partying it up with a couple of Instagram models and his usual crew; Banner, the bookish assistant he'd hired as a mercy deal in order to bang his sister, a man who seemed to be on his side and excited to be in the room, but at the same time gave a shiftiness that made Jeffrey question his loyalty. Beside him was Maurice, an old school drama queen who *'used to hang with the Krays, dear boy,'* and who was about a hundred and four, dressing like he was out for a jolly at Ascot. Jeffrey kept him around as Maurice knew everyone in the old gangster crowd, and with his elders no longer bringing him into their schemes, Jeffrey needed whatever advantages he could get to move forward with *his* plans.

And he had *big* plans and was making some *major* moves.

They were, however, about to be placed on hold, as through the throng of nightclub dancers, three determined men walked confidently towards his booth. The first was a man who looked as old as Maurice, his hair more white than grey, blowdried back and set solid, unmoving under the air conditioning, a black shirt and suit completing the ensemble. He looked like a showbiz undertaker, and Jeffrey, a little fuzzy from expensive champagne, sniggered to himself at the comparison. The men on either side were obviously muscle, and not worth anyone's time; the one on the left was no older than a kid, black with a scowl that promised a bad attitude, hoodie over his head and a sling backpack over his shoulder. On the right was an older man, broader, giving off the look of Irish muscle, with a white wife-beater vest under a blue tracksuit.

Neither of them fitted the dress code, Jeffrey smiled. *He'd need to fire the doormen.*

The man in the suit eyed up Maurice, Banner and then Jeffrey in order.

'I'm guessing you're Tsang,' he said finally, his blue eyes locked on Jeffrey's own. 'The old fart and the kid don't have the slitty eyes.'

Oh, how lovely, we're being an old school racist today, Jeffrey thought, looking to the side where Keith, his bodyguard, usually stood surreptitiously against the wall and out of the way, but still within easy reach of whomever came too close.

'Yeah, the black guy you're looking for took a break,' the man said as he smiled. 'Best decision he made all night.'

Jeffrey was about to snap some kind of bitch-ass reply when he stopped and sniffed. There was a strange, ammonia-like smell from nearby. Looking around, he stopped as he saw Maurice, his face pale, a dark stain of urine travelling down his left leg, visible through his trouser leg. The man who claimed to hang out with the Krays had literally pissed himself at the sight of this stranger and his friends. And, with a glance around, Jeffrey saw that several of the patrons were filming this; Banner had filled the place with influencers tonight, saying that they'd live stream and post about the club; and now Jeffrey knew tonight they were getting a show as well.

'What the fu—' Jeffrey started, turning back to the old man who now smelled of piss, but Maurice interrupted him, waving his hand with more force than Jeffrey was happy with, speaking to the man with more reverence than he ever spoke to him.

'Mister Lucas,' he whispered. 'I—it's good to see—I mean to say, I'm not with *him*.'

He looked back at Jeffrey with an apologetic *sorry* before backing away from him in the booth.

It was around this point that the surrounding people realised something was very wrong. *More* cameras filmed.

'Mister Lucas?' Jeffrey considered this, still deciding that offence was the best form of defence. 'You're the old fart that runs Globe Town, yeah? Johnny Lucas?'

The man looked back from Maurice to Jeffrey, his eyes cold and dead, utterly emotionless as he considered the question for a long, silent moment.

'That's my brother,' he said. 'I'm *Jackie* Lucas.'

'What you are is *mad*, mate,' Banner laughed, still drinking his flute of champagne and suffering the aftereffects of whatever he'd snorted up his nose earlier that night. 'Everyone knows there ain't no Jackie. You're just mental—'

Before he could finish, Jackie pulled out a gun, a small, snub-nosed automatic and, with no warning, shot Banner in his right knee.

Blam.

As the nightclub broke into chaos, the revellers running for the door, Jackie held the gun up, stopping Jeffrey from moving closer to the now screaming Banner as he now looked back at the gunshot victim, on the floor now and clutching his leg, tears streaming down his face. Jeffrey hadn't expected Banner to step up like that. Jeffrey had actually expected Banner to slink into the shadows. This was all going very wrong, and now Jeffrey was a little more than worried that things were about to go seriously off script, as he stared back at the white-haired man.

'Am I still mental?' Jackie asked calmly. 'Eh? Am I? Yes or no?'

Banner didn't speak, unable to utter more than a

whimper as he stared in terror at the black-suited man, now leaning down, placing the muzzle of the gun against his shattered knee.

'*Yes or no?*' Jackie repeated, his voice light, almost like someone enjoying themselves. Banner scrunched his face up, forcing the pain away as anger took over.

'Go fu—'

Blam.

The muzzle of the gun, now brought up to Banner's temple, fired again, killing him instantly, the back of his skull exploding out against the booth behind them. As Banner's screams stopped instantly and the body slumped to the floor, Jackie Lucas rose, turning back to face the now green-faced Jeffrey Tsang.

'I heard you've been spouting my name a lot,' he said. 'Saying it's time to retire. That right?'

Jeffrey cleared his throat, consciously aware of the others in the club, the ones staying in the shadows, filming this on their phones. He reckoned this had to be streaming on a dozen social media pages by now; all he had to do was to be seen standing his ground until the police came. He couldn't look weak here; no matter what the mad old bastard did to the Chinese heir apparent, if he was weak, and it was online?

He could lose everything.

'In conversation only,' he replied calmly, keeping the quaver from his voice. 'With others.'

'Those others be Nicky Simpson or the Seven Sisters?'

'Can't remember,' Jeffrey kept his face placid, but still unable to hide to the watchers and recorders how terrified he was at the accuracy of Jackie's guess; if it even was a guess. He knew what the onlookers in the club were now thinking.

Had someone grassed him up?

Jackie looked at his two goons, searching for any kind of response from them.

The hooded black goon nodded.

'He's talked to Mama Delcourt,' he said. 'I know it. Saw him there last week. Laughing like a meth head.'

Jeffrey felt his stomach flip-flop as Jackie returned his gaze to him.

'I ain't retiring,' Jackie said, his voice hoarse and whispered as he pulled out a handkerchief, wiping the back of his neck. 'But I do hate these public showdowns.'

'Yeah,' Jeffrey agreed, and the onlookers could see there was a chance for him to get out of this. 'It helps nothing. Look, it was banter, yeah? Just trying to stay in with the others, and they said way worse, I swear.'

Jeffrey looked at Maurice, who by now had backed as far away from him as he could, staring at the floor, unable to look Jeffrey in the eye. He then looked at Banner, dead on the floor.

'Maybe we can—' he started

Blam.

Live-steamed and photographed, Jackie Lucas leant in and fired a third shot at close range into his stomach. Jeffrey Tsang fell to a knee, unable to collapse to the floor as the two soldiers of Jackie Lucas pulled him, now clutching at his heavily bleeding gut wound, to his feet once more.

'I know you were planning on muscling in on my territory,' Jackie said, placing the gun calmly away as he spoke. 'I know the people you were talking to and I know who you tried to pay off. And you're right, we shouldn't have these public arguments.'

He leaned close, his mouth to Jeffrey's ear.

'So let's go somewhere private,' he hissed in a theatrical whisper, loud enough for everyone to hear.

Jeffrey Tsang couldn't cry for help as they dragged him to the back door of his own club. Everyone could see he was in too much pain, fighting to stay conscious as his intestines threatened to fall out of the bullet hole, seeing the revellers run to Banner's body as he was taken out of the main bar, seeing the look of resignation and shame on Maurice's face as he watched him, probably for the last time.

And then Jeffrey Tsang passed out, dragged between the two men as Jackie Lucas opened the door to the kitchen area and the back entrance fire escape, the four of them leaving the club, and the shocked partygoers within.

1

GRAVEYARD SHIFT

DCI Esposito was working late.

To be honest, he was always working late. Mile End was a part of London that never wanted to sleep, no matter how much he prayed to every Saint he knew for a respite.

But the Saints listened little in Mile End.

He'd been there less than a year; his predecessor, DCI Ford, had found herself removed from duty when she was not only discovered to be working for the Lucas Twins, but also had been involved in the murder of a student at the nearby Queen Mary's College; a murder that involved some kind of make-believe internet money, and the additional arrest of the Unit's cybercrime operative, DC Hart, alongside her.

Maybe 'removed from duty' was too light a term, after all. Maybe 'arrested with extreme prejudice' was more apt.

Esposito hadn't met either of them, but he knew the stories. And DS Anjli Kapoor had filled him in during her brief transfer here a month or two into his stay, before she returned to Temple Inn after her brief sabbatical. Kapoor was another who had connections to the Twins, stemming from her previous stint at Mile End as a Detective Constable-turned Sergeant, but Esposito reckoned she was less likely to fall down the hole Ford had. And, over the last six months following her transfer back, Esposito had tried to bring in a clean sweep, or new broom approach to the Command Unit, with the first plan of action being the removal of the crime lords of Globe Town, Jackie and Johnny Lucas.

Who, as everyone knew, was actually one man with a multiple personality disorder, a man who, as *Johnny* was polite as could be, but when he became *Jackie*, the *Mister Hyde* to his *Doctor Jekyll*—well, you backed out of the room as quick as possible, and bugger the consequences.

Esposito had only met Johnny once; it was after DCI Monroe's team had solved the *Magpies* case, ending with some weird face-off in the boxing club Johnny owned, one between the killers and DI Declan Walsh, with Mile End being called in to supply the muscle for the arrests.

Declan Walsh.

Another name that kept popping up, especially since it was Walsh that revealed Ford and Hart for what they were, costing him a lot of support in the force. Esposito didn't hold him any ill will, though; *bent coppers needed to be removed.* The same as wannabe East End gangsters who hadn't realised it was the bloody twenty-first century now, and the Krays were nothing but a history lesson afterthought—

His phone rang, bringing him back to the present, and after a moment of readjustment, he picked up the phone.

'Esposito,' he said, pausing as he listened to the voice on the other end of the line. 'He did *what?*'

After a moment more of listening to frantic speaking down the phone line, Esposito placed it back on its cradle, rose from the chair and walked over to the coat tree in the corner of his office. Grabbing his jacket, he pulled it on, glancing at himself in the window, the night sky behind it turning it into a makeshift full-length mirror.

Esposito was a middle-aged man, tall, lean and dark-skinned with his black hair parted on the right, while left to its own devices. He attempted briefly to pat it into place, before giving up. There would be cameras there, but *he* wasn't likely to be the one in front of them.

This was way bigger than that.

THE *HELEN OF TROY* WAS A KNOWN LATE-NIGHT DRINKERS haunt north of Soho, up a small, almost unseen side road from Oxford Street, a narrow passageway that curved gently to the right as it headed towards Tottenham Court Road, and the north.

Nothing more than the floor above a restaurant, at one time it'd been known as a journalists bar, a place for people to grab an off-the-books can of Guinness for a stupidly inflated price, but more than anything it'd become a place for the lost, the quiet, and the grieving, whether it was for a love, a job lost or the general state of the world.

At the same time though, if you wanted something out there, speaking loudly and carelessly here could find you quoted in a dozen different medias.

Jackie Lucas wanted that.

'Give me a scotch,' he said to the woman behind the bar, a short, white-haired battle-axe with a mischievous smile. This was the titular Helen of the location, and as she passed it across, Jackie slid a ten-pound note back to her, waving off the change, much as it would be. Taking a sip, he looked around the room—no, the bar. Even though this was effectively a large living room space at the top of some stairs, the tables and chairs scattered around gave it a cosy feel, half-occupied by quietly drinking men and a couple of older women.

'Any Journos here?' Jackie asked. There was a moment of silence as a reply, and then a couple of older men, men who gave the look of having drunk here for decades, one of which was working on a laptop, likely still finishing a piece, raised their hands.

'As much as one can be these days,' the laptop-using man muttered. 'Why?'

'My name's Jackie, Jackie Lucas. You might have heard of me.'

There was a muttering at this, and two drinkers paid attention now.

'I'm giving you the scoop,' Jackie continued, toasting the room with his glass. 'I'm taking down the Triad. Putting a million each on Benny and Kenny Tsang. Let's make London British again. Well, at least gangster wise.'

'Sure,' the laptop drinker replied. 'And how do we know you're not some drunk wannabe?'

Jackie nodded, finished his drink and walked over to the man who, realising he'd stuck his head above the trenches, railed back, expecting to be struck.

Instead, Jackie placed a gold signet ring on the table.

'That's Jeffrey Tsang's ring,' he said. 'Take a photo with your phone. And then ask yourself why I have it.'

As the man now took a photo, Jackie looked around.

'I'm putting the City on notice,' he announced. 'No more

scum. And if I have to burn it down? I'll do that. Remember. A million each.'

With this proclamation made, Jackie took the ring, nodded to Helen, and then left.

There was a moment of stunned nothingness, before nearly everyone in the room reached for their phones with an urgency not seen in the bar for years.

There was a *scoop* to be found here. And these days, something like this was golden.

The squad car brought Esposito to the boxing club on Bullard's Place, smack bang in the middle of Globe Town, around one in the morning. Already, the place was awash in blue lights, and regardless of the time, a small crowd of onlookers, half still in their pyjamas and dressing gowns, had arrived to see what was going on, intermingled with photographers and journalists, all jostling with the *scene of crime* officers who were valiantly attempting to hold them back. As Esposito walked towards the main doors to the boxing club, DS McAlroy; mid-thirties, taller than most of the surrounding officers, and with her dyed-red hair pulled into a ponytail emerged from inside the building, pulling her latex gloves off and throwing them into her pocket as she stopped, placed her hands on her hips and bent over, taking deep breaths.

Esposito thought she was about to throw up, but she recovered and, looking up at him, straightened.

'Don't go in, boss,' she warned, her voice unsettled. 'It's not good.'

'Go on,' Esposito glanced over at the door, deciding to hold off entering for a moment. 'What's the sit rep?'

'Jeffrey Tsang, age twenty-four, shot in the gut and abducted from his club, *Tsang City,* in White City around ten pm tonight,' McAlroy started. 'Witnesses claimed it was an old man and his henchmen who did it. Said he announced to everyone he was Jackie Lucas.'

'Ah, crap,' Esposito replied, running his hand through his hair. 'And he's in there?'

'Jeffrey Tsang or Jackie Lucas?'

'Tsang.'

'Kinda,' McAlroy admitted. 'They stripped him naked, laid him in the middle of the ring, tied a limb to each of the boxing ring corners and... well...'

She turned away, paling again.

'They took their time,' she whispered. 'Pretty much skinned him, and hacked pieces away for fun. Body has a gunshot wound, too, which matches what witnesses said happened in the West London club. There's not much of him left, unrecognisable in fact, and the doc reckons he was still alive for much of it.'

Esposito nodded, making a mental note not to enter the boxing club until someone had cleared it up. He hated blood at the best of times.

'If they took him from West London, can't the West London Met deal with this?' he muttered to himself. 'Anyone know where Lucas is?'

'Cars went to his house, but he's not there,' McAlroy read from her notes now. 'One of our informers said he has a girlfriend in Canary Wharf who he goes to see sometimes, but consensus is that if he did this, he's probably in the wind, looking for an alibi right now that saves him from—'

She stopped as, at the corner of the road, the watching crowd moved aside, and a black Jaguar F-Type SUV pushed its way slowly through them. Stopping beside an officer who looked quizzically at it, the passenger door opened and a black-suited man in a blue shirt, his almost-white hair strangely bedraggled, stormed out, pushing past the confused officer and making his way directly towards Esposito.

'What the hell are you doing in my club?' he demanded. 'I just got a call telling me the bloody circus is in town, so here I am.'

He stared at the club, watched the forensics officers walk out, his anger and bluster fading slightly as he saw a body bag being removed.

'Want to tell me what I've done this time?' he asked, more cautiously now.

'Murder, Mister Lucas,' Esposito stated matter-of-factly, nodding at a couple of officers to move in from behind. 'We believe we have the body of Jeffrey Tsang in your club. We know he's been spouting off about you for a few weeks now, and we also know you and his family aren't the best of chums. He's been shot, tortured and killed, and when he was abducted a couple of hours ago from his own premises in White City, witnesses in the club said it was *you* that did it.'

'Nonsense,' Johnny Lucas snapped. 'I've been asleep at my girlfriend's. Cheryl Jenkins. Lives in Cirque Apartments in Canary Wharf. I've been there all night. Just ask her.'

'I'm sure a person like you has no issue finding alibis, and we will indeed be speaking to your undoubtably lovely lady,' Esposito replied. 'But I didn't say you as in *Johnny*, I said you as in *Jackie*.'

Johnny faltered at this.

'Jackie's away on business,' he said.

'And if we needed to speak to him?'

'He's incommunicado.'

'Convenient,' Esposito sighed. 'Look. We have over a dozen witnesses stating it was Jackie. He even *told them* he was Jackie, while they filmed him live, sharing it for everyone to see on the internet. And the problem with that, *Johnny*, is we both know *Jackie isn't real*, don't we?'

Johnny didn't reply, his brows furrowing as he tried to work out what was really happening here.

'So let me make it simple,' Esposito continued. 'Explain to me one thing, please. When you are Jackie, do you remember being Johnny? Is it like a blackout? Or are you still there, still in control?'

Johnny looked around, realising for the first time the amount of police now standing around him.

'If, hypothetically, I was as you said, it would most likely be in the form of a blackout,' he said. 'I don't—I mean, I *wouldn't* remember.'

'And you were asleep tonight, around ten?'

'Yes.'

'Not a blackout?'

Johnny's eyes widened as he stared at Esposito.

'You think *I* did this?' He exclaimed. 'That I blacked out, became Jackie and killed him?'

'You didn't just kill him,' McAlroy snapped. 'You shot him, bragged about it to everyone there, and then took him here, tied him up and sliced him into pieces. What do you say to that?'

In a slow circle of realisation, Johnny looked from McAlroy to the boxing club, and then back to Esposito.

'I was sleeping,' he said, almost as a whine. 'I didn't do it.

If Jackie did it, you can't blame me for that. I'm not my brother's keeper.'

'You are when they're *make believe*,' McAlroy hissed. 'Boss, can we move on here? I'm still feeling queasy and this murdering prick isn't helping.'

'Mister Lucas, not only can I blame you, I'm also arresting you for the murder of Jeffrey Tsang, until your brother magically appears,' Esposito nodded to the officers behind Johnny Lucas, who now moved in, pulling his hands behind him, cuffing his wrists. 'Unless you either miraculously produce him, or find someone else who can prove your innocence beyond any doubt, then you're *mine*.'

Johnny Lucas didn't stop them from cuffing him. He didn't protest as they led him to the car.

He didn't resist at all.

Because he knew without a doubt who'd killed Jeffrey Tsang.

It had to be Jackie Lucas.

Not him.

All he had to do now was prove it.

2

HONEYMOON PERIOD

Declan stared at the engagement ring in his hand with the look of someone considering their own doom.

'It's too soon,' he said. 'It's only been like a month.'

'You're just scared of change, dad,' Jess grinned as she walked over to him from the other counter of the jewellers. 'I think it's romantic. And I also think it's adorable that you're like this. Ohh, *that's* nice. She'll like that.'

'And you're an expert on rings suddenly?' Declan muttered with a preceding scowl as he smiled at the shop assistant, passing the ring back to her. 'Thank you, but as I said, I'm—'

'Considering it,' Jess interrupted. 'A grand? For that? Actually dad, you could do better.'

Declan stared at his daughter in a mixture of annoyance and amusement. Jessica Walsh had only turned sixteen a month or so earlier, but already she was blossoming out from the gawky teenage kid he'd known for so long. Now she was becoming the woman she wanted to be, even if that was a woman with dark brown hair in a bob, Lennon specs (even though she didn't need glasses), a red plaid lumberjack shirt over a white t-shirt, a faded, retro print of the eighties movie *Red Dawn* on it and black *Levis*, with a pair of black Doc Martens finishing her ensemble.

(Although she'd explained when they met that these weren't real Docs, these were *Solovairs*, the original manufacturers before Doc Martens sold the rights to China, and they were vegan friendly, which Declan guessed meant that they weren't actually made of leather.)

'In rings, or family members?' he muttered irritably. 'Why are you here with me, exactly?'

'Because I know about rings, and I know men are rubbish when choosing them for possibly the most important question of their lives,' Jess folded her arms, smiling innocently at her father. 'And I'm staying with you for two weeks, so you have to take me out and treat me like a princess, or I'm telling mum.'

'I'm not buying you a ring,' Declan replied.

'This isn't about you buying me a ring,' Jess contrasted. 'This is about—'

She stopped as the door to the shop opened again, and a flustered and obviously nervous DCI Farrow entered the jewellers.

He looked exactly the same as he had the last time Declan had seen him; with his wire-rimmed glasses and tufty hair sticking out to the sides, the detectives who worked under him often likened Farrow to a rather irritated owl, and with the scowl he now wore, he looked even more so.

'Walsh,' he said, shaking Declan's hand. 'Thanks for coming.'

'Not my choice,' Declan gave the briefest hint of a smile in return as he glared at Jess. 'My daughter decided she wanted a say in this.'

Farrow looked at Jess, who also smiled back at him.

'Yes, I suppose she does,' he replied. 'Sorry I'm late. Can I have a quick word outside?'

Confused, Declan looked over at Jess.

'Can't whatever you want to say be said here?' he asked. Not that he didn't want to walk outside, it was that he was currently feeling a little out of his depth; the current boyfriend of his ex-wife, and up to a year ago his boss was asking his advice on engagement rings for her. The fact Declan had even turned up was a miracle.

'No,' Farrow replied simply, pushing his glasses back up his nose. 'Sorry, Declan, but I need to speak to you alone.'

Sighing, Declan nodded. He had a pretty good idea of what was going on here and, with a subtle nod to his daughter, he followed Farrow out of the Hatton Garden jewellers and onto the street.

'Look,' he started, shaking his head, speaking first, getting this over with before it became too uncomfortable. 'I get it. I'm the ex, I'm the father of Jess, I'll always be a part of Liz's life. But you really don't need to ask my blessing about this. I think it's a little rushed though, all said and done; you've only been dating her a month—'

'We've been seeing each other for about *three* months now,' Farrow replied icily. 'And I've known her for over a year. Ever since she came to Tottenham North to chew you out about something. You know, back in the normal days, before you punched a priest, arrested a DCI and then joined Monroe's band of merry miscreants.'

'Three months?' Declan raised his eyebrows at this,

genuinely surprised it'd been that long. 'Still feels a little short notice, you know?'

'Well luckily, DI Walsh, I don't need to worry about your opinion, just as much as I don't need your blessing,' Farrow adjusted his jacket as the wind picked up. It was strangely cold for August.

'Fine,' Declan's tone was sulky as he spoke, looking up the street and away from Farrow. 'For the record, I would have given it. You make her happy, and that's all that matters.'

Farrow paused, surprised at this.

'Oh,' he muttered, embarrassed. 'I assumed you'd be a bit of a dick about it.'

'Just promise me you'll let Jess decide for herself if she wants to take your surname,' Declan added, ignoring Farrow's minor character assassination.

'Of course,' Farrow nodded. 'That had been my plan, anyway.'

There was a long, uncomfortable moment on the street before Declan looked back to his onetime boss, frowning as he considered the conversation they were having.

'Why did we come out here then?' he asked.

Farrow's eyes widened as he realised he'd become distracted.

'Yes, of course,' he replied, pulling his glasses off and removing the handkerchief from his jacket pocket, wiped the lenses. 'You have a case.'

'I'm not sure if you got the memo, but I left Tottenham North a while back,' Declan smiled. 'Although, are you sure you want me back?'

'You're a funny man, Walsh,' Farrow was stone faced as he spoke. 'I can see what drew Liz to you. Your amazing humour.'

Declan nodded, conceding the point.

'So, what's the case?' he asked.

'Mile End,' Farrow glanced down at his watch as he replied; looking past him at the clock jutting out of the wall above them, Declan could see it was ten-thirty in the morning. 'They had a murder last night. Technically, two. Made an arrest in Globe Town.'

'Globe Town,' Declan mulled the words over. 'Bloody hell. They arrested Johnny Lucas?'

Farrow nodded.

'He killed Jeffrey Tsang, of the Chinatown Tsangs,' he said, as if this would mean something to Declan. It did. 'Abducted him from his club in West London, shot and killed one of his friends, took him back to that boxing club he claims makes him a legit businessman and tortured him to death. Literally sliced the skin off him while he was still alive. Body was unrecognisable.'

'As Tsang?'

'As a *human*.'

Declan didn't speak for a moment, as he tried to work through what Farrow had said. He was no fan of Johnny Lucas, but he also felt that the man he'd met many times, the man who'd even saved his boss' life, wouldn't have done something so gruesome, especially in his own club.

'And he's definitely the killer?'

'God knows, apparently he's claiming it wasn't him, and his clothes didn't have any blood spatter on them, but he could have changed,' Farrow placed his glasses back on, squinting through them as he looked around. 'Said it was his brother. Probably going for an insanity plea.'

'He's got the history for it,' Declan nodded. It was a well-known fact in the underworld that Johnny and Jackie Lucas were the same man, but two wildly unique personalities, and had been since the nineties. It actually surprised Declan Johnny hadn't used this defence before. 'But why do we get the case? Mile End is DCI Esposito. And forgive me, but you're North London, not west.'

'I know,' sighed Farrow. 'But apparently a witness, one of the clubbers recognised Johnny Lucas' muscle. Or, at least, the younger, hooded one. You know him too. I seem to recall he hit you with a baseball bat once, after you rammed a metal door into his head, and made him look a fool by taking his gun away from him.'

Declan grimaced at the memory.

'Kayas,' he replied. 'Doorman. Worked for Moses Delcourt. Or, at least, Mama Delcourt and the Seven Sisters, before Moses tried to take over and Mama Delcourt blinded herself with a paint grenade. I'd assumed he'd either sucked up to the new leader, or got himself arrested.'

'There is no leader, it's still Mama Delcourt,' Farrow shook his head. 'She copped a plea deal, and the blindness helped in her favour. Of course, when Moses was arrested, most of his crew disappeared. Simply drifted away on the wind before his trial's even started. But, as we have an East End gangster, with North London muscle abducting a West End chancer, it's been decided that we should make this a joint effort.'

'And who decided that?'

'Chief Superintendent Bradbury—'

A car horn beeped as Farrow spoke and he jumped slightly, on edge.

'Said that as you'd dealt with pretty much all the guilty parties, and as your team were at a loose end right now, you could take point.'

'Bradbury doesn't want a gang war messing up his figures,' Declan knew what was happening here. 'He knows if we screw up, he can land it all on us as a City issue.'

'Sorry,' Farrow sounded almost genuine as he apologised. 'Anyway, your Scottish boss is at the boxing club, and once he's done, they will probably need your expertise. I know this was your day off, and I appreciate the fact you were coming to help me pick a ring, but I'm afraid this'll have to wait.'

'I'm sure Jess could stay and help you,' Declan offered, looking through the glass door and catching his daughter's eye, motioning for her to come outside. 'She could give you better ideas as to what Liz likes these days than I could.'

'I'll give you even odds that she immediately tells you to take her with you,' Farrow grinned as, concerned, Jess emerged through the door to the jewellers, her gaze travelling from Declan to Farrow, and then back.

'No ring today?' she asked, a note of disappointment in her voice.

'More a case of no me,' Declan replied. 'I've been called into work. I have to go back—'

'You mean *we* need to,' Jess interrupted quickly. 'You promised, dad. I could help if something came up during the holidays.'

'Told you,' Farrow said, walking up to the door of the jewellers. 'I can pick a ring by myself, Declan. You two go be coppers. Or, at least, be a copper and his way-too-eager child.'

'Way-too-eager and soon-to-be-your-stepchild,' Declan replied.

'Fair point, well made.'

'I've placed out three rings I think mum would like,' Jess nodded back at the door. 'All in the right size, too. I suggest the second one. Don't go for anything with emeralds. She hates them.'

'But I bought her an emerald pendant last month,' Farrow frowned.

Jess grinned.

'Yes, and it's very nice, sitting in the box it came in, never to be opened again,' she said. 'I'm just waiting for Christmas, when she'll likely gift it to me.'

With a reluctant sigh and nod of appreciation, Farrow looked back at Declan for a moment, as if about to say something. Then, deciding not to, he opened the door and entered the jewellers, leaving Declan and Jess alone on the street.

'So, what's the case?' Jess asked eagerly.

'I'm not sure,' Declan answered honestly as they started down Hatton Garden, heading towards High Holborn. 'But whatever it is, you'll be spending it sitting beside Billy.'

'I'd learn more sitting beside Morten,' Jess said, her voice wistful. Declan grimaced again; he'd forgotten the crush she had on the seven-foot tall Viking police officer.

'Hey,' Jess continued. 'Are you okay? With Henry asking mum to marry him?'

Declan stopped. It felt strange hearing Farrow being called by his first name, even more so by his daughter.

'Yes, believe it or not,' he replied, waving for a cab. 'You mum deserves something good to happen. And he seems like he has his head on straight.'

'He's already written to the Pope,' Jess said matter-of-factly.

Declan paled.

'Christ,' he whispered. 'Is it because I punched that priest? That was almost a year ago now! I never—'

He stopped as Jess started laughing.

'No, you idiot,' she gasped for breath. 'It's because mum's divorced, and he wants to marry her in his church.'

She stopped, suddenly worried.

'I hope they don't work out who she is though,' she stroked her chin. 'They might ban her simply because of you.'

Declan ignored his daughter's mocking, watching the road for another free taxi. As he did so, Jess continued.

'I didn't see Anjli this morning,' she said. 'You guys fighting?'

'She's visiting her mother,' Declan replied as a third black cab went past, ignoring his wave. 'She also wanted you to have some space when visiting.'

'Usually when someone visits their mother, it's because they've had a fight,' Jess frowned. 'Are you sure you're doing okay?'

'Jess, it's only been four weeks,' Declan reached into his jacket, pulling out his warrant card. 'It's barely even begun.'

'Say that to Henry,' Jess watched as Declan opened it and walked out onto the road, holding it up in the air as a cab approached. 'He's proposing after three months, and they don't even live with each other.'

'We don't live with each other,' Declan snapped back. 'We share a house—*police! We need you to take us to Temple Inn!*'

The second part of this was aimed at the driver of the black cab, who, nodding reluctantly as Declan ushered Jess into the back, did an illegal u-turn in the middle of the road.

'Always wanted to do that,' the driver said with a smile. 'Reckoned this was the best time.'

'Come on, dad, spill the beans,' Jess urged.

Declan paused, took a breath, and turned to his daughter.

'How's—now, what's her name again?' he pretended to root around in his memory for a name. 'Prita? Prina?'

'*Prisha*,' Jess groaned at her father's clumsy investigating skills, and Declan knew with a smile that he'd caught a nerve. He knew Jess had a crush on Prisha, a student she'd met on a case in Hurley, now at the London School of Economics for the summer. And, with Prisha only a year older than his daughter, and not a mid-twenties police officer who also had a crush on *his* fellow forensics examiner, Declan was actually fine with this. 'And she's doing okay. She finishes her course in a week. We've met up a few times in Henley, and we're meeting up while I'm in London.'

'You're not in London,' Declan reminded her. 'You're in Hurley. *I'm* in London when *I'm* at work.'

'*We're* in London,' Jess contradicted. 'You promised.'

Declan sighed.

'Let's see how bad the case is first, yeah?'

'How bad could it be?' Jess' optimism was catching.

'How about the fact that the last time you helped me in a case, you were kidnapped and almost died?'

'You forget the part where I didn't die, kicked her arse and would have citizen's arrested her by myself, if Anjli hadn't turned up and hogged all the glory.'

'That's not how I heard it,' Declan scratched his head.

'Well, that's the problem, dad,' Jess settled back into the seat. 'There's two sides to every story.'

'Actually, there's three,' Declan corrected. 'Yours, theirs, and the *truth*.'

This lesson given, he looked out of the window, considering what Farrow had told him. For Johnny Lucas to be working with ex-soldiers of the Delcourts was a change, one that came out of left field.

For him to be killing rivals, brutally so, was different.

Declan hoped very much that in this situation, the truth was an answer that could explain everything…

Because currently it looked like the two sides of Johnny Lucas were at war with each other.

3

MY PRETTY PRINCESS

BILLY WAS ALONE AT HIS MONITOR STATION WHEN DECLAN AND Jess arrived at the Temple Inn offices. Looking up, and seeing Jess enter, he quickly swiped on his track pad, and a photo on the screen, likely that of the boxing club victim, disappeared.

Declan appreciated that immensely. The last thing he wanted to do right now, was give his daughter more nightmares.

'I heard it was your day off?' Billy said, straightening his blue Harris-tweed waistcoat and gold tie, immaculately tied in a Windsor knot. He was always the best-dressed officer in the squad, his blond hair expensively groomed as well, but then his family came from money, and even though he'd been cut off from the family trust, his *wardrobe* hadn't been repossessed. The average three-piece suit Billy wore cost more than all of Declan's suits combined.

'I was in Hatton Garden,' Declan pulled his coat off, opening his desk drawer and pulling out a fresh shirt and tie. He'd gone to the jewellers with a polo shirt on, felt something a little more official would be a plan right now, and luckily always kept a spare. 'I was looking at engagement rings with DCI Farrow.'

Billy's eyes sparkled with delight, and Declan immediately groaned.

'Oh, that's great news!' he cried out, clapping his hands in mock excitement. 'Did you say yes? I do so hope you said yes.'

He stopped, as he realised something terrible, his face paling.

'Wait,' he whispered fearfully. 'Does... does *Anjli* know?'

'Yeah, yeah, you're hilarious,' Declan nodded. 'I mean, it's a laugh a minute being with someone as they pick out a ring to give to your ex-wife, but sure—'

He stopped as he saw Jess' face drop.

'You're not happy about it?' she asked, as if this revelation had blindsided her.

'It's not that,' Declan turned, grabbing Jess gently by the shoulders. 'Henry Farrow's a good man, if an annoying ex-boss, and Liz is the best person to pull that stick out of his arse, but for them to be happy together just shows how badly we—I mean me and Liz—failed.'

'You didn't fail,' Jess punched Declan on the arm. 'You had me, remember?'

'I stand by my comment,' Declan smiled as he ignored Jess' mock-shocked, hurt expression once more, looking back at Billy. 'Where is everyone?'

'Monroe, Anjli and De'Geer are at the boxing club, and Doctor Marcos, Davey, and Cooper are at the West End nightclub,' Billy replied. 'Bullman's in the office, trying to find out why we're even involved in this. You do know what happened, right?'

'Only what Farrow told me,' Declan nodded, pulling off

the polo shirt and pulling on a pale blue dress shirt. 'I'd appreciate a PG-rated catchup.'

'I'm not a kid, dad,' Jess muttered.

'Fine, make it 15-rated,' Declan reconsidered.

'Jeffrey Tsang, son of Donnie Tsang and nephew of Benjamin and Kenneth Tsang, abducted and killed by what looks to be Jackie Lucas,' Billy looked back to his monitors, where several portrait-angled videos of the night were playing, all showing the same scene from different angles. 'I'm going through footage right now. The place was filled with influencers, so it was all over TikTok and Instagram which makes my life a lot easier.'

'Never thought I'd be grateful for that,' Declan smiled.

'Some of their phones are better definition than the CCTV,' Billy replied. 'Together I can use all angles and actually make a pretty good 3D mock-up. I've always wanted to do that.'

He pointed at one of the footage screens.

'Here we go. At ten pm, Jackie and two companions arrive. This is from the venue, so not that great.'

On the screen was grainy CCTV footage of the front door to *Tsang City*. On it, Declan could see three men walk to the door and, after a couple of words to the bouncers, they were waved through without a second glance.

The leader was definitely Jackie Lucas, or at least how Johnny dressed when he became his brother; his hair fell to the other side, the shirt a jet black. It wasn't the best angle, but it looked correct.

And the two men behind him were also known.

'Kayas Ashad, used to be a doorman for the Seven Sisters, primarily under Moses Delcourt,' Declan nodded. 'I wouldn't forget that face easily. Bastard pulled a gun on me. And hit me with a baseball bat.'

'In fairness, you slammed a metal door into his face,' Billy mentioned.

'Whose side are you on?' Declan glared back before returning to the screen. 'The guy beside him, I don't know his name, but he's usually at the boxing club whenever I've been there.'

'Mickey Trackies,' Billy replied. 'No, really. Nicknamed 'Trackies' because of his love for terrible tracksuits. Thinks he's from the *Sopranos*. And, as far as we know, still works for the Lucas clan.'

By now they were watching the feeds from the images and livestreams taken inside of the club; Jackie had walked to a booth at the back, and was now talking to a young Asian man, two men either side of him, a girl running from the booth as the conversation was obviously heating.

'Jeffrey Tsang,' Billy paused the image, tapping on the screen. 'The guy to his right is David Banner—'

'David Banner? Like the Hulk?' Declan frowned.

'*Bruce* Banner was the Hulk,' Billy corrected.

'No, it was David,' Declan argued. 'Watched the show every week as a kid. Bill Bixby was David Banner.'

'The *show* might have called him David, but the show was *wrong*,' Billy was genuinely getting irritated by this.'

'I can't wait to be a copper,' Jess mocked. 'To be involved in amazing cases, with intelligent conversations...'

Declan took a deep breath, shaking off the irritation.

'And who is this Banner?' he asked.

'*Was*. Childhood mate and apparently branding manager,' Billy replied. 'And yeah, it seems that gangsters have branding managers now. From what I can find, Jeffrey only reconnected recently with him because he wants to sha-I mean *date* Banner's sister, who went out with him briefly in school.'

'Bloody hell, it's a Hallmark movie.'

'If *Blumhouse Studios* did it,' Billy nodded. 'Anyway, he was the one that booked all the influencers to attend last night; the club believed some rap star was turning up and wanted people to tweet, Instagram or TikTok about it. Although after what happened—'

He stopped, looking back at Jess.

'I don't think you should see this,' he mumbled.

Jess, nodding, dutifully turned away from the monitors.

'I'll explain so you don't miss a clue, but it's a little... brutal,' Billy continued the footage, and on the screen they saw Jackie pull a gun, shooting Banner in the knee.

'Jackie shoots Banner in the kneecap, point blank, then fires a second shot into his skull at close range,' Billy explained as on the screen Jackie mimicked the actions. 'Dead instantly.'

'I'm glad you warned me,' Jess said, sounding a little queasy as she spoke.

'Who's the suit?' Declan asked, pointing at the third man on Jeffrey Tsang's side.

'Maurice Hamilton,' hiding the gruesome images so that Jess could look back, Billy pulled a browser screen up and tapped in the name. A selection of photos of Maurice, taken over fifty-plus years, appeared. In nearly all of them, he was well dressed in blazer and tie.

'Used to hang out with the Krays when he was a teenager, apparently worked for them in his teens although there's no record of it, reckoned he was in the Blind Beggar pub in

Whitechapel the night Ronnie Kray shot and killed George Cornell—‘

‘Just like a hundred east-end cabbies seemed to be,’ Declan said with a wry smile. ‘Says there he wrote a book?’

‘Yeah, when the Krays were immortalised in that film with the *Spandau Ballet* brothers, he made himself a little nest egg, writing anecdotes and stories that were based in truth, but now had *him* involved in them. Wrote three in total and then stopped in 2000, after he had the living crap beaten out of him one night in Whitechapel. Claimed it was a case of mistaken identity, but it wasn’t a coincidence the courts released Reggie Kray a week earlier after serving around thirty years, and he’d said he wanted Maurice to *shut his gobshite mouth*.’

‘So Maurice is a tall-tale teller, but it doesn’t explain why he’s with Tsang.’

‘Honestly? Tsang probably thought having someone old school like Hamilton there would give him some credibility,’ Billy shrugged, looking at the screen. ‘It’s no secret he wanted to branch off from his family’s Triad history and make it on his own.’

‘Didn’t help him much,’ Declan shook his head. ‘Do we see where they took him?’

‘No CCTV in the alley, probably because Tsang had his more dubious contacts and purchases come in through that way,’ Billy replied, tapping on the screen. ‘And surprisingly, none of the influencers filming wanted to follow the strange, scary man with the gun out the back door. We don’t know what car they used, and ANPR—that’s *automatic number plate recognition*, Jess—needs a number plate to work from.’

‘So that’s ten pm,’ Declan rubbed at the back of his neck.

He felt like someone was watching him, and it was a feeling he didn't like. 'When do we get to Globe Town?'

'Just after midnight,' Billy said, shifting in his chair. 'Jogger going past the boxing club saw the lights on, thought it odd, checked everything was okay. Found... Well, it wasn't nice. They'd stripped him, tied him to the four corners of the ring and...'

He trailed off, paling.

'And what?' Jess asked.

'Think of the worst, most painful thing you can think of inflicting on another human being,' Billy whispered. 'They did that and more. Turned him into an unrecognisable chunk of meat.'

Jess looked away again as Declan repositioned his hastily tied necktie.

'Why isn't Marcos there?' he asked, confused, folding down the collar of his shirt. Everyone knew that something like this, as horrific and brutal as it sounded, was catnip to Doctor Marcos, the *Last Chance Saloon*'s Divisional Surgeon.

'The Mile End guy's running it,' Billy explained. 'Doctor Marcos and Anjli both know him, said he's good. Ramesh something.'

'*Rajesh* Khanna,' Declan corrected. 'Worked with him on the Bernard Lau case before I came here. Yeah, he's good.'

'I helped on that case,' Jess interjected. 'Just saying, in case it helps me get on this one.'

'All you did was explain to me what crypto currency was.'

'That's *helping*, dad.'

'Well, you can help Billy for the moment,' Declan sighed. 'If that's okay?'

'Sure,' Billy smiled. 'I have some gopher work that needs

to be done. Scanning, script-kiddie filing, it's within her wheelhouse.'

Declan expected Jess to kick back at this, but instead she grinned, pulled off her fake-leather jacket, tossing it to the side and saluted.

'Where do you need me, boss?' she asked.

As Billy and Jess started discussing the day's duties, both forgetting Declan was even there, he took the opportunity to walk across the open plan office and knock on Detective Superintendent Bullman's door.

'Sorry to pull you in,' she said by way of introduction as he entered, 'but at the moment we're on a back footing.'

'It's Johnny,' Declan replied with abject certainty. 'I saw the footage. It's Johnny when he becomes Jackie.'

'You know that, I know that, half of the bloody London underworld knows that, but apparently nobody gave Johnny Lucas the memo,' Bullman leaned back in the chair, running her hand through her short, white hair as she did so. 'Go join Jock McScottie and see if you can dig up anything.'

'Yes, boss,' Declan turned to leave, but stopped as Bullman continued.

'Heard you went ring buying with DCI Farrow,' she said, and, even facing away, Declan knew she had a smile on her lips. 'I hope you don't say yes to him. You're *my* pretty princess, Walsh.'

'Never crossed my mind,' Declan replied, leaving the office and walking over to his desk. By now Jess was already situated at one of the empty spaces against the wall, a laptop open in front of her. Declan didn't want to know what she was doing; it was probably breaking half a dozen HR rules as it was. Grabbing his jacket, he nodded at his daughter as she glanced up, told Billy to text if anything new happened and then, feeling like a fifth wheel, he left the Temple Inn offices, on his way to Globe Town, a very familiar boxing club, and a confusing, unexpected murder.

KENNETH TSANG WANTED BLOOD.

He sat in his Chinatown office, staring at photos on his iPad; images taken from the previous night's abduction. On them, he could see the fear on his nephew's face as Jackie Lucas dragged him out of the back entrance.

'How many of these are there?' he asked. 'Out there?'

'You mean feeds?' Sharon Taylor, his go-to fixer, leaned against the bar, considering the question.

'Whatever these are,' Kenneth tossed the iPad across the room in impotent fury. 'People filming this, making coin off my family's suffering. I want them found.'

'You can't blame them for uploading this,' Sharon sighed, walking across the room. 'It's car crash TV. It's what people do now.'

'I want them taken down,' Kenneth hissed. 'I want these people shown that you don't screw with the Wo Shing Wo.'

'Come on, Kenny, this isn't Triad business, this is Tsang business,' Sharon almost laughed. 'This is Jeffrey having his Icarus moment and flying too close to the sun before falling to his death. And there's been no love lost there for ages.'

She looked across at the half finished chess game on the side table.

'How is the rematch going?' she asked with the tone of someone who really didn't care.

'Bad for me,' Kenneth leant back. 'Did you hear about the

Oxford Street pub? He dared to put a hit out on me! To say he would eradicate us! Twenty years we've held the peace!'

'So what are you going to do about it?'

Kenneth rose from the chair now, his build and height now fully revealed as he towered over Sharon.

'I'm going to fill the East End streets with blood,' he hissed. 'Get me my generals in here.'

He cricked his neck as he breathed in, savouring the moment, the order he'd wanted to give for years.

'We're going to war.'

4

SO YOU WANNA BE A BOXER

DCI Monroe was outside the building as Declan pulled up in what seemed to be the last remaining spot, parking around the corner of the street and nodding to De'Geer as he passed under the crime scene tape.

'Well, you took your bloody time,' Monroe growled.

'Had to get up to speed from Billy,' Declan replied calmly. 'And Bullman told me to go find *Jock McScottie*, and I didn't know who that was.'

He smiled innocently. Monroe's gruffness didn't shake him; he was well used to it by now.

'Are *you* Jock McScottie?' he asked, curiously.

'Everyone's a bloody comic these days,' Monroe complained. 'And to think, I campaigned for her to take the role. So why were you really late?'

'I had to convince Billy to babysit Jess, and then find something for her to do.'

'Oh, aye, it's summer holidays,' Monroe realised with a groan as he looked back at the entrance. 'Probably best you didn't bring her.'

'You think?' Declan raised an eyebrow half-mockingly as they started back to the steps that led to the door, already pulling on his latex crime scene gloves as he did so. 'When Billy tells a sixteen-year-old to look away from the monitor, you know it's not that great. Is the—'

'Body still in there? Nah, laddie; that's long gone. Poor bloody Khanna took that job on. When even Rosanna Marcos doesn't want it, you know there's something bloody horrid there.'

'Marcos turned it down?' This threw Declan. 'I thought she'd allowed Rajesh Khanna to continue because this was his patch?'

'First off, it's *Doctor* Marcos, and second, she has history with the Tsangs, apparently, so decided it was better to have a look at the club instead.'

Declan nodded as they entered the boxing club; he now wanted more than anything to ask what the history with the Tsangs was, but knew better than to try to solicit gossip from Monroe.

In the corner, talking to a man wearing head-to-toe PPE, a visible police turban underneath, was DS Anjli Kapoor. She noted Declan's arrival with a curt nod and returned to the conversation. Declan knew she'd been told he was turning up, so there was no surprise there. But perhaps a small part of him that'd hoped for the slightest hint of a smile.

Declan reluctantly turned his attention to the boxing ring. The body might no longer be within, but the bloodied ropes, each tied to a corner of the ring were, hanging limply, gruesome reminders of the atrocities that had taken place here less than twelve hours earlier.

'If the runner hadn't been nosey, this would have stayed

hidden until opening time,' Monroe muttered. 'What a bloody cheerful scene for the cleaners to find.'

'Do we have the runner's name?' Declan asked.

'The witness? Aye, I think the police were savvy enough to grab that,' Monroe smiled slightly as he replied. 'Why? You think there's something jinky going on there?'

'Guv, you've spent your time in the area,' Declan straightened, stretching his back muscles as he thought aloud. 'Would you go for a jog around the estate at midnight, alone?'

'No, and I wouldn't wish it on a lassie, either,' Monroe nodded. 'I thought that too, so don't get too cocky. I've got Billy checking into her. You think she's connected to Lucas?'

'If she is, she utterly screwed him over,' Declan mused, walking to the ring and staring closely at one of the ropes. 'Chances are if someone loyal to him found this, they could have kept it quiet until they could lose the body somewhere. This, added to the hunt that was happening, makes me think it's a little too convenient.'

Anjli, having finished her conversation with Rajesh, now made her way through the heavy bags and weight equipment to join them.

'Farrow get his ring?'

Declan shook his head, waving at the bloodied boxing square beside them.

'He got *a* ring, but not the one he was expecting,' he said. 'Anything from Khanna?'

'Not yet,' Anjli shuddered. 'Only thing he noted was that the rope's from the back room, and it's what they use to lace up the heavy bags.'

'Might be significant, I'll get Davey to look into it,' Monroe replied. 'Anything else?'

'There were four jerry cans of petrol beside the ring,'

Anjli read from her notes. 'I reckon they were intending to burn the body after they finished, but maybe got spooked when the runner came by.'

'Or they were using the petrol on him as they…' Monroe trailed off, unable to continue the horrific thought.

Anjli nodded.

'Possibly,' she replied. 'We've also located the girlfriend, Johnny's alibi. Cheryl Jenkins. Address on record in Canary Wharf, so I'm about to go over there.'

'Good idea,' Monroe took one last look around the boxing club. 'We'll go chat to Johnny Lucas, see if the mad bastard's come to his senses yet.'

He paused.

'Ring,' he said.

'No, come on, we've done this already,' Declan sighed.

'Not you, Jeffrey,' Monroe was scanning through his phone messages. 'Marcus Lightman. Old journo friend of mine. Said Jackie Lucas turned up last night at Helen of Troy in Soho, mouthing off that he was putting the Tsangs on notice. Showed a ring to people in there. Claimed it was Jeffrey's.'

'Was this before midnight?'

'Not sure, he didn't give a time.'

'Well, if it wasn't, I can't see how he did it while being in a Mile End cell.'

'I'll check in with him, see what he knows.'

'Johnny?'

'No, you *bampot*. Marcus.'

Declan nodded absently at this, making his own scan of the boxing club. He stopped, however, as he saw PC De'Geer emerge from the back office, waving to them. Nudging Monroe and pointing, the three detectives walked over to the uniformed officer, as ever in his motorcycle police gear, who had the expression of a man caught with a dilemma.

'What?' Monroe asked. 'You look like you've seen a ghost.'

'I think I have, boss,' De'Geer motioned for the others to follow him, leading them into Johnny Lucas' back office. 'I've been in here before, back when the *Magpies* were arrested.'

'Aye, and I was here after DI Frost tried to kill me,' Monroe mused, looking around. 'What's different? I'm guessing that's why you're here?'

'The photo frames,' De'Geer pointed at a bookshelf, three shelves filled with photos of Johnny Lucas. Declan knew them also; he'd spent his time in the boxing club, and the office of Johnny Lucas.

However, this time, all the photos were placed face down on the shelves.

'Maybe forensics did it?' Anjli asked, picking up a photo frame and looking at it. The image under the glass showed Johnny Lucas and the then-Mayor of London, Boris Johnson, at some black-tie event. Placing it back on the shelf, she frowned as she scanned the shelves.

There were two photos there that hadn't been placed down.

The first was one Declan had seen before; a childhood photo of three children, two boys and a girl, a few years older than the others, and taken in the sixties or early seventies. He'd assumed it'd been found by Johnny at a car boot sale or something, and placed on his shelf to add to the legend of 'The Twins', but now Declan wasn't sure.

The second one was new.

'That's the one,' De'Geer, seeing Anjli and Declan's gaze, replied. 'All the others are face down except for those two.

And I don't remember seeing the second one before. It's like we were supposed to see it.'

Declan walked over now, picking up the photo, staring down at it.

'It has to be Photoshop,' he murmured to himself as he looked up at Monroe, passing the photo frame over as he continued. 'It's impossible.'

The image in the frame was that of Johnny Lucas, in a club, smiling widely. It wasn't more than a couple of years old, as the Johnny Lucas in the photo was pretty much the same as Declan knew currently.

It was the *other* man in the photo that threw him.

The same height and build, his almost white hair parted opposite, and a black shirt worn instead of his brother's navy coloured one, Jackie Lucas held an arm around his brother, raising a glass to the camera.

'Either that, or Johnny Lucas isn't the mad bastard we thought he was,' Anjli whispered. 'And Jackie Lucas isn't a voice in his head after all.'

Declan looked at Monroe as he stared at the photo.

'We need to speak to Johnny Lucas,' Monroe whispered urgently. 'We need to confirm his alibi right now.'

'What aren't you telling us, Guv?' Anjli asked.

Monroe looked up at her and she recoiled, the force of his gaze hitting her dead centre.

'I need to check some things first,' he replied, his voice devoid of all emotion now. 'Declan? With me. Anjli? Go speak to the girlfriend. De'Geer? See if anything else has been moved in here.'

And with that said, Monroe turned and walked stiffly out of the office. De'Geer looked at Declan and Anjli.

'Okay, I'm not misreading that, am I?' he asked. 'Something's spooked the Guv something rotten.'

Declan nodded, watching through the door as Monroe continued through the boxing club, eyes fixed straight ahead.

'No, I think you're right there,' he replied. 'But I'll be damned if I know what it is.'

Keeping the photo frame in his hand, Declan nodded to Anjli and De'Geer, following Monroe out of the boxing club. He'd wanted to chat to Anjli, say hello, check on her mum, but that could all wait.

Because now it was time to chat to Johnny Lucas.

THEY HAD PLACED JOHNNY LUCAS IN CUSTODY IN MILE END station, so it was a quick journey there for Declan and Monroe from Globe Town. Declan drove, as Monroe had cadged a lift to the boxing club with Anjli, and during the brief ride there Declan tried to get something out of the dour Scot beside him, but Monroe didn't speak at all for the journey, eyes staring straight out ahead.

'When we get in there, let me talk,' he said as they climbed out of the car, now parked in one of Mile End Command Unit's visitor bays.

'Fine by me,' Declan replied, locking up and staring up at the building. 'You know, I don't think I've been here properly since DCI Ford.'

'Let's hope they don't remember that too much,' Monroe grinned for the first time since they'd left the boxing club. 'I don't want them arresting you before we speak to Johnny.'

Declan grimaced; before he'd joined Monroe's team, he'd been suspended from Tottenham North after punching a Catholic priest on live TV. In his defence, the priest had been arrested, and had just told Declan that Jess was going to Hell, but it was enough to put his job on the line. Mile End's DCI Ford had pulled him onto a murder case, but after a while Declan realised he was nothing more than a patsy, there for her and DC Hart to place blame on after they stole millions in cryptocurrency. Declan had, however, turned this against them, and by the end both Ford and Hart were arrested, while Declan found himself ostracised once more, this time however for turning against his own.

The fact he'd done this before they turned on *him* was irrelevant.

Entering Mile End, Declan followed Monroe as they went along the corridors leading to DCI Esposito's office, but as they reached the corridor that led into the main bullpen area, Declan hung back; already they'd passed a couple of officers who'd thrown dagger glares at him, and he really wasn't feeling the love right now.

'I'll wait here,' he said. 'I think I'm gathering a little attention.'

'Christ, man, nobody here even remembers who you are,' Monroe laughed. 'You're just way more paranoid than you were last time you were in this Godforsaken place.'

Declan accepted this and reluctantly followed his boss into Esposito's office.

DCI Esposito was there with a woman detective, taller than everyone else in the room, and with hair almost as bright red as Jess had a few months earlier. They both looked up as Monroe and Declan entered, Monroe tapping on the glass of the door, but not waiting for an invitation before walking through.

'Oh thank God,' Esposito stated sardonically. 'The cavalry has arrived.'

'Good to see you too, Alvaro,' Monroe smiled. 'Wish it was under better circumstances.'

'Hey, if you can get this off my slate, I'm more than happy,' Esposito replied, straightening. 'DS McAlroy, meet DCI Monroe and DI Walsh.'

'Walsh?' McAlroy's eyes widened. 'As in the one that—'

'Probably,' Declan interrupted. 'If you hear any kind of rumour about me, just assume it's true.'

'You here to interview Lucas?' Esposito sat back in his chair.

'If it's okay with you?' Monroe was strangely diplomatic as he replied, and Declan wondered if this was leading to something.

'I'll have him moved to Interview One for you,' Esposito looked at McAlroy, who, after a moment, realised this was her unspoken command to do so and, with a nod to the two detectives, left the room.

'Anjli's replacement?' Declan watched after her as she left. He could almost feel the anger from her, forced to leave the office and sort out the menial work while the others planned the next steps. It was something he understood well; he'd been in exactly the same position before.

Esposito nodded, looking over at Monroe.

'Yeah, she's good. Probably too good. Has a bit of the Devil in her, just like your lad here.'

The last part was aimed at Declan, and he smiled as Esposito continued.

'But she's a closer. And somewhere like Mile End, we need to close things quickly.'

'I get the message,' Monroe glanced at Declan. 'We don't want to be on this forever, either.'

'Then we're agreed,' Esposito rose, shaking Monroe's hand. 'This isn't a pretty one, Alex. Sorry you have to deal with it.'

'Ach, it's not my first dance with the Lucas way of life,' Monroe joked. 'And with him in your cells, hopefully it won't escalate.'

The conversation with DCI Esposito now finished, Monroe and Declan walked out of the office and down the corridor towards the interview rooms. As they did this, Declan wondered how true that statement actually was; with Johnny Lucas locked away for murder, the East End was now open for new business.

And that meant that *everything* would be escalating.

5

FALLEN RULERS

JOHNNY LUCAS LOOKED TERRIBLE AS HE SAT ACROSS THE interview room table from Declan and Monroe. His solicitor, a stick thin, almost skeletal man with obviously dyed-black hair cut into a wedge, with a face that could be in its thirties or fifties depending on the light, sat stock still, waiting for someone to speak.

Monroe, facing him, seemed to play a waiting game.

But Johnny looked tired and broken. His usually pristine hair was lank and tousled, a night of lying on a rubber custody cell bed likely to be the cause, his expensive navy blue shirt wrinkled and creased. But more than that, his face was haggard, *desperate* looking, even.

'What the hell happened, Johnny?' Monroe started. 'This isn't like you. Or Jackie.'

Johnny stared at the table, a far cry from the usually arrogant and cocksure man that they both knew so well.

'They say I killed the Tsang kid,' he replied. 'I don't remember doing it.'

'That's not the same as 'I didn't do it', now,' Monroe frowned. 'Are you saying you did? That you may have?'

Johnny shrugged.

'I don't remember,' he said simply.

'What my client means to say—' the solicitor started, but stopped as Johnny held up a hand.

'We don't need that,' he muttered. 'Not today, not with these two. They're not recording this.'

'Thought it better to talk off the record first,' Declan replied cautiously. 'Especially with such a unique situation.'

'How so?' Johnny looked warily at Declan now.

'Where's Jackie, Johnny?' Declan asked.

'He's in Liverpool, on bus—'

'I said, *where's Jackie*, Johnny,' Declan interrupted, his voice more demanding.

After a long moment, Johnny sighed, looked to the ceiling and slumped down in the chair.

'Jackie doesn't exist,' he said.

'Good,' Declan nodded. 'Now we can speak as adults. How does it work?'

'How does what work?'

'You and Jackie,' Monroe interjected. 'I've seen both of you. Is it a full multiple personality, or is it an act for the cheap seats?'

Johnny shook his head.

'He's real,' he replied. 'He just, well, takes over. I take a back seat. Have you ever been drunk? I mean really drunk, so pissed that you can remember everything, but it felt like someone else was in control?'

'I'm aware of the feeling,' Declan's face was emotionless as he spoke. 'Is that how it was?'

'In the beginning, I did it to keep the peace, to make sure

everyone knew if I wasn't being respected, someone *worse* would show up,' Johnny admitted. 'But after a while, it became second nature, easier to do. I wasn't acting anymore, it was like I was channelling him. I'd feel him coming, you know? Like a '*get out, run away, the bogeyman's coming*' kind of thing. I assumed it was just my darker tastes coming out for a drive, a *Jekyll and Hyde* thing.'

'So Jackie comes out, restyles his hair and changes his shirt?'

'At the start it was me,' Johnny nodded. 'I was more in control. It was like I was just buzzing, like I'd had a joint. I was more relaxed, easygoing. I changed the look so people understood. And, because I'd always been the Twins, and also because Jackie was a right bastard, everyone kept quiet.'

'What do you mean, *always been the Twins?*' Declan frowned, confused at this.

Johnny looked surprised at Monroe.

'You never told him?'

'Never came up,' Monroe replied simply. 'I'll fill him in after. Keep going.'

Johnny shifted in his chair, reluctant to continue.

'So I lived this weird double life,' he said. 'I knew what I was doing, but I wasn't fully in control. Like I was driving on cruise control, you get me?'

At a nod, he continued.

'I liked it. I got to be political, calm and considered—and when I wanted to duff someone up, I'd change shirts, go round their house and beat seven shades of shit out of them. It was strangely liberating.'

'Addictive.'

'That too,' Johnny nodded, glad for an understanding audience. 'But, after a few years, it started getting stronger.

Like Jackie was starting to really exist. And then the black-outs came.'

'Blackouts?'

'Yeah. I'd sit in my chair, in the back office and then a moment later I'd come to in a car park, or a waste ground, dressed like Jackie. I realised quickly that he'd kinda taken me over, like I was sleepwalking.'

'And you didn't think to get help?'

Johnny scowled.

'I'm Johnny bloody Lucas, the scourge of the East End,' he snarled. 'What do you think happens the moment people learn I'm a looney? I'd lose everything. Danny Martin would have been first in line, followed by every other gang in the E postcodes.'

'So, better the devil you know?' Monroe raised an eyebrow as he scratched at his white goatee. 'If things go too far, it's all part of the show?'

'You could say that,' Johnny nodded. 'Last night, I was seeing Cheryl. She's my—I suppose you could call her my *friend with benefits.* It was our anniversary. Six months. I went to her apartment—well, the one *I* pay the rent for, we had dinner and planned to have a night in, if you get what I mean, but I was wiped out. It's been a busy month.'

'Oh aye? How busy?'

'Better you don't know,' Johnny smiled, the first genuine one so far. 'Anyway, about nine, I fell asleep on the couch. Only woke up around midnight when Cheryl shook me awake, telling me the police were at the club.'

'Who told her?'

'Jason. He was my night time driver. He'd just heard and came to pick me up.'

'And he had the car all night?'

'No, I left it in the apartment car park. He'd *Uber'ed* over.'

'Mickey Trackies wasn't your driver?' Monroe asked.

'Trackies? Christ, I dunno if he even knows how to drive,' Johnny couldn't help laughing. 'I mean he has keys, but that's only because he valets it every week.'

'And Cheryl was with you all night?'

'Yeah.'

'She'll confirm this?'

'Of course.'

'And there's CCTV that could corroborate this?'

Johnny rocked back on the chair, thinking.

'It's a new apartment complex, so I'd hope so,' he replied. 'Anyway, that's everything. I thought I was having a doze, but meanwhile someone's out there pretending to be me.'

Monroe looked at Declan for a moment before reaching down and picking up the photo frame they'd taken from the club. Placing it on the table, he turned it to show Johnny.

'All the photos in your office were face down except for this one,' he said. 'Did you do this?'

Johnny peered down at the photo.

'What the hell is this?' he asked, shaking his head in disbelief. 'Your pretty boy in the waistcoat playing with Photoshop again?'

'Are you saying you've never seen this before?' Declan leaned closer. 'Because this was in your office when we arrived, upright, while everything else was flattened. And if we didn't do it, and if you didn't...'

Johnny Lucas looked up from the photo.

'I'm being set up,' he half-pleaded. 'You have to help me.'

Declan stared at Johnny's face, looking for any clue to his true state of mind. There was every chance that Johnny was playing them, but his expression was one of desperation.

'Jeffrey Tsang,' Declan started. 'You knew him?'

'Here and there. Knew his uncles more.'

'What about Maurice Hamilton?'

'That ponce? Yeah, I knew him. Did a bit of business with him a couple of decades ago, stuck with him ever since. Bane of my bloody life, he was. Reckoned he was the Krays go-to guy, when all he did was give Reggie and Ronnie a reach around. Probably.'

'So no love lost?'

'No,' Johnny replied adamantly. 'We don't run in the same circles. He likes the younger crowd, the ones who grew up on shit gangster movies and Tom Hardy biopics.'

'Ones like Jeffrey Tsang.'

'Yeah.'

'Did you and Jeffrey ever have any issues?' Declan asked.

Johnny chuckled.

'His uncles bloody hated me,' he replied. 'We made each other's lives hell for decades, but we had a what do you call it, a confidential, *mutually assured destruction* pact. If we hurt each other, we all suffered financially.'

'How so?'

'You understand what confidential means, right?'

'You understand what life in prison means, right?'

Johnny nodded.

'We were both part of a real estate deal. It was in our interests to stay friendly or lose money.'

Declan wrote this down.

'And Jeffrey Tsang?'

'Jeff spouted off a couple of times, but he was like a Terrier, you know? All bark and with his balls cut off. Was mouthing off about me a week ago, actually. I found it strangely reassuring. You know how it goes, the one thing worse than having bad things spoken about you—'

'Is not being spoken about at all,' Monroe finished.

'Got it in one, mate.'

Declan leaned back now, glancing at Monroe. In return, the dour Scot stared dispassionately at Johnny Lucas, as if trying himself to work out the truth of the matter.

'Alex,' Johnny pleaded. 'I saved your life, gave you sanctuary. Almost cost me the club. Return the favour. Clear me.'

'That's a tough favour to ask,' Monroe replied sadly. 'At the moment there's a bastard ton of plates spinning. Did you blackout, did someone pretend to be Jackie, was it the real Jackie—'

'Guv?' Declan asked.

'I said we'd get into it later,' Monroe shook his head, looking back over at Johnny. 'But, once we get CCTV proof you were in Cheryl's apartment, and a statement from her as well, we'll be better equipped to move on this.'

Johnny nodded, relaxing back into his chair as his solicitor, silent throughout, started gathering his papers together. Rising from their chairs in one singular motion, Monroe and Declan took the picture frame off the table.

'But if it was you, and you *did* do this?' Monroe added, his tone icy as he held the photo frame in his hand. 'I'll cut your balls off and make you into a Terrier myself.'

THE *CIRQUE APARTMENTS* IN CANARY WHARF WERE A NEW build estate, finished within the last few years, and boasting a view over the Thames that went all the way from the O2 Arena to the east, to the London Shard in the west, currently just about visible through the haze, as Anjli stared out of the fourteenth-floor window.

'You sure you don't want a brew?' Cheryl Jenkins asked, standing in a small kitchenette area beside the living room.

'No, I'm good,' Anjli smiled. 'Thanks. Look, I'm sorry to ask, but how much does a place like this cost?'

'You looking to rent one?' Cheryl turned from the counter. 'I also manage the estate, so I can get you a good deal. Place like this is around three, perhaps four grand a month.'

Anjli whistled.

'Yeah, I think I'll hold on that until I win the lottery,' she said as Cheryl, an espresso in her hand, walked to the sofa, sitting down. Taking the chair opposite, Anjli pulled out her notebook.

'So you're seeing Johnny Lucas?' she asked.

'*Seeing*, that's such a leading word,' Cheryl smiled impishly behind the cup. 'I prefer *shagging like bunnies*.'

Anjli nodded, writing this down, while trying desperately *not* to envision the mid-sixties Johnny Lucas in any kind of sexual situation.

'Thanks for the clarification,' she said. 'And were you, as you say, shagging like bunnies last night?'

'I wish,' Cheryl sighed. 'Johnny was over about seven. I made him his favourite, gammon and chips with an egg on top. We had dinner, snuggled up on the sofa, and then he dozed off.'

'He fell asleep?'

'Yeah,' Cheryl placed the cup onto the glass coffee table in front of her. 'Right royally pissed me off, too. I had my best undies on and everything. I'd even shaved.'

Anjli went to ask for more clarification, but then stopped herself.

Cheryl wasn't talking about beard stubble.

'Okay, and then you did what?'

Cheryl thought about the question for a moment.

'Scrolled through Instagram for a bit, read a little of the new James Patterson book, anything that didn't wake him. He's been so stressed recently. Even to the point of having *man* problems, if you get what I mean. He hasn't been sleeping at all, and he looked so peaceful. Well, at the start.'

'The start?' Anjli looked up from the notepad. 'Go on.'

'Well, then *he* turned up,' Cheryl shook her head, her voice dripping with disdain. 'I've only seen him now and then, but when he arrives, it's never good. He wants to *force* himself, you know?'

'You mean the *Jackie* persona,' Anjli wrote this down. 'Did he do anything to you last night? Force you to do anything?'

'No,' Cheryl shook her head vehemently. 'Rather the opposite, really. He got up, said hello, apologised for interrupting my evening, then went into the bedroom. Quite polite, actually. Johnny has some shirts in there, and Jackie didn't like the blue he was currently wearing. He changed shirts, put on a nice black one, told me not to wait up and then left.'

Anjli half-rose at this.

'He left?' she repeated. 'What time?'

'About nine-fifteen, maybe nine-thirty,' Cheryl replied. 'Came back just before midnight, said hello again, sat on the sofa and fell asleep.'

'Did he say where he went?' Anjli sat on the edge of the cushion now, leaning closer.

Cheryl shook her head.

'I know better than to ask him things like that,' she replied. 'Not Jackie.'

She stopped, as if a sudden thought came to her.

'There was one thing,' she finished. 'He'd changed his shirt again. Back to the blue ones he wore as Johnny. It was a Ted Baker one, and I knew he had those in his office, so he must have gone to the boxing club. And his suit was clean, too; he'd spilled wine on his jacket but it wasn't there.'

'Like he'd changed his jacket?'

'Yeah, maybe,' Cheryl faltered now, realising she'd given too much away.

Anjli rose from the chair, placing her notepad into her jacket pocket.

'Thank you for this,' she said, her mind reeling with the revelation. Johnny may have claimed he was innocent, but the dominant Jackie persona now had no alibi for the evening.

Jackie Lucas could have killed Jeffrey Tsang.

'Detective,' Cheryl stood, awkwardly wringing her hands. 'Johnny, he's a bad man, sure, but he's no killer.'

'Trust me, I know Johnny,' Anjli replied. 'I know he—'

'But that Jackie?' Cheryl interrupted. 'He's a *bastard*. And all he wants is blood.'

And with that ringing endorsement in her head, Cheryl walked over to the kitchenette and began cleaning her coffee cup as Anjli made her apologies, placed a business card with her number on the side table, and left.

6

SIBLING RIVALRY

DECLAN GLARED AT MONROE AS THEY WALKED INTO THE MILE End car park. Monroe, in turn, was managing very well to avoid Declan's eye.

'So, if you want to tell me what I obviously don't know, now would be the perfect time to do it,' he muttered sullenly. 'I don't like being kept in the dark, especially about bloody Johnny Lucas.'

Monroe stopped, sighing.

'Look at the photo,' he said.

Declan took the offered frame from Monroe and looked at the two men shown in it.

'It's a Photoshop job,' he said. 'Not that great either, because the Jackie figure has a slight halo, which means he wasn't properly cut from the photo he was originally in. Billy explained this to me a while back after I asked one too many times about enhancing a CCTV photo. Tons of technical twaddle about pixels and dots per inch, but this I remembered.'

'Look at Jackie,' Monroe urged. 'I mean, *really* look at him.'

Declan stared at the photo. He didn't know what he was supposed to be looking at, but then he stopped, peered closely at the image and looked back at Monroe.

'Jackie has a small scar on his chin,' he said. 'One that Johnny doesn't.'

'Exactly,' Monroe nodded. 'I didn't notice it until I glanced at it during the interview. If you were to take photos of Johnny, ones where he's being both personalities, merge them together and print it like this? The hair, shirt, clothes would be different, but the face would be exactly the same. At best, maybe mirrored. And there wouldn't be a scar.'

'So someone took this from a time when Johnny had a scar there that's now healed?'

'Possibly,' Monroe looked around the car park as he returned his attention to Declan. 'Or there's a different answer. Why do you think so many people believe the Twins exist?'

'Because Johnny, as Jackie, would hurt them if they didn't?'

'Well, there is that, but there's a different answer,' Monroe replied. 'There *was* a Jackie, once.'

'No bloody way,' Declan shook his head. 'You're not telling me they were twins, after all. We'd know.'

'They weren't twins,' Monroe started towards the car, motioning for Declan to follow. 'But they were brothers. Eleven months apart. Jackie was born on the fifteenth of September, and then Johnny arrived on the thirty first of August. Because of the dates, it placed them in the same year and class at school; Jackie was the oldest in the year, and Johnny the youngest. But they were almost identical, similar in height and build, and the idea of them being twins began then.'

'Why isn't this known?'

'It is known, but nobody really remembers it as fact,' Monroe shrugged. 'Remember, this was before social media and all that, and things can be altered. In the nineties, Johnny made sure that his whole family were removed from the spotlight. His parents, a sister who ran like hell from them before they became the kings of the East End... money can make a lot of things disappear, and also create stories that seem real.'

Declan remembered the photo of the three children.

'There was a picture of two small boys and a girl,' he replied.

Monroe nodded.

'Aye, but who knows if it's real or not. His whole life is now made up, so Christ knows who they were. Could be anyone's.'

'And people nowadays assume this is all part of Johnny's plan back in the nineties to fake a twin,' Declan nodded. 'Only those who knew them back then would know the truth.'

'Exactly. And they paid many of those off to conveniently forget certain things. Johnny and Jackie were boxers, just like the Krays were, even trained in the same places. By the time they were in their early twenties, they were already making a scene. And, just like Reggie and Ronnie, Johnny was the calm, assured, sensible one while Jackie was the psycho.'

They were now in the car, Declan starting the engine as Monroe continued.

'But in the late eighties, perhaps the start of the nineties even, there was an assassination attempt on them,' Monroe continued. 'Problems with a Russian gangster, I believe. After that, everyone was told that Jackie and Johnny would never be seen in the same place together for safety. And that's how it stayed until now, and the story's never changed. People knew it was Johnny playing two parts, and over the years it kind of retroactively altered his story, and Jackie faded from existence as the *fake* brother took over, to the point now that unless you were there at the time, you wouldn't know there even was a Jackie.'

'School records?'

'In the sixties and seventies, all on paper. All able to be destroyed. At one point in his life, Johnny purged everything from his past. Even his family records are missing.'

Declan gripped the steering wheel tighter as he considered the implications here.

'So Johnny subconsciously replaced his brother, creating his own multiple personality, rather than admitting he was gone, most likely killed in this assassination attempt,' he said.

Monroe nodded.

'The Twins always existed, and there was enough plausible deniability to create something out of it,' he explained. 'But here's the thing. I heard a story once, back when I—'

He paused, and Declan knew Monroe was trying to work out the best way to say *when I was being paid off by them* without making it sound bad.

'When me and your father knew them,' he finished. 'The story was how one of the rival gangs in the eighties, a man called *The Turk* in Soho, had caught Jackie's chin with a butterfly knife, opening it up. It was something to do with a girl, and as ever, the story's altered every time it was told. Hear it now, and there's no scar, and the Turk lost his finger instead. But originally, it happened.'

'Cut like that would have left a scar,' Declan nodded. 'But

if Jackie died, and Johnny's been playing both roles, how do we have an older Jackie, complete with scar, in this photo?'

'That's the dilemma, laddie,' Monroe mused. 'You shouldn't be able to. Which means it's either someone who knows the stories and is playing games and adding photoshopped scars to the photoshopped pictures, or that *is* Jackie Lucas, in the flesh, taken within the last couple of years, and placed in the photo.'

Declan stopped at a set of red traffic lights, and Monroe turned to face him.

'Here's the kicker, though,' he breathed. 'The rumour mill at the time said it was Johnny that put the hit on Jackie. He felt he was getting out of control, that he was going to get them both arrested, put away.'

'He wasn't wrong there,' Declan replied as the car started again. 'So what, we need to find out if Jackie Lucas survived, hid somewhere for thirty, forty years and has now come back?'

'Aye, pretty much,' Monroe scratched at his chin. 'I think we need to speak to someone who knew the real Jackie back in the day, who might be able to give us his impression of this new one.'

'Maurice Hamilton?'

Monroe grinned.

'You read my mind, laddie,' he said. 'But let's go grab a spot of lunch first, aye? I'm starving.'

'You didn't have to make me a tea,' Billy said as Jess passed him a mug. 'I'm perfectly capable of doing it, whatever your dad says.'

'No offence, Billy, but I had your tea in Hurley, and you don't make it right,' Jess replied, sitting back in her own chair, her own mug cupped in both hands. 'I'm sure it's what your butlers, or whatever servants you had in Downton Abbey taught you, but I prefer it to be a bit more *builder's* tea. Stick your spoon in it and watch it stay straight.'

'That's not tea,' Billy bemoaned, now looking at the mug in his hand in a mixture of concern and abject terror as to what he was about to drink. 'That's soup. Your dad is a monster for teaching you that.'

Jess chuckled as she shuffled into the seat.

'You found anything?'

Billy nodded, suddenly back to complete seriousness as he replied.

'Yeah, and it's not good for Johnny Lucas. I spoke to the security of the Cirque Apartments. They don't have night security, but they do have cameras in the lobby. They sent this over ten minutes ago.'

He tapped on the keyboard, and a small screen appeared on his right hand monitor; the CCTV footage of Cheryl Jenkins' apartment lobby.

'This was nine-thirty last night,' Billy said as he played it. On the screen a man appeared from the external door, waiting to the left of the screen, wearing a tracksuit, a white bandage on his right hand. He didn't show his face to the camera, and from his stance, Jess could see that he obviously knew where the camera was.

'I think that's Mickey Trackies,' Billy scrolled through the feed as he spoke.

'Yeah, I can see that,' Jess sipped at her tea. 'What is it about bruisers and track suits?'

'I'd say they love the cliché, but it's likely to blend in at the boxing club Johnny owns. That looks like boxing tape on his knuckles.'

'But he's not in the boxing club,' Jess protested. 'Someone needs to explain to him about dressing for occasions.'

'At the moment, I'm not sure what this occasion actually was,' Billy replied, watching the screen until a figure appeared on the right of it. He was in a black suit, with what looked to be a dark grey shirt on the monochrome screen, although this could be a reflection on the material. His hair, almost white, had been blow dried back, and parted on the side.

It was obviously Johnny Lucas. Or, more likely, his 'Jackie' persona.

He stopped in front of Mickey Trackies, they spoke for a moment, although Jess couldn't make out anything and then Mickey pulled a gun out from within his tracksuit top, passing it to 'Jackie', who placed it in the back of his trouser belt, bringing his suit jacket over it as they walked out.

'Well, *that's* not ominous at all,' Jess muttered.

'They go to this car,' Billy tapped on the keyboard again, and this time another image appeared, a static photo of a black Jaguar F-Type SUV, driving down a street, lights on. 'I've followed it through the ANPR, that's the—'

'Automatic number plate recognition,' Jess interrupted with a grin. 'Yeah, you said earlier.'

Billy opened up a browser on the middle screen, what effectively looked like a google map of central London, with little red camera symbols littered throughout.

'There are dozens of these in the city, but they only pick up the plates if the cars drive past them,' he said as he tapped on the screen, showing one in Canary Wharf. 'Johnny, or I suppose Jackie now, he couldn't miss this one as it's a chokehold lane change on the Limehouse Underpass, coming out of Canary Wharf. We miss him in Central London, but knowing where he's believed to end up, we pick him up here—'

Another click, another static image; this time one of the black Jaguar F-Type SUV pulling off a dual carriageway.

'—on the A40, just north of White City.'

Jess leaned closer, as if looking at the image from a nearer perspective would suddenly help her.

'Can you see who's driving?' she asked.

'No, they usually pick the plate up from behind, but that the car's even *there's* enough to show that someone at least connected to Johnny was too,' Billy replied. 'We then don't see the car for fifteen minutes or so, and then we get this; the SUV returning home.'

A third photo appeared on the screen; the SUV now driving down the Bayswater Road, with Hyde Park to its right.

'We can follow the car through London, as we pick it up in Victoria, then the Embankment, then out through Whitechapel,' Billy went back to the map, tapping on various points of it. 'We have a hit one last time outside Bethnal Green tube station, and then I lose it. But you can map a route, following these hits, all the way from White City to Globe Town.'

'Where the body of Jeffrey Tsang was found,' Jess nodded. 'So Lucas did it?'

'Looks like the SUV was at least used in the abduction, and we also have this,' Billy clicked his mouse button and the CCTV of the entrance of *Tsang City* appeared from earlier; on it, lit up by the neon sign as he spoke to the doormen for a moment before being allowed through, was obviously Jackie Lucas, the two men with him following in behind. 'We've seen this before, and we've seen what happens inside, so I won't return there. But that's the same Mickie Trackies, so it matches the timeline we've made here. And that's not all.'

He clicked back to the map.

'So around midnight, we catch the Jag F-Type again, heading towards Canary Wharf. We get footage again from the apartment lobby CCTV of Johnny, or Jackie Lucas, alone this time, returning to Cheryl. And, about half an hour later, we catch him leaving again on the same CCTV, a different driver picking him up this time, and returning to Globe Town, caught on the camera beside the McDonald's roundabout on the A12. Working on the time this was taken, it has to be the point where Johnny arrived while the police were examining the crime scene.'

'When they arrested him.'

'Yes. So, we can hypotheses that Johnny, as Jackie left Cheryl Jenkins' apartment, met Mickey Trackies at the door, took a gun from him and drove to White City, where he either joined a waiting Kayas Ashad or brought him in the car,' Billy surmised. 'Once there, filmed by dozens of London based influencers, he shot and abducted Jeffrey Tsang, drove him back to Globe Town, spent around an hour, maybe an hour and a half there doing unspeakable things, drove back to Cheryl's, fell asleep and then returned to the club after someone woke him up when they called him.'

'That's very convoluted,' Jess frowned as she leaned back. 'Why not just stay there, or come from somewhere else, rather than driving all over the place?'

'Maybe Johnny was still in there somewhere, and kind of homed back in on Cheryl's place, like instinct,' Billy replied, turning around in the chair to face Jess. 'Hypothetical case scenario is Jackie leaves, goes back to Cheryl's, sits down, falls asleep, is woken by Cheryl, the phone, whatever. But now it's Johnny who wakes up; the Banner to his Hulk, the Jekyll to his Hyde. As far as Johnny's concerned, he dozed off three hours earlier, and has been woken up for something completely unconnected to him, because as far as he knows, he's been there all the time. A sleepwalker doesn't know that they sleepwalk if they wake up in bed.'

'So he's innocent?' Jess shook her head. 'How does that work?'

'I never said he was innocent,' Billy closed the screens on his monitor as he considered the question. 'I said he doesn't know he did it. And that's likely what they'll use as his defence.'

'Could that get him free?'

'Insanity clauses are always dubious at best,' Billy took the mug, sipping at it, raising his eyebrows in surprise as he tasted it. 'Okay, this is good.'

'Can I ask a question?' Jess scratched at her chin. 'What if he did know?'

'How do you mean?' Billy sipped again as he watched her work through her reply.

'Okay, so you're Johnny Lucas,' Jess started. 'You've spent years being one of a mythical set of twins. Everyone knows it's rubbish, that it's just you, but they're too scared to say anything, because when you're Jackie, you can really let go, allow your baser needs to come out. And, if anything bad happens, you just change your shirt, comb your hair differently and go 'it wasn't me'.'

'So you think he *knew* what he was doing?'

'Could make sense,' Jess was on a roll now as she worked through the idea. 'He has some kind of beef with Jeffrey Tsang. Decides to take him out. Pretends to doze off, gets up, changes, goes out, does horrible things, comes back, dozes off and then 'wakes up', claiming he's innocent.'

'He'd still be arrested,' Billy mused. 'It'd be easier to get someone in to do it for him.'

'But not as personal,' Jess insisted. 'And Jackie Lucas sounds like the kind of man who does personal very well.'

Billy leaned back in his gamer chair now, the one he'd specifically ordered because of his hours sitting, and considered this.

'It's a theory,' he muttered. 'But how do you prove it?'

'You're the copper, you tell me,' Jess shrugged. 'Who knows him the best?'

Billy nodded slowly to himself.

'Don't take this the wrong way, but I bloody hope you're wrong,' he said. 'If Johnny has been consciously doing this, then he's been playing a long game, and that includes playing us.'

He rose from the chair, arching his back, stretching out his spine.

'Go through the archives, hit his file on a deep dive,' he ordered. 'See if you can find any other times he may have done this. And I hope to God you don't find anything.'

'And if I do?'

'Then we'll be pushing to have the whole 'it's another personality' thing stripped from his defence,' Billy patted Jess on the shoulder as he passed. 'I'll let the boss know.'

He stopped, though, and once more looked back at the screens, showing the various points of Jackie Lucas' night-time jaunt.

'I just can't get the feeling out of my head that I've missed something,' he muttered. 'Something small but really important.'

Shaking his head, he continued towards Bullman's office.

'And no touching my monitors,' he muttered as he left.

Now alone at the monitor, Jess stared at the blank screen. She knew the history the *Last Chance Saloon* had with Johnny Lucas; he'd saved Monroe's life, but she'd also been told by Anjli once that Johnny Lucas had tried to blackmail her into working for him, holding her mother's privately funded cancer treatments from her if she didn't, classing it as a 'business agreement'.

Johnny Lucas was a bad guy. End of.

So why did she still feel that he was innocent here?

7

QUEEN SACRIFICE

PC COOPER HAD ONLY BEEN WITH THE TEMPLE INN COMMAND Unit for a few months, but in that time she'd seen rock bands try to kill each other, chefs go to war and, even though she hadn't been with them at the time, heard all about the illegal military duelling club the team had overthrown, while hunting illegally designed, Chinese-based laser weapons.

Somehow, a shooting in a White City club seemed almost pedestrian in comparison.

The West London Metropolitan Police had happily passed this one across when Doctor Marcos arrived with Cooper and DC Davey; they knew her reputation and were aware that if anyone could work the crime scene, it would be her. And, in fact, the local Shepherd's Bush CSI crew had even taken time off from their other duties to come and assist her, as it gave them a chance to see how Doctor Marcos worked.

PC Cooper didn't know if Doctor Marcos was aware she was giving a masterclass to the others, and didn't really want to mention it, just in case she'd read the situation wrong. One of the local coppers, PC Davison, a strawberry-blond man in his thirties, had stayed to liaise, and Cooper had chatted to him as they controlled the onlookers; Davison was a long-time beat copper for the area, and had known Jeffrey Tsang—or at least had been following his actions with professional interest—for quite a while now.

'Never thought it'd be the East End that took him out,' Davison muttered as he glanced back to the nightclub across the street from where they stood. 'I always thought it'd be the north or the south.'

'How come?' Cooper didn't really know much about the gangs of London, apart from what she'd read in the Unit's records; a previous case involving a gangland war, where the sons of several of the gang leaders attempted a coup, was pretty much the maximum information she had right now.

'Tsangs had issues with the Elephant crew,' Davison spoke with the authority of someone who had researched this fully.

'Elephants?' Cooper frowned. 'You don't mean—'

'Elephant and Castle,' Davison shook his head. 'South of the Thames. Christ, don't they teach you City plod anything?'

'They teach us not to be dicks to fellow officers who aren't as clued in,' Cooper replied icily. 'Who runs south of the river, then?'

Davison looked uncomfortable at the admonishment, but sniffed as he considered the question.

'People reckon Nicky Simpson's one of the major players,' he said.

'The YouTube guy?' Cooper was surprised at this. 'My mum and dad do his keep fit video every morning.'

Davison nodded.

'Yeah and he's got good lawyers, so we don't actually know

if that's correct,' he added. 'However, the name gets bounced around. He's never been arrested for anything, and technically, he's squeaky clean, with excellent legal bods who sue anyone who even hint at his family business. But his dad was a known wrong'un, his grandad worked with the Richardsons, and we know the Elephant crew have been having issues—with the Seven Sisters.'

PC Cooper knew about the Seven Sisters. They were a matriarchal gang based in Tottenham that worked as a committee of women, but in the same way that Johnny and Jackie Lucas was a story told to keep people in line, so were the Seven Sisters, as the real power there was Janelle, or 'Mama' Delcourt, who'd controlled the Sisters until earlier this year, when she'd blinded herself with a simunition paint grenade, all while trying to kill DCI Monroe and DI Walsh.

Now, relaxing and with gossip to provide, PC Davison was in full revelation mode, pointing out that the rumour mill he caught here and there claimed one of the other Sisters, Anita Taborsky, had risen to the role of 'assistant' to the now blinded Mama Delcourt, while in effect controlling the organisation; the power behind the throne, so to speak.

But at the same time, Janelle's daughter Molly, thirteen-years old going on thirty, and into ponies more than gangsters, had been groomed by the other Sisters for a seat at the table; a way to keep the Delcourt name at the top, and while the infighting could destabilise everything, especially after Moses Delcourt's attempted coup, the Sisters could continue somehow.

Davison believed Mama Delcourt could have instigated the war between Jeffrey Tsang and Johnny Lucas just to deflect from her own issues. Which actually made perfect sense, but didn't explain why one of her old soldiers, or rather one of *Moses Delcourt's* old soldiers, was now hanging out with the East End crime lord.

Cooper almost felt sorry for the detectives trying to make sense of this, and not for the first time since joining the Unit, felt grateful that she was mainly just the uniform that kept the paparazzi away from the crime scenes.

On that subject, Cooper had noticed a car pull up near the back of the crowd; a Ford Focus, it was driven by a woman in her mid-thirties, her long, slightly curly black hair pulled back into a ponytail, olive skin and a striped blue suit over a cream blouse, a woman who, once the car came to a stop and the engine was turned off, climbed out of the driver's side and walked towards them. She looked officious, maybe police or perhaps something more legal.

As if knowing her importance, the crowd of paparazzi seemed to part before her, and she stopped at the crime scene tape, pulling out a warrant card holder, showing it briefly to Cooper.

'DI Reckless, Vauxhall Met,' she said, placing the black leather holder back into her jacket. 'Who's in charge here?'

'Currently it's just forensics, Ma'am,' Cooper said as she held the tape up for DI Reckless to walk under. 'The divisional surgeon has been calling the shots. That's Doctor Marcos, of the City Police.'

'Rosanna Marcos?' For a second, it looked like DI Reckless faltered. 'Shit.'

'Ma'am?' Cooper hadn't expected such a response. DI Reckless stopped, almost holding back from approaching the club.

'We have history,' she replied simply. 'An old case. Got her into trouble, not my fault. Probably best if I don't talk to her. What's your name?'

'Cooper, Ma'am.'

'Okay then PC Cooper, why don't *you* get me up to speed here? Was it Jackie Lucas, or was it someone else?'

Cooper went to reply, but stopped herself before she could start.

'I'm sorry, Ma'am,' she said carefully, aware she was about to walk into a potential minefield. 'But what's your connection to the case? I was under the assumption we were working with Tottenham and Mile End, not south of the river?'

'Good call,' Reckless nodded. 'You pick up a lot, don't you? I can see that.'

She looked around, ensuring they were alone before leaning in.

'Look, although north, south and West London are being represented and all that, South London, and by that I mean pretty much *everything south of the river Thames* is being represented by yours truly. All of this could be connected to a case I'm working, and if it is, I could put down a really nasty bastard for a long time. You heard of Nicky Simpson?'

Cooper glanced back at Davison, currently dealing with a bolshy reporter at the crime tape.

'Someone was just talking about him,' she replied. 'Is he—'

'The Peckham version of Johnny Lucas?' Reckless replied with a smile. 'Yeah. Pretty much.'

PC Cooper watched DI Reckless for a moment. The detective seemed on edge, uncomfortable to be here.

'Perhaps I can find someone to speak to you who isn't Doctor Marcos?' she asked.

Reckless, as a response to this shook her head and turned to leave.

'I'll get my DS to speak to her,' she said as she looked around the scene, presumably looking for the Detective Sergeant she'd mentioned. 'If I can find the soppy idiot. Probably chatting up some of the public. It's probably best if I don't reopen old wounds.'

She stopped, her head whipping back to look at Cooper.

'Or you could just give me the cliff notes?' she asked with a grin.

Rosanna Marcos stretched her back, hearing the audible clicks of her spine as her muscles, compressed after an hour or two of crouching over, groaned their way into movement once more. Pulling off the hood of her custom fitted PPE suit, she ran a hand through her hair, freeing it as she walked over to DC Davey, rising from her current position of peering under a nightclub booth.

'Anything?' she asked, not really expecting a positive answer. And, in return, Davey shook her head, pulling her own mask and hood off.

'Not for this case, anyway,' the DC replied, placing a Q-Tip swab into a clear forensic baggie. 'Although by now I think we could close this place down for a dozen different violations.'

She nodded at the deep burgundy wallpaper, stark and unwelcoming in the harsh light of the forensics team's lamps.

'I mean, we could get him on style choices alone,' she smiled.

'Anything on the gun?'

'Same as the witnesses said,' Davey started walking with Doctor Marcos back to the nightclub's entrance. 'We found a bullet lodged into the skirting board at the back of the booth Tsang was sitting in, or rather standing in front of; it's most likely the one Jackie Lucas fired when he shot the victim through the skull.'

'*Possible* Jackie Lucas,' Doctor Marcos corrected. 'We're not sure it's him yet.'

'Aren't we?' Davey stopped, hands on hips, still stretching. 'It's becoming a little difficult to argue that right now. Witnesses alone are fingering him for this, Billy's got CCTV footage and livestreams from a dozen people where Jackie's near as dammit gurning for the cameras...'

She shrugged.

'If it looks like a duck, and quacks like a duck...' she tailed off, the point made.

'Tell that to a duck hunter,' Doctor Marcos shook her head. 'They have duck calls and fake ducks; enough to convince the poor, tasty little buggers to come over and get shot.'

'You still think this is a setup?'

'I think there's a duck hunter with a bloody good duck call,' Doctor Marcos nodded. 'But I don't know how or why.'

She pointed back at the booth.

'Something's been bothering me for the last hour, Jo. Looking at it time and time again? All I can see is the blood spatter isn't right,' she complained. 'Gunshots are impactful. Blood sprays away from the body, basically in a mist. Banner's knee did it, as you can see the blood spatter all over the booth. Likewise, his skull.'

She pursed her lips.

'But Tsang's gut wound, it's almost like a stab wound instead.'

'Lucas moved in close, so maybe the body blocked the

main spatter, and the blood on the floor's from where he bled out?'

Doctor Marcos shrugged.

'Yeah, maybe. Anything else?'

Davey nodded.

'Two things. First, the back door to the place had a message scrawled on it in marker pen,' Davey pulled out her smartphone, opening it so she could give the correct information. 'Looks like a chess move.'

Doctor Marcos stopped in the nightclub entranceway.

'Chess?' she asked. 'That's not what I'd expect to see on the door of a crime lord's nightclub. What does it say?'

'*Queen to C-7*,' Davey replied, showing a photo on her phone. 'I thought I'd snap a shot, in case it was relevant. There was dried blood on the surrounding door, but I couldn't work out if that was because they'd leaned against it while writing, or left blood marks when they pushed it open later.'

Doctor Marcos stared at the image on the phone, and Davey could see her eyes narrowing, as in her head Doctor Marcos was already moving through every feasible option here.

'We need to speak to the kitchen staff,' she eventually replied. 'I need to find out if any of them wrote this.'

'I already did, and none of them remember it being there before Jackie left,' Davey frowned. 'You know what it means?'

'Possibly,' Doctor Marcos nodded. 'But it's a bit *out there,* if you know what I mean. My dad was a national champion level player of chess. He had tons of books on it, read them to me all the time when I was a kid, hoping I'd follow in his footsteps.'

'Did you?'

'God no. But it taught me how to think several moves ahead, so *go dad*, I suppose.'

'And this is connected to that?'

Doctor Marcos looked across the nightclub as she brought back a move she'd last seen decades earlier.

'Later in life, sure. This is about thirty years ago. *Queen to C-7* is a particular move, known as *Meier's Spectacular Sacrifice*. Rated as one of the five best winning moves in history. But it's not a pretty one.'

'How so?' Davey, not really a chess fan, was still intrigued.

'It's a deflection tactic,' Doctor Marcos replied, 'but with three possible directions. All of black's pieces are overloaded, defending too many things on the seventh and eighth lines. Getting any of those pieces off what they're defending can lead to a win—but at a significant cost. Meier placed his Queen on a place where three black pieces could take it, but each one is taken by a *different* piece. Here it was Rook takes Queen, but then that opened up a check by Meier's own Rook. Muller's Queen stopped that, but was taken in turn by Meier's *other* Rook.'

'Okay...' Davey was uncertain where this was going.

'Muller's Rook takes *that* Rook, and Meier moves his Bishop to check the King again. Muller's first Rook blocks, the Bishop takes it. *Check*. Second Rook blocks, Bishop takes, and Black King finds himself trapped between both Bishops. *Checkmate*. It's a brutal and very dispassionate series of moves, because you're not trying to keep any of your pieces. You're sacrificing everything for the endgame.'

'So why have this on a door?' Davey shook her head.

'Maybe because it's a bloodbath in there?' Doctor Marcos considered. 'The Queen's sacrifice starts a chain of events that takes her, the other Queen, three Rooks, better known as

Castles and the rival King out of the game. Bodies everywhere.'

Doctor Marcos shuddered, as if a sliver of ice ran down her spine.

'This isn't a chess-playing Easter egg, this could be a statement of intent,' she mused. 'Jackie Lucas is making a play and there are more bodies coming.'

There was a long moment as both of them considered the ramifications of what Doctor Marcos was suggesting.

'Shit,' was all Davey said. 'Who knew chess was so brutal?'

'You'd be stunned at the stories I have,' Doctor Marcos smiled. 'So, that aside, what was the second thing you found?'

'Piss,' Davey wrinkled her nose at the thought. 'There was a statement by one girl that had been with Tsang when Jackie —I mean, whoever was claiming to be Jackie—arrived, stating that when Jackie faced them, the old guy, Maurice Hamilton, stood to the side and wet himself. I'm guessing the ammonia smell and the urine stains came from that.'

Doctor Marcos mused on this for a moment.

'I met Hamilton a couple of times when I was doing the Tancredi case,' she said, thinking back. 'He was a bit of a chancer, reckoned he was bigger than he was and all that, but he never struck me as a coward. Sure, he was good at making sure he wasn't in the firing range, but not to the level he'd soil himself.'

'Must have been something that terrified him,' Davey, blinking twice as they walked out into the afternoon sun, said. 'Do you want to grab a late lunch before we—'

She stopped as she realised that Doctor Marcos was already moving away from her, picking up her pace as, across the street and beside the police cordon, PC Cooper was looking up at the approaching doctor, a black-haired woman beside her.

'Oi!' Doctor Marcos cried out. 'What the hell are *you* doing here?'

PC Cooper turned to Doctor Marcos, walking towards her, hands up in a placating gesture, as if aware that this was the starting of a very uncomfortable scene.

'DI Reckless was just asking about the case, Ma'am,' she said. 'I've heard you and her have a history, and I just wanted to calm the situation down before DI Reckless and you—'

'DI Reckless *doesn't exist*,' Doctor Marcos hissed as she glared at Cooper. 'Did she show you her badge? Did you—'

The second part of the comment was aimed at Reckless, Doctor Marcos looking back to where the detective had been standing but a second earlier; but all that was there was now an empty space and a gap in the onlookers, wide enough for someone to have pushed their way through while exiting the scene of the crime rather quickly. In fact, it had been so quick that as Cooper's brain caught up to the fact that DI Reckless was no longer there, the Ford Focus she'd arrived in sparked to life, screeching off before Doctor Marcos could chase after her.

'I'm sorry, I didn't know,' Cooper moaned, looking from Davey to Doctor Marcos. 'She had a warrant card; it looked real. She told me all about the issues you had. It sounded genuine.'

'The issues and the warrant card are real,' Doctor Marcos muttered irritably, her face scrunched up in anger. 'It's just the card's no longer valid. You weren't to know.'

'Problems?' Davey asked, walking up to join them.

'I don't know,' Doctor Marcos replied. 'Ellie Reckless used

to be a DI in the South London Met. Good one, too. Closed a lot of cases and pissed a lot of bastards off.'

'So what happened?' Cooper asked, nervously.

'She murdered a witness in an organised crime case,' Doctor Marcos explained matter-of-factly. 'Stopped Bryan Noyce from testifying against a wicked bastard in the Elephant and Castle. The police couldn't prove it though, and had to eventually toss the case out. Noyce had information on a lot of people, so most of the London underworld was pretty bloody happy he was gone, and lined up to give alibis to show she couldn't have done it. She was never convicted of the murder, which is still unsolved, and tried to return to her job as if nothing happened. Police did the only thing they could; they found another way to get her out.'

Davey stared off down the street, the Ford Focus long gone.

'What did you tell her?' she asked.

'I didn't know,' Cooper bemoaned. 'I thought she was a copper.'

'I get that,' Davey nodded soothingly, her voice calm. 'But I'm guessing she turned up saying she needed information?'

'She said she was working on a case that would nail some guy called Nicky Simpson,' Cooper stated, trying to regain a little of her professionalism as she spoke. 'I know a Simpson, but he's a TV guy or something, and PC Davison over there said he might be the guy who runs South London.'

'I'm sure she was working on something that involved Simpson,' Doctor Marcos nodded. 'He's the bugger who wanted Bryan Noyce dead.'

'What did you tell her about the case?' Davey repeated.

Cooper slumped a little.

'Everything,' she muttered, almost a whisper. 'I thought she was one of us.'

'Shit,' Doctor Marcos looked up to the sky, letting out a long, frustrated sigh. 'I need to call Monroe.'

'Ma'am?' Cooper looked horrified. 'Does DCI Monroe really need to know what I did—'

'It's not you,' Doctor Marcos smiled, placing a reassuring hand on the officer's shoulder. 'Ellie Reckless has conned bigger and older than you over the years. You weren't to know. Take the lesson here never to trust someone you don't know until they've jumped through a dozen flaming hoops. But yeah, I'm going to have to tell Monroe that she's around again.'

She pulled out her phone, staring at her screen.

'You see,' she finished before typing a number, 'Ellie Reckless was his protégé once. In fact, DCI Alex Monroe trained her in everything she knows, before she betrayed the force, took Nicky Simpson's blood money and murdered her *boyfriend,* Bryan Noyce.'

8

MOTHER'S DAY

JANELLE DELCOURT HATED WAITING.

As the head of the Seven Sisters, she believed strongly she shouldn't ever have to wait, but over the last six months, she'd found herself more and more in a position where she would sit, waiting, until someone could arrive to help her, speak to her, tell her what the merry hell was going on in her own manor.

Coincidentally, she'd been *blind* for the last six months.

It was her fault; she knew it. As the police had burst in on her and the other crime lords in a secret meeting in a Manor House, held in the middle of nowhere, the older generation about to be executed by their successors, her own son Moses holding a gun to her head, she'd seen her rivals go down in gunfire and handcuffs, and realised that a life in prison was very much her next stage in life.

She didn't know why she did it; it was a knee-jerk, gut reaction. There had been a grenade on the counter, brought in by one of the coppers, the Scottish DCI that had been kidnapped and brought there. She'd grabbed it, deciding at that moment she'd rather die than be taken in, or at least take down some of the bastards that had done this to her, who'd ended her reign as queen of the Sisters, and had pulled the pin.

Of a sodding *paint* grenade.

Who even brings one of those to a gunfight?

The explosion, pretty much at point-blank range, had blinded her; even now, over half a year later, she could only make out the faintest of shadows and shapes, relying on recognition of voices to know who she was talking to. She'd been arrested and taken with the others, but this had weirdly helped her, as the officers had taken pity, diverting her to a hospital to have her eyes seen to, which meant she wasn't processed with the others, and could make her own arrangements, and when her legal team had pushed for a plea deal, the powers that be had listened and sympathised, classing the explosion as an accident in the heat of the action, and ultimately agreed to let her go free, on the condition she told them *everything* that happened, and *kept on* telling them.

She wasn't a grass, though. Snitches were bitches and bitches got stitches. She simply saw this as getting her revenge on the people who screwed her over; people like Danny Martin, once a right-hand man of Johnny Lucas, and others like her son Moses and the bastard Byrnes from Birmingham. Between them all, as well as a fake Catholic priest who—and she still didn't quite understand how—was leading this, they had all tried to destroy her life.

A life that was effectively over.

The doctors had said with luck she would regain a small amount of sight eventually, and they'd worked hard to remove as much paint from the corneas as they could, but there had been vicious trauma, the eyes were permanently damaged and all she had to look forward to was a lifetime of blurry shadows and shapes. She knew if someone was in the room but she didn't know who it was until they spoke.

She was a hindrance, and she knew it.

And the Seven Sisters knew it, too.

Janelle stretched the kinks out of her neck as she sat in the chair; she also knew there were members of the Seven Sisters who wanted her out, and not only since the attack; she'd known for years she was a controversial choice to lead, a legacy pre-determined by her mother, the *original* Mama Delcourt, rather than some of the more 'deserving' candidates, people who believed their own press and weren't that important at all, and over the years had struggled; not only with the ambitions of her son but also with the back stabbing of harsh, brutal feminists.

She'd hoped to stay in power long enough for Molly, her daughter, to move into place, maybe four, five years from now, if she even wanted it, that was; Moses, the more likely and if she was honest preferable choice had never been considered, having the distinctive flaw of having a penis hanging between his legs, and it was this decision by the Sisters, based on their own 'no-males' charter, short-sighted or not, that had brought them to blows, with Moses now in Belmarsh Prison, and Janelle reliant on others.

Others like Anita Taborsky.

Anita had been a friend of Janelle's mother; a haggard harridan of a woman, bordering her seventies and with long white hair pulled into a bun, she'd been Janelle's enforcer, always taking the Matriarch's side when it suited her, before the accident. She was a no-nonsense East Ender, who had joined the Sisters back in the nineties after her husband had died during a years-long constant fight with the Twins.

But in recent months, Anita Taborsky had taken it upon herself to become Mama Delcourt's personal assistant, making sure Janelle could attend meetings, meet with the same people she once did when she could see, and make decisions still for the organisation. Besides this, she took a grandmotherly interest in Molly too, making sure her grades stayed high, and that losing her brother to the prison system didn't affect her too much.

Janelle grimaced at this thought; she hated the fact that, through her own actions, she'd made sure she couldn't look after her daughter in the manner she was accustomed to. And in the process, Anita Taborsky had skilfully wormed her way deeper into the organisation, making sure that she was the one constant in Janelle's life, the one person who now managed to be in all places at all times.

If someone wanted to make a play for the throne right now, Anita Taborsky was in the perfect spot.

But Taborsky was old now; she'd had her opportunities several times over the decades. She had no ambition to be Queen, and this meant she had to be laying the groundwork for someone else to move in.

But who?

Janelle couldn't work that out yet, and it irritated her greatly. She always worked out what was happening, but this was something she couldn't plan for. All she could do was hope Anita's plans somehow meshed with her own.

There was a cough at the table, and Janelle was brought back to the present, and the Seven Sisters board meeting that she was heading.

Today, she was sitting in the main chamber of the Seven Sisters' headquarters, a dining room containing an enormous table with chairs all around it. On these chairs sat five more women of varying ages, including Taborsky, with Janelle at the head of the table; beneath the room were a row of shops including an international supermarket, a cab company and a Brazilian café, standing shoulder to shoulder, facing the housing estate on the other side of the road.

And above these businesses, where the women now sat, the houses above these shops had been smashed through, refurbished and turned into one enormous *mansion* several years earlier; a secret, stately home in the middle of Tottenham, and accessible by several entrances. Two-storeys high and seven shops wide, there was enough space here for several families' living space and multiple offices, but although the Seven Sisters were seven individuals, only one family had ever lived here since the renovation.

The *Delcourts*. Janelle, Molly and Moses. Until Moses was reassigned new lodgings in prison, that was.

Now, of course, there were new people living here; people who were at Janelle's beck and call whenever she needed it, servants, all controlled by Anita Taborsky, who currently sat to Janelle's right.

'Are you ready?' Anita asked softly, loud enough only for Janelle to hear. Imperceptibly, she nodded.

'Bring him in,' Anita said commandingly to the man at the door. 'Let's see what he has to say.'

She paused, looking at Janelle, who sensed the movement.

'That is, if it's okay with you?' she asked loudly for all to hear. Janelle appreciated the gesture. Even though Anita was making the order, it still came from Mama Delcourt.

'Of course,' she replied. 'I want to see what excuses he has, too.'

There was a motion as the door opened, and Janelle felt

bright light enter the room as her blurred nothingness whitened slightly; it was from the windows the other side of the double doors, most likely. She heard the footsteps enter, but couldn't tell if the new arrival had sat down or stayed standing.

She guessed standing; only *women* could sit at the table.

'Kayas Ashad,' Anita Taborsky spoke the name condescendingly. 'You'd better have a damned good excuse why you were seen at the abduction of Jeffrey Tsang last night.'

There was silence, and for a moment, Janelle wondered if Kayas had even arrived, or whether this was some sick pantomime for her benefit.

'Well?' Anita snapped. 'What do you have to say?'

'I don't speak to the monkey, I speak to the organ grinder,' Kayas replied, his voice calm and considered. Janelle had realised that she could pick up the nuances in voices far better now; it was one of the few benefits of the accident.

'Then speak,' Janelle stated.

'Mama Delcourt, there's been a misunderstanding,' Kayas came closer, his voice louder. 'I was at *Tsang City*, yes, but I didn't kill the boy.'

The boy. Janelle almost laughed. Kayas was younger than Jeffrey Tsang by two years.

'Then why do I have witnesses telling me you were there as he was taken, and his companion brutally executed?'

'Because I was,' Kayas admitted. 'I've had it tough, Mama. Since Moses went rogue, which I knew nothing about, I swear, I've been cut off, ostracised by the Sisters—'

'You tried to kill Mama Delcourt!' Another of the Sisters spoke out. 'And when her son was arrested, you ran!'

'From the police!' Kayas was desperate now. 'The man who arrested Moses was the same man I hit with a bat! That I aimed a gun at! I thought I was next! My sister's ten years old and I have to look after her! I couldn't go down! I couldn't see her put into foster care! And I never helped Moses, I was the doorman here! Nothing more! He never told me what he was doing because he knew I'd run to you. I'm loyal!'

'As tragic as your story is,' Anita Taborsky's tone was almost mocking now. 'You still haven't got to the point of why you came here today.'

There was a silence, and Janelle wondered whether Kayas was too scared to speak, or if he was working out his story.

'I was approached,' he said eventually. 'Approached by Jackie Lucas.'

'Jackie or *Johnny?*' Janelle asked. 'Be very sure. It's important.'

'I dunno,' Kayas admitted. 'I mean, sure, it was Jackie last night, he was a maniac, but when he first contacted me, he was calmer. Wore a blue shirt rather than the black one he wore last night. That means something, right? Someone told me once that meant something.'

Blue shirt. Johnny Lucas.

'So why did you turn up last night?' Janelle continued.

'Because he offered me ten grand to be there,' Kayas admitted. 'Said he just needed an extra muscle, I wasn't to do anything, just witness, like the others.'

'Others?'

'Whole place was filled with people with cameras. Like they knew something was going to happen. All there to witness, like me.'

'You keep saying that word. Witness what?' Anita's voice again.

'What he did,' Kayas was sullen, almost argumentative at this. 'We all were.'

'The people with cameras weren't there by chance?'

'Nah, the people in the club? Most of them were invited.'

'Who by?' Janelle asked.

There was no answer.

'Who by?' she repeated.

'I don't know,' Kayas replied, and Janelle felt she could hear the honesty in his voice. 'I think it was Jeffrey himself.'

'Were you involved—' Anita's voice cracked a little. '—In the *skinning?*'

There was no answer from Kayas.

'I said—'

'I heard you,' Kayas was belligerent now as he replied to Anita. 'And yeah, I was there. I didn't kill him, I just took the body in. I was paid ten grand, and by this point, having seen what he was capable of, I was too scared to say no. and besides, I was there as a spy. On my cognisance, nothing connected to you.'

'And why would you do that?' Another of the Sisters asked.

'I got crew in the gangs around there,' Kayas explained. 'The Tsang boy was grooming them, getting them to put diss tracks out about us. He wanted us to be seen as a joke, a whole gang of mummy's boys who weren't allowed to make our own decisions. I wanted to know why.'

'So you killed him.'

'I didn't know that was happening. The old guy, he came to me, offered me money, explained we had the same issues. Enemy of my foe is my ally and all that. Said you and him? You had an old school working arrangement, and that was being threatened.'

'Enemy of my enemy,' one of the Sisters corrected.

'Yeah, whatever. That's why I did it. And as I said, I got a sister. I needed the scratch.'

There was another lapse in conversation, and Janelle assume everyone was waiting for her judgement.

'Looks like the Tsangs aren't as close as they used to be,' Anita Taborsky muttered. 'It looks like there's a war about to happen and we're in the middle. Maybe this boy needs to re-learn where his loyalties should be.'

'You had loyalties to the east once as well,' Janelle replied coldly at her. 'You forget where you came from and the family *you* once had. I could say the same to you, as you do to him.'

'My loyalties to the east died the day I married,' Anita stated smugly. 'And my loyalties to the Sisters began the day they *killed* him.'

There was a moment of unease in the room. Many of the women there knew the rumours, the legends of Anita Taborsky's abusive Russian husband, and how he was found savaged by dogs one Christmas, many years ago, dogs sent by the Lucas Twins. Nobody wanted to continue this line of questioning.

'Tell me exactly what Jackie or Johnny or whomever it was told you about our so called working arrangement,' Janelle said slowly, ensuring that Kayas felt every syllable. 'And remember, what you tell us will have a large effect on your future with the Seven Sisters.'

After a moment to consider this, Kayas told them everything he knew.

9

COLD SOLDIERS

MAURICE HAMILTON LIVED IN A MODEST TWO-UP, TWO-DOWN house a few blocks north of Bethnal Green, situated down a quiet side road, and surrounded by nameless, unified housing estates. It had a small garden at the front, no larger than a postage stamp, the stucco on the outside of the building was an off-white and, unlike the surrounding houses, was completely bereft of any graffiti or damage.

Must be great having the Krays as sway, to keep the teenagers away, Declan thought to himself as he stared up at it.

'Have you met Maurice before?' Monroe asked, his usually gravelly voice soft, almost reverential.

'No,' Declan replied, glancing over. 'Have you?'

'Aye, a couple of times,' Monroe nodded. 'Not the man he used to be, though. Remember that when you speak to him.'

This suggestion given, Monroe then walked up to the door, knocking hard on it. There was no bell to be seen, just a simple brass door knocker, and it surprised Declan; nearly every other house had some kind of Wi-Fi-enabled doorbell camera on the front, presumably to keep unwanted visitors at bay.

Obviously, Maurice didn't need to worry about that, Declan mused. *Either that, or he didn't want a video record of them.*

After a moment the door opened, and a white-haired man in a smoking jacket opened the door the briefest crack, glaring out into the open air.

'What?' he asked, his voice cracked and gravelly, as if he'd been eating cigarettes.

'DCI Alex Monroe and DI Declan Walsh,' Monroe held his warrant card up. 'You know why we're here. Can we have a chat?'

Without saying another word, Maurice Hamilton opened the door, allowing Monroe and Declan entry, closing the door behind them and, with a magnanimous wave of his arm, ushered them into his living room.

The living room in question was a cluttered, house-length space, narrow but long, and split in the middle into a sitting room with sofas and TV at the front, and a small dining area, complete with a pine six-seater table, and a weird-looking hexagonal mirror on the wall, with gold painted cherubs on the corners, at the back. Every recess was shelved, the books double deep and with more resting on top. There wasn't a single space to place another novel; even the mantelpiece over the fire—well, a modern-looking radiator anyway—had at least a dozen hardbacks on it.

As they went to sit down, Declan could see some titles of the books. He wasn't surprised to see that every one of them was a true crime novel, most likely something that either involved Maurice, or a book he'd contributed to.

On the other walls, almost covering the rather sickly green-painted wallpaper, were pictures and frames of varying sizes; photos of Maurice throughout the years, usually standing beside someone else; West End stars, movie actors, Princess Margaret (or at least someone who looked like her) in the seventies, a collection of recognisable old-school gangsters with a young Maurice seen in successive photos beside Ronnie Kray, Eddie Richardson, and an older Maurice next to a man who Declan believed was the Essex drug lord Pat Tate, made popular recently in a ton of bad 'Essex gangster' movies.

Interspersed among these were stage play posters and movie four-sheets, an artwork four-sheet of the film *The Long Good Friday* positioned in pride of place over the mantelpiece and books.

'You a fan?' Maurice, noting that Declan had stopped at the poster, asked.

'Yes, I remember seeing it as a kid,' Declan replied. 'Bob Hoskins and Helen Mirren, right? And Charley from *Casualty?* Yeah, it was good. I'm trying to work out the autographs, though.'

There were five or six unfamiliar black squiggles in the bottom corners of the image.

'Barrie Keefe is that one,' Maurice waved at one squiggle. 'He wrote the screenplay. I knew him when he was a cub reporter for the *Stratford Express*, you know. They hired a whole load of us old school guys for a scene where Bob Hoskins rallies his troops when he gives out all the shooters, and I got a few of them to sign this back in the nineties when we had a reunion.'

Declan resisted the urge to comment at Maurice's clipped, well-spoken accent saying the word *shooters* rather than *guns* or *weapons*, and stayed silent as Maurice now peered closely at the signatures.

'Can't make out a single bloody one of them nowadays,' he admitted. 'They all merge in my memories.'

'You were in *The Long Good Friday?*' Declan asked.

'I've been in a load of these,' Maurice boasted. 'I'm the go-to guy for many people, mainly because of my extensive knowledge.'

Monroe failed to hold back a snort for this; Maurice didn't notice, but Declan did.

'Anyway,' Monroe continued. 'Can we have that wee chat now?'

Maurice flattened his white hair with his hand, and Declan observed it was a strange, yellow-white, like it had aged in the same way pub ceilings did in the days when smoking was allowed. He was slim, but at the same time had a face of a man who was once larger. The smoking jacket was plush and navy blue, and Declan couldn't help but wonder whether it was all for show, thrown on quickly when he realised someone was at the door, or whether Maurice Hamilton was playing one last role.

'Last night,' Monroe started. '*Tsang City.*'

'Yes, I was there,' Maurice nodded.

'We know you were there,' Monroe interrupted, pulling out his notebook. 'We have your DNA all over the floor.'

There was a long, awkward moment of silence as Monroe smiled at the irritated Maurice.

'Not my proudest moment,' he eventually said. 'Old man, small bladder. Should have gone earlier.'

'So why *did* you piss yourself?' Monroe continued. Declan had seen Monroe use this style of interviewing before; it wasn't so much *good cop, bad cop*, as more a kind of *good cop, really piss you off cop*, with Monroe relying on anger and insult to cause mistakes in witness testimonies.

'Why? Because Jackie Lucas turned up, that's why.'

'Yeah, but you know as well as I do that 'Jackie' is nothing more than Johnny with a different shirt on,' Monroe leaned in. 'Or do you know something else?'

Maurice's eyes flitted from Monroe to Declan.

'Why were you there last night?' Declan decided that softer inroads were needed here.

'I was there last night because Jeffrey asked me to be.'

'Asked, or paid you to be?'

'I was his *consigliere*,' Maurice rose in his armchair slightly. 'The *Tom Hagen* to his *Michael Corleone*.'

'Aye? Well, you did a shite job of that, then,' Monroe replied, writing this down. 'I hope he wasn't paying you too much because you totally failed to earn your fee. So, you advised Jeffrey on what?'

'How to get out of the shadows of greater, yet pettier people,' Maurice leaned back in his seat, placing his hands together as if praying. 'I'd had my time under the shadow of monumental egos, and Jeffrey's uncles were just as bad. I was helping him find his own way.'

'And one of those ways was to publicly insult the Twins?'

'That wasn't my idea,' Maurice shook his head. 'Bloody idiot. Forgot that old lions still have teeth.'

'So why did he do it?' Declan asked.

There was a pause, a slight twitch in Maurice's face, as if he was mentally changing his answer.

Probably still thinking about lions.

'Because Johnny outbid him for Jack Spot's knife,' Maurice eventually shook his head. 'It was on auction recently. Not the usual channels, of course.'

Declan had heard of Jack Spot, a Jewish gangster from before the Krays, and his infamous love-hate relationship with Billy Hill. He was also known for the *Battle of Cable Street,* where he gathered a mob and charged into Oswald Mosley's fascist Blackshirts during a rally in 1936.

'Is the knife important?' he asked.

'It was stolen from the police's black museum when they moved locations, so I'd say so,' Maurice sniffed, reaching behind for a vodka. 'Drink, anyone? I think I need one today.'

With nobody agreeing to take one, Maurice poured a generous measure into a mug on the coffee table in front of him.

'Jeffrey didn't know Jack Spot, didn't even realise his real name was Comer, but he knew that possessing the knife gave him a link to the old days. Older than the Twins, older than the Krays. Legitimacy, in a way. It's probably why Johnny was bidding, too. But when Jeffrey won, he rubbed it in Johnny's face. Even threatened to use it on him.'

'And Johnny—or rather Jackie—decided enough was enough?'

Maurice sighed, looking around the room.

'Johnny was fine with it, laughed it off,' he said. 'And Jackie, come on, it's all for show. But this wasn't Jackie. This was *Jackie.*'

Monroe glanced at Declan at this and shifted closer in his seat.

'The original?' he asked.

'You know the story?' Maurice lowered his voice and Declan couldn't tell if this was because the aged ex-gangster feared talking aloud, or was just reading his audience, ever the showman.

'That Jackie died and Johnny continued to be him? Aye, I know that. Even met the original once, when I was a kiddie up in Glasgow,' Monroe nodded. 'Well, that is, I *think* I did. And I know about the chin scar.'

'That's how I recognised him,' Maurice was nodding as well now, vigorously agreeing with the detective. 'I was there when that happened. The Turk was this fat, greasy pig of a man, and he'd tried to court Johnny's older sister. Johnny closed it down though at her request, but the Turk didn't believe this and went for him one night when Johnny was in one of his Soho clubs.'

He took a sip.

'Bloody idiot didn't realise it was *Jackie* instead. Johnny was at a boxing match in York Hall that night.'

'So the Turk cut Jackie's chin?'

'Yes, and Jackie pulled out a machete and took a *finger* as retribution,' Maurice's eyes sparkled as he regaled the story, and Declan felt a shiver run down his spine. Maurice wasn't just a sad old man trying to keep hold of his past glories; he revelled in the violence, the danger, the brutality of those days.

'So what happened to Jackie? The real one?' Declan tried to change the subject. 'How did he die?'

'He didn't,' Maurice tapped his nose in a secretive manner. 'Well, between us and the vicar, the story was he *did*, but honestly? Jackie Lucas never died.'

There it was again. The showman selling the story.

'Go on,' Monroe urged.

Maurice swirled the mug now, watching the liquid inside as he considered his response.

'There was a drug deal going on in the late eighties or early nineties. I can't remember when. Johnny and Jackie were trying to pull in a massive coke deal because the Baron —he was the law in Acton at the time—did a lot of that back then, and wouldn't cut them in. So they tried to bypass him. Jackie went to South America to discuss trade with a couple of the cartels down there.'

He took a swig of vodka, warming to the storytelling now.

'Anyway, legend goes that Jackie had been shagging Johnny's girlfriend around this point and as they *weren't* identical, there was no way she could claim mistaken identity, you see? Johnny found out, and they argued. Jackie pointed out as the older brother, he was technically in charge and as *he* was the one always gutting fish—'

'Fish?' Declan frowned.

'Taking out the rivals,' Maurice explained. 'Jackie liked to do the job personally. Anyway, as Jackie was the one people were terrified of, us in the know, who were inside the room? We knew Johnny was soon to be *retired*.'

He mimed a knife across the throat.

'Jackie would kill him?' Declan was surprised.

'You're basing that response on what you know of the Twins, and that's information gleaned from the last couple of decades,' Maurice shook his head. 'Johnny's version of Jackie was always going to toe the party line, because that's what Johnny wanted the original one to do. But in all honesty, they absolutely detested one another. Always trying to gain an upper hand. Johnny was the careful planner, always the youngest in the class, smallest in the room, while Jackie was the dickhead with a gun. More visible.'

'So Johnny retires Jackie before he can do the same to him,' Monroe nodded.

'Pretty much,' Maurice continued. 'Someone gave him the news that Jackie was about to take him out—' Maurice puffed out his chest, '—I couldn't possibly say who, of course, and Johnny played it cool, pretended not to know. When Jackie went to bongo bongo land or wherever the hell it was, Johnny made sure the cartels knew Jackie was a liability. At the time the US had a war on drugs that was actually a *war*, Johnny got picked up on a boat near Haiti—god knows why he was there—and he got dumped in a shit hole jail in Bogotá, left to rot forever.'

'Obviously not forever,' Monroe commented dryly, 'if he's returned.'

'Yes, quite,' Maurice's hand trembled as he took another mouthful. 'Somehow he's escaped, or been let out and now he's back and taking what's his.'

'Do you think Johnny knows?' Declan asked.

Maurice shook his head.

'Nobody did,' he replied. 'Christ, I thought he was there for *me* when he turned up, thought he'd heard rumours of me grassing him. That's why I was... well, why I was scared.'

'Aye, I'd piss myself too,' Monroe said soothingly. 'So he shoots David Banner dead, takes Jeffrey and leaves. How did he have one of Johnny's guys with him?'

'And one of Mama Delcourt's, too?' Declan added.

'No idea,' Maurice admitted. 'I guess he pretended to be Johnny, or that Michael—'

'Michael?'

'Michael Kent. You know him as Mickey Trackies,' Maurice rose from the chair, walking to the window. 'His father worked with them in the day too, so Michael may have had loyalties from his father leading to the real Jackie Lucas.'

'And Kayas Ashad?'

'Is that the black kid? No idea,' Maurice shrugged. 'Probably had issues with Jeffrey.'

'He used to roll with Mama Delcourt,' Declan added. 'Any issues there with Jeffrey?'

Maurice stopped drinking, pausing, his mug held halfway up to his mouth as he stared out of the window.

'I don't know,' his voice was almost a whisper. 'I can't help you.'

'Look,' Monroe said, walking to Maurice. 'I'm sure we—'

'You need to get out,' Maurice turned to face Monroe, and his expression was one of anger. 'Now. Go, please.'

Declan now rose, hands up in a placating gesture.

'Whatever the problem here is—'

'I said go!' Maurice shouted now. 'Am I under arrest? No? Then get out!'

'Come on Declan,' Monroe nodded to Maurice. 'I'm sure we can always chat again with Maurice.'

As they walked out of the door and back out onto the estate, Declan saw Monroe writing a number in his notebook.

'Mister Hamilton,' he said, looking back at Maurice, half hidden behind his door. 'I'm sure we can find a way—'

'*And don't come back!*' Maurice hissed as he slammed the door in his face.

'What the hell?' Declan bemoaned as he followed Monroe onto the street. 'One minute he's fine, and then the next minute...'

'The next minute he looks out of the window,' Monroe replied, nodding up the road where a battered Rover could be seen driving off. 'And as I approach, that car drives off. I've written the number, so let's go chat with wee Billy and see who Maurice Hamilton is scared of.'

'You already know, don't you?' Declan raised an eyebrow. 'You have that look.'

'I recognised the car, yes,' Monroe walked to Declan's Audi. 'But I could be mistaken.'

'And who do you think it was?'

'Scroat of a thief I used to run into about five, ten years back,' Monroe said as he climbed into the passenger seat. 'My protégé brought him in a couple of times, in fact. Ramsey Allen.'

Declan stood by the car looking up the road; the Rover was long gone.

'Who did he run with?' he asked, climbing into the car and already knowing the answer.

Monroe stared out of the window, and Declan wondered whether he was looking at the estate outside, or whether he was remembering a different estate from long ago.

'Ramsey Allen worked for a lot of the London names,' he breathed. 'But the people he was always closest to were Johnny and Jackie Lucas.'

'Then let's get confirmation, make sure it was him, and then bring him in,' Declan started the engine. 'Because I, for one, am sick of all roads leading back to Globe Town.'

10

DATES AND TIMES

It took Declan another half an hour to drive back to the Temple Inn offices of the Last Chance Saloon, the morose and constantly grumbling Monroe sitting beside him. And by the time they arrived, it was already evening, and Declan's stomach was rumbling.

'Skip breakfast?' Monroe asked as they entered through the double doors, the sergeant on desk duty already buzzing them through.

'Running to help Farrow, but Jess has me on this intermittent fasting thing,' Declan explained. 'I can only eat from noon until eight in the evening.'

'And how's that work out for you?' Monroe grinned.

'Not great,' Declan admitted. 'But Jess manages it just fine.'

'Your daughter lies,' Monroe said ominously as they walked up the stairs. 'She's probably snaffled all the biscuits since she got here. And you should have had lunch.'

'I offered,' Declan muttered. 'Late lunch before we spoke to Maurice, remember?'

'Oh, aye,' Monroe smiled. 'We should have done that.'

'How are you not hungry?' Declan threw his jacket onto his chair, surprised to see the office was an almost full house; Jess and Billy worked at the monitor station, Anjli was discussing something with De'Geer, and the only people not there were PC Cooper, Doctor Marcos and DC Davey, and the latter two were most likely in forensics downstairs, as Declan had noted the door was closed as they walked past.

'Oh, I had a big breakfast,' Monroe replied. 'Full English. It's one of the few things you Sassenachs do right.'

Monroe walked over to the monitors.

'Billy,' he smiled, holding out his notebook. 'Do me a favour and run this licence. I think it'll come up as Ramsey Allen, thieving scroat extraordinaire, but I want proof.'

'On it,' Billy nodded.

Declan sat in his chair, quickly checking his emails, resisting the urge to look over at Jess. He didn't want her to think he was monitoring her.

'You okay?' it was Jess that spoke first, looking around at Declan. 'You look like the weight of the world is on you.'

Declan forced a smile, looking at his watch. It was already gone six in the evening.

'I'm really sorry,' he said. 'This isn't how you expected to spend your summer holidays.'

'Are you kidding?' Jess rose from her seat now, smiling widely. 'This has been great. I got to play with the *Holmes 2* network!'

'Actually, you don't play with the—' Billy started, but gave up. 'Sure. She played with the incredibly expensive computer network that links the entire police network together.'

'Should she even be using it?' Monroe, leaning against Anjli's desk, having not made it to his own office yet, asked.

'Well, that depends on how liberal you are on the terminology of 'only police officers',' Billy shrugged.

'I don't want to know, laddie,' Monroe shook his head, now heading to his office.

'Do you want some dinner?' Declan asked, a little apologetically. 'I'm waiting for some emails to come in, so I'm unlikely to be able to leave yet.'

'No sweat, dad,' Jess smiled soothingly. 'I guessed you'd be busy, so I texted Prisha. We're going to catch up.'

'On a date?'

'It's not a date,' Jess corrected. 'It's just a—'

'You're going out with the girl you have a crush on. Does she have a crush on you?'

'I'm not sure.'

'Well, if she does, it's a date. Was she eager to meet up?'

Jess blushed a little.

'Yeah,' she said, the smile still there.

'Where are you going?' Anjli, walking over to her desk with De'Geer and having overheard the conversation, asked.

'We don't know yet,' Jess admitted. 'Prisha's only been in town a couple of days.'

'I thought we saw her here a month or two back?'

'She was going for her interview then,' Jess was getting irritated now. 'Get with it, dad.'

Declan held back from replying; it was one thing to rib his daughter a little, but you needed to know when to stop.

'Come out with me,' Anjli offered.

Jess, surprised, looked at her.

'I'm meeting mum in an hour in Shoreditch,' Anjli explained. 'We're off to see a Kate Bush tribute band. Cheesy as hell, but should be fun. You can bring Prisha, it's public and at the end, I can drive you back to Hurley.'

'There's no need for that,' Declan waved a hand. 'You're staying with your mum.'

'I need an excuse not to,' Anjli replied slowly. 'I love mum but Christ, she's doing my head in. If Jess comes, I can use this as an excuse, leave around ten. That good?'

The last part of this was aimed at Jess, who was already texting.

'Totally,' she replied. 'If dad's okay?'

'Oh, he'll be fine,' Anjli grinned as she looked over at Declan. 'When we leave after the gig, he'll likely still be here.'

'She's not wrong, sir,' De'Geer added.

Declan looked up at him.

'Whose side are you on, anyway?' he asked. 'You're supposed to be mortified that my daughter has chosen another over you.'

'Oh, I am,' De'Geer said, winking at Jess as she reddened. 'Absolutely heartbroken. But I'm sure I'll get over it.'

Anjli grabbed her coat.

'Great,' she said. 'See you back at home then. Jess, you can send Prisha the details en route.'

'I thought we were meeting your mum in an hour?' Jess gathered her own jacket now.

'We are, but I'm not bloody eating with her,' Anjli grinned. 'There's an awesome diner on Shoreditch High Street we can go to. Superb Vegan food, apparently.'

With Jess now pulling her jacket on, Anjli walked over and kissed Declan on the cheek.

'I'll make sure she's okay,' she whispered. And before Declan could answer, the two women had left the office.

'She'll make a great step-mum,' Billy muttered, laughing as he ducked a thrown notebook from Declan. 'Sorry, I forgot, it *wasn't* you that bought the ring today!'

Monroe walked back out of his office, watching the antics in front of him.

'Right then, I'm ordering pizza,' he said. 'Who's up for a lad's night in?'

'That include lassies?' Bullman's voice echoed out of her office, the Scots drawl of *lassies* a deliberate mockery of Monroe's own accent.

'Aye, you're more bloody hardcore than the rest of us,' Monroe grinned. 'Bring your expensive whisky out so we can share a dram.'

'Not me, I'm driving,' Declan held a hand up. 'I'll raid the vending machine for a coke.'

'Or we could just pop over to the pub,' Bullman walked out of the office, staring at Declan, De'Geer, Billy, and Monroe in succession. 'You've all been working long hours, you all need a break and we can escape for an hour.'

'Ma'am, I need—' Declan started, but Bullman waved him silent.

'Walsh, you're on your day off,' she said. 'We're across the road. We'll get everything that comes in, and Billy'll likely be glued to his laptop there, anyway.'

She smiled.

'Besides, we have some extra petty cash that needs to be spent, and I'm buying.'

THE OLD BANK OF ENGLAND, A PUB BASED ON THE OTHER SIDE of Fleet Street from the entrance to Temple Inn, and therefore only a couple of minutes away from the offices, was an imposing Grade II-listed building, once the Law Courts branch of the *Bank of England* from 1888 to 1975. However, after years of falling into disrepair, it was eventually restored by *Fuller's* brewery in the nineties, a full redesign in neoclassical style, complete with marble, specially commissioned murals, chandeliers and sculptured high ceilings. Now a *McMullen's* brewery, the pub was situated over a onetime gold bullion vault where the Crown Jewels were rumoured to be briefly held, and the marketing for the pub even hinted at connections to *Sweeney Todd,* the demon barber of Fleet Street.

Fictional barber, that was, Declan thought as he sat at a circular table, a pint of Guinness in his hand.

In the end, De'Geer, Billy, Monroe and Bullman had joined him in the bar; Declan felt bad that Anjli and Jess weren't there, but at the same time he didn't want to ruin a possible bonding experience with what was likely to be a boring works drink. Monroe had texted Doctor Marcos and DC Davey, letting them know they were in the bar, but had received a reply saying that both forensics officers would be unlikely to appear before they finished their food and returned.

On receipt of this, Monroe had to visibly order De'Geer to sit back down, so eager was the PC to assist them.

'So, what's the conversation about?' Bullman asked as she sipped at a brandy.

'Jackie Lucas,' Declan replied, looking at Monroe. 'The real one.'

'Laddie, that's not really a polite dinner conversation.'

'Alex, they all know your past,' Bullman replied. 'What do we have, and is it going to result in us letting Johnny bloody Lucas out on bail?'

Monroe considered this.

'I was a kid,' he said. 'I was working with the Hutchinsons, you all know that. My brother wasn't happy about it, but at the same time he was always out, so he didn't really have a say. One day, and I must have been about fifteen, I was working lookout for the firm, making sure nobody interrupted—'

'You mean police?' Billy asked.

'Aye, and other nefarious types,' Monroe shrugged. 'The Whites, a couple other gangs. This was a important meeting. They held it in a hotel south of Glasgow; I'd never seen so many tooled-up bruisers in one place before. It was the criminal equivalent of a Queen's visit, you get me?'

'Johnny and Jackie?' Declan asked.

'Aye, it was,' Monroe replied. 'They were young, in their early twenties, and making a name for themselves. They were looking for distributors, whisky experts to help bring down some bottles they'd gained in Aberdeen. Wondered if we'd be up to moving it on, while taking a little for ourselves.'

Declan listened, noting quietly that Monroe was using the terms *we* and *our* when mentioning the Hutchinsons.

Monroe sipped at his drink before continuing.

'I'm down by the door when the car turns up, told by someone, possibly Sutton, because he was there too, to *go open the door*. I run over, but they're already emerging, and the sight of a teenager running at them throws them into an alert mentality. Guns come out. Guns pointed at me.'

'This explains a lot about your personality,' Bullman mocked.

'Aye, probably,' Monroe nodded. 'Anyway, Jackie has also come out, and he's not bothered at all. Waves the guns down, passes me a pound note, tells me to slow down, and they don't need airs and graces. Then Johnny comes around and blanks me. Totally. Jackie winks, walks on with his brother. I didn't see them again.'

'So Jackie was the one that stopped the fight?' Declan asked. 'Doesn't sound like the Jackie we've heard of.'

'That's because this was early Jackie,' Monroe leaned into his chair. 'He wasn't as bad back then. It was only when he started on the coke that he got worse. Sutton told me this when I first arrived in London. It's also how I worked out Johnny and Jackie were the same person by then.'

'How?' Billy leaned closer.

'Because when I met Jackie for the first time, and remember I was a brand new shiny detective at this point, I mentioned this meeting, but I screwed up the punchline. I didn't mention he'd given me money. But 'Jackie' said he remembered it perfectly, even described me to a tee.'

De'Geer frowned.

'So how did you know?' he asked.

'Because he didn't ask for his pound back,' Monroe smiled. 'Johnny never saw me take it, he came out of the other door. He never knew, so obviously *this* Jackie didn't know either.'

He shifted in the chair.

'Also, the Jackie I met in Glasgow had a small scar on his chin. One that later Jackie didn't have, probably because it would be a problem to play with prosthetics every time he wanted to go knife someone.'

'A scar that's in the photo,' De'Geer nodded.

'So is it Jackie?' Bullman asked. 'Because if it is, that's a good chunk of the evidence needed for Johnny Lucas' lawyers to get him out.'

'I'm not sure,' Monroe shook his head. 'Maurice said he was rotting in a Bogotá jail.'

Declan sipped at his Guinness.

'Anyone know a friendly Colombian diplomat we can ask?' he suggested, leaning back as a server arrived with the first two plates of food. 'After we've eaten, that is.'

JESS ALMOST DIDN'T MAKE IT TO THE TRIBUTE BAND.

To be fair, she'd wanted to, and Prisha even sounded keen to go, but after eating in the Shoreditch diner that Anjli had suggested, a meal that had been a little stilted and awkward, mainly as Anjli was nervous about being alone with Jess, she'd wondered if spending a whole evening like that could be a problem. However, Prisha had joined them in the diner halfway through the meal and, with a third person to bounce off, Anjli seemed to relax a little, turning the attention to Prisha and Jess as they ate.

Prisha was the same as she'd been the last time; wearing a denim hoodie that zipped up at the front, opened up to reveal a *Strokes* t-shirt, a pair of *Bosé* headphones around her neck, a pair of khaki trousers over *Nike* sneakers. Her hair was in a bob, and her makeup was minimal, and she'd been more relaxed than either of them as she arrived. Anjli and Prisha got on well, and Jess relaxed; this was the evening she'd hoped for. And, when the meal was finished, the three of them left to walk to Shoreditch High Street overground station, where Anjli's mum was supposed to meet them.

However, as they were walking down Redchurch Street, Jess had glanced along a side road and stopped.

There was a crowd of young people outside a door to a building; it didn't look that special, and there was no signage above it, but one of the people outside looked familiar.

'What's that place?' she asked.

Anjli looked, shrugged.

'Shoreditch House,' she said. 'Swanky members' club with a pool on the roof. I had a friend bring me here once.'

'A rich friend?' Prisha asked jokingly.

'Eden Storm,' Anjli replied matter-of-factly. Jess smiled at this; although she knew that after having the *Last Chance Saloon* clear his name of murder, tech magnate billionaire Eden Storm had courted Anjli. And, while the feeling wasn't reciprocated, a couple of drinks and a meal or two later he got bored and moved on, promising to stay in touch. Jess didn't know if he had, but watching Prisha's expression as she realised who Anjli meant and recognising it was priceless.

'And the people?' she asked, returning to the reason she asked.

'Either members, or people trying to get in, all hanging around outside until a friend can get them past reception,' Anjli replied cautiously. 'Why?'

'I recognise someone there,' Jess said, nodding to a brunette woman in a dress way too skimpy for her, a young man in a white muscle t-shirt beside her, as they spoke into a phone. They could have been video calling, but Jess knew it was a video blog. For this was one of the influencers at *Tsang City* the previous night; one of Jess' jobs today had been to check up all the people who'd recorded that night, and this person was called—

'Hey, Laura Bloom, right?' Jess shouted as she approached. 'Big fan.'

Laura Bloom stopped whatever recording she was doing and turned to Jess, a weary smile on her face.

'I am,' she nodded. 'You watch my vlog?'

'It's wicked,' Jess lied. 'Although last night was mental. I'm just so glad you got out in time.'

'Oh my God,' Laura looked at the man beside her, and Jess had a feeling he was called Alfie, or Archie, or something vaguely forgettable. 'Worst night of my life. Biggest audience, obviously, but it's not about the numbers. We were so lucky to get out. I could see he was mad, you know. He'd looked at me earlier.'

'I was about to stop him,' Alfie /Archie said. 'I know Tai Kwon-do, and I'd just prepared to move in—'

'When he pulled out the gun?'

'Yeah,' Laura interjected. 'Can't outfight a bullet, babes. We're just lucky to be alive.'

She looked at Jess, and seriously placed her hands together.

'*Hashtag blessed*,' she said, without a hint of irony.

'So how come you were there?' Jess asked, and by now Laura had clocked Anjli and Prisha behind Jess, her stance becoming a little more defensive.

'We were invited,' Laura sniffed, glancing back at the doors to Shoreditch House as if thinking that by stating this, they would magically open. 'Davey Banner put the word out—'

'The guy that was killed?' Jess asked, wide eyed.

'Yeah, oh God, that was mank,' Laura nodded. 'He told us all to come, that something massive was gonna happen. We thought it was a rap drop, you know, a new tune or something, not that.'

'Bouncers were in on it though,' Alfie / Archie muttered. 'Mate was in the queue. Said they just let them through.'

'What was your mate's name?' Jess asked, and from the expressions on Laura and her boyfriend's face, she knew she'd pushed her luck.

'Who are you, anyway?' Alfie / Archie said, moving protectively in front of Laura. 'Press? Some other channel? Get lost.'

'Hey!' Prisha muscled in now. 'Don't talk to her that way!'

'Oh yeah?' Laura, her 'nice' persona now gone, pushed Prisha away. 'And what's your connection to her, anyway?'

'She's—uh—she's my girlfriend,' Prisha snapped, and then paled as she realised what she said. 'I mean, a girl. Who's my friend. Yeah.'

'Go on, piss off,' Alfie / Archie raised his voice now. 'We don't talk to press.'

'What about police?' Anjli, tired of this, now stepped forward, waving her warrant card. 'Because I'm sick of this shit, sick of the pair of you, and my mum's waiting. So how about you answer her questions, give me your contact details and get this over with, so we can go to a gig I've been waiting for all week?'

Laura baulked at the tone, but stopped when she saw the warrant ID.

'Well, of course I can answer the questions,' she said. 'We'd both love to. Always happy to help the police, especially to catch that maniac.'

However, after saying this she smiled; a shy, hopeful one.

'But can I film it while we do?' Laura started to record on her phone. 'Not live, I'll edit it. And if you like and subscribe, I can let you know when it goes out.'

Anjli looked at Jess, at Prisha, and then at Laura.

'No,' she said. 'But I can happily arrest you for refusing to cooperate, while muscles there films you.'

Sulking, Laura turned off the camera.

'I bet you down vote videos,' she muttered.

At this, Anjli grinned.

'Babes,' she mocked. 'I *live* for down voting videos. *Hashtag blessed*.'

11

POST-DRINK THEATRE

AFTER THEY'D FINISHED THEIR PUB DINNER, THE MEMBERS OF the *Last Chance Saloon* had returned to the office, finding an unsurprising lack of advancement in their case. De'Geer had made his excuses and left, stating something about helping Doctor Marcos and DC Davey in Mile End; the body of Jeffrey Tsang had been placed there earlier that day, and the two forensics experts had gone over there to help with the autopsy.

Bullman had returned to her office, where she was currently on the phone to Chief Superintendent Bradbury in Scotland Yard, giving an update of the day's work, but mainly still asking why this poisoned chalice was dumped on their lap, and Declan and Monroe were now deep in conversation in Monroe's office, going over the notes they'd taken from Maurice Hamilton.

Billy had returned to his monitor station; it was now well past nine in the evening, but with others in the office still working, he felt bad for leaving early—if nine in the evening was classed as such. However, Declan was likely waiting for

Jess to return, Monroe was probably hanging around until Doctor Marcos came back, and from the laughter that emanated from Bullman's office, Billy wondered if the relationship she had with Bradbury was strictly business.

Billy's only relationship was with his monitors, and he was very aware of how creepy that sounded.

There was a *ding* of an email arriving, and Billy checked it; nothing more than a sales email asking him if he wanted to beef up his home security with some Wi-Fi cameras.

Cameras.

There was still something in the back of his mind, something wrong with the footage he'd seen in the Cirque Apartments; opening it back up, he worked through the CCTV video again. He could see Mickey Trackies to the side, waiting as Jackie Lucas came to meet him. Then, later on, Jackie returned alone.

What was he missing?

He was so engrossed in the hunt that he missed Declan returning to his desk, Monroe and Bullman both leaving for the night and Anjli and Jess finally arriving back from the gig they'd gone to. In fact, it was only Anjli tapping Billy on the shoulder that brought him back to the present, noting that the time was now gone ten pm, and he'd lost an hour somehow. *Was this how Johnny felt when he became Jackie, losing time in the process?*

'He's been like that for ages,' Declan looked up from his computer. 'Fun gig?'

'It was okay,' Anjli replied noncommittally. 'Interestingly, it was more fun beforehand.'

She nodded to Jess to continue.

'We found the influencer from last night,' Jess beamed. 'One of them, anyway.'

'Jess did, that is,' Anjli added. 'Laura something.'

'Laura Bloom,' Jess looked to Billy, who, hearing the name, started tapping onto the screen. 'She's a YouTuber who's moved more onto TikTok these days.'

'Got her,' Billy was already working through Laura Bloom's social media profile, scanning images and moving on without a second thought.

Jess watched for a moment.

'You know, with those skills, you could be a really effective stalker,' she commented. Billy grinned.

'Who says I'm not?' he asked innocently. 'Okay, what am I looking at?'

'She said that David Banner invited her to *Tsang City* last night,' Anjli read from her notebook now. 'Said that he'd emailed her the time and place, but she couldn't find the email in question. Reckoned she'd deleted it, as she got *thousands of emails a day, darling.*'

'Hashtag blessed,' Jess replied, and the two of them started laughing.

'Do you have her email?' Billy looked over at Anjli, who, putting her serious face back on, showed him the notebook page.

'Too many numbers and letters to explain properly, so just copy it from that.'

Billy had already done so, and was already working through Laura Bloom's security pages.

'It's a cloud-base browser, so I should be able to get into it somewhere,' he said. 'Wait.'

'What is it?'

Billy had been scrolling through Laura Bloom's Instagram feed. It was mainly a selection of selfies of Laura in exciting looking places; there were a few of Laura in a gym, or some kind of health spa, and these were the ones Billy paused at.

'That's Simpson's Health Spa,' he said, pointing at a logo in one of the image backgrounds. 'She's been there a few times, from the looks of things.'

'Maybe she's a member?' Declan pursed his lips together as he considered this. 'Could be nothing, but very interesting if these so-called invited guests all have connections to Nicky Simpson.'

'Simpson wants a public fight between east and West London, so he makes sure it goes viral,' Anjli considered. 'But how would he know about this?'

'That's the problem,' Declan stretched, rising from his chair. 'In the real world, he wouldn't. If Nicky Simpson knew that Jackie Lucas was going to *Tsang City*, it was because he'd aimed him there, or because Jackie Lucas had told him he was going.'

'Do we need to bring Simpson in?' Jess asked.

'*We* need to go home and sleep,' Declan smiled. 'We'll come back to this in the morning. Simpson's not stupid, and we can't nick him for working with influencers, considering his whole public persona is based in the same world.'

He looked at Billy.

'The feeds you have of the attack, the influencers we've already found,' he mused. 'Can you go through their Instagram pages, or whatever they're posting on, and see how many others have connections to Simpson's Health Spa?'

'Sure, but it'll take a while.'

'It's not important, do it tomorrow,' Declan suggested. 'I think we've all done enough for today.'

As Anjli and Jess grabbed their things, Billy shook his head.

'I'll have a quick look now,' he smiled, nodding at the monitors. 'I'm still working through something else and if I don't find an answer, it'll be winding me up all night.'

'See you in the morning,' Declan nodded before looking at Anjli. 'Share a car home?'

'Ah, no, sorry,' Anjli looked apologetic. 'In the end I promised mum I'd pop back after bringing Jess back here. I ought to stay with her one more night.'

'No problem, see you tomorrow,' Declan replied, pulling Jess gently by the arm. 'Anything else exciting happen tonight?'

'Prisha called me her girlfriend,' Jess said as they walked out of the office. Billy didn't catch Declan's reply to this, but he wished more than anything to be a fly on that wall.

Anjli was still standing beside her desk, staring at the door.

'So, what's the problem?' Billy asked.

'What do you mean?' Anjli asked. There was a *ding* from Billy's computer; another email, but he ignored it for the moment.

'You and Declan,' he said. 'You're pulling back. Why?'

'You're mistaken—'

'Anj, *what's the problem?*'

Anjli sighed, leaning back against her desk.

'It's been good,' she said. 'Nice, comfortable, you know? It's not like the usual relationship thing, as we've worked together almost a year and lived as housemates before we—well, before we, *you know*.'

'So what's the *problem?*' Billy repeated.

'Jess,' Anjli replied. 'I think she's great, don't get me wrong, wicked smart and we get along fine, but it's...'

She struggled for her words.

'You're worried about being less of a mate, and more of a mum now?' Billy rose from his chair now, walking over to Anjli. 'It's okay, you know. You're going to double-think this, it's human nature.'

'Well, human nature sucks,' Anjli forced a brief smile.

Billy held out his arms.

'Gay best friend hug?' he waggled his hands. 'Come on, let uncle Billy make everything right.'

Anjli gratefully moved in for the hug.

'You really shouldn't call yourself uncle Billy,' she said into his shoulder. 'It makes you sound like a—'

'Yeah, I heard it the moment I spoke the words,' Billy grinned, pulling away. 'Look, I've seen you and Jess together. She's a good kid and you're a good friend. And you and Declan, as much as it sickens me to say it, you guys work.'

Turning, he walked back to his monitor station as another email *dinged*.

'So stop stressing about the small things and enjoy it. I mean, honestly, it could be worse. You're inheriting a girl as a surrogate stepdaughter, who's pretty much an adult. She could have been a *toddler*.'

He shuddered, but then stopped, as a realisation took hold.

'How much of this is Farrow?'

Anjli knotted her eyebrows at this. 'How much of what?'

'I'm serious, Anj. You have the twitch at the same time Henry Farrow looks to propose to Liz Walsh? It can't be coin cidence.'

'Well yeah, what if Declan wants to do the same?' Anjli couldn't help herself as she spoke. 'We've been together for weeks, Bill. Just weeks. I don't know if I'm ready.'

'Has he said anything?' Billy held up a hand. 'Made any motions towards asking you?'

'I suppose not,' Anjli admitted.

'And did you see how he reacted himself to Farrow? He's convinced it's too soon, and Liz and Farrow have been together three times longer than you.'

'Yeah, but we live together.'

'Exactly!' Bill clapped his hands together, turning to check the email. 'You're practically married in everything but name. Just enjoy the bloody honeymoon period and stop trying to destroy the relationship before it even gets started. That's usually reserved for me to...'

He trailed off as he read the contents of the email.

'You alright?' Anjli started towards him.

'Friend of mine in Scotland Yard,' Billy looked away from the screen. 'He monitors a lot of the dark web forums, all the *Web two-point-oh* stuff.'

'Which means nothing to me.'

'Anj, it's the forums where illegal things are discussed with no fear of being found. Where things are offered, illegal things, or even more illegal services.'

'Okay,' Anjli said carefully, unsure where the conversation was going. 'And what's he just sent you?'

'Someone's just put a two million dollar hit out on Johnny Lucas,' Billy pointed at the screenshot he'd been sent. 'Not Jackie, not Jackie and Johnny, but simply Johnny. Two million dollars on proof of kill.'

Anjli whistled.

'If I'd known he was worth that much, I'd have done it ages ago,' she joked.

'That's the thing,' Billy sat in the chair, already typing a reply. 'He hasn't been. There's never been a hit put on him that's stuck. People have been too scared. But within twenty-four hours of Jeffrey Tsang's murder, someone does this?'

'This is an escalation of the war,' Anjli nodded. 'Monroe mentioned earlier that someone looking like Jackie claimed a million pound hit on the Tsang brothers last night. Someone's taking it up a notch. It has to be the Tsangs.'

'You'd think,' Billy scrolled through some lines of data. 'They have the money, and they also have the motive right now. But I don't think we can find out properly without a confession.'

'I'm calling Mile End and Esposito,' Anjli was already picking up the phone on her desk. 'Johnny Lucas is still in custody, and he's about to get a ton of unwanted attention.'

Monroe had intended to go home; Rosanna Marcos was likely pulling another all-nighter, and he had little sleep the previous night. But a text from Marcus Lightman had brought him into Soho, and the Nellie Deane pub west of Soho Square.

It was a small, cosy pub, a long bar on one side and small tables along the other. It was busy; late night drinkers and after-show visitors filling the space, but in the corner was Lightman, standing at a small tall table around a pillar, sipping at a pint of bitter.

'Alex,' he waved as Monroe entered. 'I'll have a pint.'

Snorting, Monroe bought two drinks and took them over.

'Thanks for meeting me,' he said, sipping at one of them. 'It's been a shitty day.'

'Oh yes? Care to say anything on the record?' Lightman grinned.

'If I do decide, you'll be the first to know,' Monroe raised his pint as they clinked glasses. 'So tell me about Jackie.'

'I was in Helen's,' Lightman began. 'End of day, didn't really want to be around anyone. I also had a piece going in a Los Angeles blog and had to upload by six pm their time.'

'So two am.'

'Yeah. Helen lets me use the Wi-Fi there, so I intended to finish it up over a hideously expensive drink, upload and then go home.'

'But that changed?'

'Not really, but there was an interruption,' Lightman nodded. 'You probably already know, but Jackie Lucas came in. Made a big announcement, said he was putting a million each on the Tsangs, proof of kill required. Then he walked over to me, told me to take a photo of this ring he had.'

Lightman showed Monroe the image, a gold signet ring on the table.

'I've seen it before,' he whispered. 'It used to be Donnie's.'

'Jeffrey's father?'

'Yeah. Makes sense the boy would have it after his death. Anyway, he shows this, finishes his drink, makes this big proclamation of *no more scum, and if I have to burn it down I'll do that*, and then leaves.'

'Why wasn't this in the press?' Monroe frowned.

'We had it spiked,' Lightman leant in conspiratorially. 'Someone on high didn't want this coming out right now.'

Monroe nodded at this. It wasn't uncommon for Scotland Yard to lean heavily on editors, to make sure certain aspects of a crime didn't come out at the wrong moment.

'It'll come out, though,' Lightman added. 'Maybe not the photo, but the news will hit the smaller digital news services, the ones that don't give a shit about warnings. And then a bloody big war will begin, Alex. One you don't want to be in the middle of.'

'The war's already begun,' Monroe ominously prophesied, finishing his drink. 'All I can do is hope we can triage it before it bleeds everywhere.'

He considered the news.

'You hear anything from north or south? Sisters or Simpsons?'

'Nothing. Sisters are sabre rattling but nothing more, and south of the river is its own world.'

'Anything on Maurice Hamilton?' Monroe placed the glass on the table.

'Sorry, no.'

'No worries. If you hear anything, let me know, aye? Stay safe, Marcus.'

And, now burdened with more fears of London burning in flames, Monroe left his informer, the pub, and his faith that *things would get better before they got worse.*

12

DOUBLE-TAP

ALTHOUGH THE *PEKING PALACE* CHINESE RESTAURANT IN ACTON had closed around eleven the previous night, the basement casino still ran underground games of poker, blackjack and roulette until the early hours of the morning, alongside other more regional games such as mahjong and fan-tan; the banker's bell for the latter running a melodic counterpoint to the cheers, shouts of anger and general background conversations that these close-knit places gave out.

Both locals and overseas visitors played for high-end money, with thousands of pounds in chips being bet on the fall of a card, or roll of a die, at any time.

Lu Hanbing sat at the bar, sipping his matcha green tea from a small, ornate cup; it was strong and concentrated, the equivalent, he supposed, of an espresso. But he hated coffee, and the watered-down alcohol behind the bar, freely given out to the gamblers, wasn't there for him or his staff; it was there to be drunk, to make *them* drunk, and to make them overconfident, enabling them to *lose*.

Hanbing was Chinese for *cold ice*, and Lu had spent his

life trying to fit that name. It was because of this he'd worked his way up through the ranks of the Tsang family; from barman, to banker, to manager and now owner.

The casino was a more pop-up shop, however; every few months it would move to the basement of another club or restaurant; always changing, always on the go. The regulars and the trusted friends would be given the new address and password—after all, what was a casino without the desperate addicts that lost their money there nightly—and, after a couple of days settling in, it would be business as usual.

Lu knew that he'd outstayed his welcome here, though; they'd become complacent, and the previous night's attack on the Tsangs had unnerved him slightly. He'd met the Lucas Twins—or, rather, Johnny Lucas a couple of times, usually on neutral ground. But now? Now he was concerned.

He was also worried at the lack of Benny Tsang, the dominant force around here, in the casino. Like Lu Hanbing, Benny was a mainstay of the casino, a known and expected face to be seen, keeping the tea-drinking overlord company as they watched the gamblers lose, and the profits rise.

But Benny hadn't arrived last night, and he was a no-show again today. Today Lu understood, as the chances were the brothers Kenny and Benny had been told to stay secure after the attack and murder of Jeffrey, and the subsequent hit placed on them both, but he wouldn't have known last night, would he?

Lu frowned. *It wasn't the first time a family member had been betrayed by another, and the brothers had been arguing of late.*

Lu was brought out of his thoughts and back to the casino by the sound of a shotgun going off.

Looking up, he saw four men, in balaclavas and kevlar vests, all with holdalls around their shoulders and all with weapons. Two had assault rifles, one had the shotgun he'd heard fire; but the last one was unarmed, it seemed. Judging him to be the leader, and knowing that the gunshot would have brought more of Lu's men out of the counting room while the others placed tonight's takings in the safe, Lu rose from the chair, hands in the air.

'Relax everyone,' he said calmly, facing the lead masked man. 'I'm sure this is something that can be settled peacefully.'

'Yeah? You reckon?'

Lu could see now that three of the four men were Caucasian, with the lead man black, or possibly Indian. Definitely dark skinned.

'The money's in a safe,' Lu replied, still keeping a level tone to his voice. 'It's guarded by half a dozen men, all better tooled than you seem to be.'

As if on cue, the back door opened and two young men, both with pistols in their hands ran through; however, they stopped when they saw the weaponry aimed at them.

'No need for any of you to die, we ain't here for money,' the lead man replied, nodding to his three friends who, as one, started opening their holdalls. 'We're here to give a message.'

Lu frowned.

'What kind of message?'

The three men now pulled five litre-petrol cans out of the holdalls and, as the gamblers and staff all backed into a corner, they poured the liquid over the tables and the bar.

'A message from Johnny and Jackie Lucas. *Gambling time is over.*'

With that, the lead man pulled a flare gun from his pocket

and fired it at the roulette table, the flare igniting the petrol they'd liberally tossed around the room.

'Tell Kenny Tsang we said hello,' the man laughed as, with his three men behind him, he backed out of the room.

'Get everyone out!' Lu shouted, waving to a back door, now with flames licking around the edges of the doorframe. 'Get them out now!'

As the guards escorted the terrified gamblers out through the back, Lu Hanbing stared around the casino, now engulfed in flames.

They'd lost money tonight, and more so they'd lost face. People would know that the Lucas Twins had taken down a casino without a fight. But at the same time, there *couldn't* be a fight, not with the civilians in the room.

Lu knew he would have to explain this to the brothers. If he even saw Benny and Kenny again.

The question was, what would they do to retaliate? And, more importantly, why hadn't the message been to Kenny and Benny?

What did Jackie and Johnny Lucas know that Lu Hanbing didn't?

MICKEY TRACKIES HADN'T BEEN ABLE TO SLEEP.

He'd known from the moment Jackie had met him the previous night that something was wrong; Jackie was far more confident, far more focused than usual, and when he'd received the call to action by text, he'd almost been reluctant to turn up. It had been a good few years since he'd been asked on such a journey, after all. He didn't know if he still had it in him.

He'd expected it to be a standard threat night, a *back off or I take what's yours* night. More old school villainy, not a bloodbath. The kid who'd appeared, the black kid in the hoodie who Mickey was sure came from Mama Delcourt, and who had driven the SUV, had also seemed shocked. But the money had been good—man, the money was *always* good working for the Lucas Twins, but this time it'd been flowing—and Mickey had some poor bets to pay off. He needed the work.

But not this kind of work.

They'd gone to the club, they'd faced off with Jeffrey Tsang, and his mate, the weaselly one in the glasses, had gobbed off, opened his mouth a bit too much. Jackie had snapped, shooting the poor bastard dead. And what for, making a comment? *Taking the piss?*

Not for the first time, Mickey Trackies considered going to the police, telling them what he knew. He'd already heard the rumours, seen that Johnny had been arrested. He knew the boxing club was under deep scrutiny, that the body had been found and—

And that they didn't have a clue what they really had there.

Mickey glanced at his hotel room clock; it was one in the morning. Sighing, and giving up on sleep for the moment, he rose from his bed, walking over to his phone, currently charging on the small desk. It was a burner phone, and pretty much untraceable, but he could use it to connect to his cloud-based email without fear of being found. Well, at least he thought he could. Honestly, he didn't really know if he was as off the grid as he wanted.

There were around ten messages on his phone from Elaine, his wife; the police had been to their house in Bethnal Green twice during the day, but she didn't know where he was, and they wouldn't know where he was right now, as he'd paid cash for the room. He'd turned the phone off, unsure whether it could be tracked or not. But, turning on the phone, he'd seen the messages. The reports.

Johnny was taken.

The war that Jackie wanted had begun.

Jeffrey Tsang was dead.

There were hits out on the Tsangs from the Lucas clan.

Everything he already knew or suspected was there in black and white on his screen. Half of his contacts wanted to buy Mickey a drink, the other half wanted him to get out of the country fast.

There was an email that stood out, though; forwarded to him by an associate of the Lucas family.

Mickey.

Watch your back.
Two million dollar hit put out on Johnny. Not sure who.
Might be connected to last night. Heard you were there too.

Might be time to get out of town for a bit.

Mickey stared at the message with a sense of utter dread.

If they were spending two mil on Johnny, then how much was he worth?

Looking around the squalid room, Mickey realised he was too exposed here. This wasn't the secure location he'd thought it would be, and as for a place to lay his head, he was too wired now to even consider sleep. He'd booked it late the previous night, paid cash and given a fake name, and had spent the whole day and evening in the room, watching TV, waiting for things to cool down, only popping out to grab fast food for lunch and dinner, before staying a second night. He'd expected to stay here a couple of days until everything died down a little; this was the playbook from the old days, where you went to ground for a couple of nights, maybe read a book or two before re-emerging... but he'd known from the start this wasn't like the old days.

Two million dollars.

Mickey decided to get out of there before someone linked *the quiet man in the tracksuit who paid cash* to *the man who'd been beside Jackie Lucas in the club the previous night*. If the police knew, then others did, and he'd not been as careful as he should have been when he bought his food. Someone could have seen him, recognised him.

Two million dollars.

He walked into the shower, allowing the cold water to wake him. He'd been doing cold showers for years now; When you got older, the injuries from fights took longer to heal. This was a way to speed his metabolism up, to fix himself faster, ready for the next one. And Mickey reckoned he needed to be fitter than ever right now.

Rivulets of blood still streamed off his body, into the shower's drain plug. He stared down at them, absently. It wasn't his blood, and he'd thought he'd washed it all off before going to bed the previous night, but it'd been late, and he'd been...

Nobody should see what he saw last night.

Turning the shower off, and towelling himself down, he threw on a new tracksuit and vest from his 'go bag', the one he always kept in his car just in case, pulled on his trainers and, his mind made up, he grabbed his phone and keys, leaving the hotel room. He knew eventually the police would work out he was there, in the small three-star hotel in Stepney. He'd needed to blow off steam after, well, after *that*. Something violent, something filthy, and he'd known a place where the whores were clean and up for anything.

And a place his wife wouldn't find out.

He needed to go to the police now. He could pick his things up later. If he got there tonight, he could make a deal, maybe keep out of the firing line. Witness relocation, perhaps? He was there when it happened, sure, but he was an accessory, not the actual murderer. He didn't know what was going on, nobody had told him.

He was just the muscle.

And the cash couldn't be traced. Cash was cash. Even when there was a lot.

He was so deep in his thoughts as he walked westwards down the Mile End Road, stopping at the crossing with Cambridge Heath Road, the White Hart pub to his right and the Blind Beggar, the most notorious pub in Whitechapel across the road in front of him, he hadn't noted the hooded Asian man that had been following him from the Genesis Cinema. He was in a grey, pull-over hoodie, his hands in his pockets, head down and hood up, watching Mickey from a distance, as if stalking him.

And, as Mickey walked past the Blind Beggar, still open, but soon closing for the night, restraining himself from entering before last orders and having a last, dutch courage drink for the road, walking past the parked vans that were already setting up for the following day's vegetable and fruit market, the Asian stalker picked up his pace, walking up to one van and, pulling out a small hammer, swinging it hard at the window, smashing it as he walked on quickly, the van's alarm ringing out shrilly in the cool night air, drawing the attention of anyone walking the street towards it.

This done, the Asian walked up behind Mickey Trainers and, as the tracksuit bruiser looked back to see what the noise was, pulled a small gun from his other pocket with his left hand, revealing what looked to be a snub nose silencer on the end and, at close range, shot Mickey Trainers in the face twice, with two quick shots.

Snap-snap.

Mickey had recognised his attacker, his eyes widening in surprise as the bullets entered between them. Dead instantly, the blood splattering out of the hole in the back of his skull as he fell, Mickey Trainers collapsed to the floor as the Asian, now with the gun back into his pocket and darting through the vans, clambered into a waiting car, and drove off the other direction, back towards Bow Road.

As the other night time partygoers on the street, many standing outside the Blind Beggar as the music thumped from within, finally realised what had happened, the screams began.

But for Mickey Trainers, there was no scream. No last word.

Mickey Trainers would never box again.

Nor would he tell the police the truth about what happened the night before—or about the identity of his killer.

13

JACK SPOT'S SCAR

BILLY HAD GOT THE NEWS THE MOMENT HE ARRIVED IN THE office.

'You hear about Mickey Trackies?' Anjli asked from her desk, looking up as he pulled off his tweed jacket, hanging it up on a hook on the wall beside his desk. 'Shot twice in the head outside the *Blind Beggar* in Whitechapel.'

'Yeah, had a message from a mate in vice about it—'

'Christ on a cross, they're really going for the gangster tropes, aren't they?' Monroe fumed, interrupting Billy, walking into the office and dumping his jacket on a spare desk as he looked over at Anjli. 'Outside the George Cornell pub? Bloody hell. Did they just wait until he went past something old-school gangster specific? Maybe he could have walked past the *Lion & Unicorn* from *The Long Good Friday* and had the damn thing blow up on him?'

'I think that was demolished years ago, Guv,' Anjli replied. 'Sorry to destroy your dreams.'

'Aye, well, at least he kept to the Krays trope, eh?' Monroe grimaced. 'Any idea of the shooter?'

Billy was already logged in and typing on his keyboard as he spoke.

'Asian male, in his twenties, jumped into a car and drove off eastwards. Someone pegged the licence, but when they checked it, the car was classed as stolen earlier the same day in Westminster.'

'Asian? That could be the Tsangs, getting revenge for their nephew,' Monroe considered this, scratching at his white goatee beard as he did so. 'Apparently, both sides have hits out on each other now. Looks like we have a bona fide gang war on our hands.'

Billy leaned back in his chair as he looked back.

'So you've heard there's a bounty on Johnny,' he said.

'Aye, I heard,' Monroe replied. 'I know you class two million as pocket money, but maybe if DS Kapoor and I put our heads together, we could share it?'

'Any bounties being paid are going to me,' Doctor Marcos now entered the office. 'Joanne and I know the best ways to kill, and we can always use the money.'

'I should have known you'd know about Johnny Lucas' contract,' Monroe replied.

At this, however, Doctor Marcos frowned.

'Johnny Lucas has a contact out on him?'

'Yes, two million,' Anjli looked up at the divisional surgeon. 'What were you talking about?'

'Oh, definitely that,' Doctor Marcos smiled, but considering the conversation, it seemed a lot more sinister than it was before. And the conversation now over, Doctor Marcos continued through the office, heading towards the back staircase and the coffee making facilities, while Monroe continued into his office, hanging up his coat as he did so.

Billy went to speak to Anjli, but paused as his phone rang.

'DC Fitzwarren, Temple Inn,' he said into the receiver.

'Hi, this is DI Buckley,' the voice down the line spoke. 'I'm the curator of the Metropolitan Police Crime Museum. You left a voicemail last night?'

'Yes, thanks for calling back,' Billy grabbed a notepad and pen. 'I needed a confirmation from the Black Museum for something.'

'Well, we don't call it that,' Buckley's voice was already irritated. 'We changed the name when we moved buildings a good while ago.'

'Sorry, my mistake,' Billy grimaced. 'I need confirmation from the Crime Museum, then.'

'Okay, what can I help with?' Buckley relented slightly.

'Jack Spot's knife,' Billy read from his notebook; notes he'd taken when Monroe had told him about his conversation with Maurice Hamilton while they ate dinner the previous night. 'I understand you had it in your collection, but lost it when you moved buildings?'

'I'm sorry, DC Fitzwarren, but I don't know what you mean,' Buckley was confused now. 'There are two blades that could be called Jack Spot's knife, but neither is that important. Spot never had a specific knife he'd use.'

'What are the two blades you mean, then?' Billy was already opening a browser as he spoke.

'Well, the first one was August 1955,' Buckley started, and Billy wasn't surprised to see that a curator for a crime-based museum was knowledgeable about crime. 'There was a vicious knife fight in Frith Street, Soho, between Jack Spot and a friend of Billy Hill, who Spot was trying to overthrow, an Italian known as Albert Dimes. There was an argument, Spot chased Dimes into the Continental Fruit Store, slashing him in the process with his blade. In the struggle, though, it changed hands and Spot was also cut. Both men ended up in hospital and both were arrested.'

'And the other?'

'A year later, May 1965, Spot got his famous scar on Cabbell Street, when 'Mad' Frankie Frazer, also connected to Billy Hill, once ambushed him and slashed his face with razors,' Buckley explained. 'But again, that wasn't a knife. The only one that fits your narrative is the Frith Street one. And I'm afraid nobody knows where that is.'

'And you never owned it?'

'Here? Definitely not. It's not that important to be kept, I'm afraid. All I can think is that it's simply a case of urban legends; two distinct moments being merged into one scene, creating a different, yet incorrect narrative in the process.'

Billy thanked DI Buckley for his time and disconnected the call, leaning back in his gamer chair.

Maurice Hamilton had lied to Monroe.

It may have been a harmless mistake, but it was definitely something that needed to be looked at. And yet, there was something else there, something said that once more irked at his memories.

'Two distinct moments being merged into one scene, creating a different, yet incorrect narrative in the process.'

Billy felt a sliver of ice run down his spine as he realised finally what it had been that concerned him with the CCTV footage.

'Guv?' He whispered, before replying with a sturdier '*Guv?* I think I have something.'

Monroe emerged out of his office, walking over to Billy as, through the door, Declan and Jess entered.

'Sorry we're late,' he said.

'You're early,' Monroe checked his watch. 'It's just that

we're earlier. And you're just in time for a Billy Fitzwarren revelation.'

He looked at Billy, who, now realising he had an audience, paled a little.

'Well, I might not have it, but I *think* I have it.'

'And already, the wee laddie backtracks,' Monroe sighed theatrically.

'Okay, so look at this,' Billy tapped on his keyboard, and on the screen several of the influencers' livestreams, taken in *Tsang City*, appeared on the screen. 'This is when Jackie Lucas, or at least a man we believe is Jackie Lucas, abducts Jeffrey Tsang.'

'Do we need to watch it all?' Declan asked, nodding at Jess.

Billy shook his head.

'Actually, all I need is this image,' he replied, zooming in on Mickey Trackies. 'Note here that Mickey Trackies, a known Lucas operative—'

'Operative is a bit grand for him,' Monroe chuckled. 'He hits people. *Hit* people, I suppose. Past tense and all that. Not really James Bond levels here.'

'Associate then,' Billy continued, waving the mouse cursor on the screen around Mickey's right, un-bandaged hand. 'See here? Mickey has no bandage on his wrist.'

Anjli noted this down. 'Should he have been wearing one?'

'Yes,' Jess leaned around now, replying to Anjli, realising where Billy was going with this. 'If you're looking at the apartment footage, that is.'

'I knew something was wrong, but I couldn't work out what it was, and why it was niggling at me,' Billy opened up another CCTV window on the monitor screen. 'Here's the footage of 'Jackie' leaving the apartment half an hour before he arrives at *Tsang City*.'

The Unit watched as, on the screen, a track-suited man that had to be Mickey Trackies appeared from the external door, waiting to the left of the screen, a white bandage on his right hand. When 'Jackie' entered from the other side, Mickey Trackies passed him a gun, one that Johnny or Jackie placed behind in his trouser band.

'Note this,' Billy rewound the footage slightly, and froze the image as Mickey gave the gun in his right hand. 'Mickey has a bandage on. And, looking at the gradients here, Jackie looks to have a lighter shirt on, which is Johnny's MO.'

'And the parting's wrong,' Anjli commented. 'Now you look at it. Although it could just be the angle.'

'So he took the bandage off while driving?' Declan suggested.

'I'll let Jess answer that,' Billy grinned, looking over at her. 'In her background checks yesterday she picked it up, but we didn't click how relevant it was.'

As if realising how important this moment was, Jess ran to the desk she'd been using and picked up the notepad she'd been writing in, flicking back a couple of pages.

'I checked the boxing club website, and last week Mickey Trackies, in his boxing name *Mickey 'the fist' Kent* had a bare knuckle match there,' she replied, reading from her notes. 'One of the visitor reviews on the page commented he beat his rival so bad they had to bandage his punching hand up.'

'We need to check the body, and see if the hand still has those injuries,' Monroe glanced at the rear door, where but minutes earlier Doctor Marcos had left. 'We can do that in a minute. But if forensics confirms the injuries *are* a week old, that means this footage isn't from last night. It's from shortly after the fight.'

'And we look at the hair and possible blue shirt, it's of Mickey and Johnny, not Mickey and Jackie,' Declan added. 'Someone hacked the system, changed the footage when they sent it to us. Who can get into the apartment complex's security?'

'Cheryl Jenkins could,' Anjli looked over at him. 'She manages the apartments as well as renting one. She could have taken a piece from the last time Johnny was there and spliced it into last night's footage. Probably didn't realise about the bandage.'

'Johnny's woman set him up?' Bullman, watching from the door to her office, shook her head. 'No honour among thieves.'

'Bloody hellfire,' Monroe started. 'When did you turn up?'

'I never left,' Bullman replied, straight-faced. 'I never leave. I'm always here.'

There was a moment of pause, and during this, Doctor Marcos now entered, watching the crowd around the monitor.

'Did I miss a Billy revelation?' she asked.

Billy looked around, rising to meet her gaze.

'The Mickey Trackies murder, Ma'am,' he said. 'Do you have a report on him yet?'

'Billy, because you were polite to me, I shall answer your question and you *shall* go to the ball,' Doctor Marcos sipped at her coffee. 'From what I know, there's nothing yet, but Khanna was on the scene last night, and I believe DC Davey is assisting him with the autopsy right now in Mile End. What do you need?'

'Is he wearing a bandage on his right hand?' Billy replied. 'Or was he when he died? We need to know about—'

'About bruises on his right knuckles,' Jess interrupted eagerly, before looking, ashen-faced at Billy. 'Sorry. I got excited.'

Nodding, Doctor Marcos passed her mug to Anjli to hold, tapped out a text on her phone, and sent it.

'Soon as I hear, you'll hear,' she said as she took the mug back from Anjli. 'I hope your chilly hands haven't altered my drink's temperature.'

As Anjli looked at the doctor in a mixture of confusion and annoyance, Declan spoke quickly to move the conversation on.

'If she lied about Johnny leaving and set up a fake video to prove her story, then she did more than simply set him up,' Declan mused. 'She planned the whole story. Which means she must have made sure that Johnny—'

'Was drugged,' Doctor Marcos spoke now. 'Yeah, I was going to mention this in the briefing. We checked the bloodwork. He had GHB in his system.'

'Are you sure?' Monroe rose straighter at this, and Declan understood why. GHB, or rather *Gamma Hydroxy butyric Acid*, better known as Liquid Ecstasy was known as a date rape drug, and had been the poison of choice to use on Monroe back in Birmingham a few months earlier, when DI White, under the orders of Macca Byrne and Moses Delcourt had drugged him, before taking his unconscious body to Beachampton.

Doctor Marcos nodded.

'More than that, Alex,' she replied. 'From the report, it looks like a near as dammit match to the stuff you had in your system. Likely from the same source.'

'Bloody hell,' Declan muttered. 'So Cheryl drugged Johnny, he goes to sleep, and she sets the CCTV up to look like he leaves. But if he doesn't leave, who was Jackie?'

'Maybe it was actually Jackie Lucas,' Monroe stared up at the first CCTV image on the monitor, where Jackie faced Jeffrey Tsang. 'According to Maurice Hamilton it was, anyway.'

Suddenly remembering, Monroe looked back at Billy.

'Anything on that car registration, by the way?'

'I'm not magic,' Billy muttered as he tapped on the keyboard, checking the system. 'It takes a while to—oh, wait—yes, it's Ramsey Allen's Rover. You were right yesterday.'

'So, Ramsey Allen is out there playing silly buggers, and Maurice knows,' Monroe looked at Doctor Marcos, who had a slightly queasy expression on her face. 'Now what?'

'I wasn't going to tell you, but as it's likely connected, I probably should,' Doctor Marcos spoke slowly, trying to keep Monroe calm. 'But Ellie Reckless was at the club yesterday afternoon, trying to get information.'

'And you were going to *keep this from me?*' Monroe exploded in anger as he stared at the divisional surgeon. 'My protégé, the murdering scum, and the prick she hangs around with? *Together, both involved here somehow?*'

'I said nothing because I knew this was how you'd react,' Doctor Marcos snapped back in response. 'It's a hole in the jigsaw. A piece on the chessboard.'

'I'll *wipe the piece off the bloody board* when I see her,' Monroe hissed, but stopped as Doctor Marcos' phone beeped.

Looking at it, she glanced back at Billy.

'No bandage,' she said. 'But Davey says there are signs of bruising, about a week old.'

'Bloody hell, Johnny Lucas *is* being set up,' Anjli muttered.

'Aye,' Monroe, his temper subsiding slightly, agreed. 'Looks like he might be. Framed for a murder, and when that doesn't work, put a bloody hit on him so big he can't escape.'

Turning away from the group, Monroe stormed off back to his office, muttering to himself as he did so.

'Briefing room, now,' he grumbled audibly. Watching this, Declan walked over to Anjli.

'Who the hell is Ellie Reckless?' he asked.

Anjli, as confused as he was, simply shrugged.

'We both know Monroe collects broken toys,' she said, gathering her notes and already starting for the briefing room. 'Maybe this one couldn't be put back together again.'

Declan considered this silently for a moment, and then stopped as a hand tugged at his sleeve.

'Can I be in the briefing too?' Jess asked. 'I've never been in a proper briefing before.'

'Do you have anything to add to it?' Declan asked, half-amused by Jess' eagerness and innocence.

'Actually, I think I do,' she smiled. 'But all things in time, dad.'

And with that, she almost skipped past him, back to her desk, papers in hand.

Suddenly, Declan felt an irrational fear that his own daughter was going to outshine him here.

14

KNIGHT TAKES ROOK

'ALRIGHT KIDDIES, LINE UP TO AMAZE ME WITH YOUR DETECTIVE prowess, and remember to keep your words to a PG rating, as we have a twelve-year-old in the room,' Monroe said, nodding at Jess. 'Who, if she wants to be helpful, could get us all a drink.'

'Let her stay,' Declan replied, noting Jess' crestfallen face. 'You can call it an apology for calling her twelve, Guv. Besides, she says she has something.'

Fifteen minutes had passed since Monroe had grumpily marched into his office demanding a briefing, and in that time both De'Geer and Cooper had also arrived, although the latter was conspicuous by leaving the room quietly and heading to the back as Monroe had started the briefing

Doctor Marcos walked into the room, nodding to Bullman, standing by the door, but then stopped as her phone beeped, pulling it out. After reading the message, she swore, punched the door and stormed back out of the briefing room, heading back to the main doors and the stairs down to her forensics lab.

'So much for PG rated,' Monroe muttered, watching through the glass windows as she left. 'Where's PC Cooper gone? I'm sure she was here a minute ago.'

'Making the teas,' Billy sat at the side of the briefing room, connecting his laptop to the plasma screen. 'She felt it was inhumane and offensive that the youngest member of the team, even if on a temporary basis, would miss her first briefing because you needed a coffee, and decided to selflessly gather our morning caffeine requirements. *Boss.*'

'I'm glad you ended that with boss, because it sounded remarkably like insubordination,' Monroe raised an eyebrow at Billy's tone.

'Sorry,' Billy reddened. 'No sleep. Needing the aforementioned caffeine.'

'Aye, we know that one way too well,' Monroe smiled as he looked over at Jess. 'Are you sure you want to join up? All you get is grief and attitude.'

'She's joining,' Bullman smiled from the doorway. 'I want her on the team eventually. Has a good head on her shoulders. Worth a Declan and a half, so I'd have the equivalent of two working Walsh officers by then.'

'Well, while we wait for Rosanna to come back, let's go through what we know,' Monroe suggested, before Declan could comment on Bullman's maths. 'Who's first?'

There was a silence in the room. Nobody wanted to go first in such a complicated case.

'Anything more from Hamilton?' Bullman asked, breaking the silence.

'Nothing major, he baulked the moment he saw Ramsey Allen outside the house,' Declan replied. 'Reckoned he was only there to help Jeffrey Tsang become legitimate. He said something about Jackie though, that he was left for dead in

South America, rotting in a jail, but a body was never found.'

'While Johnny created his own version,' Billy shuddered. 'Imagine coming back and finding that.'

'Was there anything connecting the Tsangs and the Twins?' Monroe asked. 'Maurice said something about a knife auction, but I hadn't heard anything.'

'I just heard from the Metropolitan Crime Museum,' Billy nodded. 'There isn't a 'Jack Spot's Knife', as such and even if there was, it was never on their records.'

'So Maurice Hamilton invents a fictional feud,' Monroe looked at Declan. 'Or, they didn't realise they were bidding on a fake. Ramsey Allen is a known forger.'

'You think he worked with Maurice to sell it to them?' Declan rubbed at his chin. 'Possible. We've seen people fight for less.'

'Let's see if we can find another way for them to truly hate each other,' Monroe pondered. 'One that perhaps brings in Mama Delcourt and Nicky Simpson.'

Jess meekly held up a hand.

'Go on, lassie, no need to wait.'

'Thank you, sir. There's talk, well, notes in forums I found—'

'On the dark web?' Declan asked, and was answered by a click of the teeth and an eye roll by his daughter.

'Not everything's the dark web,' she sighed.

'But the best things usually are,' Billy grinned.

'Carry on,' Monroe urged Jess. 'Before DC Fitzwarren tries to sell us illegal arms and contraband artwork.'

'Well, what I found were people talking about the whole *Crossrail* infrastructure, and how buildings are now going up where the construction work has finished,' Jess read from her notes. 'And someone said on a London based *Reddit* thread that the Tsang brothers and the Twins had been working together for years to build up Soho, in particular the land taken down by Crossrail.'

'Aye, Johnny told us yesterday they were both part of a real estate deal. In their interests to stay friendly or lose money,' Monroe sighed, cricking his neck as he spoke. 'Must have been investing in this before they hated each other.'

'What if the Tsangs killed Jeffrey?' De'Geer spoke aloud. 'Maybe he was screwing up their business by going legit, trying to carve his own way? It's known that the Triads are all about family—until they aren't.'

'It's a thought,' Declan noted it down. 'Someone has to have been bankrolling the real Jackie Lucas, though.'

'It still feels weird saying that out loud,' Anjli replied. 'The crazy old gangster's past is now catching up with him.'

'The crazy old gangster left his brother to die, so he deserves it,' Declan shifted in his chair. 'Although, with what we have, we will have to let him go now.'

'Shame,' Monroe agreed ruefully. 'I was hoping he'd gain some humility.'

'I think he might gain that the moment people try to kill him,' Anjli mused. 'After all, two million is a hell of a payday.'

'Maybe we can't release him yet,' Monroe considered the alternative. 'I'd rather he was captured than dead. And we still don't have conclusive proof it wasn't him.'

'The CCTV?' Jess looked confused.

'Maybe done deliberately to free him,' Declan replied. 'Deliberately made himself the prime suspect, just so we had to let him go. I'd suggest we keep him in the cell for as long as we can.'

'Agreed,' Monroe nodded.

'Any news on the jogger?' Anjli suddenly asked. 'The one that found the body?'

'We had a statement taken,' De'Geer read from his own notes now. 'That is, Mile End police did. She gave a name and address, but neither of them are real.'

'How do you know?'

'Because I looked for her yesterday evening, and she doesn't exist,' De'Geer looked apologetic as he spoke. 'I'm not going to throw aspersions on Mile End, but I'd have been a little more thorough.'

'In fairness, it was gone midnight in a bloodbath,' Monroe took a whiteboard marker, writing on the plasma screen. 'I wouldn't be surprised if everyone was shaken. Who spoke to the witness?'

'A Detective Sergeant McAlroy,' De'Geer read. 'I've not been able to get hold of her yet.'

'McAlroy,' Declan checked through his notes. 'We met her yesterday. She was the one told to move Johnny into the interview room.'

'Well, let's check into her a little,' Monroe carried on writing.

Declan nodded, noting this down.

'So Johnny is drugged and footage doctored to make him look guilty,' Monroe said as he wrote JOHNNY on the whiteboard. 'Cheryl must have known something. Mickey Trackies was there and must also have known something was up, but he's now dead, killed by an Asian man who could be connected to the Tsangs.'

He wrote three names on the screen;

JACKIE

CHERYL

JEFFREY

'What else?'

'Jogger finds the place at midnight, and this makes sure Johnny can't hide the murder if he returns later that night,' Declan suggests. 'And Kayas Ashad, who was last seen with the Seven Sisters, is beside Jackie as he confronts Jeffrey.'

'What about Hamilton or Banner?' De'Geer asked.

'Maurice has connections to everyone on the board,' Monroe mused. 'And Banner seemed to be in the wrong place, wrong time.'

'Although he invited everyone who was there filming, it seems,' Jess noted.

'Many of whom were influencers connected to Simpson's health clubs,' Billy added. 'Good catch, by the way.'

'Anything else?'

'The GHB,' Bullman piped up from the door. 'If it's the same source, then that means it came from the Byrnes or the Delcourts, as Macca and Moses gave it to DI White.'

'Aye and the Byrnes are now gone,' Monroe nodded, looking over at Bullman. DI White had been her partner while she was in Birmingham, and even now she took it as a personal fault that she didn't realise before he died he was corrupt, and in Macca Byrne's pocket. 'We need to chat to Janelle Delcourt.'

Declan raised a hand.

'I'll take that one, sir,' he replied. 'I have priors in the place.'

'Good man. And while you're there, try not to steal guns and have fights with people with baseball bats this time.'

'I'll do my best,' Declan added with a rueful smile.

'Right then,' Monroe muttered as he looked back at the plasma screen, pen still in his hand. 'What else is there, or are we now at the end?'

'There was a fire in Acton last night,' Billy read from his screen. 'Believed to be an illegal, off-books casino. Witnesses say four armed men came in, said *Johnny and Jackie Lucas says gambling time is over* and torched the whole place. Didn't even go for money. Scorched earth attempt from the looks of things.'

'Bloody marvellous,' Monroe sighed. 'I was hoping the gang war would take a little more time to start. Let's talk about our track-suited friend, anyway. What do we have?'

Declan leaned back.

'Definitely Asian, definitely following him, left-handed according to witnesses.'

'He wasn't anywhere near his house, and we'd been knocking all day,' Bullman said from the doorway. 'He would have gone to ground. Find out if he had a preferred flop house or knocking shop, see if we can locate where he was staying. Maybe there's stuff of his still there.'

'Good plan,' Monroe replied as, through the door and struggling with a tray of mugs, PC Cooper re-entered.

'They're all white coffee, no sugar,' she apologised. 'I realised as I started making them I didn't have a clue how any of you took them. Sorry.'

'It's hot and filled with caffeine,' Monroe smiled as he took a mug labelled *WORLD'S BEST BATMAN*. 'It'll do fine, lassie. Place them down and take a seat. De'Geer will update you, and you'll be with him today.'

Surprised at this, most likely expecting more crowd control, Cooper wandered over to De'Geer, as he showed her his notes from the briefing.

'There's also the chess move,' Anjli read from her own notes. 'Drawn in a marker pen on the door as you exited the back of the club, where Jackie, Mickey Trackies and Kayas

Ashad left with Jeffrey Tsang. *Queen to C-7.* Doctor Marcos said it's a move called *Meier's Spectacular Sacrifice*.'

'Written by Lucas on the door? A message perhaps?'

De'Geer looked up from his notes.

'Maybe he knew Jeffrey's last move and was taunting?'

'Has to be something like that,' Declan scratched at his neck as he replied. 'I never really saw Jackie as a chess player. Unless it was speed chess. With knives.'

'It's a strategy game though,' Monroe mused. 'And one thing Johnny is good at, maybe Jackie too, is strategy.'

Anjli nodded.

'Has to be a message.'

Monroe went to reply, but stopped once again; this time it was Doctor Marcos who walked into the briefing room, her face a mask of fury.

'Stop everything,' she ordered. 'We're being played for fools.'

'How so?' Declan frowned.

Doctor Marcos tossed a piece of paper to the desk beside her as she addressed the team.

'I had a concern when I saw the blood spatter at the scene yesterday,' she said. 'Banner, the friend who was killed? His blood spatter around the booth was like mist. A blood explosion, if you want. Jeffrey Tsang, however, was more of a constant drip, like a stab wound.'

'Maybe the bullet went into the gut, but Jeffery Tsang held the blood in as he doubled over?' De'Geer offered.

'That's what Davey thought,' Doctor Marcos nodded. 'But at the same time, there was something off. Like it was more staged than real.'

'Banner's execution looked pretty real to me,' Anjli

muttered, closing her book. 'Or was that to legitimise what you're saying?'

'I think you might be onto something there,' Doctor Marcos leaned against the front desk as she faced the room. 'It wasn't right, so I sent the blood to be checked. Just a sample, that is.'

'And?' Monroe was impatient. 'Get on with it, lassie.'

'I'll ignore the fact that you told me to hurry, because you called me *lassie*, and your accent makes me tingle,' Doctor Marcos smiled back at Monroe. 'But there's not much to say. DC Davey got the results back and texted them to me a few minutes ago. I just confirmed them.'

Doctor Marcos shook her head, unable to believe what she was about to say.

'The blood wasn't fresh,' she said to the room. 'Estimated to be removed from the body a few days earlier, and kept from deteriorating by some anti-coagulants, most likely in the bag they stored it in.'

'The blood was fake?' Monroe exclaimed.

'No, the blood was blood, and was also Jeffrey Tsang's blood,' Doctor Marcos continued. 'But *this* blood also came out of him days before he was shot, and was spurted around like it—'

'Was squirted from a blood bag,' Declan finished the hypothesis. 'The third gunshot was fake. Jeffrey Tsang had to know, to hold the bag, maybe taped up under his shirt.'

'It would also explain why Banner brought in a ton of people with cameras,' Anjli added. 'Poor bastard didn't realise he was the opening act.'

'Jackie had to be in on this,' Doctor Marcos replied. 'But we won't know until we speak to either Jackie or Jeffery about it.'

'I think speaking to Jeffrey might involve some mediums and a ouija board,' Monroe frowned. 'Unless you have something else?'

'Oh, yeah, I forgot to tell you,' Doctor Marcos hadn't finished, and her anger was building again. 'The skinned body in the boxing club is a different blood type to Jeffrey Tsang.'

'It's not Jeffrey?' Billy rocked back in his chair. 'Then who is it, Ma'am?'

'We don't have a DNA match yet, and to be honest, we hadn't looked because we believed we knew the identity,' Doctor Marcos replied to Billy, but spoke to the entire room. 'However, it looks like the man who was tortured, skinned alive and killed in Globe Town wasn't Jeffrey Tsang. As far as I know, the *real* Jeffrey's still alive and out there, held hostage by the *real* Jackie Lucas.'

'I think I'm getting why every bloody Command Unit dumped this on us,' Monroe moaned. 'If it's not Jeffrey, do you have any ideas about who it might be?'

Doctor Marcos shook her head.

'Not a single bloody clue,' she muttered. 'And believe me, that pisses me off greatly.'

'Right then, change of plans,' Monroe straightened. 'This isn't a murder enquiry—well it is, but that can hold for a moment—now it's a missing person's enquiry. Where is Jeffrey Tsang, and who took him?'

He looked around the room.

'De'Geer and Cooper? Change of plans. Bring me Cheryl Jenkins. I want her to explain why she changed the CCTV. Doctor Marcos? Find the identity of this mysterious John Doe and give us anything you can on Mickey Trackies' death.'

'Sir,' De'Geer rose from the chair, Cooper following him out.

'Billy, take young Miss Walsh and hit the forums, the Reddits, the whatever you guys do. I want a solid connection to Nicky Simpson, and more on where the hell Jackie Lucas has been, how he got back, and where he's staying. Also, check more into Maurice Hamilton. Where's he getting his money from, and who's he dealing with? I didn't believe for one moment he was exclusive with Jeffrey Tsang, but now I think the whole bloody lot of them are playing some kind of game.'

'Sir.'

Monroe turned to Anjli now.

'DS Kapoor, I think it's time we talked to the Sisters.'

'I thought Declan was going there?' Anjli asked, surprised at the change of plan.

'Aye, he was, but I think he's going to have to come with me,' Monroe was visibly trying to keep his anger in. 'He's going to stop me doing a murder.'

'Sir?' Billy asked, concerned.

'Ellie bloody Reckless,' Monroe snapped. 'It's time we go have a wee chat with her.'

Declan followed Monroe, grabbing his coat as he did so, chasing his boss as he stormed out of the office, down the steps, through the entrance area and out into the car park.

'Want to tell me where we're going?' he asked, eventually catching up.

'*We're* going nowhere,' Monroe muttered. 'You're sitting in the car and listening to the footie while I kill a bloody—'

He stopped, sighing, kicking a discarded drink can away with more force than required.

'I trained her,' he said sadly. 'I trained her, and she betrayed me when she killed Noyce.'

'Then let's go see her,' Declan opened the door to his Audi. 'Unless you want to call a cab?'

'Bloody comedian,' Monroe muttered as he clambered in. 'All right. We're going to Farringdon.'

15

DINER DATE

Ellie Reckless' "office" was in a parade of shops between Farringdon Station and Smithfield Market, surrounded by sports bars and coffee shops, and deliberately placed amid a growing, gentrified populace.

The irony wasn't misplaced on Declan as he stared up at the signage above.

'*Caesar's Diner?*' He said, half in disbelief. 'The woman you're so pissed off about works in a café?'

'As the sign says, it's a diner,' Monroe grumbled as he opened the door, walking into the premises. And, as Declan followed, he realised what his superior meant.

The inside of Caesar's was to enter a fifties diner, with the floor a checkerboard black and white design; the walls tiled white. There were tables in the middle and along the side were large, opulent red-leather booths, easily enough for six or seven people to sit and eat in. On the wall were fifties advertising posters for milkshakes, burgers and soft drinks, and on each table was a small jukebox, where for a 20p piece you could change the fifties song to *another* fifties song. It was a typical city diner, and from the looks of things, its clientele were often rich, hungry and nostalgic.

Its clientele also included a woman with dark, curly hair and a leather jacket, who sat at the back of one booth, talking to an older man, possibly in his sixties, dressed in a three-piece pinstripe suit that would make Billy salivate, over a white Eton shirt and navy striped tie, his greying hair cut short, a trimmed moustache his only facial hair, and a third person, wearing an olive-coloured German Army coat and blue jeans, her curly blonde hair pulled back and placed under a tatty baseball cap.

Only the man looked like *money*, but Declan felt that of the three, he was probably the hardest up.

Declan also assumed that one of the two women was ex-DI Ellie Reckless, as Monroe hadn't even looked around before striding determinedly over to them.

'You've got some nerve,' he hissed at the woman in the leather jacket.

'Oh, hello Alex, grab a seat,' Ellie waved for the older man to move around. 'You know Ramsey, don't you? This is Tinker Jones. She's my… well, let's say *driver,* for now.'

She looked up at Declan, standing behind Monroe, and smiled.

'Hello, DI Walsh, I'm Ellie Reckless,' she stated as the other woman, apparently named Tinker, also moved aside for Declan to join Monroe at the booth.

Monroe, however, hadn't moved.

'You keep away from my crime scene,' he hissed. 'I don't want you and your criminal mates muddying up the waters.'

'Oh, shut up and have a cup of tea, you bloody drama queen,' Ellie sighed, waving for the waitress to come over. 'You think I haven't been waiting for this visit? I knew you'd turn up since I heard Rosanna Marcos was on the scene yesterday.'

She looked at Declan.

'He told you about me yet?' she asked.

Declan shrugged.

'A little,' he admitted. 'Mainly that you were his protégé, but you got in with the wrong crowd and killed a man.'

Ellie raised an eyebrow as she looked back at Monroe.

'Who'd I kill?' she asked, a little too innocently, like she knew the answer and wanted Monroe to speak it aloud.

'You know damn well what you did.'

'No, Alex, tell me,' Ellie leaned closer now, and Declan felt the atmosphere around the booth change, darken somehow.

This wasn't a conversation anymore, this was a fight.

'Who did I kill?'

Monroe paused, shifting his stance. Surprisingly, he didn't answer.

'That's right, Ellie snapped back at him. 'I didn't kill anyone. They accused me of killing Bryan Noyce, but the jury cleared me. I was bloody innocent, but I was damned by bad press and opinions.'

She looked over at Declan now.

'When you were called a terrorist and had to go on the run—yes, I know all about you, Mister Walsh—did Monroe believe in you?'

'Yes,' Declan replied simply. 'Although, to be transparent, he was suffering from a vicious head injury at the time.'

Ellie chuckled.

'Then he has more faith in you than he ever had in me,' she stated. 'Because if he had *any* faith, he would have taken me at my word.'

There was a long, awkward moment of silence.

'Oh, for God's sake Alex, sit the hell down. Both of you,' Ellie waved to the two empty spaces again. 'I'm not your enemy. Never was.'

'Then explain why you appeared at a crime scene waving a badge that doesn't belong to you,' Monroe sullenly sat on the red leather booth seat.

Ellie considered this and then looked at Declan.

'So let me get this right, Alex told you I was his protégé, but one that hung around with villains and killed Bryan Noyce?'

'In a roundabout way, I suppose,' Declan admitted. 'No solid facts or anything. He doesn't want to talk about his past with you.'

Ellie chuckled.

'Christ, it must be bad then, because Alex there *loves* to talk about his past,' she said. 'Let me tell you the story. See what you think. I became one of the youngest DCs in police history, quickly made it to DS, and then joined Monroe at Mile End. Worked with your father too, briefly. Good man. I was sorry to hear he'd died.'

'Thank you,' Declan didn't know what else to say.

'When Monroe there gained his DCI promotion and moved to Vauxhall a couple of years after this, he brought me with him,' Ellie continued.

'And then you threw it all away,' Monroe hissed.

'Actually, I'll agree with you there,' Ellie nodded at Monroe before turning to Declan. 'Full transparency; I started an affair with a confidential informant. Not one of those scummy drug dealers, this was an accountant.'

'Bryan Noyce.'

Ellie stopped and fixed Monroe with a glare.

'If you don't stop interrupting, you miserable bloody Scot, I'll stop with story time.'

Declan couldn't help himself; he liked this woman. Anyone who gave as good as they got from Monroe couldn't be all bad.

'Tell me about Noyce,' he said.

'He was part of a case, I got a little too close, we started sleeping with each other,' Ellie replied blankly, as if stating facts. Her tone was devoid of all emotion, and Declan couldn't help but wonder if this was some kind of compartmentalising technique. 'He was married, with a son. I had a husband and Millie—'

'Daughter?' Declan couldn't help himself.

'Cocker Spaniel, five years old,' Ellie replied. 'Nathan—that's my ex—is holding her above me right now. He hates her, never enjoyed having a dog, but he's keeping her out of spite. I'm about to fight for custody.'

'I remember the Noyce case,' Declan shifted in his seat, nodding thanks as a waitress brought over a mug of tea that he hadn't ordered. 'But I don't remember any scandal like that.'

'Nobody knew about the affair,' Ellie interrupted. 'I'm explaining it now for transparency. Noyce got in too deep with a right vicious bastard and was killed for it. They found me with his blood on my clothes.'

'How?' Monroe leaned back in his chair. Declan wondered whether he was waiting to argue this, or was genuinely curious of the answer.

'Because I'd punched Bryan in the face earlier that night,' Ellie replied calmly. 'We'd split up. We both knew it was wrong, but apparently I knew this better than he did. Bryan got mouthy, started shouting, went to slap me.'

'And you broke his nose?'

'Bloodied it, nothing more. But that was enough to link me. And then after they found his body, other things appeared; meetings I never had appearing in my online diary, cash appearing in my locker I'd never seen.'

Ellie's face softened.

'I swear to you, boss—I never did the things they accused me of. I'll take that to my grave.'

Declan noticed Monroe start slightly at the mention of *boss*; he looked around the diner, rather than catch her eye.

'They accused you of corruption,' he stated.

'And never convicted,' Ellie pushed back. 'The people who wanted me gone knew they had nothing. Just enough to damn me in the court of public opinion, just like your man there.'

She indicated Declan.

'Or did you forget he had his photo on the front page of half a dozen national newspapers when they thought he was *terrorist suspect number one?*'

'She has a point, Guv,' Declan said. 'You stood beside me, even when we thought we were about to be executed.'

Monroe sipped at his mug at tea, the long, silent moment stretching uncomfortably, interrupted only by the sounds of the *Righteous Brothers* on the jukebox.

'So what's your reason for invading my case?' Monroe watched Ellie intently as he spoke, nodding at Ramsey. 'For sticking *this* thieving scumbag outside Maurice Hamilton's house? Looking to break in, perhaps?'

'I'd appreciate you not insulting my associates like that,' Ellie's tone darkened. 'Mister Allen here has paid his price, done his time. He's a free, honest man.'

'Who happens to be one of the best safe breakers and

burglars in town, and works for you now,' Monroe looked around the diner. 'In a greasy spoon.'

Ellie nodded to Tinker and Ramsey.

'Give us a minute,' she said.

Monroe and Declan slid back out of the booth so they could leave, and Ellie Reckless watched her associates reluctantly walk out of the diner before continuing.

'First off, I didn't fake entrance to a crime scene,' she said. 'I was never fired, I walked. They never took my badge and technically I'm still at the rank of Detective Inspector. So, when I arrived—'

'*Come on, Ellie!*' Monroe, unable to hold his anger, finally exploded. 'You were one of the good ones! And now you're a gopher for criminals!'

Ellie grabbed the mug in front of her and took a mouthful of tea, swallowing it, letting the moment draw on as she formed a reply.

'They took everything from me, Alex,' she said. 'That smug bastard killed my career with a PR company and some gossip. They—' she motioned at the two outside, '—help me, but they don't know the true story.'

'And that is?' Declan asked.

'Robbie Lewis, my lawyer during the trial? He was pissed that they screwed me over, and when he moved jobs, working for an insurance investigator in the city, he brought me with him.'

'You're an insurance investigator,' Monroe almost shook his head.

'It's honest work, and I could create my own team,' Ellie retorted. 'Ramsey was the best, and you know it. I was the only one that caught him, and when he got out, I offered him a job. But yeah, I started working for criminals. I worked off books. Solved problems. You have something stolen? Go to the police. You have something stolen that you can't tell the police about? There's few options. I fill that void. I'll sort the issue in return for a favour. Freely given, a chit of any size to be called in at a time and place of my choosing, and unable to be refused.'

'And what do you intend to do with these favours?' Monroe rested his head on the back of the red leather seat.

'I intend to bank enough of them, so when I trigger them all at once, it'll be a domino effect that not only clears my name for good, it'll also take down the bastard who killed Bryan Noyce,' Ellie replied with utter conviction.

'You could have come to me,' Monroe said, his voice softening now. 'I could have helped.'

'Nobody from my past life can help,' Ellie shook her head. 'And I don't want to bring anyone in who can get hurt. My team? All new. None of whom know my past life except for what they saw in the papers. Oh, apart from Tinker, who I knew in Hendon briefly, before she got kicked out, and Khanna, who helps from time to time.'

'Rajesh Khanna?' Declan straightened at the name.

'Was my CSI when I was in Vauxhall,' Ellie explained. 'It was his testimony that saved me from prison. He reckons he still owes me though, and I'm not turning that guilt trip down.'

'We still haven't got to why you were there yesterday, or why your man Ramsey was at Hamilton's house,' Monroe continued. 'You're working for Johnny Lucas, aren't you?'

'I am, and I have been for a couple of weeks,' Ellie admitted. 'He had a problem he needed sorting, and I needed a couple of favours from him.'

'So it wasn't about clearing his name?'

Ellie shook her head.

'It probably would be now,' she smiled. 'But a week ago, it was about getting to the source of some rumours saying his brother had returned. I'm guessing you've worked out by now that Jackie, the original one, is back in town?'

'We had considered this,' Monroe replied cautiously.

'Consider it harder,' Ellie tapped the counter. 'It's him, he's back and someone's bankrolling him.'

'How do you know this for certain?' Declan asked.

'Because I burned a couple of favours to find out,' Ellie stated. 'The rumours on the street say he got out around a year ago. Some regime change or something where he was being held, added to the recent chaos of the Bogotá mayoral race. From what I heard, he walked out the gates with no issues and went to find an embassy.'

'Johnny never signed anything official stating Jackie was dead,' Monroe nodded, realising. 'He couldn't if he wanted to keep the myth going. Jackie Lucas could have sorted out a new passport and a flight home.'

'But he didn't,' Ellie held up a hand. 'Yes, he got a passport, but according to my sources, he went to Hong Kong. Straight into the heart of the *Wo Shing Wo Triad*.'

'The Tsangs?' Monroe glanced at Declan, already writing this down.

'Their bosses, more likely,' Ellie said. 'He disappears there and doesn't show until a week ago, where he's in London, has money and is talking with an old friend in the Seven Sisters.'

'Janelle Delcourt?' Declan asked, and Ellie nodded.

'Met up in Battersea, so I hear,' she said.

Monroe pondered the information.

'So Jackie and the Sisters are making a play for the east and the west. But why Tsang? Why watch Maurice?'

'I didn't say he was *working* with the Sisters,' Ellie smiled, watching her old mentor struggle. 'I said he was with the Triad. And with Maurice.'

'Maurice pissed himself when he saw Jackie,' Monroe pursed his lips. 'That's not a simple thing to do unless you're scared.'

'It is when you want everyone to consider, with no doubt, that you weren't allies, or connected,' Ellie said. 'That's why we're watching Maurice. He's more involved than anyone likes to think.'

'Who's the body in the boxing club?' Declan asked.

At this question, Ellie paused.

'It's not Jeffrey?'

'No, and you know this,' Declan replied, tiring of the dance. 'Because you were the runner that called it in, weren't you?'

'He's good,' Ellie leaned back in the seat, nodding to Monroe. 'You picked well. Yes, I called it in. I'd been watching the boxing club after the police radio announced the abduction, waiting for them to turn up. After a couple of hours of nothing, with nobody going in or out, I wondered if they'd got in some other way, so went and had a look.'

She paled slightly at the memory.

'I didn't expect what they did. It was horrific,' she said. 'But you're saying it wasn't Jeffery Tsang?'

'I never said that,' Declan smiled. 'I asked who it was.'

Ellie waved him off.

'You wouldn't have asked if you didn't suspect,' she replied. 'I don't know for sure, but you might want to hunt around for his uncle Benny. From what I hear, he's not been around since lunchtime yesterday.'

Her phone buzzed, and she looked down at the screen.

'Johnny's lawyer,' she said. 'Must have heard the news of his client's new fame in the assassin community. Good to see you Alex, but I think chat time is over.'

With a curt nod, Monroe motioned for Declan to join him as they left the diner, walking back out into the Farringdon morning. As they passed, Ramsey and Tinker watched them cautiously before they walked back in to join their boss.

Now alone on the street, Declan looked at Monroe.

'You believe her?' He asked.

'I'm not sure, laddie,' Monroe mused. 'But I think we should try to find Benny Tsang. Because if she's right, not only do we have a candidate for the skinned, dead body, but we'll also have a solid reason for a war in London on our hands.'

16

VIKING RAIDERS

De'Geer and Cooper had arrived at the Cirque Apartments shortly before noon, but there was no Cheryl Jenkins to be seen. Nobody was answering the main entrance buzzer, and eventually someone leaving the double doors beside them allowed the two officers entry to the building, so they went to the fourteenth floor via the elevators, marched to the door of the apartment and knocked once more.

Again, no answer.

'Maybe she's working?' Cooper suggested. 'We hadn't mentioned we were coming, so she could be downstairs, or at the shops, maybe she could have gone to Mile End, to see Mister Lucas?'

'Or she's dead,' De'Geer replied, trying to peer through the door's peephole. 'Wouldn't be the first time we've turned up to find a body.'

'Thanks for reminding me of that,' Cooper looked up and down the corridor. 'She worked for the building, right? So there must be administration offices somewhere.'

De'Geer reluctantly gave up his attempt to look through

the peephole, following Cooper as she headed back to the elevators at the end of the corridor. They'd managed about thirty yards when the door to Cheryl Jenkin's apartment opened, and a tired-looking man leaned out, removing a pair of headphones.

'Can I help you?' he asked, wiping his hands on his jumper. He was in his thirties, short brown hair left to dry wildly, giving him a wind-swept look.

'We're looking for Cheryl Jenkins,' De'Geer said, walking back to the door.

'And who's that?' the man asked, genuinely confused.

'Well, according to our details, she's the woman who lives here,' Cooper pointed at the door. 'Unless you know differently?'

The man stopped, frowning as he looked back into the apartment.

'This one?' he asked again. 'No, you're wrong. Sorry. I've been here for six months now.'

'Can I ask your name?' De'Geer looked back through his notes.

'Paul Burston,' the man, or rather Paul, replied.

De'Geer looked at the door number.

'Were you here yesterday?' he asked.

'No,' Paul shook his head. 'Only got back in this morning. I've been away for a few weeks.'

'May we come in?' Cooper asked, and the tone of her voice made it very clear this wasn't a request.

'Sure,' Paul stepped back as the two officers walked in.

The apartment was spotless, apart from a large wheeled suitcase, a checked luggage tag on the handle, placed in the middle of the living area. It looked like Paul had been correct and had just arrived.

'Been anywhere fun?' De'Geer looked around the living area. It was white-walled and modern, a full wall of glass looking out onto the Thames, a kitchenette to the side. Paul walked over to it, pouring himself water from a drinks dispenser on the front of the expensive-looking fridge.

'Madrid,' he replied, sipping the water as he looked back at the two officers. 'Went about a month back. Was supposed to be a short-term thing, ended up taking way too long.'

'What's your line of work?' Cooper walked to a side table, where a pile of bills and letters lay unopened, most likely recently picked up.

'I work as a wellness associate and advisor,' Paul waved the non-glass-holding-hand at Cooper. 'Could you not go through my mail, please?'

'Anyone else live here?' De'Geer spoke now, diverting Paul's attention back to him.

'No,' he frowned. 'What's this about?'

'And does anyone have a key?'

'It's a company house, so I suppose so,' Paul was getting angry now. 'What the hell is going on?'

'We could ask the same of you, sir,' De'Geer replied calmly. 'Yesterday. Detective Sergeant Kapoor of the City Police came to this apartment and spoke to a woman named Cheryl Jenkins about her movements the previous night. We were led to believe this was her property, that she also managed the building.'

'Look mate, nobody came in here, I wasn't about and you probably have the wrong floor,' Paul placed the glass on a coffee table. 'And don't take it the wrong way, but I don't—'

'It's definitely the right address,' Cooper said, bringing Paul's attention back to her, as she picked a business card, half hidden by the discarded envelopes off the side table, holding it up to show him. 'This is DS Kapoor's card. She would have left it after the meeting.'

Paul stormed across the floor, snatching the card from Cooper's hand, peering closely at it as his expression changed from anger to bemusement. Lowering it, he looked around the living space.

'The cleaner,' he said, as if this explained everything. 'She was probably in. Your boss more likely spoke to her.'

'Mister Burston,' De'Geer placed a hand on Paul's shoulder, and the man looked up at him, realising, at close range, how imposing the tall policeman truly was. 'Let me explain something. There's a gang war going on in London, with three dead so far and one missing.'

'I don't see what this has to do with me?'

'The catalyst for this war,' De'Geer continued, cutting off Paul, 'was a brutal attack from an East End gangster, a man that left this very apartment to commit the crime, returning in the early hours of yesterday morning.'

'I wasn't here,' Paul's voice had dropped in volume, as he realised the potential trouble he could be in right now. 'I have proof, hotel receipts—'

'We believe you,' De'Geer smiled, but it wasn't a soothing one. 'But, that doesn't stop the fact that someone used your apartment, while you were away, as a base, convincing their gangster boyfriend they lived here. Now, we believe this gangster had been here several times over the months, so I'm assuming this would also tally up with days you weren't staying here, trips you took over the last six months?'

'I travel a lot for my company,' Paul whispered. 'I'm a—'

'A wellness associate and advisor,' Cooper interrupted. 'Yes, sir, you've said. And who do you do that for?'

'It's contracted,' Paul sat on the sofa now, his eyes glazed over as the enormity of the situation hit him. 'I work on a consultancy basis for Simpson's Health Clubs.'

'Nicky Simpson?' De'Geer glanced quickly at Cooper before regaining his composure.

'Yes, do you know him?' Paul looked up at De'Geer. 'He's expanding out into Spain, and I was there checking everything over.'

'Was this trip your decision or Nicky's?' De'Geer continued. Paul thought about this for a moment before replying.

'I think it was a mixture of both,' he eventually said. 'The Madrid operation's been going for a while now, and I've been back and forth a few times. Why? Is Nicky involved here?'

'I'm sure he's not,' Cooper intervened now, a smile on her face as she glanced at De'Geer. 'But at the same time, someone's been living here while you've been away.'

'Nah, I'd know,' Paul shook his head. 'And even if they were, nothing seems to be missing, so I'm sure it's not that bad.'

'The man believed to have been here two nights ago has a two million dollar hit out on him,' De'Geer stated matter-of-factly, taking a silent delight at Paul's paling face as he heard the number. 'If people believe he was here, they might think he's *still* here. They might come looking. But as you said, it's not that bad.'

'Do I need police protection?' Paul rose from the sofa.

'I don't think so, everything's quite secure,' De'Geer smiled again, this time a real one. 'And if you're that worried, perhaps you should talk to your boss about a relocation.'

'The cleaner I mentioned,' Paul now said, bargaining for some goodwill from the officers. 'I have a cleaner, she comes in three times a week. She'd have seen if anyone was living here.'

'Excellent,' De'Geer pulled out his notepad and pen, passing it across. 'Just write their contact details here, and we'll leave you alone for the moment.'

Nervously, Paul did so.

STANDING IN THE LOBBY OF THE CIRQUE APARTMENTS, De'Geer looked at Cooper as they took a moment to reflect on the previous conversation.

'Thoughts?' he asked.

'I don't know anyone who, when they hear strangers have been in their apartment, just wave it off,' Cooper muttered through clenched teeth. 'Even the thought of someone being in my room, going through my things, wearing my underwear? Puts my teeth on edge.'

'I don't recall anything being said about underwear,' De'Geer frowned.

'Nobody ever *says* anything about the underwear,' Cooper hissed. 'But you know it happens.'

A security guard walked over to them; short and stocky, he was no more than five feet in height, but still gave the impression of someone who could hold his own, and more so, in a fight.

'You needed to speak to me?' he asked, suspicious, expecting to get some kind of reprimand.

'Depends. Are you the person who deals with security footage?'

'Aye, I am,' the man nodded, holding a hand out. 'Ant McGann. What do you need?'

'CCTV footage,' De'Geer nodded up at the camera in the

corner. 'Who controls the feed, and how can they alter it, if needed?'

'I do, and it can't be,' McGann shrugged.

'What about Cheryl Jenkins?' Cooper asked.

At the name, Ant McGann became a little more agitated.

'Bloody Jenkins!' he hissed. 'That's the fourth time I've heard that name this week!'

'You know her?' De'Geer moved closer. 'I understand she manages the estate?'

'Oh, is that what she's saying now?' McGann shook his head. 'Bloody woman.'

'You're going to need to explain yourself a little more,' De'Geer now loomed over McGann, almost two feet higher. 'She's a witness in a murder investigation.'

'Aye, I heard about that,' McGann replied. 'And I told the copper who asked the same thing I'll tell you. Cheryl Jenkins used to work here about six months back, but then left. More fired, really.'

'Fired for what?'

'She'd squat in people's flats,' McGann sniffed. 'Like, she'd find out when people were away for a couple of weeks and move in. She claimed it was a *house sitting* style of arrangement, but it was basically just Cheryl drinking expensive wines and taking food from people who were too rich to notice.'

He pointed up at the ceiling.

'There's a Russian fellow, owns the top floor. Whole thing made as a penthouse. Never visits it, maybe twice a year tops; Fashion Week and the BAFTAs, usually. Rest of the time he just has a cleaner in. Cheryl got a copy of the key and lived there for three months before someone worked it out.'

De'Geer noted this down. From the looks of things,

Cheryl's exclusive apartment wasn't hers. *Did Johnny know? Monroe had said Johnny claimed to be paying the rent; was Cheryl pocketing a few grand a month while lying to her boyfriend?*

'What was her job?' Cooper asked. 'While she was here?'

'She manned the security desk,' McGann scratched at his neck. 'Some owners have Wi-Fi CCTV in their properties, so she would deal with them, show them their cloud footage if an alarm went off, all that stuff. It's why she was so good at getting in.'

'So if she was fired, how is she still getting in?' De'Geer asked.

'Anyone can walk in or out if they have the right key fobs,' McGann pulled one out of his pocket; it was on a lanyard, and he waggled it at De'Geer, forcing the larger man to step back to get a better look. 'We took her work one from her, but she probably has a dozen of them, and we can't police every entrant to the building. And because of cutbacks we don't have a night team anymore, and we have a massive turnover of staff, so even if they saw her, they probably wouldn't confront her, she'd be just another resident, of which we have hundreds in here.'

'Do you have a current address?' Cooper pulled out her notebook. 'It'd help a lot, and get us out of your hair.'

'Bloody hell, don't you guys keep in contact?' McGann pulled out his phone, swiping through his phone list. 'I gave the other guys all this.'

'What other guys?' De'Geer felt his mouth go dry as he asked.

'The other coppers!'

'What other coppers?' De'Geer was more forceful this time. 'Where were they based?'

'They said they were City police,' McGann stopped

scrolling now and whitened slightly, realising something was very wrong here.

'*We're* the City police,' De'Geer hissed. 'Nobody else has been sent from our Unit. What did they look like?'

'I dunno! They all look the same to me!' McGann struggled to remember. 'Early twenties, both Asian, I think Chinese—'

'How long ago?' De'Geer grabbed McGann's arm. 'What did they ask?'

'About half an hour back,' McGann whispered. 'They wanted Cheryl. I gave them her address.'

'Control, this is De'Geer,' De'Geer spoke into his shoulder radio now, glaring at McGann. 'I need a car sent to—' he clicked his fingers at McGann, and the now incredibly nervous security guard turned the phone to show him. On the screen was an address. '—to address two-five-seven, Rotherhithe Street, SE16 right away! Two Asian men, possibly impersonating police officers, maybe looking to kidnap or kill Cheryl Jenkins.'

Getting an affirmative through the radio, De'Geer looked back at McGann.

'Kidnap or kill?' McGann looked like he was about to throw up.

'There's a two million hit on her boyfriend, and she was with him here, two nights ago,' De'Geer nodded. 'Chances are someone thinks she can help, so they want to interrogate her. Or, they want to kill someone he loves and hurt him, and she's the logical choice. What were they driving?'

'I didn't see,' McGann moaned. 'I heard one of them mention Rotherhithe Tunnel is closed, and they'd have to go through the Blackwall Tunnel. That's a good thirty, forty minutes.'

'Dammit, and they have a half hour lead on us,' De'Geer was already marching to the southern door, Cooper and McGann following.

'Maybe not,' McGann replied, pointing to the left as they walked out of the apartment complex and onto the promenade. 'Just over there's the Thames Clipper jetty. There's a ferry that goes back and forth to the *Doubletree by Hilton* hotel across the river.'

'And how does that help us?' Cooper looked confused, as McGann, realising he had a chance to redeem himself, puffed his chest out.

'Because the other side of that is Rotherhithe Street, and Cheryl lives about a hundred yards from the jetty, as she used to use the boat to get to work and back.'

De'Geer ran now; across the promenade, and down the jetty. At the end was a white and blue single level ferry with large, open windows and *DOUBLETREE BY HILTON* written in black on the side.

'*Police!*' he cried as he leapt onto the deck, half-scaring the woman standing at the entrance to the waiting room inside the ferry. 'We need to get across the river right now!'

By now, Cooper and McGann, there for the ride, had also joined him.

'Ant?' the woman asked quizzically.

'No time to answer questions, Danielle, we need to get going right now!' McGann said with a renewed sense of urgency. 'Someone's life hangs in the balance!'

Danielle didn't need to be asked again, and after casting off the rope and radioing the ferry's captain, apparently named Doug, the ferry shuddered and departed the eastern dock at speed.

'Sorry for the change of plans,' Cooper said into the

inside space, where two terrified looking Indian tourists now stared at her, clutching the handrails on the seats in front of them for dear life. Walking over to the side of the ferry's entrance ramp as the ferry cut its way across the Thames, Cooper grinned as the hotel dock loomed up in front of them.

'People always say you look like a Viking,' she said to De'Geer, now standing on the prow. 'I never really saw it, but now, as we're sailing on a boat towards battle, I really get it.'

De'Geer didn't reply immediately; instead he looked over to the side, where a stainless steel boat hook, the metal end mounted into the top of a piece of wood, was resting against some coiled rope on the deck. Grabbing it, he hefted it in his hands, checking the weight as the ferry connected hard with the dock.

'For Odin,' he said with a wink as he jumped off the ferry.

17

CHINATOWN

THE JOURNEY FROM FARRINGDON TO CHINATOWN WAS ONLY two miles, but at this time in the afternoon, it took Declan almost half an hour to drive it, all the while with Monroe muttering how he could walk it quicker.

Declan lasted until the fifth complaint before he stopped and suggested that Monroe could do just that. Unsurprisingly, Monroe chose not to.

The Tsangs operated out of a bar and restaurant on Gerrard Street, situated in the middle of Chinatown's main pedestrianised area. Known as *The Opium Den and Dim Sum Café*, it was a tongue-in-cheek reference to the older days of the town, where for a small fee, addicts could recline on comfortable benches and hold their long opium pipes over oil lamps, heating the drug until it vaporised, allowing the smoker to inhale the vapours and drift off into whatever dream they wanted.

Declan had first heard of these places in *Sherlock Holmes* novels, but it wasn't until he joined the police that he realised the places were more historical fiction than fact, most likely originating in a Charles Dickens story or two. And, more importantly, they didn't really begin in this sanitised, tourist-heavy location, just west of Piccadilly Circus; instead it was Limehouse, five miles to the east and closer to Canary Wharf where the original Chinatown slums had been, a place where the English novelist Sax Rohmer had created the headquarters of the mysterious *Fu Manchu,* which went a long way in vilifying Asians as villains and drug fiends.

It took another well-known villain to change this; Hitler's bombing raids on London destroyed much of the area, and as the rebuilding began, the influx of Asians moved closer to the centre of the city, where they stayed until this day.

Declan had never met the Tsangs, and there was a small part of his mind that wondered whether they'd be similar in style to those old Fu Manchu stories, or more the way of business suits than flowing robes and twirly moustaches. He hoped it was more the latter; he'd always found the Fu Manchu movies to be a little stereotypical and racist.

'Right, let me do the talking,' Monroe said as they parked up behind the Soho Fire Station on Newport Place, leaving the car and walking towards the large Chinese entranceway that welcomed you to the pedestrianised part of Chinatown. The afternoon and pre-early evening crowd was already arriving; tourists, enjoying their day of exploration were mingling with the theatre crowd, arriving for an after-matinee show buffet, walking in tandem with the day-long partygoers, the couples simply out for a stroll, the office workers catching a late lunch and the many others that frequented the area on a more constant basis.

'Who are we talking to?' Declan followed Monroe along the street, breathing in the smells of the dumpling shops and Chinese restaurants that lined the sides.

'If Benny isn't there, we'll speak to his brother, Kenneth,' Monroe suggested.

Declan almost choked.

'What it is with gangsters and linked names?' he asked. 'Johnny and Jackie, Benny and Kenny—'

'He's Kenneth, and Benny is better known as Benjamin,' Monroe scolded as he stopped outside the Opium Den and Dim Sum Café. 'Don't think these are cartoon caricatures. I dealt with both a few years back; if they feel threatened, they can turn into violent buggers who'll make Jackie Lucas look like a choirboy.'

'Great,' Declan muttered as they entered through the main door. It was a narrow, five-storey frontage painted blue, with a shopfront at the bottom, a menu in the window promising an *all you can eat Chinese Hot Pot*. Inside, the room felt claustrophobic, with every available space filled with tables, usually big enough for four people, white cloths over all of them and with plates of random food items scattered randomly across the top, as the diners sitting at them used forks, spoons and chopsticks to pick their way through their meal.

The floor was red-carpeted; a deep shag pile that threatened to engulf Declan's shoes, and the ceiling looked more akin to an office floor than a restaurant, with square, white polystyrene tiles across the width of the room. There was a narrow bar at the back, a barman glaring at them as he cleaned a glass, and a staircase at the side that led both up and down, most likely leading to more floors of tables.

A Chinese man in a black shirt and trousers walked over. Looking back at the barman, Declan realised that the black ensemble was likely the working uniform for the restaurant.

'Good evening, gentlemen, table for two?' he asked, his

accent flawless, his English perfect. Monroe flashed the warrant card.

'Kenneth Tsang.'

'No Tsang here,' the man replied, instantly falling into the typical staccato 'speak no English' style that was stereotypical for many situations Declan had been in over the years, where the person being asked questions *really* didn't want to continue the conversation. 'You go elsewhere.'

'Amazing how you lost the ability to converse with us by the utterance of a simple name,' Monroe smiled, placing the ID away and leaning in, whispering into the waiter's ear.

'Tell Kenneth we're not here officially, and it's about his brother.'

The waiter paused, and Declan knew he was internally debating whether to bluff this out, claim once more there were no Tsangs on the premises, or disappear quickly and tell his boss. This could, however, reveal that a Tsang family member was indeed on site, and he could get into trouble for this—but he'd get into worse if he didn't tell his boss about a potential issue with Benjamin Tsang.

'Downstairs,' the waiter nodded sharply, turning, barking out an order in Chinese to the barman, who picked up a phone and spoke into it. Declan hoped it was to arrange a comfy chair for them rather than a welcome committee.

Downstairs was exactly as Declan had expected; the same as upstairs, just without the full-length windows at the front, although at the back was a small, unobtrusive brown door that the waiters walked in and out of. Passing through this, the surly waiter that had met them, now speaking English well again, led them through the kitchen area and down a back corridor, stopping beside a sturdy-looking wooden door to the side. Giving it four knocks, the waiter looked back at Monroe and Declan and, before they could say anything, walked silently past them, out into the restaurant and presumably back to his place at the door.

After a moment, the door opened, and a large, vicious looking Chinese man in a well fitting suit stared down at them.

'IDs,' he ordered, and Declan brought his warrant card out to show before he realised he was doing it. After a moment, the man nodded and stepped back.

'In.'

Declan and Monroe walked into the back office, the muscle closing the door behind them. It looked more like a library than an office, with shelves along each wall, filled from ceiling to cabinet with books. Many of them had Chinese writing on them, so Declan couldn't guess at the contents, but some were in English; books on the human body, on chess masters, on financial trading, there was no distinct grouping for them.

It was as if someone had raided every part of a library at once.

At the other end was a large mahogany desk, and to the right, beside the bookshelves, was a small square table with an ornate chess set on it, a game in progress.

Behind the desk sat a small, bespectacled man with greasy black hair parted sharply on the right side. He wore a suit, ill-fitting and cheap, and he looked up with irritation as he spoke, glancing at the muscle before looking at Declan and Monroe.

'What you want?' he asked.

Declan guessed this was Kenneth Tsang, as Monroe moved closer.

'Mister Tsang, we're detectives working on your nephew's abduction.'

'I heard it was murder,' the bespectacled man replied dismissively with a wave of his hand.

'It was murder, yes, but we're unsure whether it was Jeffrey that was murdered or not,' Monroe said calmly, looking at the muscle as he walked to the side of the desk. 'We're worried it could be your brother, Mister Tsang.'

The muscle stopped, a slight hint of a smile crossing his face, as if impressed with Monroe's swerve. Declan, meanwhile realised, a little too late, what Monroe had already seen.

'How did you know it was me?' Kenneth asked. 'Why not this man, sitting behind the desk, barking orders?'

Monroe shrugged.

'DI Walsh?'

'Your suit is better made and more expensive than your 'boss' over there,' Declan started. 'Your English is better, you carry yourself with an assuredness that rarely shows in hired muscle. I can't be sure, but I think he looked at you before speaking, and you probably gave him a brief nod to start as well.'

As Declan finished, Monroe walked over to Kenneth, only a little taller but far wider than he was, before continuing.

'And you look almost the same as you did when I arrested you, ten years back, and there's no way you could have shrunk in that time—'

He looked at the man at the desk.

'—to that,' he finished.

Kenneth Tsang looked at the man at the desk and, after a guttural Chinese order, the elder man rose and left without another word, Kenneth taking his place at the desk.

'One of our rice chefs,' he explained. 'Over the years, I've found it far easier to stand and watch people than have them watch me.'

He waved for Monroe and Declan to sit.

'I remember you now,' he said, watching Monroe. 'You had more colour to your hair. Still that terrible Scottish accent, though. You made my life quite awkward.'

'Sorry about that,' Monroe shrugged. 'Goes with the job and all that.'

'My man said you had news on my brother, but here you say he could be dead,' Kenneth leaned back in the chair, an ominous creak sounding as his muscled weight pushed hard on the hydraulics of it. 'And you also say it wasn't my nephew murdered. That sounds ominous, gentlemen.'

'Aye, it is.'

'Benjamin's been missing a couple of days now,' Kenneth continued. 'What do you know about this?'

'Possibly nothing,' Monroe replied carefully. 'Just that there's a chance that the body we found in the boxing club isn't Jeffrey Tsang's.'

Kenneth looked at the table.

'My brother wasn't big like me,' he said. 'He was more like Jeffrey is. Slim, wiry.'

'Did your nephew get on with Benjamin?' Declan asked.

Kenneth looked at him, weighing him up before speaking, resting his hands on the desk.

'No, not really. Blames Benny for his father's death. Only really ever speaks to me, and that was because we have a game on.'

'A game?' Declan looked back at the chessboard. 'That game?'

'Yeah,' Kenneth leaned back in his leather chair once

more, once more creaking, as he let it tip backwards slightly. 'Little bastard was about to lose, too. I had him in five moves.'

'May I look?' Declan rose from his chair at a nod and wandered over to the board. As he did this, Monroe continued.

'When was the last time you saw Benjamin? And Jeffrey, for that matter?'

'Benny? I'd say the lunchtime rush, couple of days back,' Kenneth considered. 'He always came in before the food was out, as it was the only time it was peaceful here. He had some business to attend to, took a meeting in here, and then he left to see a friend.'

'Name of the friend?'

'No idea, but her escort service will be on his credit card bill,' Kenneth smiled. 'Benny always paid for the top.'

He looked away, staring into the corner of the room as he tried to recall an answer to the second half of the question.

'As for Jeffery? He turned up at the same time. There was a bit of a row, actually. Jeffrey's started a new club in Shepherd's Bush somewhere and he's worried we're gonna push in on him, claim a little of it ourselves. That's the reason for the game, actually. A gentleman's bet. He wins? I back off. I win? We negotiate for the club in good faith. Benny got a little cocky though, started telling Jeffrey what he was gonna do to the place when he took over. Jeffrey's a bit of a hothead.'

'They fought?'

'Not fists, but it was close,' Kenneth nodded. 'Benny left, Jeffrey stuck around. We talked some business, and then he left around two.'

'What sort of business?' Declan asked, looking up from the board.

'Business that I'm not gonna give out to you two,' Kenneth

smiled, and it was more a baring of teeth than calming gesture. A shark, considering how difficult it would be to turn his current prey into dinner.

'Okay then, one hypothetical question,' Monroe stated. 'And then we'll leave.'

Kenneth nodded acceptance, and Monroe continued.

'Jackie Lucas takes Jeffrey. The original one, not Johnny's other personality—'

'Jackie Lucas is alive?' Kenneth's eyebrow raised.

'I'd believe your surprised expression a lot more, if I hadn't heard rumours that the Wo Shing Wo Triad paid for his travel home,' Monroe smiled.

'Bullshit,' Kenneth snapped. 'I knew about Jackie because two nights ago he put contracts out on me and my brother, and says he's going to gut Chinatown. Now, you tell me. Does that sound like someone working with the Triad?'

'Depends on whether the Triad wants you both gone,' Monroe surmised. 'But that's not part of my question. Jackie Lucas takes Jeffrey, but let's say it's Benjamin that's found dead. Why?'

Kenneth frowned, not answering.

'Do you mean why would Jackie Lucas kill him?' he eventually asked. 'That's simple. They've had bad blood for years.'

'Jackie? Or Johnny playing Jackie?' Monroe interjected, accepting Kenneth's nod of acceptance before continuing, his voice cold and emotionless. 'No, the question I'm hypothetically asking is why would Jeffrey team up with Jackie Lucas, fake his death and then kill his uncle.'

There was a brief pause in the conversation as Kenneth Tsang mulled the question over in his head.

'I think the time for such fanciful questions is over now, and you should leave,' he answered, his immense form towering over Monroe as he rose from his seat. 'Come back with warrants. I'll bring my solicitors. And don't forget to grab some complimentary prawn crackers as you leave. On me.'

Monroe considered this, nodded, and then rose. His phone beeped; as he looked at the message, Declan felt his own phone silently vibrate. Pulling it out, Declan saw the same message Monroe had just read, sent from Billy.

De'Geer and Cooper chasing Asian assassins, hunting Cheryl Jenkins. Police called to Rotherhithe.

'Another question,' Monroe continued, looking up.

'You already asked your one question.'

'Yes, and you didn't bloody answer it, so I'm having a do-over,' Monroe snapped. 'What are your current plans for Johnny Lucas?'

'I wasn't intending to go drinking with him, if that's what you mean.'

'You know about the hit on him?'

'Everyone knows about the hit, detective,' Kenneth shrugged. 'Two million for proof of death. And no, I didn't put the bounty on him. I'd want to kill him personally.'

'So you haven't sent two of your men out to kidnap or kill his girlfriend?' Monroe asked. 'Because currently we've got officers facing off against them, and if you did? I'd seriously consider calling them off before they get hurt.'

'Before *they* get hurt?' Kenneth was amused by the statement, but Monroe was stone faced.

'Aye,' he replied coldly. 'You haven't seen the size of the officer facing them. Makes you look like a wee baby in comparison.'

'I'm sorry to spoil your day, but I sent nobody,' Kenneth replied. 'But the organisation has many captains in it, and any of them could have done this. I will check, and if this was us, I'll tell them to stand down, if you promise me one thing.'

'What is it?'

Kenneth paced behind the desk.

'When you confirm it's Benny, you let me know,' he asked.

'You're next of kin,' Monroe nodded. 'We'd tell you, anyway. You'd need to officially identify the body.'

'And that could take days,' Kenneth snapped. 'I want to know *immediately*.'

'I'll see what I can do, and thanks for your time,' Monroe replied, glancing at Declan. 'Time to leave this man to his work, laddie. You done?'

Declan turned from the chessboard on the table.

'Jeffrey Tsang beat you,' he said matter-of-factly. 'His last move brought you in for a kill shot.'

Kenneth frowned at this.

'No he didn't, I had him lined up.'

He walked over, examining the board.

'You play?'

'A little,' Declan replied, 'But not to this level. There was a chess move written on the door, the one Jackie took Jeffrey through two nights ago. Queen to C7.'

He pointed at the chessboard.

'It was Jeffrey's next move, right?' he asked. 'The Queen is here, and it can move to C7 there, taking the Rook.'

Kenneth nodded.

'It's plausible,' he said, leaning closer to the board. 'But it's a suicidal move—'

'It's a winning move,' Declan interrupted as he moved the

queen, taking Kenneth's Rook. 'It's a known finish. In five moves, he's beaten you.'

He looked back at Kenneth Tsang, tossing him the taken Rook. Tsang caught it in midair, his huge hand engulfing the tiny piece.

'But you already know that, don't you?' Declan finished, joining Monroe by the door. 'Just as I'm sure you'd already been told about the move, scrawled on the door in permanent marker, Mister Tsang.'

Kenneth glared at the two of them.

'Get out,' he hissed.

Leaving the back office and making their way through the restaurant, Monroe and Declan didn't speak until they were out of the building, complimentary prawn crackers in hand, and halfway down the street.

'So, what did you get from that, laddie?' Monroe asked.

'Kenny Tsang knows his brother's dead, and that his nephew's alive,' Declan replied.

'Oh, aye? And how did you get that?'

Declan reached the driver's door of his car, thinking back to the conversation he'd just had.

'The tenses he used when describing his family,' he answered. 'When he spoke about Jeffrey, it was present tense. He said Jeffrey's started a new club, and *he's* worried, not *he was* worried. But when he mentioned Benny and the escorts, he said Benny always *paid* for the top. Past tense, like he wasn't going to do it anymore.'

Monroe nodded as they climbed into the car.

'Aye, I caught that, too,' he said. 'But what does that give us?'

'Jeffrey faked his death and wrote his next chess move on

a door,' Declan replied. 'A game that decided whether Jeffrey owned his club outright.'

He started the car.

'I'm wondering if this was him stating he didn't want to play the game anymore,' he added.

'No, I think this is worse,' Monroe mused as Declan pulled the car quickly out onto Shaftsbury Ave, heading towards Piccadilly Circus, the Thames, South London and Rotherhithe, the blue lights flashing and the siren sounding. 'As you worked out, Jeffrey was going to win in a couple of moves. This was a statement of intent. Of what, though, we still have no bloody idea.'

'Maybe we'll know better when we get to Rotherhithe?' Declan asked, weaving through the afternoon traffic.

'Laddie, if De'Geer's involved, it'll be over before we even get there,' Monroe smiled.

18

WRONG ADDRESS

When the two Asian hitmen had left Canary Wharf, en route to their target's recently gathered address, the last thing they could have expected on arrival was to face a furious-looking Viking, dressed in a police uniform and brandishing a vicious looking spear-like weapon as he sprinted down the street towards them.

The car they were in was old, and had been stolen easily earlier that day, but this meant that it was unfamiliar to them, and as the driver quickly fumbled with the gears, trying to remember how to put the vehicle into reverse, the other hitman started screaming, pulling out a wicked-looking blade from within his fluorescent vest.

They'd decided not to bring guns; Canary Wharf was a place that had security checkpoints, and armed police throughout, because of the financial nature of the companies that held offices there. It was rife for terrorist attack, and therefore every vehicle that passed through had the chance of being stopped. And, although they were wearing police uniforms, if they had been held at a checkpoint, and their IDs checked, they may at least have bluffed their way out.

If they had found a gun, that wouldn't have happened.

Besides, this was an old woman, they'd been told. She would be easy to constrain, to subdue before they removed her. As 'police', they could even get her out of the building and into the car before anyone realised what was going on. A gun was simply one complication too many right now.

But right now, a gun would have been very helpful.

The officer had run out of the entrance to the hotel they were approaching; he was obviously looking for them too, as the moment he locked eyes on the driver, he immediately ran at them.

'Get out of the car!' he maniacally screamed at them, brandishing his weapon like a warrior from the dark ages. *'Get out now!'*

By now they slammed the car into reverse and, as the maniacal police officer chased them, the two hitmen started backwards, away from the hotel. The passenger noted two other people emerging from the same entrance; a smaller female officer and the same security guard from the Cirque Apartments they had spoken to earlier.

Dammit, there must have been a ferry.

It hadn't mattered though, as even with the ferry, they would still have needed a vehicle to place the target in once captured; this was simply terrible timing on their part.

And adding to the bad luck, a bus had appeared behind them, blocking the way, now reversing as well, as the car approaching was forced to stop momentarily—

The steel hook at the end of the spear-like weapon slammed into one of the car's front headlights.

'You're under arrest!' The officer shouted as he smashed the other side now.

'Get out of here!' The passenger hitman shouted at the driver hitman, and, with the giant now to the side of the car, the driver slammed the stolen vehicle's gearstick into first and the car leaped forward, almost running the Viking over and speeding off southwards, away from the police, the hotel, and the target.

Now free, the driver looked at the passenger and laughed.

'Did you see that?' he wheezed. 'Bjorn Ironside! From *Vikings!* Bjorn Ironside!'

Laughing hard, the two of them didn't even notice the police car speeding down Salter Road, until it went into the side of them.

BACK AT THE ENTRANCE TO THE DOUBLETREE BY HILTON, De'Geer bent over, holding his sides, the boat hook dropped to the floor. He wasn't out of shape, and although the sprint from the dock had involved a lot of ramps and stairs, the stitch in his side and the sudden exhaustion were mainly from the adrenaline leaving his system.

'What if they'd had a gun?' PC Cooper asked, running up to him. 'You're an idiot, Morten! They could have killed you!'

'They got away,' McGann muttered sadly. 'Shame.'

'All I wanted was for them not to reach Cheryl Jenkins,' De'Geer, his breath returned, straightened now, looking back at McGann. 'What number was it again?'

'Two-five-seven,' McGann replied, pointing up the road. 'I think it's beside that pub.'

The pub in question was *The Blacksmiths Arms*, a three-storey mock Tudor building, with painted black timbers and white brickwork, with three separate entrances on both sides and the middle, with small flower beds in window trays built in between each. It was an old style building between two modern brick rectangles, a building named Canada Wharf on one side, and a narrow, three-storey residence on the other side, with no signage bar a single wooden door on the right.

'This one, perhaps?' De'Geer went to knock on the door, but was stopped as a middle-aged, portly, and balding man emerged from the pub.

'Everything alright?' he asked nervously; the sight of a large policeman smashing car headlights wasn't something you saw every day.

'Yes, sorry,' De'Geer replied, as, in the distance, he could hear police sirens. 'Do you know if this house is number two-five-seven?'

'No, it's not,' the man pointed at the pub he'd just walked out of. 'This is two-five-seven. Blacksmiths Arms. Has been for a hundred and fifty years.'

'And I don't suppose you have a Cheryl Jenkins living there?' De'Geer didn't wait for an answer, already turning to McGann. 'Well, this was a waste of time.'

'I don't understand!' McGann complained. 'That's the address we have on file!'

'And you didn't follow up on it, check if she'd given the real one or not?' Cooper shook her head. 'Marvellous.'

'It's not my role to check up,' McGann protested, realising that once more he was in the position of trying to explain a screw up. 'I didn't hire her, after all! She just worked in the building!'

De'Geer was about to reply, as the blue lights of a squad

car lit up the southern end of the street, and a police officer leaned out of the window.

'You De'Geer?' he shouted out.

'I am,' De'Geer, forgetting McGann, now started towards the officer.

'PC Mantel, Surrey Quays,' the officer called back. 'Just letting you know we caught your guys.'

De'Geer raised a hand in thanks and looked back at Cooper.

'Okay, so we have the scary people we didn't know about in custody,' he drawled, looking around the street. 'But where the hell's the woman we originally came for?'

Acorn Walk was a gated community of apartments that backed onto Rotherhithe Street, with an entrance that was situated opposite Nelson Dock, and the nearby Doubletree by Hilton hotel. The complex was nestled in between Rotherhithe and Salter Street, and for the main was a secure, quiet location.

Currently, Cheryl Jenkins was grateful for that, as she watched out of her second-floor window, down at the pub that could be seen through it, and the police standing outside. She recognised that wanker McGann, too; as they stared in confusion at the pub, she knew he'd set her up, taken them right to the address she'd given, back when she'd started working there.

'Bollocks,' she muttered to herself. *She'd gotten too complacent, and she'd let them tell her what to do, where to go.*

She wouldn't be going back to Cirque Apartments again. She had only gone back to remove anything that could incriminate her the previous day, and it was sheer bloody luck that the female copper had caught her there. She'd called her bluff, played the game, just like she did with Johnny, but it had cut too close. Cheryl knew the owner was returning the following day, and he'd want his place back.

He'd probably want his network privileges back, too.

Cheryl had chuckled a little at that. The police had blindly accepted what she sent them, the 'security footage' of the night in question, footage that showed Johnny—poor, idiotic Johnny—leaving the apartments at a time he believed himself to be asleep.

Of course he was asleep. She'd given him enough GHB to knock out a bear.

Cheryl regretted what she'd done, mainly because it meant she'd lose the money; Johnny had been gallantly paying her 'rent' while she was with him, and bar a couple of times when she claimed the builders were fixing small issues, she could usually hack the master key to gain entrance to Paul Burston's apartment in time to fix it up; lose anything to do with Paul, and gain a lot more 'Cheryl' in style.

Security had never hassled her in all the time she'd been doing this; the ones that knew her assumed she was back working for them, the other ones assumed she was a resident. And most of the time, nobody was there; no night crew meant no hassle. And, nobody to ask why she was re-editing video footage at one in the morning, making a whole new narrative.

Cheryl sighed; the money *had* been good. When they'd aimed her at Johnny, when they'd explained what she needed to do, she'd complained, said she wouldn't do it—but they'd been watching her for months, had a dossier on her activities. They knew where she'd been, what she'd taken, and which residents would press charges once they knew that *someone had been sleeping in their bed.* And unlike Goldilocks, they gave Cheryl no option to refuse.

The problem was, she'd actually liked Johnny once she got to know him. He was clever, funny and looked good for his age. And of course, it didn't hurt that he was bloody good between the sheets. She would have stayed seeing him just for that, not because he'd offered to cover her rent in the apartments when she'd raised the possibility of moving out.

And then she stabbed him in the back.

Cheryl regretted what she did. But at the same time, she worried others were after her for this. She'd heard the first crash of glass outside when washing up some plates in the kitchen. Looking out of the window, she'd seen the tall, blond police officer screaming at the two men in the car to get out. With hindsight, she now knew the police had likely been looking for her, as McGann, that sneaky, creepy little shit being with them was pretty much proof positive—but who were the two men in the car, and what relationship did they have with what she'd done to Johnny? Were they looking for her, too? And if so, were they there to punish her, or was it something worse?

Picking up her phone and walking away from the window, Cheryl dialled a number and waited, phone to her ear.

'What?' the voice at the other end was irritated.

'The police are looking for me,' Cheryl said. 'They came to the address I gave them.'

'So?' the voice, a woman's one, replied. 'You knew they'd come looking, you're his alibi, remember?'

'They were arguing with two guys in a car,' Cheryl had to

force her voice from quavering. 'There was an incident with what looked like a hook, or a spear.'

'Who were the guys in the car?'

'I don't know, I could only see one,' Cheryl thought back. 'Looked like they were wearing police uniforms, but I don't know if they were real. I saw the driver, he was Chinese I think, maybe thirties?'

'Probably sent by the Triad,' the voice mused. 'There's a hit out on Johnny. They either wanted you to tell them where he is, or to be used as bait.'

'Everyone knows where he is!' Cheryl exclaimed angrily. 'And it's because of me he's there! If they come for me, I'm telling them everything, Anita! I swear it!'

'And what exactly is everything?' Anita Taborsky's voice was crisp and calculating as she replied.

'That you told me which apartment to use, and that Simpson knew and was okay with it,' Cheryl replied. 'That Jeffrey Tsang gave me the GHB to use on Johnny, and that Jackie Lucas is hiding in your bedroom!'

There was an uncomfortably long moment of silence on the line, and Cheryl had to pull the phone away from her ear and check the display on the screen, just to make sure she hadn't been disconnected.

'So, what do you want?' Anita asked dispassionately.

'This wasn't what I signed up for,' Cheryl sobbed again, shaking as the tremors started once more. 'I want out, Anita. I want money to start a new life. A new name. I want this behind me.'

'Fine,' Anita replied, bored by the conversation. 'It'll take a while to get everything sorted, if you really want to disappear. Are you in the apartment?'

'Yes,' Cheryl watched out the window again; a second squad car had arrived now, talking to the blond officer.

'Can the police find your address?'

'No, I'm not on the council tax. It's another of Nicky's houses.'

'Stay there then,' Anita ordered. 'Don't leave. Don't even order food to be delivered. Don't let anyone know you're in there. By tomorrow, we'll bring you money and a new identity. And, once this is all over, you can return to your old life. Deal?'

'Deal.'

'One other thing,' Anita said before hanging up. 'Once we're done and you're on your way? Lose this number. If I ever hear from you, if you ever ask me for something again, I'll hunt you down and slit your throat. You understand?'

'I understand,' Cheryl whispered as Anita Taborsky disconnected the call.

And now, alone in the apartment, and with the sounds of sirens outside her window, Cheryl Jenkins clutched at her sides, rocking back and forth as she silently sobbed.

19

SCHOOL REUNION

DS McAlroy was feeding ducks in Victoria Park when Ellie Reckless arrived.

'You shouldn't do that,' Ellie said as she sat on the bench beside the officer, currently breaking slices of bread up and tossing them out. 'The ducks will become reliant on you, follow you home and then you'll have this mercenary duck army out there that you won't know what to do with.'

'I think you'll find your life goals differ wildly from mine,' McAlroy smiled fairly as she emptied the remnants of the bag the bread came in onto the ground before looking over at her. 'What's so important we had to meet?'

'Monroe,' Ellie replied, as if this one word would explain everything.

'The Scottish guy?' McAlroy was confused by the name. 'What's he got to do with anything?'

'He knows me,' Ellie leant back on the bench, shutting her eyes, feeling the sunlight on her face. 'And he knows I was the jogger. Which means at some point he'll work out that you must have known me when you interviewed me two nights ago.'

'Did he work it out, or did you tell him?'

'Does it matter?'

'Christ, Ellie, of course it matters!' McAlroy hissed, lowering her voice as an elderly couple on the next bench glanced over at the raised words. 'You might be in the wind, but I still have a career! One they'll bloody end when they realise we were in the same class as each other!'

'We were never in the same *class*, Jules,' Ellie grinned. 'You were always the diligent one, while I was the screwup.'

'And yet you were the one making Inspector, while I just scraped Sergeant,' McAlroy looked away, fury on her face. 'This might be a game to you, but this is my life.'

'And that's why I'm here,' Ellie placed an arm around McAlroy's shoulder, an arm that was quickly shrugged off. 'You've heard about the hit on Johnny Lucas?'

'Two million. Yeah. So what?'

'So what? So every gun for hire in the City is going to try to break into Mile End, just to end him,' Ellie said. 'Do you want that?'

'Sure, that's totally what I want,' McAlroy mocked. 'Look, what do you need, Ellie? I'm on the night shift soon, and Esposito asked for me in by six.'

'How much do you trust Esposito?' Ellie suddenly asked, and the question threw McAlroy.

'I trust him okay,' she replied cautiously. 'I mean, he's my boss, so of course I do. Why?'

'I knew him,' Ellie took the bread bag, holding it upside down, shaking it so that any last crumbs fell out. 'Straight die, by the book fellow. He still like that?'

'I suppose,' McAlroy narrowed her eyes as she stared at Ellie. 'Again, why?'

'Because someone wants Johnny Lucas dead,' Ellie rolled up the bag and tossed it into the open bin beside the bench. 'And part of me thinks it's a stage, you know? Johnny dies, and only then does something else happen. We won't know what it is until this happens. And, maybe, once it happens, everything changes.'

'But we won't know, because Johnny won't be dying soon.'

'You sure?' Ellie looked at her watch. 'His thirty-six hours ended at noon. By now his solicitors will push for a release by morning.'

'We can keep him for up to ninety-six hours,' McAlroy smiled. 'You're forgetting the basics, ex-DI Reckless.'

'Only if you suspect him of a serious crime.'

'Murder is a serious crime, Ellie. I don't know if you realise that—'

'The relevant word isn't serious, Jules. The relevant word is *suspect*,' Ellie rose from the bench now, stretching her back as she looked around. 'You can't suspect him of a crime when the evidence is corrupted. Monroe's people have already worked out the CCTV footage was tampered with by now, and will have realised that Cheryl Jenkins is on the run. How long do you think it'll take for a competent brief to have his charges thrown out? As I said, he'll be out by morning. And the moment he walks out?'

She placed her index finger against McAlroy's temple.

'Blam,' she said as McAlroy irritatedly batted it away.

'So what do we do?' she asked. 'Keep him in some other way? Use the terrorism act and keep him for two weeks?'

'I was thinking of a more permanent solution,' Ellie

shrugged. 'After all, there's two million waiting to be picked up, and a ton of people out there waiting to do so...'

McAlroy rose now, facing her onetime friend.

'Are you suggesting what I think you're suggesting?' she whispered.

'Probably,' Ellie replied enigmatically. 'And now we're on the same page, let me ask you again. How much do you trust DCI Esposito?'

DECLAN AND MONROE HAD ARRIVED AT ROTHERHITHE AROUND half an hour after the two Chinese men, now identified as Wen Xinyu and Li Xiaoyu, both known Triad operatives, were taken by Special Branch; the detectives had passed De'Geer their details and told him to get Bullman to call them—this was no longer just a 'little murder', as far as they were concerned. If a full scale war was about to happen, then the Last Chance Saloon were woefully outmatched.

De'Geer had agreed with them. However, he also pointed out that if the gangs of all four compass points had a war, then all the police together might still find themselves outmatched.

Arriving at the end of this, Monroe had made a lot of obscene comments on the subject, mainly around Special Branch, and what they had that was 'little'. But the message was passed on, and Declan had wondered whether this was Special Branch's way of raising a complaint about the small City police unit gaining another high-profile case.

To be honest, if they were that bothered, they could take it on themselves.

With De'Geer and Cooper already back across the

Thames, gathering up their squad car and returning to base, and with Cheryl Jenkins nowhere to be seen, Declan and Monroe had reluctantly followed suit, arriving back at the Temple Inn offices around seven in the evening. They'd gone over what they'd learnt from Kenneth Tsang, and discussed what to do about the missing gangster girlfriend, but with nothing appearing immediately, Declan knew the best thing to do was step back and consider the bigger picture, rather than chase the small things.

Interestingly, Jess, in the meantime, had actually found something concrete; a company formation around the turn of the millennium, *Shand Properties* was only a name and a London address so far, but thanks to Billy's help, she'd found that the company had been set up anonymously through a London based legal firm, one that, when you went on the webpage, showed a familiar-looking solicitor. With the name *Fabian Kleid* underneath his face, Declan recognised the same hard-faced, stick thin, almost skeletal man with obviously dyed-black hair cut into a wedge that he'd seen beside Johnny Lucas the previous day.

Billy had checked into this and had confirmed that the solicitors that Fabian worked for had represented the Lucas family all the way back into the nineties. Which meant that when they created this company, it'd been while they worked for the Lucas brothers. And, more importantly, there was a Chinese investment firm connected, one that, after a few back searches in more delicate areas, showed that the Tsangs had a hand in this as well.

Perhaps this was the name of the mutually assured destruction that had kept the peace for almost two decades, Declan thought to himself. But, until they could bring some names out, there was nothing to do. Johnny would likely be out by morning, and Declan knew he wouldn't speak to anyone about this.

By this point, having drawn a blank with the Seven Sisters, Anjli had also returned to the Unit, furious that after an hour of waiting around, she'd been given the brush off and told to make an appointment. Declan had begun to make a comment about smashing in doors and stealing guns being the best way to get through, but decided against it after seeing her furious expression. And, after she'd learnt of Cheryl's deception the previous day, and after providing a few new expletives of her own, Declan used this tirade from Anjli as an excuse to call it a day, citing that everyone was getting angry on the case, before taking Jess home for the evening, as nothing new was likely to arrive before morning.

Surprisingly, Anjli asked if she could cadge a lift back with them; Declan had assumed she'd be looking to stay with her mother again, but Anjli had explained she'd started to get a little cabin fever staying there. And besides, this way she could spend the evening talking about the case with Declan and Jess, while she couldn't at her mum's.

Declan had hoped there were other reasons Anjli wanted to join them, but he was happy to take the win, no matter how small. And, knowing that they were likely discussing the case until the late hours of the evening, he offered an invitation to De'Geer, mainly because he only lived a few miles down the road from them.

Unsurprisingly though, De'Geer took a rain check on the offer, explaining that he wanted to help Doctor Marcos and DC Davey downstairs, as they were both still working through a multitude of autopsies, and trying to confidently identify the first body found—the common belief was that this was indeed Benny Tsang, but Benny had done remarkably well in hiding his DNA and records over the years, making it nigh on impossible to confirm the body's identity, if it was him. It was well known that although a uniformed officer, De'Geer had an interest in moving to forensics, and Declan nodded politely, glad that De'Geer wasn't actually turning up, if only because the poor man wouldn't spend the entire evening trying to avoid Jess' teenage advances.

Although apparently Jess had a girlfriend now. Maybe.

Arriving back at Hurley around ten past eight in the evening, Declan was almost tempted to try for the *Olde Bell* and see if there were any tables going, maybe try to book a last-minute dinner, but was outvoted by Anjli and Jess, who both wanted Thai from a place in Henley that delivered. And it was pointed out that by the time they actually rocked up to the pub, the food would probably have stopped.

Declan had never been a fan of Thai food, but he was however a fan of keeping the people he cared for happy, so he dutifully ordered a few dishes more than they probably needed, having no idea of their size, making sure he checked Jess' constantly changing dietary requirements. This done, he made some teas in the kitchen, as it was a little too late for coffee, and sat down in the living room with Jess and Anjli, leaning back in the sofa and sipping the hot drink with a sigh, borne not from satisfaction, but irritation at the whole damned scenario.

'So, what are your thoughts?' Anjli asked eventually, swirling her cup in an attempt to cool the drink down.

'Honestly? I'm not sure,' Declan stared up at the ceiling. 'From what we've found out, Jackie exists, and is physically separate to Johnny. But does Johnny know for sure? We know he hired Ellie Reckless to look into it. We have Jackie apparently leaving a South American prison recently, but was it official or just a rumour?'

'And if they paid his ticket home, why would the Triad send him after the Tsangs?' Jess asked. 'And what's with the chess move?'

'That's a message, it has to be,' Declan nodded. 'But who to? He was playing with his uncle, Kenny, and Kenny seemed to know that his brother was dead and Jeffrey was still out there. His present and past tenses were all over the place.'

'Could it have been a dialect issue?' Anjli suggested. 'English as a second language and all that?'

'Maybe, but I'm not sure. Kenny seemed remarkably relaxed for a man that was learning about a death in the family.'

'Could be because he's lived with death for so long.'

'Well, that's bloody grim.'

There was a long moment after this, with everyone sipping their drinks.

'So, a boathook,' Jess smiled. 'Am I the only one that wishes someone filmed that?'

'We should make boathooks the new standard weapon for police,' Anjli grinned.

'I'll keep the extendable baton, thanks,' Declan laughed.

'When do I get one?' Jess asked, seriously. 'I mean, I'm part of the team right now, shouldn't I have one?'

'You'd just get into trouble,' Declan shook his head. 'You need to know how to use one. Look at last time you were here, when Ilse captured you.'

'And think how much quicker I could have beaten her if I'd had a baton,' Jess said, innocently rising her eyebrows. Declan laughed, rummaging in his jacket, lying beside the sofa, and pulled out his own baton, tossing it to her.

'Here,' he said as Jess quickly snaffled it away before he thought better and asked for it back. 'I have a spare. Just don't break anything with it.'

'Like an arm?'

'Like one of Billy's screens when you pretend you're a Power Ranger, and you—' Declan started, but paused as the doorbell went. '—Bloody hell, that's fast service.'

Walking to the door, he grabbed his wallet from the sideboard, ready to pay for the food, but as he opened it, he found himself not facing a delivery driver; instead, he was facing Janelle 'Mama' Delcourt, sunglasses over her eyes, a teenage girl standing beside her. On the curb at the end of the garden was a black Mercedes, a scowling black man in the driver's seat, glaring at Declan as he looked over.

'Oh, hello,' was all Declan could think of.

'Sorry to bother you,' Janelle Delcourt stated, a little stiffly. 'I hoped we could speak. And, as the last time you came to see me, you turned up at my door, I thought I'd return the favour.'

20

HAPPY FAMILIES

DECLAN STARED AT THE BLIND JANELLE DELCOURT ON HIS doorstep, her young daughter beside her.

'Of course,' he said, stepping back and waving before realising Janelle probably couldn't see the invitation. However, the girl, most likely Molly Delcourt, the younger sister of Moses, took her mother by the arm and escorted her into the living room.

Anjli and Jess were already moving from the sofa as they entered.

'Can I get you a drink?' Declan asked.

'A water, please,' Janelle smiled as they led her to a chair. 'We can't stay long. They'll wonder where I am soon.'

'Where are you supposed to be?' Anjli asked. Janelle looked up, surprised.

'That's DS Anjli Kapoor, my housemate,' Declan explained. 'Also in the room is my teenage daughter, Jess.'

'Maybe your daughter could keep mine entertained while we speak?' Janelle asked, but Declan couldn't help shaking the feeling this was an order. Nevertheless, Jess grinned, nodding to Molly to follow her upstairs.

'It's Molly, right?' she asked. 'Come on, let's go have the important chat while the old people gossip.'

Molly didn't look happy to leave her mother, but dutifully followed Jess upstairs as Declan sat on the sofa, watching Janelle.

'DS Kapoor, I'm sorry I couldn't speak to you when you came to my house today,' Janelle started as Anjli entered the kitchen. 'I hope you understand why I couldn't be seen with you.'

'Sure,' Anjli replied stiffly from the doorway. Noticing this, Declan started the ball rolling.

'Last time I saw you, Janelle, you were trying to kill everyone in the room with a grenade,' he said, a little more coldly than he intended.

'No, DI Walsh, the last time you saw me, I was trying to kill myself,' Janelle replied haughtily. 'Amusingly—well, not that amusingly, I suppose, that was also the last time *I* saw anything.'

There was a long moment of awkwardness here; Declan wanted to comment, to say how she was damned by her own actions, but she looked so helpless, staring off into nothing, her dark glasses hiding the true scars of her injury.

'Now your daughter is gone, do you want to tell me why you're here?' Declan asked. 'And why we have this cloak and dagger game going on right now?'

'I'm head of the Seven Sisters,' Janelle replied. 'They know the only reason I didn't go to prison last year was because the court felt sorry for my blindness.'

'And the fact you worked out a deal,' Anjli muttered, walking back into the room, a glass of water in her hand. She placed it on the coffee table. 'There's water just in front of you. Do you need me to—'

She stopped as, with a soft test of the area with her fingers, Janelle took the glass.

'True,' Janelle smiled, looking vaguely in Anjli's direction. 'But what they don't know is that my deal is ongoing, and the information I provided back then…'

'Is also ongoing,' Declan realised. 'You're an informant. That's why you didn't want your daughter hearing.'

Janelle shifted back into the chair, contemplating her answer.

'I don't want this life for my daughter,' she said. 'I want out. My son wanted to kill me—kill his own momma for power. Will I get that from Molly down the line? And what of the other Sisters? They're not gonna let me eke out my time on the throne. Molly's not even fourteen. Over four years until she can make a play for the crown, and that's even if she wants it.'

'She doesn't want it?' Anjli asked.

Janelle shrugged.

'She's a teenager. It changes constantly. Last week, she wanted to be a vet. This week I think it's a professional rock climber. Honestly, I'd be happy with either of those.'

'So what's stopping you from getting out?' Declan asked. 'You're here now. Just keep driving. Don't look back.'

'What, and lose everything?' Janelle sucked in through her teeth. 'My mama and I? We've made the Sisters, between us. Lived like Queens.'

She sighed.

'Queens who can't leave the house,' she continued. 'The man in the car? That's my cousin, Barry. Been with me for years. Every time I go out, Anita Taborsky follows. Stick-thin witch, it's like I'm being haunted by a pencil. Only times I can get out alone is when I have to take Molly somewhere.'

'So, where are you tonight?'

'Dress fitting for a friend's fourteenth birthday party,' Janelle smiled. 'Few days ago I met with someone, trying to find a way out of this, and instead I told the Sisters I was looking at uniforms for the next school year.'

Declan nodded.

'A lot of effort to sneak out after curfew,' he said. 'This must be important for you.'

'It is,' Janelle's voice was calm, but Declan could sense this was an act. Either Janelle wanted to stay emotionless, or she was fighting to aim Declan at a particular narrative. He couldn't work out which one, though. 'Someone wants to kill me, remove me from the hierarchy of the Seven Sisters for good. And if I go, they'll take out Molly too. It's the smart choice, removes retaliation down the line.'

She leaned forward, her vacant gaze now fixing on Declan, or at least giving the impression that she was.

'I don't care if I die, I'm too far involved in a lot of things to get out cleanly anyway, DI Walsh. But you took my son away from me; please don't let them take my daughter.'

'So what music do you like?' Jess was connecting her iPhone to the speaker by the bed, Molly sitting on it, staring around the room with an expression that bordered on disgust, like she'd found the whole room on the sole of her shoe, and needed to throw it away.

'Got any Ye?' she asked, half distracted. Jess tapped on the screen, and a moment later, the sounds of Kanye West filtered through the speakers.

'Do you want some chocolate?' she asked, walking over to her rucksack. 'I might have some Dairy Milk.'

'Nah, I don't like UK chocolate,' Molly shook her head. 'I'm a Hershey's girl.'

'I've never had that,' Jess looked back from the rucksack, where she'd pulled out half a bar of Cadbury's Fruit and Nut. 'No, wait, are they the people who do Reese's Pieces? They're okay.'

'Okay?' Molly was stunned by the comment. 'They're more than okay! They're amazing! The *Milk Chocolate With Almonds* bars are to die for. I'm addicted to them. Mum knows an American store in Tottenham and they bring boxes of it in just for me.'

'Well, I don't have any, sorry,' Jess snapped off a piece and offered it. 'You'll just have to do with good, old-fashioned UK chocolate.'

Molly reluctantly took a piece and ate it, staring around the bedroom as she did so.

'Your room's... nice,' she said. 'Mine's bigger, and I got an en suite, but I'm not allowed to put posters on the walls.'

'That sucks,' Jess slumped onto a beanbag chair to the side, the remains of the chocolate bar in her hand. 'This isn't my actual bedroom, though.'

'Divorce?'

'Yeah.'

'Two bedrooms, though? Nice,' Molly smiled, but Jess felt it was mocking, slightly.

'True, but I don't live in a mansion like you.'

'You don't know me,' Molly snapped back, the anger within the thirteen-year-old evident. 'You live in your country house with your copper dad and you know nothing of my life.'

'I don't live in the country,' Jess replied calmly. 'I visit my *divorced* dad on holidays. I actually live in a tiny house in Tottenham North, near the retail park.'

She leant closer.

'Near your *mansion*,' she smiled.

Molly moved back against the wall, nodding acceptance of this.

'Still spend time in a sleepy village,' she replied with disdain.

'A few months back, this sleepy village tried to kill me,' Jess shrugged. 'I fought for my life in a garage, less than half a mile from here, with the daughter of a serial killer as she tried to strangle me with a length of chain.'

'Shut up,' Molly leant back in, suddenly interested. 'What happened?'

'I slammed the base of a cordless drill into the side of her head,' Jess replied like it was nothing.

'We should trade numbers,' Molly grinned. 'You could teach me how to fight.'

'You aren't taught already?'

'Mum don't want me learning,' this visibly annoyed Molly. 'So I got my brother's mate to teach me. Kayas ain't that good, though.'

'You mean Kayas Ashad?'

Molly nodded.

'He used to be around all the time,' she said sadly. 'Until the Sisters fired him.'

'Why did they fire him?'

'Because he helped Moses,' Molly replied, like it was the most natural thing in the world. 'You wanna be a copper?' she asked suddenly. 'Like your dad? I've heard of him. He put my brother away.'

'Yeah, I'd like that,' Jess replied. 'Not to put people away, but to help people. And your brother, from what I heard, was trying to kill your mum when he was arrested.'

'Can't be perfect all the time,' Molly smiled.

'How about you? Do you want to follow in your mother's footsteps?' Jess asked now. 'Run the Sisters?'

'Not really,' Molly shook her head. 'I'm gonna go legitimate. Though I could if I wanted, yeah? I know mum's holding on until I take over.'

'But how long will that take?' Jess leant closer. 'You're what, fourteen?'

'Almost,' Molly straightened as she spoke, almost as if she was trying to look older while sitting on the bed. 'But I been in this gangster world since I was born, innit? I've seen the problem mum deals with, and I'm harder than she thinks. I've seen dead people.'

'So have I,' Jess mused. 'But I'd rather I hadn't.'

'What don't kill you strengthens you,' Molly nodded. 'You get me, I know it. And one day I'll live by it.'

Jess got Molly. She got that this was a girl enamoured by power, who was going to find it very difficult to move on, living in a normal, unexciting, crime-free world.

'So how is your mum planning to get out?' she asked.

'She's taking meetings,' Molly replied. 'Financial types. Pension advisors. She's channelling funds into offshore accounts.'

'And you're sure of this?' Jess couldn't see a teenage girl being brought into such meetings.

'Yeah,' Molly pulled out her phone. 'She's been building for the big one since they announced the Olympics. Every ten years the fund she's in moves into something else, and this month the deadline hits. She gets a choice to stick or twist, and this time she's cashing out.'

She sniffed.

'I see them. I'm told to hang back, but as I'm the excuse to get mum out, I have to be around. This is the guy she saw earlier this week. He's helping her get out.'

She showed a photo on her phone; one of Janelle sitting at a cafe table with a man, in what looked like a white walled dining area. The man was old, with grey, almost white hair. They were deep in conversation, unaware of the photo.

And Jess recognised something.

'Can I get a copy of that?' she asked.

'I dunno,' Molly was suddenly reticent to do this. 'If it gets out, it can only be me that gave you it.'

Jess understood and pulled out her phone.

'Is your car still outside?' she asked. 'Could you have a quick look? I thought I heard it drive off.'

Molly, frowning, left the phone, photo still open on it as she climbed across the bed and looked out of the window, peering down at the black car on the kerb.

'Yeah,' she said, looking back. 'Why?'

'I just needed you to look away,' Jess smiled, showing her own phone; it now had a photo on the screen, a photo taken of *Molly's* screen. 'This way you didn't give me anything, and I conned you to get it. It gives you plausible deniability.'

Molly grinned.

'Oh, we should really hang out more,' she said.

'There's a play going on for London, but you've probably guessed that now,' Janelle explained. 'Jackie Lucas is back and killing his old enemies.'

'You're sure?' Declan played innocent. 'Jackie Lucas is a personality in Johnny Lucas' head.'

'That's not what I've heard,' Janelle spoke with a hint of smugness. 'And I know you know this too.'

'Okay, so hypothetically he's back. So what?' Declan sat forward on the sofa. 'How does this affect you right now, and scare you enough to make you come here?'

'I didn't want to come here, or speak to *you*,' Janelle snapped, 'looking' straight at Declan now. 'Molly suggested it. She knows I won't take help when needed. For twenty years now, London's been in an uneasy truce. The Twins in the east, the Sisters in the north, Simpson in the south, father and son, and the Tsangs in Soho and the west.'

'I thought there were more groups out there,' Anjli muttered. 'I know at least two Indian gangs, one Albanian—'

'Of course there's more than four,' Janelle replied. 'But they all fight at our command, make loose alliances. I gave you the *compass points* answer for ease and quickness. But if Jackie returns, he topples that peace. The body count goes up.'

Declan nodded, forgetting once more that Janelle couldn't see this.

'You mean Benny Tsang's disappearance, and Jeffrey's death,' he said, deliberately making sure he didn't give away any of their newer information.

'The west is in disarray and at war with the east, now leaderless with Johnny arrested for the murder of Jeffrey,' Janelle nodded. 'That will escalate. And the north and south will capitalise.'

'How?'

Janelle looked away, as much as someone who was blind could do so.

'We've had a company,' she said. 'Started it back in 2002. Johnny, the Tsangs, Max Simpson, and me. I'd just become Mama Delcourt, and I was the honorary girl, I think.'

'What sort of company?'

'Real estate,' Janelle replied. 'Olympics. We heard London wanted it, and they were looking to submit a bid to host in 2003. A lot of the land being looked at was on Johnny's turf, but there were things happening at Greenwich, Wembley, Wimbledon, all over the place. Johnny couldn't afford to buy up all the land, so we came in. All invested equal amounts and created a shell company led by an impartial CEO.'

'Let me guess,' Declan sighed. 'Maurice Hamilton?'

'He knew everyone,' Janelle smiled faintly. 'Anyway, the Olympics were a success, the Olympic Delivery Authority, or the ODA offered us a stupidly large cheque, which was pennies considering they had a nine billion budget, we took the money in August 2012, and invested it again.'

'In what, this time?'

'Crossrail,' Janelle fumbled for the glass of water, taking it and sipping. 'People in the ODA had moved across and said it was guaranteed money. It had just been accused of black-listing when picking partners, so things were being moved around and tenders were artificially low, and it perfectly timed us to buy prime real estate that the alternative routes would pass by. It was supposed to finish in 2019, but it got delayed until now. And our ten-year options expire this month, so we need to move fast if we want to stay in, or move on.'

'So, the war is because people don't want this?'

'Jesus, no,' Janelle laughed. 'We all want the money. But now Max isn't in power down there anymore, and his son, Nicky is sniffing around—and Nicky has a better idea of how this all works. There's a new generation who aren't involved in this, and they want their slice of the pie. Which I get, I really do. If it'd been me, I'd feel the same. But it's not their time, and they didn't *earn* this. And if they don't get it...'

'They'll make sure nobody does,' Anjli nodded. 'And a gang war, a public, violent one, would lower your profits a lot, I'm guessing. And this is where Jackie comes in? Another who lost out on this?'

'I didn't want to be involved in that,' Janelle sighed. 'But one of the Seven Sisters is involved, planning in corners with the enemy's foot soldier, and with history involved with the East End.'

'Foot soldier. You mean Kayas Ashad?'

Janelle nodded again.

'He blames me for Moses. Only person he listens to is Anita Taborsky. And she's the one with the history.'

'And she wants your throne?'

Janelle laughed.

'She can have the damned thing when I'm gone. No, I said *history*. Taborsky is her married name.'

'What's her maiden name?' Even though he didn't know for definite, Declan almost expected the answer. The photo of the three children was once more in his mind.

'It's not Russian for sure. She's an East End girl. Anita *Lucas*,' Janelle's voice darkened as she finished.

'She's the elder sister of Johnny and Jackie.'

21

MYSTERIOUS MEETINGS

Billy had stayed in the office another half an hour after the others had gone, mainly as he wanted to go over some last CCTV footage he'd received from the night of the murder, along a shopfront on the Roman Road near Globe Town, but also because he currently felt a little awkward around Declan, Anjli and Jess.

Not that he was unhappy at their budding relationship status, or that he felt they shouldn't be together; the simple fact was two of his closest friends in the office were discovering a new level to their relationship, while Billy Fitzwarren was painfully single.

Granted, this was by choice; the last actual date he'd had was months earlier, and it'd been scuppered when industrialist Rufus Harrington appeared instead of Simon, his dinner partner for the night, who'd been easily bought off, despite their previous relationship. After that, Billy had been a little more cautious about who he ate with; or, rather, who he even hung out with. Recent events had mainly been linked to work outings, the occasional dinner with his estranged uncle

Chivalry—that was, estranged by situation, with Chivalry trying to repair long-standing family issues between Billy and the rest of the Fitzwarren clan—and a couple of tentative, but mostly fruitless blind dates, mainly set up by well-wishing colleagues on the *uniform* side.

Billy decided early on that for the moment, he was destined to be single for a while.

Doctor Marcos tried to place him on one of the two blind dates; a CSI she'd worked with a couple of times, but they'd spent the entire dinner gushing about how great Doctor Marcos was, and Billy quickly worked out that they only went out with him to gain more information about *her*. Learning about this, she'd threatened to make things right, find him another 'hottie', to use her own term, but he'd politely refused, claiming workload as the excuse.

By now it was almost eight in the evening, and his stomach was rumbling. He didn't really want to travel once more to the local Pret or Tesco Express, and the nearby pubs were likely to be filled with tourists, so Billy grabbed his jacket and, closing up shop for the evening decided to make a night of it, albeit solo, heading down to *Simpsons in the Strand*, a restaurant so steeped in police history that it was literally the go-to dining place for *Sherlock Holmes*.

Of course, this was also mainly because it was across the road from the onetime offices of *The Strand Magazin*e, publishers of Conan-Doyle's original tales, and they'd likely convinced the author to add them, in possibly one of the first licensing deals in fiction ever.

Set within walking distance of The Savoy Theatre, Somerset House and The National Gallery, Simpsons was a favourite for pre-theatre drinks and meals, but Billy hoped he could bypass the queues now the shows would have started.

And, after a ten-minute stroll, Billy entered the restaurant through its extravagant main doors, smiling at the Maitre d' as they recognised him, taking him upstairs to a large, oak-panelled room with an ornate, cream coloured high-ceiling that was known as the *Grand Divan.* It felt and looked like a stately house, and for a moment Billy felt at home, as they led him to his small square table for one, two red-cushioned chairs awaiting him.

Opened in 1828, Simpsons was then one of London's great *chess* rooms. Roast dinners would be wheeled round to the tables under shiny silver carving trollies, and attended to by the Master Carver, so the games would not be disturbed. The chess games no longer happened, but the trollies were still in evidence as they wheeled around the room. Billy chuckled, wondering if the onetime chess connection subconsciously brought him here, but quickly shook it away as he ordered a red wine, a lobster soup to start and a roast saddle of lamb, complete with roast potatoes, savoy cabbage, homemade mint sauce and redcurrant jelly. It was a far cry from the microwaved kale macaroni and cheese he had been considering earlier.

It was a lot more expensive, too; but Billy needed it. He needed to feel somewhere that was 'home', and not part of an investigation into the lowlifes of London.

His bottle of 2003 *Chateau Lynch-Bages Pauillac*, a savoury, classic and rather expensive red wine, had only just arrived when the stranger appeared. Billy rarely ordered expensive wine, mainly as the people he'd drink with, often colleagues, couldn't afford to return the favour. But alone, he knew he could truly savour it.

The stranger was young, maybe late twenties at most. Olive skinned and brown eyed, his short black hair was styled and picked at, giving the impression of carelessness, while being fastidiously set, matching the uniformed grooming of his stubble. He wore a dark grey suit with pale blue shirt, no tie, and his leather shoes were black and shined to excess.

He looked stylish and of money, but Billy felt he gave the vibe more of an official, or diplomat, than someone who would usually dine here.

'William Fitzwarren?' he asked, his voice soft and melodic, the slightest hint of a South American accent on it. 'May I speak with you?'

'Call me Billy, please,' Billy kept the conversation casual until he knew what was going on here. *Was he about to be served papers? How had they even known he was here, when this was an impulse decision?*

He waved at the chair opposite.

'Wine?' he showed the bottle. 'I won't manage all of this.'

'If you're sure? Then thank you, please,' the man smiled, and Billy couldn't help noticing how attractive he was.

Christ, man. Put it back in your trousers. He came looking for you. He's trouble.

'I'm Andrade Estrada,' the man started shyly. 'From the Colombian Embassy. I—I was told to find you and speak with you.'

'Colombian embassy?' Billy considered this. 'Are you here about the enquiry I made about Jackie Lucas?'

'In a way,' Andrade replied, taking the glass and raising it. 'Salut.'

Billy clinked glasses, watching the newcomer as he sipped.

'Interesting taste,' Andrade considered the glass. 'Big, rich, dark fruit flavour. Still a little tannic and astringent.'

He gave an impish smile.

Oh, you're dangerous, Billy considered. *No, think business.*

'I applied for information pertaining to Jackie Lucas—I mean *Jackson* Lucas' release from La Modelo jail in Bogotá in an email late last night,' Billy said. 'I hadn't heard back.'

'No, because we wanted to speak to you personally about this,' Andrade was definitely nervous. 'If I can ask you, how much do you know about the prison?'

'Only what I've seen on Wikipedia,' Billy admitted. 'It's overcrowded, people die in there a lot. Oh, and a few years back, you found like a hundred corpses in the drains.'

Andrade paled a little at this.

'Not one of their better stories,' he replied. 'You said in your enquiry that you'd been told that we released Jackson Lucas within the last couple of years after a regime change?'

'That's what we'd heard,' Billy sipped at his own glass now. 'But as I also said, I took it as a rumour rather than fact, until proven. If I'm wrong, please let me know.'

'We indeed sent Jackson Lucas to La Modelo, we have the paperwork,' Andrade spoke quickly now. 'However, there can be no record of his release, because he did not live long enough to be released.'

'He died?' Billy placed the glass down now. 'When?'

'It was a dark time,' Andrade started. 'In 1999, there were tunnels discovered. Eugenia Aguilar, director of the National Penitentiary and Prison Institute, was told that in each courtyard a tunnel had been found, and because of this ordered the prison to be closed to visitors. Inmates started to die, and then Aguilar left office, replaced by Police Colonel Laureano Villamizar. He found another twenty tunnels, and there were big fights. Armed clashes. During one of these, Jackson Lucas was shot and killed. Nobody knows if this was deliberate or not, but we knew he was an agitator during his time there.'

'Do you have a death certificate for this?' Billy leaned back in his seat as he considered the story.

Andrade shook his head.

'Unfortunately, no, which is why we have a problem,' he said. 'Jackson Lucas is on a list of dead, but they found no body. And as you said, bodies, many of which had been there for decades, were found in the sewers. We believe many of these were murders by other inmates, and we're still trying to identify all of them.'

Billy nodded. Jackie Lucas had been set up by Johnny and then dumped in La Modelo. And, a few years later was believed dead in a riot.

Believed dead. Not proven to have died in the riot. Not proven to be dead at all, actually.

'Thank you,' Billy smiled. 'Although you could have just emailed me this.'

'True,' Andrade tipped his head in a nod. 'But my supervisor, she wanted me to show you what a good friend we could be. To you... or *your* friends.'

And just like that, the penny dropped.

'Oh,' Billy's voice darkened. 'You mean Charles Baker.'

It was no secret that recently elected Prime Minister Charles Baker classed the *Last Chance Saloon* as allies; not only had they saved his life frequently, but they'd also forced his opponent to back out of taking the role, after her past caught up with her, allowing him to be fast-tracked into the position. However, none of these actions were performed because of a loyalty to the man; indeed, there was an unspoken rule in the office that, if they could, they'd take Charles Baker down a peg or two, especially as the jury was still out on whether his *Star Chamber* antics caused the death of Kendis Taylor at the start of the year.

Billy considered how to phrase his response, but before he could speak, Andrade held up a hand.

'Look, Billy,' he said carefully. 'I am just a messenger. I do not care what you decide to do with the information, or whether you continue the relationship with my embassy afterwards. That is for higher-level people to decide.'

He smiled, looking around.

'I just wanted to see this wonderful place for myself when I saw you enter.'

'You were following me?'

'Yes,' Andrade spoke it as a matter of fact. 'I was intending to meet your superior at your office, but you were leaving as I arrived, and you, shall we say, *caught my eye.*'

Billy nodded at this, hoping he wasn't blushing at the implied compliment. If he was aware, Andrade didn't comment.

'And so I followed, and hoped to perhaps find a time to make my introductions.'

He raised the glass, saluting Billy.

'I am glad I waited until now,' he smiled.

Billy couldn't help himself. He smiled too.

'So am I,' he replied. 'Well then, now we've fulfilled the business part of the evening, would you care to join me for dinner?'

'I would be honoured,' Andrade replied. 'Although you must allow me to pay, as I can claim it as a diplomatic endeavour.'

'I'm liking this idea even more,' Billy laughed as he settled back in his chair. The evening was turning out quite nice after all, even if the news was incredibly concerning.

But for once, the news could wait until tomorrow.

JANELLE DRANK SOME OF HER WATER AS SHE WAITED FOR Declan and Anjli to digest the information she'd just given them.

'Why doesn't anyone know this?' Declan asked. 'Why didn't *we?*'

'No, we knew there was a sister,' Anjli corrected. 'That is, Mile End knew there was. But she'd been gone for years. Out of sight, out of mind and all that.'

'Anita Taborsky has been a pain in my side since this,' Janelle motioned to her dark glasses. 'And yes, I'm aware of the irony of doing this to myself.'

'When did they last speak?' Declan asked. 'The Lucas family?'

'She's talked with Johnny many times over the years,' Janelle replied. 'Either as himself or as Jackie. Not once did they give away they were siblings. I learnt over time that she'd walked from the family when she was young, married a Russian mobster, one of the guys who helped the Turk in Soho, and took his name. And when Jackie, real Jackie injured Sergei—that was the husband—in a gunfight in Clerkenwell back in the early nineties, an injury he passed away from days later in hospital, she kept the name, swore revenge on the family and came to Tottenham.'

'So it wasn't dogs attacking him, then?'

Janelle laughed.

'Ah, the power of a wonderful tale,' she smiled. 'No, it was quite pedestrian, really. But Anita was always incredibly theatrical.'

Realising she was drifting, Janelle returned to the conversation. Declan noted Anjli frantically writing in her notebook, recording everything Janelle said. It might have sounded like a careless comment, but Declan knew Mama Delcourt. Everything she did, or even said, had a reason behind it.

'Anyway, after that my mama took her into the Sisters, where she's been ever since,' she finished, holding up her hands in a '*what can I do*' motion.

'Is she a threat?' Declan asked.

'To me? Definitely. To your case? I don't believe so. She hates the Lucas family, and I believe she has no issues with the Tsangs.'

There was another knock at the door, and Janelle jumped.

'I shouldn't have stayed here so long,' she whispered fearfully.

Declan, however, rose from the chair.

'It's likely our takeaway,' he said as he opened the door, nodded thanks to the delivery driver, took the carrier bag of food from her and brought it back in, closing the door behind him. 'If you want to stay and join us, you can. I'm sure there'll be enough.'

'No,' Janelle rose. 'It'll take an hour to return to London. I'll need to eat at a drive-through to give an excuse for the delay. McDonald's wrappers are better proof than receipts, these days.'

There was a noise from the side of the room as Molly and Jess came down the stairs.

'Who was it?' Molly asked, concerned, glancing nervously at the door. 'Was it Barry?'

'Dinner,' Jess grinned, spying the bags on the table. 'Told you so.'

'We should go, little one,' Janelle reached out blindly,

waiting for Molly to take her hand, leading her to the door, the outside world and the still-waiting Barry in the black Mercedes.

'Mrs Delcourt,' Declan said, refusing to use her gangland title as Janelle passed over the threshold. 'If you truly want to get out of this life, let me know. I can help.'

'Stop the war first, and then we'll talk,' Janelle smiled, following Molly down the steps that led through the front garden. Declan watched them walk to the car, Molly helping her mother into the back seat before Barry, glaring one last time at Declan, revved the engine and pulled off, a little too forcefully, speeding away down the road.

Chuckling, Declan returned into the house, closing the door behind him.

'Sorry about that,' he said to Jess. 'I know you'd have preferred to be downstairs with us. But—'

'Actually dad, it's fine,' Jess replied, pulling out her phone and opening it. 'I think I found a major clue.'

'Oh yes?' Anjli walked over now. 'Given by the daughter or taken?'

'Bit of both,' Jess showed them the photo she'd taken of Molly's phone, complete with the image of Janelle Delcourt and the financial advisor. 'I took it when Molly was distracted,' she lied.

'What is it?' Declan looked at the scene, confused. 'I mean, I know what it *is*, but what did Molly—'

'Molly said that she went with her mum earlier this week to talk to financial advisors,' Jess explained. 'People to channel her funds out of the Sisters, so she can live comfortably once she goes. The exact line she said when showing me this was that this man is helping her mum get out.'

'You know who that is, right?' Declan looked up at his daughter, who nodded.

'I've been looking at CCTV of him all day beside Billy,' she said. 'Jackie Lucas, the guy we saw in *Tsang City*, And, more than that,' Jess tapped the image, zooming on a logo on the wall. 'Recognise that?'

Realising that neither adult in the room did, she sighed.

'YouTube has it all over his videos,' she said. 'That's the logo of *Nicky Simpson's Health Clubs*.'

Declan looked back at the photo.

The queen of North London, meeting the king of East London, in the home of the king of South of the Thames.

'So is that the fake Jackie, or Johnny being Jackie?' he asked.

'Hopefully, Billy can work that out,' Anjli suggested.

Declan sighed.

'For once, just once, I'd like a simple case,' he said. 'One where we arrive and the killer's still there holding the knife. Done and dusted.'

'You'd be bored in ten minutes,' Anjli was opening the carrier bag, examining the contents. 'Come on, let's eat before dinner gets cold.'

And with that suggestion found to be imminently agreeable to all parties, and with all thoughts to the case now put aside for the moment, Declan, Anjli and Jess started arguing about who'd ordered what, as they prepared a late dinner; the blind woman and her teenage daughter, now driving home in a black Mercedes, completely forgotten.

22

LIFE AND DEATH

JOHNNY LUCAS SAT ON THE EDGE OF THE CUSTODY CELL'S BED and stared up at the corner of the room. He'd been staring at it for the better part of the day now; there was a harvester spider in it, a tiny, spindly thing, and apart from the times they allowed him out of the cell for either interviews or his solicitor meetings, it was the only other living thing he spoke to.

The room was square, white-tiled and boring. To his right was a toilet and paper, a small, incredibly basic sink beside it. Above him was a mirror in the cell's corner, angled into the room so anyone entering had a full view of it, in the same way that some houses had them on country roads to show if anyone was approaching when the owners pulled out of their driveways.

On the opposite corner, not the one with the harvester spider, but at the end of his bed was a conical CCTV camera, probably watching to see if he tried to hurt himself. The red light under it flashed, a constant reminder that *big brother was watching him.*

Tiring of the surveillance, he looked back at the spider.

'So, what are you in for?' he asked with a smile. 'Really? That's harsh. They'll throw the book at you for that. Probably squish you in the process.'

He chuckled at the joke, but the smile quickly faded as there was a noise at the door, a key in the lock being inserted before being turned. As Johnny rose from the rubber mattress that doubled as bench and bed, he saw DS McAlroy enter; the door left half-open behind her.

'It's a bit late for visitors, isn't it?' Johnny looked at an imaginary watch on his wrist. 'Has to be what, ten?'

'Eleven thirty,' McAlroy said, uncomfortable to be there. 'You should be asleep.'

'I've always been a night owl,' Johnny shifted now, unsure what was going on. Looking up at the CCTV camera, he noted the red flashing light was no longer visible. 'You letting me go yet? I'll guarantee my solicitor will have words. He's probably already outside.'

He smiled.

'Is that what this is?' he asked, glancing around the room, looking for a weapon.

Something was about to go down, and he didn't like his chances.

He had a thin bed sheet, the same sheet he'd slept under the previous night, but at best he could whip it around and try to strangle anyone who attacked. 'Is he here already? It's good to see you though, Jules. You've done well. I—'

'Don't,' DS McAlroy held a hand up to interrupt him. 'We're not doing that right now. Don't make this personal.'

'Don't make *what* personal?' Johnny asked. 'What aren't you telling me—'

He stopped, his words dying in his throat as a second person walked into the room.

'What the hell are you doing here?' he snapped. 'I paid you to sort things out, not leave me in a cell. Some copper you are. Oh, wait, I forgot.'

'Johnny, it's not a copper you need right now, it's a priest,' Ellie Reckless replied, ignoring the insult. 'There's a lot of people who want you dead out there. Someone put a two million dollar hit on you, and poor Jules here has been fighting off attempts to get into the station all day.'

'Who'd dare put a hit on me?'

'Someone who thinks you're playing doubles and finishing rivals and loose ends before they can get a hit in back, perhaps?'

'I'd say Jeffrey Tsang, but he's the reason I'm in here,' Johnny suggested. 'Who else am I supposed to have offed? What loose ends am I tying up?'

Ellie shrugged.

'Mickey Trackies and Benny Tsang for a start.'

Johnny stared open mouthed at Ellie for a long moment.

'Mickie's dead?'

'Yeah, sorry,' Ellie gave an apologetic smile. 'I'm super shite at sugarcoating things.'

'But I'm in here,' Johnny spoke to McAlroy now. 'How am I supposed to have done this?'

'Many people run empires from prison,' Ellie continued, pulling a small rucksack, one that Johnny hadn't noticed from behind her shoulder. 'But that's not your problem, is it? Your problem is that now, the police know it wasn't you that did it; it was your brother. And eventually you'll be set free.'

She placed the rucksack on the floor now, unzipping it.

'So I'll be free,' Johnny frowned. 'Where's the downside to that?'

'The downside is,' Ellie replied as she pulled a length of bedsheet out of the bag, 'that the Triads and the Sisters, and probably even the Simpsons, are all gunning for you. They want you dead. They want you destroyed. And as I said, there's a two million dollar hit on your head. You won't even make it to your solicitor's car before you're taken out.'

'Then you need to help me,' Johnny smiled winningly. 'This is how you work. I'll owe you a favour. I'll owe you two. How's that sound?'

'Sounds like a dying man clutching at straws,' Ellie looked around the room, the bedsheet in her hand; a bedsheet that Johnny could see had been cut into strips and tied together at each end, making a long, thin cord. 'Where the hell do we support this?'

'In the corner,' McAlroy said, walking past Johnny and standing on the bench, kicking aside the blue rubber mattress as she reached up to the corner mirror, using her height and strength to yank it off its fixings. Behind it, hidden, was a heavy bracket. 'A paedo hung himself a month back this way. Security didn't notice until he was purple.'

Johnny looked over at Ellie Reckless, still crouching over the rucksack; he saw one end of the bedsheet was tied into a noose.

'Ladies, come on,' he said, suddenly realising what was happening here. 'Jules, I helped you get in here. Ellie, I can help you.'

'Help me how?' Ellie asked, tossing the end of the makeshift rope to McAlroy, who fed it through the bracket. 'You're a dead man, Johnny. And when you're out there, shot in a drive by, you'll be a martyr to the cause, causing more blood to be spilled.'

She rose now, pulling a taser out of her pocket.

'Best you die here,' she said with a faint, sad smile. 'Best you die forgotten, in a cell, with no one the wiser, while we show proof to the payer, split the two million and go lay on a beach, earning ten percent. Now, we can either do this my way, or...'

She sparked the taser.

'Or *this* way,' she said, as DS McAlroy moved in behind Johnny Lucas, grabbing his arms, placing a hand over his mouth to stop him from screaming for help.

'My way,' Ellie said as she placed the homemade noose over Johnny Lucas' head.

WHEN THE DOOR TO HER APARTMENT BUZZED, CHERYL JENKINS nearly jumped out of her skin with surprise and fear, conflicting thoughts running through her head as she stared at it from across the hallway.

They've found me

They're here to kill me

They've come to arrest me

The doorbell buzzed again, and Cheryl slowly walked towards the door, expecting it to burst open at any moment. Which was stupid, because whomever was pressing the button wasn't doing it from the other side of the door, they were doing it from the main entrance downstairs.

She still had time to run.

'Hello?' she asked warily, pressing the intercom button. 'Who is it?'

'A mutual friend sent us,' the male voice at the end of the line replied. Looking up at the tiny CCTV screen above the phone, Cheryl could see two young men, both wearing hoodies. The one that had spoken was leaning into the intercom, the hood blurring his features. 'They said you were dealing with an *identity* crisis.'

Cheryl's finger paused on the OPEN button. *What did they mean by that? Was this a veiled message from Anita, and did one of these strangers have a new set of identity papers for her?*

Or was this a trap?

'How can I trust you?' she asked.

'Lady? I don't care if you trust me or not,' the man leaning close to the speaker said. 'It's late, we're tired and we've just come out to the middle of nowhere to speak to you.'

'Who sent you?'

'I'm not gonna say on this thing,' the man was getting irritated now. 'This might be recorded. You let us in or we walk. And if we walk, you do your own thing, got me?'

Cheryl bit her lip, nervous. There was every chance that this was the meeting Anita had promised, and the veiled threat was that if they left, she was on her own. No new identity, no chance to escape.

Reluctantly, she pressed the OPEN button, hearing the faint buzz from downstairs as, on the screen, the two men walked through.

No—three men. Because at the moment the camera clicked off, a third figure, wearing what looked to be motorcycle leathers, appeared behind them.

Shit.

Running to the kitchen, Cheryl pulled out the drawers, tossing them to the floor; one advantage of dating a gangster, even if it was for show, was that sometimes you could pick up things. And two nights back, when Johnny had left the apartment in a hurry, he'd left his gun behind. A gun that, for the last two days, had been taped under one of the side drawers. She just didn't remember which one.

It was an automatic pistol; black with a white ivory handle, gold highlights and screws set around it. That was as far as she went with guns though, apart from the knowledge that when in trouble, you pointed it at the person you wanted to kill and pulled the trigger.

She didn't even know if the gun was loaded, although she bloody hoped so. Surely, Johnny wouldn't have walked around with an empty gun.

For the first time, Cheryl hoped Johnny Lucas really was the psychotic bastard everyone said he was.

She looked for a place to hide; there was a large cardboard box by the kitchen, where she'd had a new washing machine arrive two days ago. She hadn't got around to chucking it yesterday, and she wondered briefly whether she could hide behind it, or even within it.

Yes, because cardboard boxes are well known for blocking bullet and knife attacks, she thought to herself, dismissing the idea as fallacy.

The front door to her apartment was knocked upon now, three slow knocks that sounded ominous in the night's silence.

'Who is it?' she asked, holding the gun tight as she walked to the door.

'Bitch, don't leave us hanging,' the man said through the door. 'I'm not feeding this under the door.'

'You lied to me!' Cheryl shouted, now on the other side of the door, staring through the peephole. 'You said there were two of you. I saw three.'

'I didn't give no number,' the man replied irritably. Through the peephole, Cheryl could see him clearly now; he was young, barely in his twenties, black and with a small scar on his cheek. His accent was London, but not south of the river. He looked to his right, backing away from the door as the third man, the one in the biker jacket and helmet, walked into view.

'Can you see me?' The voice was muffled as the biker spoke.

'Yes,' Cheryl said, nodding—although who she was nodding to was lost on her. Accepting the answer, though, the biker reached up and pulled their helmet off, revealing the furious face of Anita Taborsky.

'Good,' she said. 'Then open the goddamned door before someone else sees me.'

Chastised, Cheryl quickly opened the door and stepped back, the gun now behind her back. She felt stupid; she should have opened the door at the start, trusted that Anita would do the right thing.

Anita and the two men, both black and hooded, entered the apartment.

'Nice,' Anita said as she looked around. 'Amazing what *Shand* money can give you.'

'I'm sorry,' Cheryl blurted out. 'I was scared.'

'Understandable, but naïve,' Anita replied, holding the helmet loose in her hand now as she ran her other hand through her white hair. 'I came by bike; that way nobody could make out it was me. I knew you'd be too chickenshit to accept a call if I wasn't there.'

'I'm sorry.'

'I told you I would make you disappear,' Anita continued. 'You should have been ready. Are you ready?'

'Yes,' Cheryl replied, followed by, 'I don't know. Can I contact my mum while I'm away?'

'You can,' Anita nodded. 'If you want to see her murdered by Tsangs, too. They'll likely be watching your whole family.'

'But you said—'

'I said once this was *over*, you could return to this life,' Anita interrupted. 'And this minor war is going to last awhile, unfortunately.'

There was an uncomfortable pause in the conversation as Anita just stood there, the slightest of smug expressions on her face, waiting for Cheryl to come to the same inevitable ending as she'd already explained.

'Fine then. I'm ready,' Cheryl nodded again, finally sure. 'You have the money and identity for me?'

'No.'

As Anita said this, Cheryl saw one of the two men, the one that had spoken to her through the intercom, pull out a sharp-looking blade.

'I'm sorry, Cheryl, I really am, but I've decided it's better to tie off all loose ends after all,' Anita replied. 'But thanks for letting us in. I didn't want to make a scene.'

The man with the blade started towards Cheryl, but rather than back away, she pulled Johnny's automatic out, holding it out, aiming it at the man, his friend, and Anita in quick succession.

'I don't want to shoot you,' she said. 'I just want to get out.'

The man had stepped back, glancing at Anita for further orders. Anita, meanwhile, was staring intently at the gun, or more importantly the ivory handle.

'I recognise that,' she said. 'That's Johnny's. Taurus PT92, nine millimetre, five-inch barrel.'

'You know your guns,' Cheryl replied.

'I know *that* gun,' Anita leant closer. 'Late eighties design, when they stopped trying to mimic the Beretta. Cost a fair bit too, when I bought it for him.'

'You bought...' Cheryl started, but ran out of words as she glanced at the gun. 'Well, back away and maybe you won't see its bullets close up.'

'No fear of that,' the man with the blade sneered. 'I can see from here the safety's on.'

Cheryl looked back at the gun, checking the gold highlighted safety catch—and that spilt-second pause was all Anita Taborsky needed, as she swung the biker helmet hard at Cheryl's head, connecting on the side with a sickening crunch of noise.

As Cheryl slumped to the floor, the gun clattering out of her fingers, Anita leant down and picked it up, turning it in her hand as she admired it, clicking off the safety catch.

'Now what?' Kayas muttered.

Anita looked around the room, spying the box beside the sink.

'Pick her up, put her in that,' she said, walking over to it. 'We can take her out of here as if we're replacing broken white goods.'

She looked down at Cheryl; her face bloodied.

'Which I suppose she is,' she considered.

Closing the front door, Kayas Ashad placed away his knife and nodded to his companion.

Together, they hefted the unconscious Cheryl up now, Kayas avoiding the trickle of blood that seeped from her left ear and ran down her chin, as they opened up the top of the box, removed the styrofoam from within and tipped the unconscious woman into it, closing the top.

Cheryl Jenkins was going to disappear, after all.

DCI Esposito had only just reached his apartment when the call came in.

He hadn't even had time to change out of his suit, so it was a still-dressed-for-duty and incredibly pissed off DCI who re-entered Mile End Command Unit at just past midnight.

'Who found him?' he snapped at the officer on the desk. He didn't need to say who the *him* was; everyone knew.

'I did, Guv,' DS McAlroy walked out to intercept Esposito. 'The CCTV had gone out in his cell, and as I was nearby, I went and had a look. I found this.'

She opened her phone; on it was an image. A brutal, grotesque one. Johnny Lucas, hanging by his neck, in his cell, his eyes rolled up, his tongue lolling to the side, his torn bed sheet tied around his throat.

'Christ,' Esposito muttered as they were buzzed through the main door. 'Keep a lot of these kinds of pics on your phone, Jules?'

'I took it before Khanna cut him down,' McAlroy bristled, nodding to another officer as they walked to the custody suites. 'He's checking the body now. But with the press all outside still, he's taken it to the forensic science laboratory in Lambeth to do the autopsy.'

By now they'd entered the cell; It was claustrophobic, with several other officers and forensic crew all huddled into the room with them, dusting surfaces and taking photos. As Esposito looked up, he saw the torn sheet around the bracket was still there, although it'd been cut when the body had been pulled down.

'Thoughts?' he asked, mainly to McAlroy, but also to any of the other people in the cell listening to him.

'Johnny realised he was about to enter a world of shit. Decided to top himself,' McAlroy surmised. 'Or someone got in. Not the first time a dirty cop has given entrance in Mile End, and for a percentage of two million? That's enough to tempt most people.'

'Would it tempt you?'

'No, Guv.'

Esposito nodded.

'Someone came to kill him,' he replied. 'Turned the camera off, hanged him and left. Shit.'

'There's something else,' McAlroy pulled Esposito to the side. 'The press know.'

'How does the bloody press know?' Esposito was livid. McAlroy pulled up a page from a news site, showing him.

'Whoever did this, put it out there,' she said. 'It came up about ten minutes after we called you.'

EAST END CRIMELORD HANGS SELF RATHER THAN FACE CRIMES

Under the title was a photo, similar to the one McAlroy had shown; Johnny Lucas, hanging by the neck.

'Get that off the bloody site,' Esposito hissed. 'Go outside, find the bugger who did this, and arrest them until they tell us who gave them the scoop.'

'Yes sir,' McAlroy spun on her heel and walked out of the cell as Esposito sighed audibly. One forensic officer, a young, too-innocent-for-the-job type male, looked over at him.

'Johnny Lucas was about to be freed,' he said. 'He

wouldn't have done this. Someone got into the cell and killed him.'

'Why?' Esposito asked. 'Revenge? Hit money?'

'Maybe this was a chance to build the war up or end it?' the forensics officer suggested.

'Possibly, DC... Moseley?'

'Yes sir,' Moseley smiled.

'Keep up the good work,' Esposito said as he left the cell and walked back to his office.

In it, McAlroy was waiting for him.

'You put the photo out?' he asked after closing the door.

'Yes,' McAlroy nodded. 'Thought it was the best way to confirm the hit, to show the people who put it out that they owe money.'

'And you have someone doing that?' Esposito walked to the desk, resting his hands against it. 'I don't like this, Jules. This goes against everything I've stood for.'

'Don't worry, boss,' McAlroy smiled. 'If it all goes tits up? We'll just blame Ellie Reckless. It was her plan, after all.'

'Yeah, and I signed off on it.'

Deciding not to answer this, McAlroy went to leave.

'Anything else?' she asked as she reached the door.

'Actually, yes,' Esposito looked up at McAlroy. 'Forensics chap. Moseley.'

'Yeah, I know him. Good lad.'

'Possibly too good,' Esposito grimaced. 'Monitor him. If he gets too close to what actually happened? Pull him out.'

'Sir.'

'Oh,' Esposito sat in his chair now. 'Actually, one thing. Get down to Khanna. Make sure he's indisposed for a while. Rosanna Marcos is likely going to want to see the body, confirming the 'suicide', and we don't want her realising the truth.'

'And if she realises the truth, sir?'

DCI Esposito sighed.

'Do whatever it takes to stop her from doing something stupid,' he ordered.

23

MEET THE NEW BOSS

After Janelle left, Declan had a troubled night's sleep, not helped by the phone call from Monroe at shortly past four in the morning, giving him the news that Johnny Lucas was dead.

Anjli, half asleep in the bed beside him had jerked awake at that, and knowing that the rest of his night was now ruined, Declan had tiptoed his way downstairs to make himself a coffee, with Anjli joining him half an hour later, after she too had failed to get back to sleep.

They had decided not to wake Jess; it was a kindness that she still slept. At least someone wouldn't be falling asleep at three in the afternoon.

Anjli and Declan had sat in the living room reminiscing about Johnny; it felt weird at first, as the man was a rather psychotic criminal with multiple personality disorder, but he had assisted the Unit on multiple occasions, and had even saved both Monroe and Declan's life, both times in the boxing club that now had such a macabre end.

They'd moved from reminiscing into hypothetical suggestions on who would replace Johnny; would one of his own soldiers take over, would other East End gangs rise, or would one of the other major players, like the Seven Sisters or Nicky Simpson, take over?

By seven, Jess was awake, dressed and more than a little surprised to find Declan and Anjli, showered, fully clothed and drinking coffee as they waited for her. Eventually, after she gathered her things together as well, they all clambered into Declan's police-issue Audi, to make the long commute into London.

It was during the drive that Anjli told Jess the news they'd heard; Jess had replied she already knew, as one of the news blogs she read had shown it. She'd guessed this was why they'd been up early, but didn't want to press.

'Everyone's going to be concentrating on Lucas,' Declan said as they reached the end of the M4, when it changed into the A4 at Hogarth's Roundabout. 'Even the criminals who might not be too involved. Maybe we should see what we can find out about Simpson's Health Club?'

He nodded back to Jess, sitting in the back seat.

'That image you took last night, are you sure it's the logo?'

'Definitely,' Jess nodded. 'Simpson's all about the branding.'

'Can you send the image to Billy too?' Anjli suggested.

'Already done,' Jess smiled. 'Although Billy said without the original though, he can't really go through the metadata, or check whether layers have been fixed. Instead, he's going through photos of Johnny as Jackie, to see if any of them match the look.'

'It has to be the same bloke who shot Banner in the club

and made the announcement in Helen of Troy's,' Declan tapped his fingers on the steering wheel. 'But who the hell is it?'

'Whoever it is, he's got to come out now. Johnny's gone,' Anjli stared out of the window, watching the buildings pass by. 'There's a lot of property damage about to hit. You remember the London Riots back in 2011?'

Declan did. The riots weren't just kept to London itself; thousands of people rioted in cities and towns across England, which saw looting, arson, and the deaths of five people during it.

'It started in Tottenham Hale,' he said, thinking back to that day. 'Near to where we lived at the time.'

'I was five, and I remember mum yelling at me to stay in my room,' Jess shuddered. 'I was terrified.'

'I'd just started in Tottenham North, and DI Salmon had me investigate the Mark Duggan death, which kicked it all off,' Declan glanced at his watch. 'It's the anniversary this week.'

'Fitting,' Anjli muttered as she stared out the window still. 'They reckoned there was about two hundred million in property damage.'

She looked back at Declan.

'If this war happens,' she said, 'that'll look like weekend beer money compared to the bill this time. And we're already up to four deaths, before we've even started.'

SHANE MCCARTHY DIDN'T APPRECIATE BEING ORDERED INTO work this early in the morning.

He'd only got off shift four hours earlier and had only just dropped off to sleep when the message had come though; the same message that the other men and women, now standing around the inside of the Globe Town boxing club, had all received.

The King is dead. Long live the Queen. Boxing club. 8am. Be there or be unemployed.

Shane was a burly man in his forties, a man who had spent most of his adult life working out on the heavy bags currently beside him, bags he didn't want to walk near now, in fear of getting too close to the ring in the middle of the club.

The ring was sanitised, and a cleaning crew had been in for the last twenty-four hours, trying to remove the stench of death from it, but although the ring itself looked the same, the canvas had been left, and was now nothing but a mottled square of dried blood.

They'd all heard the news about what happened within it, and everyone there had not only been involved in some small way in keeping Johnny and Jackie Lucas' empire going, they'd also spilt blood in this club; either their own, or the person they were 'sorting out' for the Twins. Shane himself was known as a bit of a 'punchbag' man, placing debtors into leather heavy bags, zipping them up and then going to town on them, getting a full workout, including cardio, before allowing the battered debtors finally to crawl out.

He never *killed* anyone, though. That was a job for some of the nastier bastards in the room. And there were a ton of them.

They'd all heard *that* news as well, although it was still to be officially announced and confirmed; Johnny Lucas had been found in his Mile End cell, having taken his own life. Nobody could believe it; Johnny would never have gone out that way—that was a *cuck's* way out. Johnny would have kept swinging, kept fighting until the end. The way many of the men and women in the club right now wanted to go out.

Of course, none of them had a two million bounty on their heads, either.

Mickey Trackies had been a shock to Shane; he'd sparred, debt collected, and even shared threesomes with the man over the years, and Mickey was as close to a brother as Shane could ever have. And when he'd heard that some Tsang family wannabe had killed him, Shane had wanted revenge. He'd wanted to go into Chinatown and take down as many of those chopstick-kissing bastards as he could, before they took him down.

But he didn't, because he was a soldier. And his orders were yet to arrive, as his general was in custody.

No. His general was dead.

This was the problem that many of the people here had right now; *who sent the message telling them to be here?* It had to be someone who had access to Johnny's contact list; it had to be someone high in the organisation. But, although Johnny had several lieutenants, many of those were here too, just as confused with the situation as he was.

Everything that had happened over the last forty-eight hours was confusing. Nobody understood why Johnny had done this, nobody could work out if it had been *Jackie* instead, and everyone was concerned that one of the Seven Sisters wide boys had been by his side, when it should have been one of them.

'This is stupid,' Ramsey Allen, standing close by, muttered. 'I should be in bed.'

'We all should,' Shane replied, nodding. He knew Ramsey in passing, and was surprised to see him there. Although Johnny used a lot of freelancers, so perhaps Ramsey came into this through a window rather than a door; the way he was more used to entering, so the legends about the thief said. There was a creak of a door opening, and the murmurs and conversations stopped as a shadowed figure walked into the club. It was now half-past eight, and nobody else had arrived for at least twenty minutes, everyone now in fear of being seen as tardy on such an auspicious day.

After a moment the figure moved into the light, no longer back-lit from the doorway, and there was a slow groan from the attendees, as many of the street thugs and soldiers of the firm recognised the smug, smiling form of Maurice Hamilton.

'You're in the wrong place,' someone shouted. 'The Krays disappeared half a century back.'

'Yeah, piss off and write another tell-all book,' another called out.

Others shouted out now, with insults like *grass* and *snitch* and worse, echoing around the boxing club. Maurice, to his credit, ignored these jibes, walking through the crowd and, after checking the ropes in front of him for dried blood, used them to pull himself onto the boxing ring apron, crouching though the ropes and walking to the middle.

'Ladies and gentlemen!' he cried out, and the audience, realising that for Maurice to enter the ring meant something more than just an old man, desperate for a shot at the big time turning up to watch from the back, quietened down as he finished. '*Let's get ready to rumble!*'

After a moment, he coughed, laughing.

'Michael Buffer, legend,' he said, looking around. 'Come on, none of you have wanted to do that? Be serious.'

'What do you want, Hamilton?' a voice called out.

'This ain't the time for jokes,' another, more angry voice shouted. Maurice raised his hands, lowering them, motioning for silence. Shane looked at Ramsey, surprised that he had shouted nothing, considering his history with Hamilton, but was surprised to see he'd disappeared, moving to the back of the crowd.

What does Allen know we don't?

'I knew Johnny Lucas when he was a kid,' Maurice started now. 'I knew the whole family. So believe me when I say I have more right to be here than most of you.'

There was a low grumble at this; Hamilton may have been a grade A pain in the behind, but he wasn't lying.

'But I didn't turn up to mourn the past,' Maurice straightened up in the ring. 'I'm here to demand vengeance. Old school, bloody vengeance.'

'We on about that bloody film again?' Shane called out now; it was well known that Maurice had an unhealthy fixation with *The Long Good Friday*. 'We gonna dress like Bob Hoskins and get our *shooters* out?'

There was a murmur of laughter at this, and Maurice looked over at Shane. However, the expected glare was missing, and Maurice Hamilton simply smiled.

Shane had a sudden feeling that he'd just made Maurice's job, whatever it was, easier.

'I do love that film,' Maurice nodded. 'And I'm sure I've bored nearly all of you with my stories about the filming. But the reason it's such a good film is because it's timeless.'

He paced around the ring now, warming up.

'Take Bob Hoskins, or rather *Harold Shand*. He's a straight up gangster, who's had a simple life for ten years, and is trying to go legit, making big land deals and believing his own press. Sound familiar?'

There was another grumble as an answer, and Maurice continued.

'And then it all goes to shit, as his crew starts getting killed, and his businesses get destroyed. And Harold, poor stuck-in-the-past Harold, can't work out what's going on. It's a different type of war, one he hasn't fought in years. He's past his prime. He can't keep up to his IRA enemy, and more importantly the nameless killer played by Pierce Brosnan, in his second ever film role, by the way, who took his organisation apart, piece by piece. Again, sound familiar?'

There was no murmuring or grumbling this time. People were starting to wonder whether Hamilton had a point here. The ferocity of the attacks on Johnny and Mickey Trackies was hefty, and several small businesses had also been attacked by soldiers of the Triads over the last couple of days, ever since Johnny, or Jackie, or whomever it had been started torching casinos and killing heirs.

Maurice stopped walking now, fixing the onlookers with a piercing gaze.

'You're in a war,' he breathed. 'And the Sisters and Simpson are watching from the side, waiting like vultures to pick at the corpses. Johnny's been dead hours—'

'You watch what you say about Mister Lucas!' An elderly man with mutton chop sideburns warned loudly, but Maurice simply nodded, holding a hand up to pause his heckler.

'Johnny's been dead hours, and the gangs are already preparing to strike at you, seeing you as weak, leaderless.'

'We *are* leaderless,' mutton chop replied. 'With no Lucas to lead us—'

'And there you go,' Maurice smiled, holding up his hands. '*No Lucas to lead us*. You may wonder why I'm here, so let me explain. When you get an autograph, maybe a footballer signed a shirt and you've bought it, or maybe you have a signed movie poster, you need someone to authenticate it. Someone who has respect, who knows their subject matter. Someone whose word people trust.'

'And we're supposed to trust you?' Shane couldn't help himself.

'Personally, darling, I don't give a shit what you think of me,' Maurice sniffed. 'But you *will* give me the respect I deserve. And, when I tell you that in my opinion someone is what they say they are, you *believe me*.'

'So what,' Shane was belligerent now. *He'd managed three hours' sleep for this? Bollocks to that.* 'You're gonna lead us now, are you? Finally step up and be the Kray you always dreamed about?'

'Wet dream, most likely,' someone muttered in the crowd, and there was a low wave of laughter.

Maurice waited for it to die down before replying.

'No,' he said. 'But *she* is.'

As he spoke this, he pointed at the doors of the club. There, standing in the shadows and now finally emerging, was a tall, thin, white-haired woman in her late sixties or seventies. A woman everyone there recognised.

'Taborsky?' someone hissed. 'We work for the Seven Sisters now?'

Anita Taborsky climbed into the ring as Maurice spun back around now, catching the speaker with a steely eye.

'No,' he replied. 'Anita *Lucas*. The last surviving family member, and elder sister of Johnny and Jackie. A woman who for decades has made alliances with the north, allies that can help you take back your pride, avenge your fallen friends... and *leaders*.'

He let the last line hang for a moment.

'After all, when you look at yourself in the mirror, do you see yourselves as Bob Hoskins, the old, forgotten gangster—or as Pierce Brosnan? The future, created from fiery vengeance?'

With this said, Maurice stepped back, nodding at Anita, who now moved forward, facing the crowd.

'My brother is dead,' she said, simply. 'And yes, I went to the Sisters many years ago. Some of you even remember why, but those days are long gone. And over the last couple of years we'd even reconnected, started working together.'

There was a muttering to this statement; denial, disbelief, even confusion. Anita had expected this, however, and continued, pulling out an ivory handled black gun.

'Recognise this?' she asked. 'Of course you do. I bought it for Johnny, and he gave it back to me. A gesture of friendship, or reconnection.'

It was a lie, but Anita didn't care as she carried on.

'But over the last few weeks, things got worse. Johnny, as Jackie went off the rails, and in the last few days did terrible things—' here she waved a hand around the ring, '—to our rivals. And the Sisters, led by the now blind Mama Delcourt, made deals with the Tsangs.'

Now the background noise shifted; the Tsangs and their

kind were an enemy the men and women in the room understood.

'Yesterday, several East End business were attacked, in retaliation for what Jackie did, but Jackie's original acts were based on information he'd received from Mama Delcourt, information I now know was given purely to start a war between east and west, with the north and south profiting.'

Anita smiled. The noise levels were rising as the anger took hold.

'Mama Delcourt is laughing at us,' she said. 'We all know she grassed up Danny Martin when she blinded herself. She sold him for her freedom, one of you, and he's in Belmarsh because of her.'

She waved a hand around the club.

'You're all tired, I get that. We work the darkness. But so do they, and while you're here, angry and looking for a fight? They've just gone to bed. They're not expecting a war. And later, they'll not be expecting our attack. They're easy to take down, especially with me showing you their weaknesses. I have many who'd side with me over Delcourt, and when we ally, we can take down the Tsangs as well!'

Now there were cheers emerging from the crowd. Anita nodded, as if understanding the anger.

'And one last thing,' she said, holding a hand for silence. 'Mama Delcourt, Kenneth Tsang, these are the cowards who put the hit out on Johnny. Who couldn't face him one on one. So, who wants to help me *put a hit out on them?*'

There was a roar of noise in the boxing club, but this time, it wasn't one of confusion or mistrust.

Now, it was full-throated approval.

And, in the ring, Anita Taborsky—no, Anita *Lucas* drank it all in.

'You intend to go with them?' Maurice asked softly as he smiled for the audience.

'God, no,' Anita smiled back, more a gritting of teeth, if you looked closely. 'I want to meet the man behind the curtain. You're the CEO of *Shand Enterprises*; arrange an emergency board meeting. I think it's time for a takeover.'

24

UP TO SPEED

It had surprised Doctor Marcos that Rajesh Khanna hadn't taken the body of Johnny Lucas down to the Mile End Command Unit morgue, but when she considered it, she realised it was actually a stroke of genius. Lucas was a known Mile End face, and with the Unit now under scrutiny for letting it happen under their own noses, Khanna taking the body to an external location, and a location where the press couldn't get to, was a far better idea.

Parking her car on the junction of Pratt Walk and Lambeth Road, Doctor Marcos climbed out of her Mercedes and stared across the street at the four-storey brown brick and glass building on the corner. Although housing the *Metropolitan Police Central Communications Command Centre,* it was also the home of the *Metropolitan Police Forensic Science Laboratory*, where somewhere, deep inside, Rajesh Khanna was poking around inside Johnny Lucas' body.

That wasn't fair, she thought to herself. *She wanted to be the one that poked around inside Johnny Lucas.*

It was a Brutalist style police complex with external

concrete staircases, brick infill and a large concrete ventilation shaft that protruded out on the street corner, and Doctor Marcos, although familiar with both the inside and the outside of the building was not a fan of it. The last time she'd even been here, in fact, was during the time Declan was on the run for terrorist charges; while this was happening, Doctor Marcos had taken Monroe, badly injured and suffering a major head wound, out of the hospital before military contractors arrived to kill him. And, while he hid in the Globe Town boxing club of all places, she had come here to gain intelligence on a potential murder weapon that would clear Declan and uncover a conspiracy.

That she relied on the good grace of Johnny Lucas back then, and now returned to see his body, was not wasted on her.

The last time she'd been here, she'd also been barred from entering because of a six-month suspension handed to her after the Tancredi case, and had to discuss the findings in a police-friendly café next door. She'd been released from that exile by D Supt Bullman a few months earlier, and it was with her head held high that she entered the reception, scanned her ID, explained why she was there and was then directed to the basement, where Rajesh was known to haunt when he wasn't at Mile End.

Rajesh Khanna was there, but the body wasn't.

'Rosanna,' it surprised him to see Doctor Marcos as she entered. 'I wish you'd called ahead. I could have waited with the autopsy.'

'It's done already?' Doctor Marcos was confused by this. 'Findings?'

'Suicide,' Khanna walked over to his phone, tapping on it as he picked it up, reading from it. There was a faint *whoosh* noise from it as he did so. 'He tore up his bed sheet and knotted it, tied it around his throat, the other end to the bracket in the corner, and hanged himself.'

Doctor Marcos nodded calmly at the diagnosis. 'So nobody *assisted* him with his expiration?'

'Unlikely,' Khanna shrugged. 'But then we all know that Mile End has had a few rotten apples over the years. DCI Ford, DC Hart, they're just the ones we know.'

'True, the ones we know,' Doctor Marcos replied, angling around, so she was no longer with her back against the wall. 'What are you hiding, Raj?'

'I don't know what you mean.'

'I mean, you're being very evasive, and I've also heard that you've been helping Ellie Reckless, who's very high on my shit list right now,' Doctor Marcos continued. 'And, who seems to have been working for Johnny Lucas, has happily killed before, and could easily do with two million dollars hit money. Was that who you just texted? To tell her I've turned up?'

'You think I'm dirty?' Khanna's face purpled at the accusation. 'I was the only clean one in Mile End at one point! What about *you?*'

'What about me?'

'Tancredi case. I know you got suspended for playing tea party with dead gangsters. Really handy that.'

'What's that supposed to mean?'

'I mean, I saw the report, Rosanna,' Khanna hissed. 'I know why you were *really* suspended. Which Tsang you were *sleeping with*.'

Doctor Marcos stopped moving, her mouth opening and shutting.

'I thought to myself, why would Rosanna Marcos not

want to get her hands on this juicy murder scene,' Khanna continued. 'Why would she prefer to go investigate blood and piss in White City? And then I realised. You didn't want to have to tell Kenneth what happened to his nephew, because it meant seeing him again.'

'Kenny Tsang was a long time ago,' Doctor Marcos snapped. 'Where's the body, Doctor Khanna?'

'Where nobody will find it,' a voice spoke; a male voice. Doctor Marcos spun around to see DCI Esposito, a yellow police issue taser in his hand. 'Johnny's dead, and that's all you need to know.'

'Oh bloody hell,' Doctor Marcos shook her head. 'You went for the bounty, didn't you? So what, you kill Lucas, Get a thorn out of your hair and provide for your pension? This won't stay secret!'

'It doesn't have to,' Esposito nodded. 'But it's not what you think. We're ending a war.'

'By killing Johnny?' Doctor Marcos was pacing now. 'Someone else will just replace him! They're probably discussing that now!'

'It's Anita Taborsky,' Esposito explained, the taser still aimed. 'She's the last Lucas. She's set everything up, but you already know that. We need to end it.'

'And by killing Johnny Lucas, you do this?' Doctor Marcos shook her head, glancing from Esposito to Khanna. 'Please, I beg you. Explain to me how this works.'

Nodding, and lowering the taser, Esposito did so.

MONROE STOOD BESIDE THE PLASMA SCREEN AS HE LOOKED AT his currently reduced team; DC Davey stood at the back, waiting to be called, Cooper and De'Geer were by the window, and Billy sat beside the laptop, already connecting it to the plasma screen. Declan sat on the other side with Anjli and Jess, and by the door Bullman loomed menacingly at her usual haunt, half visible in the doorway. The only person missing was Doctor Marcos; after the morning's news had hit, she'd left to help Doctor Khanna, and had promised an update as soon as she had one. Currently, she wasn't answering her phone or replying to messages, which both Monroe and Davey agreed was *usual behaviour, when elbows deep in a body.*

'Tell me about Johnny Lucas,' Bullman said from the doorway.

'Found hanged, shortly before he was due to be released,' Monroe said, and Declan could see the tightness in his face; whether it was sadness, anger or disbelief, he didn't know. 'CCTV was cut, and the station was almost empty for the time of night. Someone came in, hanged Johnny and left.'

'Or he hanged himself,' Declan added. 'Just playing Devil's advocate, Guv. Maybe something was about to come out? Until we get the results back, everything's speculation.'

'Who was on security?' Davey asked. 'Surely they would have seen the feeds go down?'

'Apparently they did,' Billy looked up from his laptop now. 'They looked into it while DS McAlroy went down to check on Lucas in the cell. She was the one who found the body.'

'There's a two million dollar hit on this man that's about to be paid,' Monroe snarled. 'If he was killed, someone's gonna be looking to cash in. I want everyone involved watched like a hawk. If someone even thinks of buying a jet-ski or an expensive holiday, I want to know.'

He slammed his fist onto the desk beside him.

'With Johnny dead, we now can't confirm whether he was or wasn't Jackie. The CCTV shows fixed footage, but that doesn't mean he *didn't* go along with his two buddies to *Tsang City*. We have no fingerprints, no DNA, just a dodgy, photo-shopped image in a frame and a ton of badly filmed phone footage. And if we go on the current belief that someone impersonated Jackie, then we have to assume that Mickey Trackies was also taken in by him as easy as Maurice Hamilton was. But, on the subject of our dear, departed, track-suited friend, do we have anything else from him?'

'Shot twice in the head, face first,' Davey read from her notes. 'Nine millimetre, likely from a Glock 17, and there's a million of those in London, boss.'

'Reports from witnesses there say the killer walked up behind Mickey, waited until he turned, fired twice with his left hand and escaped in a waiting car,' De'Geer read from his own notes now. 'Car was found in Bow, discarded. A couple of witnesses, having a smoke outside the Blind Beggar, believed they saw Mickey recognise his killer, said he relaxed when he realised who was behind him.'

'That'd be nice,' Monroe mused. 'Would mean his last moments on this earth weren't surprise and fear. Do we know where he was staying?'

'Knocking shop in Stepney,' Billy replied. 'Central surveillance office backtracked him there using CCTV street cameras. Apparently it's a known haunt for Lucas' men, and his room had a bloodied tracksuit and vest, a machete and an envelope with just shy of ten grand in fifty-pound notes still in it.'

Monroe whistled.

'Good money for a night's work,' he said. 'And the blood

makes me believe that our Michael there was in the club when the body was, well—'

'Filleted?' Davey suggested.

'Well, I for one won't be eating fish again for a while,' Monroe sighed. 'Okay, let's discuss the body. We know it's not Jeffrey, so is it Benny?'

'Yes, boss,' Davey replied. 'It took a while, as Benjamin Tsang took great care to make sure his identity was untraceable. Probably because he was usually on the other side of the knife. We went through a dozen databases trying to link the blood, dental records, anything. Eventually found a report, forgotten from the late nineties. Benny has his teeth caved in by a baseball bat in some scrum in Chinatown, had three implants put in. Kept it off the books, but the dentist in question was a confidential informer for vice, and passed them the serial numbers of the fake teeth. One of Billy's searches popped a link, and they confirmed the tooth in the body. Definitely Benny. Also, there was no blood in the boot of Johnny's SUV.'

'So Benny wasn't taken in it?'

Davey moved through her notebook now, flipping the pages as she searched for something specific.

'No, sir. We think Benny was brought by other means. And another thing; once we started looking deeper, we realised that the blood in the club was older than we thought. There was a lot, but some of it was over twelve hours old. Which meant it had to have bled onto the ring—'

'Before ten pm,' Monroe nodded. 'So what, Benny was tied up and murdered before the attack on Jeffrey?'

'Probably,' Davey nodded. 'We checked with Mile End, and apparently apart from Johnny, only Mickey Trackies had keys to the place, and as it was Johnny's date night, they closed early.'

'Mickey Trackies closes at six, maybe seven.' Anjli worked through the timings. 'Johnny goes out the front door, Mickey opens the back door, they bring in Benny—Christ, Jeffrey could have done that to his uncle himself, before heading off to his club.'

'Makes sense,' Billy leaned back in his chair as he looked at the others. 'They could then take hours on him.'

Monroe *hmmed* to himself as he stared at the screen, now showing the aftermath of the boxing ring on it.

'Official story is they take Jeffrey, go to the club, and then at midnight the jogger, who we now know was Ellie Reckless, calls the cops. That's an hour tops.'

'They took longer on him,' Davey nodded. 'The draining of the blood alone would have taken that. I'd say they started around seven, and then left the—the *remains* to drain out around nine-thirty.'

'Just in time for Jeffrey to change, meet up with his friends at the club, and be 'abducted',' Bullman growled. 'Gives him a great alibi, removes a thorn in his side and starts a war.'

'One which he can return to later, and be seen as the hero avenging his family,' Monroe looked away from the screen. 'It also explains how Jackie Lucas can appear on Oxford Street around the same time. So now we have Jeffrey Tsang, Mickey Trackies, Kayas Ashad and this mysterious Jackie working together. What do we know about that?'

'Either the Jackie imposter or Jeffrey funded this,' Declan pursed his lips as he spoke. 'I can't see Kayas having ten grand to pass out. Unless the Sisters paid him.'

'Okay, so let's talk about the Jackie imposter,' Bullman

said. 'What do we know? And how does pretty boy's secret rendezvous last night help?'

'It wasn't a secret rendezvous, it was a dinner,' Billy muttered, reddening as everyone looked at him. 'He—Andrade—was a nice man. A believable man. He was giving this information because he thought, that is his superiors thought, that by helping us, we'd put a favourable word in with Baker.'

'And I hope you put that idea straight out of their heads,' Monroe growled. 'Charles Baker is no friend of this unit.'

'True, but if we're going to get help because of him, I'm all for that,' Declan smiled. 'And Billy gets his first proper date in months.'

'He has a fair point,' Billy deadpanned. 'But if what they say is true, then Jackie Lucas died. And this new one is either a bloody good impersonator with a solid family resemblance, or...'

'Or Johnny Lucas played us all,' Monroe interrupted. 'And now the bloody fool's dead, we might never know if he left or not.'

'The only one who can truly tell us that is Cheryl Jenkins, Guv,' De'Geer spoke, almost too softly to be heard. 'And she's in the wind.'

'Ah yes, and now we get to the fun part,' Monroe grinned. 'Our own Viking warrior attacking two internationally wanted Chinese hitmen with a boathook in the middle of a London street.'

'It was the first thing I had to hand,' De'Geer stared down at his feet as everyone looked at him. Declan noted, however, that Davey was watching De'Geer with a little more than curiosity. There was definitely some admiration going on there.

'What do we have on them?' De'Geer asked, deflecting the attention.

'Wen Xinyu and Li Xiaoyu, both from Hong Kong, both work for the Wo Shing Wo, both have connections with the Tsangs,' Bullman spoke now, moving into the briefing room. 'They claim they were hunting the bounty, decided to use Johnny's girlfriend as bait, but Special Branch has been on their case for a while now, and they were seen heading to Canary Wharf from Chinatown.'

'So basically, Kenny Tsang sent them,' Monroe replied. 'Makes sense. He believed at the time that Johnny, as Jackie, was starting a war.'

'Was he?' Declan interrupted. 'He spoke of Benny in the past tense, and Jeffrey in the present when we saw him, and this was at the same time De'Geer faced off the killers. He might not have killed his brother, but he already suspected his nephew was involved, I'm sure of it.'

'Aye, this was a murder to make a point, or to hold her ransom until we freed Johnny from jail and he came in on his own accord,' Monroe acknowledged. 'Luckily for us, she'd already made sure nobody could find her.'

'She'd been staying in several of the apartments, according to security,' Cooper spoke now. 'She'd been let go because of it, but had made copies of the key cards that got her back in. And the owner of the apartment she'd used with Johnny Lucas had been away for a month, and didn't want to press charges.'

'That's because the owner of the apartment wasn't the guy who lived in it,' Monroe muttered. 'The guy who owns it is Nicky Simpson.'

'Who hired her,' Billy added.

'*What?*' Most of the briefing room spoke as one as Billy

tapped on the laptop, and on the plasma screen, a list of names appeared. Third from the top was NICHOLAS SIMPSON.

'He's on the residents' committee, was one of the building investors, and they have final say on all hiring. He would at least have seen her name and photo.'

'Does he have a lot of properties around there?' Monroe asked.

'I can look,' Billy replied.

'Look for any near Rotherhithe Street,' Monroe suggested. 'The address was too specific to be random. She might be in the area.'

Billy started working through lists as Monroe glanced back at Declan.

'Right, laddie,' he smiled. 'Tell the class about your night time antics with blind people.'

'Janelle Delcourt came to me last night, mainly because she knew I wasn't dirty,' Declan said. 'Seems that nicking her son proved this. She's been a confidential informant for Special Branch for a few months now, and is trying to get out of the game, if only to keep her daughter, Molly, safe. Said that her right-hand woman, Anita Taborsky, was pushing to take over, and that Anita's maiden name was Lucas.'

Declan hadn't mentioned this before, and the second unified intake of breath from the others in the room in as many minutes was quite audible.

'Sister?' Bullman, who hadn't heard this news yet, asked. 'Aunt?'

'Elder sister,' Declan replied. 'Left the family when her husband was killed by Jackie.'

'Hence joining the sisters,' Bullman nodded. 'Good motive too.'

'True, but it's been decades, Ma'am,' Billy stated. 'Surely she'd have made her move before now?'

'Mama Delcourt wasn't weak before now,' Monroe suggested, scratching his beard. 'Now she's a prime target for a takeover. Tell us about this nest egg.'

Declan nodded at Anjli, who pulled out her notebook.

'Twenty years ago, Johnny, Janelle, Max Simpson, Maurice and the Tsangs started a company, with Maurice as CEO,' she said. 'All investing in the Olympics. And, when that was done, they started on Crossrail. The money matures this week, and Janelle wants out. She thinks the fighting is because the new crowd is pissed the old guard has this nest-egg.'

'And violence always lowers postcode prices,' Monroe nodded. 'Any idea on where the company is, or who is—'

'I have that,' Billy looked up. 'That is, I think I have it. I have account details here for a *Shand Properties*. It's a shell company, no board members shown.'

'And you're sure it's connected?'

Billy smiled.

'Harold Shand was the lead character in *The Long Good Friday*,' he said. 'I'm guessing they allowed Maurice to pick the name. They have three or four properties listed in London. One's at 14 Acorn Walk, part of a gated community of apartments, most of which back onto Rotherhithe Street.'

'Which is across the road from the Blacksmiths Arms,' Cooper said as she glanced at De'Geer. 'Cheryl could have been watching us from the window.'

'If she was there, that means she's connected to Shand Properties,' Declan fidgeted in his seat as he worked through the possibilities. 'And if she was connected, then maybe that's why Nicky Simpson made sure she was in the apartment complex.'

'So now we have Nicky actively working against his father's wishes.'

'Could be a motive.'

'Right then,' Monroe nodded, checking his phone as it beeped. 'Mister Walsh, how do you feel about fitness?'

'Not a massive fan of it,' Declan admitted.

'Tough,' Monroe smiled. 'Go have a chat with Nicky Simpson. Take DS Kapoor and Jess.'

'Jess?' Declan raised an eyebrow at this.

'Aye, Jess,' Monroe looked at the individual in question. 'She knows all about this TikTok and YouTube bollocks. Might put him off his guard as you ask the questions.'

'And you, Guv?' Declan was already rising. Monroe waved his phone as if this was the answer.

'Doctor Marcos wants to meet,' he said. 'Claims she's found something I need to see personally. Billy—'

'Actually, I have a couple of leads I want to move on,' Billy replied. 'Is it okay if I ask Marcus Lightman to pop in for a chat?'

'As long as you're not selling the story of this Unit, go wild, my boy.'

'And the rest of us, boss?' De'Geer asked.

'Laddie? You're off to find a missing squatter, hunt down a ghost and stop a war,' Monroe smiled. 'So bring your boathook and your war paint, because you're going to bloody well need them.'

25

LET'S GET PHYSICAL

NICKY SIMPSON HAD SEVERAL HEALTH CLUBS SOUTH OF THE river, but only one where he had his YouTube studio; a three-storey building in the middle of the recently reinvigorated Battersea Power Station, one that alternated between health club, gym and hot-desk workspace, with the main offices for Nicky's empire on the top floor. There were even rumours of a private pool on the roof, according to Jess, but nobody had seen it.

Nicky also had a club near The Oval cricket ground, north of Camberwell, and it was believed that, as he'd built this on property he'd inherited from his grandfather, then this was his primary location for criminal activities. Because although Nicky Simpson was a YouTube sensation and darling of the over-sixties, he was also a third-generation *villain*. His grandfather, Paddy Simpson had taken over clubs and scams south of the Thames when the Richardsons were arrested in the late sixties, his father, Max, had replaced *him* during the turn of the millennium until an onset of Parkinsons had forced Max to retire, and now, young, hungry and looking to go legit, Nicky was the face of the future.

A face Declan hadn't wanted to meet.

The health club Declan had travelled to was in the new residential block in what was known as *Circus West Village*; this was a new world, a self-contained estate for the elite, with new high-class shops, restaurants and entertainment venues opening every day, with adverts for spin cycle classes and even military fitness classes with Bear Grylls being advertised on giant LED screens as they parked up outside the venue.

Inside, it looked more like an *Apple* store than a health club; the lobby was expansive and minimalistic, the café to the side looking modern and light, the walls an eggshell aspect against bright white, with bright orange and green chairs scattered around various square tables that looked to be made from Perspex or glass.

Declan recognised the logo on the wall moments before he recognised the café; this was definitely the place in the image.

The woman on the reception desk was dressed in sportswear; Declan assumed it was to keep branding on point, but with this and the muscled personal trainers walking around, mingling with the tanned, rich toned elite, Declan couldn't help but feel podgy and overweight. He'd played rugby while in the forces and had even kept on afterwards, but the workload added to the stress of having a child had—

Come on Declan. Your love for pork pies and sausage rolls did this.

A beep of a phone brought him back; Jess had a text.

'Everything okay?'

'Not sure,' Jess said as she read the message. It from a

number she didn't recognise.

J it's Molly I need your help

A moment later, a second one appeared

Mum's losing it. News about JL in the news. Anita missing. Worried she gonna do bad thing

Worried Anita is about to make a play. If she takes out mum she takes me out too

She showed Declan and Anjli.

'Looks like it's going down today,' she said, typing a quick reply.

I can bring dad, we can help you.

'She'll say no,' Declan looked around the health club once more as he spoke. 'I'm a man.'

'Probably, but what options do we have?' Jess replied, as her phone buzzed with another message.

No men coppers sisters are stressing out

'Tell her you'll bring me,' Anjli suggested. 'She saw me, she might trust me. And we can go directly after this.'

Nodding, Jess dutifully typed in the message.

I'll bring Anjli. You met her last night. Can you hold out an hour?

Sure thing

Thanks

'Can I help you?' the receptionist, noting the three unknown visitors, none of whom looked either rich or ready for a fitness session, asked, a plastered, obviously fake smile on her face.

As Jess put her phone away, Declan and Anjli both pulled their warrant cards out, showing them.

'Need to speak to your manager,' Declan growled, deciding that he wanted to be out of here as quickly as possible, and if this included making them help him just to get him out, he was happy with that. 'Now.'

'Logan's with a client.'

'Fine, we'll wait,' Anjli nodded at the café. 'I'm guessing we can wait over there?'

'I'd prefer you didn't,' the receptionist once more evaluated Declan with a piercing glare before looking back at Anjli. 'Maybe I can help?'

'We need to see your security footage from earlier this week,' Anjli replied.

'We don't record sessions,' the receptionist's smile was becoming irritating now. 'We do, however, have an app where—'

'What about those?' Declan pointed up at two small, unobtrusive Wi-Fi cameras in the café's corner. 'Can we see those?'

The receptionist pursed her lips, sucked through her teeth, and looked around before replying.

'Look, what's the problem?' she hissed. 'You shaking us down for a reduced membership or something?'

'The *problem* is we're investigating a murder, and you're standing in our way,' Anjli leant closer now, hands on the reception's surface. 'So how about you tell us who we can speak to about getting hold of that footage before we take a real close interest in everything here?'

'There's no need for that,' a male voice spoke, and Declan looked around to see a young man walking towards them, a wide, beaming smile on his face. He was muscled and lean, wearing *Simpson Health Clubs* branded jogging bottoms and sweatshirt, the logo visible on both, his wild dark hair roughly pulled back into a small ponytail, the shortest strands escaping, framing his shaven, tanned, smiling face.

'Nicky Simpson,' Jess whispered, so Declan knew who he was looking at; however, when he glanced at her, he realised she'd just breathed the name in awe and shock.

'Mister Simpson,' Declan started. 'I'm—'

'I know who you are, Declan,' Nicky smiled. 'And you, Anjli. We all watch the news. You're quite the detective celebrities out there. Saved the Queen, cleared your name while on the run, stuff of legends.'

He turned his dazzling white smile onto Anjli now.

'Eden Storm's an *Every Club* member,' he said. 'He speaks very highly of you.'

'Really? He never mentioned your name once,' Anjli snapped back, obviously embarrassed by the mention of her kind-of ex. Declan wanted to comment too; Nicky's casual mention of their first names rather than official titles was obviously a power move, but instead he held it, to bank the slight in his memory for later usage.

'Look, what can I do for you?' Nicky asked, stopping beside the receptionist now, placing a protective arm around her. Declan couldn't help but note the slight stroke of his index finger on her bare shoulder, and wondered whether or not this was consensual.

'We believe that Janelle Delcourt, best known as—'

'Yeah, I know who Mama Delcourt is,' Nicky waved Declan quiet. 'Sorry to interrupt, but you obviously know my past. I might be a legit and legal entrepreneur, but my family wasn't, and I spent a lot of years in that world. Still get information on it. I know the Johnny Lucas people, the Seven Sisters, the Triads—half of them even have memberships. So what did Mama Delcourt do this time?'

'From the looks of things, met with Jackie Lucas in your café,' Declan showed the photo.

Nicky looked at it, grinning as he did so.

'Is this evidence in a crime?' he asked, the slightest upturn on his lips as he asked. 'Feels weird being the other side of it for a change.'

He pointed over at a chair against a table in the middle of the café.

'Mama Delcourt was over there,' he said. 'And yes, she was with Mister Lucas.'

'You remember much from the day?'

'A little.'

'Do you remember if Molly Delcourt was there?'

Nicky shook his head.

'She went off into the shops,' he indicated out of the main windows to the club. 'Poor girl doesn't get many options to shop, you see. I think she asked her driver to keep an eye on them.'

'Them being...?' Anjli asked.

'Jackie and Mama Delcourt.'

'Do you remember who the driver was?' Declan forced a smile in an attempt to disarm Nicky slightly. 'It could help. Was his name Barry, perhaps?'

'No, I remember exactly,' Nicky nodded. 'It was that

ponce, Hamilton.'

'Maurice Hamilton?'

'Oh, you've had the joy of meeting him too?' Nicky chuckled. 'Creepy bastard spent most of the time ogling the reception staff.'

Declan glanced at Jess; she was writing notes down dutifully, and he wondered whether she'd picked up that Molly must have taken the photo before leaving for a shopping trip, which meant she wasn't watching her mum's back as she'd promised.

Looking back at Nicky, he put on his best *official* face.

'I was wondering if you had any CCTV of the day in question?' he asked, his tone giving the impression this wasn't a request that could be refused.

'It was a week or so back, and nothing bad happened in here, so no,' Nicky shook his head. 'We have a two day, or forty-eight hour turnaround on footage. A lot of places do. If we pick up something? We save the file. If nothing happens? We delete it.'

'Convenient,' Anjli muttered to herself.

'I'm sorry, is there a crime committed here, apart from terrible hairstyles?' Nicky smiled. 'Looks to me like two friends out for a coffee. We get a lot of these.'

He stopped, frowning.

'Although, with Mama Delcourt being blind, I do hope she knew she was conversing with a known criminal.'

'Do your members *know* they share space with criminals?' Anjli asked. At this, Nicky burst into laughter.

'Half the members live upstairs in the Power Station, in stupidly expensive million-pound apartments,' he said. 'They're the daughters of oligarchs and hedge fund owners. MPs with multiple income streams and Saudi princesses with gold cards and a love of spandex. The question should rather be, *do our criminals know they share my clubs with civilians?*'

'Civilians,' Declan noted. 'That's a very militaristic way of looking at people.'

'We have a military boot camp next door,' Nicky shrugged. 'Must have picked up the terminology by osmosis.'

Declan smiled back at Nicky, but again, his was humourless.

'So there's nothing you can do to help us with this meeting?'

'No, apart from saying I came and said hello briefly. They both had dealings with my dad, and I was always taught that manners maketh man and all that.'

'These dealings,' Declan continued, digging. 'They involve Shand Properties?'

'That's my dad you need to be speaking to,' Nicky smiled. 'And he's not really well enough to talk these days.'

'So, you have no interest?'

'Of course I do,' Nicky snapped, and for a moment the facade dropped. 'But what my father did won't direct what I do. I have my own plans. And besides, that all ends today.'

'Why so?' Anjli looked at Declan, concerned. 'What happens today?'

'Twelfth of August,' Nicky's smile had returned, and he seemed to relax as he spoke. 'Board members meeting. The company's likely to be dissolved, anyway.'

'You don't think new members might want to join?' Anjli leant closer. 'Jeffery Tsang, Anita Taborsky perhaps?'

'Now we're in the realm of ghosts and witches, and I think we're done here,' the conversation ended, Nicky Simpson rummaged in the reception drawer and pulled out two plastic cards.

'Here,' he said, passing one each to Declan and Anjli. 'Have a free month's membership on me. Over eighteens only.'

He glanced at Jess.

Sorry, he mouthed with a grin. And then, having finished the conversation, Nicky Simpson nodded twice and turned to leave.

'One other thing,' Declan said, stopping him. 'You ever heard the name Cheryl Jenkins?'

Nicky returned his gaze to Declan, a faint smile plastered on.

'Should I?'

'She was living in one of your apartments,' Declan replied. 'She took Johnny Lucas to it the night he allegedly kidnapped Jeffrey Tsang.'

'She was squatting,' Nicky snapped back. 'That apartment was a corporate one.'

'Oh, so you have heard of her then,' Declan's face broke into a triumphant smile.

'Not her name, but I knew there was an intruder,' Nicky kept his smile, but his eyes held murderous intent. 'Now, if you'll excuse me?'

No longer even trying to pretend he was happy Declan and the others were still there, Nicky Simpson stormed off, leaving the receptionist alone once more. She glanced at the cards in Declan and Anjli's hands.

'So, shall I validate those for you?' she asked.

Leaving the club, Declan wanted to slam a fist against the wall in frustration, but he didn't want to give Simpson the pleasure of knowing he'd got to him.

'We'll find another way,' Anjli said, looking around. 'As he said, there's a ton of stupidly rich people here. And one thing they like is security.'

She pointed up around the shops and cafes that surrounded them.

'I count at least five different cameras,' she said, already taking photos of the buildings with them on. 'Nicky Simpson may have taken the footage from inside and shredded it, but maybe someone here gives us something, anything we can use.'

Declan nodded, turning in a slow circle as he looked around, and Jess jumped as her phone buzzed with a new message. Pulling it out, she paled as she read it.

Men arrived. Took mum by force. Hiding. Come quick. No police until I know what's happening.

'Um, guys?' Jess said, showing the text. 'Someone's making a move on the Delcourts, by the look of things.'

'I'll call Farrow,' Declan said. 'He's nearby—'

'No, she said no police, dad.'

'But—'

'I'll go with her,' Anjli replied. 'Look, she mentioned me earlier in the texts, and Molly was okay with it. Molly's talking past tense, so they've been and gone. If I find any problems, I'll call. And DCI Farrow's Unit isn't more than five minutes away.'

Declan considered this.

'Okay,' he said. 'Take the car, use the flashing lights and break every road law you need to. I'll get the train to the office. But keep me updated.'

Nodding, Anjli grabbed the car keys from Declan and, with Jess beside her, ran off towards the car park.

Sighing, Declan started towards the main road, the recently opened *Battersea Power Station* tube station a five-minute walk away. On a spur of the Northern Line, he could at least reach Embankment, and from there change to a Circle Line to Temple. Judging from the traffic, he could even arrive at the office before Anjli and Jess reached Tottenham and the Seven Sisters.

Pulling out his phone, he texted Billy and Monroe.

Problems with Sisters. Jess and Anjli going to pick up Molly Delcourt. Back in 30. Billy, check all CCTV around here, look for M Delcourt arriving for meeting - NS a dead end.

Considering this, he added another line.

Also, check Shand for head office address - possible meeting today.

He'd barely put the phone away, though, when an unexpected message from Doctor Marcos arrived.

Hear you're near Vauxhall. Stay where you are. Am picking up Monroe and then coming to you.

Declan stopped, confused. Something was going on and he didn't know what it was.

And that always annoyed him.

26

HOME INVASION

Billy was grabbing a coffee when front desk informed him he had a visitor. Wandering back to his monitor station, he arrived just as a confused Marcus Lightman entered the office, led by one of the desk officers. At a wave from Billy, he walked over.

'I thought I was meeting Alex Monroe?' he looked around slowly, probably taking in every detail for some future piece.

'Sorry, no, it's me today,' Billy smiled. 'DC Fitzwarren. I work under DCI Monroe.' He waved to a chair. 'I just grabbed a coffee. I can get you one too, if you want? It's very good.'

'I'm fine,' Lightman shook his head, glancing at one of Billy's screens. On it, a series of words were flashing up at speed, as it seemed to work through three documents at once.

'What's that?' he asked. 'Sorry, professional curiosity.'

Billy shrugged the apology off. 'It's a word-based algorithm,' he explained. 'I've got all of Maurice Hamilton's books on PDF, and I'm now going through them, seeing how many times certain words turn up.'

'Far easier than reading that drivel,' Lightman smiled. 'Walter Mitty's an amateur fantasist compared to him.'

'So I hear,' Billy replied. 'Look, sorry to bring you in, but I was hoping you could help.'

'I already have one promise of a scoop from your boss,' Lightman rocked back in his chair, getting comfortable. 'What will I get from you?'

Billy considered this.

'A lighter sentence?' he suggested.

Lightman almost fell off the chair as he sat back up, reddening in indignation.

'Now, you listen here—' he started, but halted as Billy held up a hand.

'Let me tell you what I have so far,' he said. 'Maurice Hamilton has written eight books over the last thirty years. All of them 'tell-all' style novels, more fiction than fact, yet all with juicy gossip, and suggestions that the life of crime isn't that glamorous anymore.'

He pointed at the screen.

'Now, interestingly, going through this, I'm seeing mentions of Krays, Richardsons, Sisters, Twins, Triads, everyone. Everyone, that is, except for the Simpsons. Paddy, Max, Nicky, they're mentioned here and there, but significantly less than everyone else. Like he's deliberately shielding them.'

'Or he doesn't know them that well.'

Billy nodded.

'True,' he acknowledged. 'But then we have the articles, the interviews, the newspaper spreads. The fluff pieces his publishers sort out every time he releases a book. Samples from the novel in question, a story about his life of crime nobody's ever heard.'

'Commonplace marketing tactics.'

'Oh, I'm sure. But I also used this algorithm on that, Mister Lightman. And I learnt very quickly that three-quarters of the interviews out there? Were with you.'

Lightman shifted uneasily now.

'And?' he snapped. 'So what? I'm a journo. It's what we do.'

'I also noted that you did additional interviews with him over the years; interviews where there was no book to promote.'

'The papers need inches,' Lightman was very uncomfortable now. Billy, in turn, sat stock still, waiting. 'I do what I have to.'

'In these interviews, these other ones, you talk about every family, apart from the Simpsons. And, roughly a week after each one, there's usually some kind of financial deal involving the Sisters, the Twins, whoever, that goes sour. Every time, Mister Lightman, every time—the Simpsons swoop in and steal that deal.'

'You can't pin that on me!'

'True, you're just a journo, and you can't go against your paymasters,' Billy nodded, tapping a key on his keyboard. The middle monitor burst into life, showing a webpage browser, a Vox-Pop post on it.

'Like this one,' Billy said, watching Lightman swallow visibly. 'An excellent piece, well written, and finished at the last minute, moments before the six pm Pacific Time deadline. This was why you were in Helen of Troy's, right?'

'Yes.'

'When Jackie came in?'

'Yes.'

'And gave you the photo of Jeffrey Tsang's ring?'

'I keep saying it, but yes.'

'I spoke to the publishers of this website,' Billy steepled his fingers as he spoke. 'They said you had an extra day, that your piece came in early. They said you knew this. So, it seems strange that, knowing you weren't on a deadline, and that you finished work four hours earlier, you'd be sitting in Helen of Troy's, the moment Jackie Lucas walks in, looking for a sympathetic ear, one he knows will tell the story he wants?'

Marcus Lightman stared at the ground.

'How much did Maurice Hamilton pay you?'

'Three grand.'

'And you know who Jackie Lucas truly is?'

Lightman nodded, tears appearing in his eyes.

'I think you should tell me,' Billy said, leaning in, patting Lightman's knee. 'Before you get arrested as an accessory to murder.'

MONROE HAD ARRIVED AT ROSANNA MARCOS' HOUSE expecting to see her Mercedes already there; instead, there was a blue Ford Focus in the driveway.

Entering the house, using his key, Monroe didn't walk into the Living Room; instead, he tiptoed up to the bedroom, moving across to Rosanna's side table, sliding it out gently, and removing the Glock 19 pistol placed within. This now in his hand, he made his way carefully down the stairs, pushing open the door to the living room, and leaping in, gun already pointing at the intruder.

'*Get on the floor!*' he shouted.

'Come on, Alex, let's not be so dramatic,' Ellie Reckless

placed down the cup of tea she'd been drinking. 'I'm here for the same reasons as you.'

'I somehow doubt that,' Monroe waved the gun as he spoke, motioning for her to rise.

'Where's Rosanna Marcos?'

'Oh, do put down that gun,' Ellie was getting annoyed now. 'Unless you want to blind me with paint, like you did Mama Delcourt.'

She waited a moment as realisation crossed his face.

'Yes, she told me all about the simunition pistol she stole once, and how you'd try to bluff with it,' she said. 'Surely that should tell you she's okay?'

'Depends on how she said it,' Monroe hissed.

In response, Ellie looked out of the window, nodding at it.

'You can ask her yourself,' she said.

Monroe wasn't stupid; he wasn't going to fall for the it's behind you trick, so he backed to the wall, angling so he could check the door.

It opened, and Doctor Marcos walked into the room.

'As much as I appreciate the sentiment, put the bloody thing down before you ruin the carpet,' she said. 'I'm fine. I told her to meet us here.'

'Did you give her a key?' Monroe lowered the gun now.

'Come on, Alex,' Ellie grinned. 'When have I ever needed a key?'

'What's this about, Rosanna?' Monroe asked. 'Your message said it was life and death.'

'A bit of both, actually,' Doctor Marcos stepped aside as a police officer, his cap pulled down low, walked in.

'Allo, allo, allo,' he said, pulling off his cap to reveal a smiling Johnny Lucas. 'What's all this then?'

As Anjli and Jess pulled up outside the Brazilian café that fronted the main entrance to the Seven Sisters, Anjli frowned as she climbed out of the Audi.

'There's usually a guy there,' she said, pointing at a bookmaker to the side. 'He watches who goes in, makes sure the people upstairs know.'

Walking up to the door, Anjli noted the SORRY WE'RE CLOSED sign was still showing. Looking through the glass door, she could see no movement; no staff, no customers. It was past opening time, but the café was a graveyard.

With a slight push, Jess tried the door, and was surprised to find that it swung into the café.

'Well, that's not ominous,' Anjli considered as they made their way into the building, walking past the bar and through the back door, leading to the stairs that took them into the heart of Seven Sisters' territory.

Jess was trying the phone again.

'She's still going to voicemail,' she said.

'Probably turned it onto silent the moment she hid,' Anjli was now walking up the stairs, noting the metal door that usually barred the way was also left open. Jess nodded, typing in a text.

We're here. Where are you?

Entering the home of the Delcourts, it surprised Jess how opulent it was. The wallpaper was a deep red with gold accents, with mahogany furniture on a thick burgundy carpet. As they continued through, Jess saw a large oil painting on the wall; a portrait of Janelle Delcourt and a young man she didn't recognise.

'That's Moses, her son,' Anjli muttered as they walked past. 'Tried to take over, I'm stunned it's still up. Although I suppose a mother's love and all that.'

'Must have really bitten at Molly,' Jess replied. 'Imagine having to see that every day, proof your mum really does have a favourite child.'

Now they were walking through a side corridor, Anjli had brought out her extendable baton in one hand, and a yellow X75 taser, taken from the Audi in the other. Seeing this, Jess pulled out the one she'd been given by her father, clicking it open.

'Be careful with that thing. You break your wrist, I saw nothing,' Anjli said, opening the door—

And stopping.

'Turn around slowly,' she said to the white-haired man facing away from her, across the bedroom they entered, and behind the double bed between them. 'I'm serious. Turn—'

She halted, taking in a breath.

'A bloody dummy,' she continued, walking over to it, turning it around.

It was a male mannequin, wearing a black shirt and suit, a white bouffant wig on top. Attached to the face were pieces of latex, a fake chin, complete with a scar, a fake nose, and two fake eyebrows.

'Shit,' Anjli looked around. 'This is the Jackie Lucas that faced Jeffrey, that spoke in the pub, that met with Janelle. Here all along.'

'It's Anita Taborsky's room,' Jess was checking the side drawer. 'There's an old prescription paper in here with her name on. *Aripiprazole?*'

'Christ, that's an anti-psychotic,' Anjli walked over now. 'It's used in the treatment of schizophrenia and bipolar disorder.'

'Looks like Anita Taborsky is keeping with the Lucas family branding.'

Anjli looked at the mannequin.

'In more ways than one,' she said as she took some photos, sending them to Billy. As she did this, Jess' phone beeped with a new message.

In a hidey hole in my bedroom.

'Molly!' Jess walked out into the corridor, calling out. 'It's Jess! I'm here with Anjli! We're alone, there's no one else here!'

There was a faint clatter, and after a moment Molly, hugging herself and moving cautiously, appeared from a door down the corridor.

'You okay?' Jess asked as Molly, seeing them, rushed to her, grabbing Jess into a hug, sobbing uncontrollably.

'They took mum,' she sobbed. 'It was Anita. She brought men. I don't understand, I thought she was my friend.'

'I don't think Anita's been your friend for a while now,' Anjli showed the mannequin. 'Look familiar?'

Molly stared at it for a moment, frowning, before her eyes widened with the realisation of what she was looking at.

'The man mum met with?' she whispered.

'We'll discuss this later,' Anjli was reading a message that had just appeared on her phone, already leaving the room, leading Jess and Molly down the corridor and back towards the stairs. 'We need to get out of here. I know you don't want the police involved, but your mum's in danger.'

There was a noise from outside the window; Anjli looked out, and from the vantage above the shop that she had, she paled as she looked down.

'What is it?' Molly asked.

'Five cars, each with three or four men, armed with baseball bats, crowbars, or knives,' Anjli urged the two girls away from the wall. 'Coming in through the café.'

'That's not right,' Molly frowned. 'Nobody—'

She stopped as Anjli ran to the metal door and slammed it shut, pushing down a bar to hold it tight.

'We're trapped,' she said.

'There's an underground way out,' Molly, deciding not to continue whatever she was about to say, pulled at Jess' arm. 'It's down here.'

She smiled at Anjli's surprised expression.

'What,' she said. 'You think the Sisters spend all this money building a fortress and don't give themselves an emergency exit? Come on, it's this way.'

Running into a kitchen area, one the size of a small restaurant, Molly opened one of the three walk-in freezers, entering quickly. Following the teenager in, Anjli realised this freezer wasn't refrigerated at all; and, behind a shelving unit at the side was a door leading to a small alcove, where a spiral staircase led down.

'This is in a crawl space,' Molly explained as they made their way down the staircase. 'Takes us out to a tunnel, and that leads to an underground car park.'

Nodding, Anjli followed, hearing the crashes behind her as, on the first floor, the new arrivals were trying to break open the door. There hadn't been any keys left in the lock, so the bar was the only thing stopping them from entering; and from the sounds of the effort they were putting in to opening it, the bar wouldn't be holding for long.

Pulling out her phone, she realised there were no bars. Expecting this, she placed the phone back into her pocket, heading deeper underground, wondering how she was going to explain to Declan what she was doing with his daughter right now.

27

RE-SPAWN OF THE DEAD

'A LOT OF PEOPLE WANTED ME DEAD,' JOHNNY LUCAS EXPLAINED as he sat on the edge of the sofa. 'You already know about Shand Properties, I'm guessing.'

At a nod, he continued.

'It was a personal thing, you see? Me, Benny and Kenny, Janelle and Max. We knew we could keep the others in check. It was only gonna be for ten years, until the Olympics, but then we got greedy.'

'When did others find out?' Monroe asked.

'Couple of years back,' Johnny admitted. 'Danny Martin knew, and he probably told Moses. Would explain why he went for the throne a year back. And Jeffrey and Nicky both moved up, although Nicky was far easier to do so, with Max coming down with Parkinsons. Poor bastard sits at home and shakes all the time now.'

'But Nicky doesn't inherit the deal?'

'No,' Johnny shook his head. 'And you can only make changes once a year at the AGM. New members, releasing assets, all that.'

'The AGM is today,' Doctor Marcos explained. 'Exactly ten years from the end of the London Olympics.'

'So they need to put leverage on you, which makes a vicious gang war a week or two before the valuation a very interestingly timed battle,' Monroe stroked his beard. 'War starts, major players die or get arrested, Jeffrey, Nicky, maybe others buy in, and then magically end the war, allowing the prices to go back up.'

'Currently they think Benny and Johnny are dead,' Ellie now spoke. 'I-'

'Aye, you,' Monroe spun to face his onetime protégé. 'What do you think you're bloody doing, faking deaths and screwing around with a police investigation?'

'I was channelling my inner Alex Monroe,' Ellie spat back. 'We knew people were coming for him. We had someone on the inside, kind of. McAlroy knew me from Hendon, vouched for me and my plan to Esposito, and Khanna knew me from before. We knew that the only way to stop people trying to kill him was to kill him first.'

'She had the right idea, Alex,' Doctor Marcos replied soothingly. 'And this gave them plausible deniability. With Johnny not around anymore, the players could make their moves.'

'Like who?'

'Like my dear, darling sister,' Johnny replied icily. 'Who, a couple of hours ago, took over my empire with Maurice Hamilton at her side.'

'Is she the one who took Janelle from her home?' Monroe asked, and was pleasantly surprised to see all three others look confused. 'Aye, you've been out of the loop. Anjli and Jess have gone to pick the wee bairn up.'

'That's not right,' Johnny shook his head. 'They would have taken Molly too. They'd have wanted leverage.'

'Maybe they had a different leverage in mind?' Doctor Marcos replied.

BILLY FELT ANTSY. IT WASN'T THAT HE WAS ALONE, OR THAT HE felt like he wasn't providing any assistance, it was just that he felt there was still something, just out of reach, that, if it was clear, would explain everything.

But what that was, Billy had no idea.

He'd heard from De'Geer and Cooper; on arrival at 14 Acorn Court, they'd found signs of a struggle, but no Cheryl Jenkins. And all Lightman had given was that there was a change in power about to occur, with the new generation demanding what was theirs. The only new piece of information was recently downloaded footage from a CCTV camera in the Circus West Village, one that showed the entrance of Simpson's Health Clubs, but nothing more. And Billy had it speeding through at ten times speed, unsure of when the meeting was, apart from a three-day, seventy-two hour time frame.

This could take hours.

As it was, it didn't; using the date he already had, and guessing the rough time of day for the meeting based on the angle of the sun in the photo, Billy knew it was likely between eleven and twelve in the morning, and this was where he started. And, after twenty minutes, he stopped the scanning, returning a few seconds to once more watch a black car arrive, and Maurice Hamilton exit out of the driver's side. He walked to the back, opening the door, allowing Janelle to climb out, helping her stand as he closed the door.

So far, everything we knew, he thought to himself, watching as Molly emerged from the other side.

And then, as the passenger door opened, and a fourth person emerged, Billy hit pause.

Jackie Lucas had just left the car. He'd been in there the whole journey.

Molly had claimed she didn't know who this man was, but he'd been in the car with her. And, having seen the photos Anjli had just sent, he knew this was actually Anita Taborsky.

Taking the blind Janelle Delcourt to a health club owned by Nicky Simpson.

There was no way Molly didn't know this.

There was no way Molly wasn't part of this.

What had Anjli and Jess let themselves in for?

Dialling Anjli's number, Billy cursed as it went straight to voicemail. Calling De'Geer now, he was already rising, pulling on his jacket.

'It's a setup!' He shouted down the line as he ran down the stairs, already waving at a couple of uniforms from the front desk to join him. 'Get to the Seven Sisters right now!'

SHANE MCCARTHY HADN'T SIGNED UP FOR THIS, BUT HE HAD to admit, it felt good trampling around the Seven Sisters mansion, picking up the expensive, likely hard to replace items the bitches had gained over the years, and smashing them against the walls, taking out the hideous wallpaper at the same time.

A few of the more hardcore crew had gone into the kitchen; they knew someone was still here, as they had barred the door from the inside. And that meant someone they could grab and play with, torture, perhaps. Anita had promised them all the loyal members of the Seven Sisters had already joined their cause, while any found here still were nothing but traitors paid for by the Triad.

And anyone connected to the Triad was fair game.

There was a painting on the wall; Mama Delcourt and her son, Moses. Shane knew Moses Delcourt; he'd followed the trial when Danny Martin had been sent down. He didn't know how, but he knew Moses was involved somehow. Another reason to hate the Sisters and their kin.

Pulling the painting off the wall, he slammed it onto the long, boardroom table with a whoop, pulling out a vicious-looking hunting knife and stabbing down, the tip of the blade piercing both picture and frame, pinning it to the table as Shane raised the blade again, repeatedly stabbing down, mangling the image, turning it into nothing more than torn strips of canvas, the faces on it shredded. This done, he climbed onto the boardroom table and, still whooping with pent-up excitement, he unzipped his jeans, and pissed on both table and painting.

Across the room, Ramsey Allen stared at the surrounding scenes in horror. He'd agreed to go with the crew, to see what they did and report back, but this was primal, this was animals staking their claim, marking their territory.

Somewhere deep in this building was likely to be some poor soul who didn't get out in time.

Ramsey quietly picked up a poker from beside the fireplace. It was wrought-iron and heavy, but with everyone around him finding weapons to use in tearing down the house, nobody commented.

Ramsey headed towards the kitchen; he remembered a story of a secret passage down there.

If anyone was still alive, they'd be down there.

Unfortunately, others had the same idea before him, and as he entered the kitchen, he saw the door to one freezer was hanging off its hinges.

'Ah, shit,' he muttered, texting and sending a quick message, taking a deep breath to steady the nerves, and then making his way into the freezer.

THE TUNNEL UNDER THE SHOPS WAS MORE LIKE A MAINTENANCE route than mysterious, home-made hack; thick power lines ran above them as Molly led Anjli and Jess along the concrete corridor, heading as far from the house as they could.

'How long has this been here?' Anjli asked, panting now.

'Oh, we didn't make this,' Molly explained with the calm breaths of youth. 'This was something to do with the Victoria Line expansion about fifty years back. We just built into it.'

She waved ahead.

'This takes us to an underground NCP car park. We can probably get a signal there.'

'Who do you think the men coming in were?' Jess asked.

'Probably connected to Johnny Lucas,' Molly replied. 'Coming for revenge after his death.'

'Great,' Jess wasn't happy about that. 'But who took your mum if it wasn't them?'

'It might have been them as well,' Molly shrugged,

glancing back as a faint rumble passed. Realising it was likely an underground train, Anjli continued.

'It's chaos up there. As far as we know, the whole East End could be a battleground right now.'

'Anita wouldn't send the soldiers to hurt me,' Molly said as they reached a large metal door with NO ENTRY on it. 'She needs me.'

She pushed at the door, but it was stiff, and only moved a few inches. Anjli went to ask what Molly meant by this, but a crash further behind them, and the faint sound of yelling meant that the crowd of men had finally worked out where they were.

'Come on,' Anjli said, slamming her shoulder into the door, forcing it open a few feet now, ushering the others through before placing her shoulder against the other side, pushing it closed. Looking frantically around, with Molly and Jess watching, she saw a discarded mop in a bucket against the wall; grabbing it, she slammed it between the handles of the door, wedging it, as if hoping it'd give them enough time to find a way out.

Looking around, she realised they were now on the lower ground floor of a car park, a couple of cars and a grey Transit van the only other vehicles to be seen.

'What if they're waiting for us?' Molly asked, running towards the van. 'What if we come out and they're there?'

Anjli nodded, as she'd been worrying about this as well.

'I'll go, try to get a signal,' she said. 'We need to find a place for you to hide.'

'No, I'll go,' Jess said. 'I'm younger.'

'Absolutely not,' Anjli stopped, typing a message on her phone. 'I'll try to send a message too, and hopefully if I can't call, it'll get out. But I'm not letting you risk yourself for me. Your dad would kill me.'

She showed the text message to Jess.

'If you don't hear from me after half an hour, go here and wait, okay?' she ordered.

Jess paled as she read the instructions, and glanced at Molly before swallowing and nodding.

'You sure?' she asked.

'Hey, this van is open,' Molly said as she pulled the back door aside. 'We can hide in here and lock the doors. They won't know we're there.'

Anjli nodded, her expression darkening.

'Yeah, I'm sure,' she said to Jess, pushing her at Molly. 'Hide in the van. I'll get them to follow me. When you get a signal, call your dad.'

Jess followed Molly into the van as Anjli closed the door behind them. Then, hearing the click of the lock from inside, she nodded to herself, turned for the exit and ran for it.

'*Come on then you bastards!*' she shouted, typing a new message and pressing send on her phone. '*Come get me if you can!*'

THE INSIDE OF THE VAN WAS SPARSE AND DARK, WHICH HELPED A lot; the seats at the front provided a wall to hide behind, and there were no other windows in the back or sides of it, so for the moment, Jess and Molly were safe in what seemed to be a decorator's van, snuggled in between paint pots and rollers, thankfully clean and dry, amid a large pile of painter's cloths, the sheets laid on the carpets to stop spillages when working.

Jess heard Anjli shout, and could hear her footsteps leaving. Hunkering down, she glanced back at Molly.

'You okay?' she asked.

Molly nodded quietly.

'We'll find your mum,' Jess continued. 'It'll all be fine.'

Molly nodded again, staring at the wall of the van, hugging herself. Jess wanted to say something else, reassure her; but the message Anjli had showed her kept returning to her mind.

And all Jess Walsh could do was sit on a pile of painter's cloths, and hope that Anjli or her father would come here and save her soon.

DECLAN HAD RECEIVED A SECOND TEXT, WITH AN ADDRESS ON the Albert Embankment, this time from Monroe, and it was with an element of frustration and confusion that he waited outside the entrance to Vauxhall Pleasure Gardens, to the east of the Embankment, and the train lines that ran above the arched buildings.

There was a car now approaching; a blue Ford Focus. In it, Declan could see Doctor Marcos and Ellie Reckless, the latter driving the car. Pulling up beside him, Doctor Marcos motioned for him to get into the back.

'Can someone explain what the merry hell is going on?' he snapped. 'I thought Monroe was meeting me?'

'He was, but then a problem came up in Tottenham,' Doctor Marcos explained. 'Don't worry, it's all under control. He's gone with Johnny Lucas to stop a war.'

'Of course he's still alive,' Declan chuckled. 'So what's going on here, then?'

Doctor Marcos pointed at the back doors of one of the arches.

'In there, that's where the takeover's about to happen,' she said. 'Shand Properties is about to have a very strange AGM, and the new king is about to be crowned.'

'Don't you mean queen?' Declan asked. 'I thought this was all about Anita Taborsky getting what's hers?'

'Not quite,' Ellie muttered, turning off the engine. 'Apparently, from what I've heard, it's Maurice Hamilton pulling the strings on behalf of Nicky Simpson.'

Declan took the information in silently, considering it for a moment.

'So what's the plan?'

'Well, there's five people in the company,' Doctor Marcos explained. 'Max Simpson, Janelle Delcourt, Johnny and Jackie Lucas, Kenny and Benny Tsang, although the last two count as one vote each, and Maurice Hamilton as CEO. He's mainly there to break ties on voting.'

'Let me guess,' Declan worked through the numbers. 'Johnny's dead, so his vote is gone, Janelle's being held away from her daughter to confirm her quiescence, Max isn't likely to be there... So it's a two-to-one vote against Kenny.'

'That's pretty much it,' Ellie nodded. 'The plan is to replace all the heads of the table. Anita for Johnny, Jeffrey for Kenneth, Nicky for Max...'

'And Molly for Janelle,' Declan rested his head back on the seat. 'Of course. So how do we stop this?'

Doctor Marcos held up her phone with a smile.

'Well, for a start we're going to bring back the dead,' she said. 'Shall we go gatecrash a meeting?'

28

UNDERNEATH THE ARCHES

KENNETH TSANG HADN'T REALISED THIS WOULD POSSIBLY BE the last meeting of his life when he entered the seemingly abandoned bar underneath the Vauxhall arches.

He'd gone for a fight, that was true enough, but he'd expected to verbally spar.

Instead, he walked through the back entrance, up the stairs and into the upper room bar to find his own, believed-dead nephew holding a gun at him.

'So you're alive,' he said calmly, walking over to the bar on the right of the room. The room was spacious, with brick walls, ornate mahogany and leather booths, and a solid, walnut-coloured floor; however, all of it was fake.

The walls were concrete with fake bricks used to give the impression of a bare wall, the 'mahogany' was simply stained to look that way, the leather nothing more than fancy PVC, the floor was made of Karndene, or similar.

Just like its owner, the bar made itself look more than it was.

'Kenny, I don't want to do this,' Jeffrey said, putting the

gun down on a low table. 'You're family. You're a part of my life.'

'And you don't want the Triads hunting you for the rest of your life,' Kenneth nodded as he looked over at the others in the room. 'Which one of you hid him?'

'I did,' Anita Taborsky, that white-headed witch, stepped forward now. Beside her was that fop Hamilton, to his right, a black kid in a hood, who Kenny assumed was the one with Jackie the night of the abduction.

'You sent Jackie there?'

'I *was* Jackie.'

Kenny considered this, pursed his lips and slow-clapped.

'Well done,' he replied. 'You started a war.'

'No,' Anita smiled. 'You and Johnny Lucas did that. And now he's dead, and they arrested your own men the same day for trying to do the same thing to his girlfriend. Both of you, putting out hits like you're *Scarface*. Looks to me like you've had a bit of a vendetta out on each other.'

Kenny took in a deep breath, finally realising, as he glanced at his nephew.

'You've learned well,' he said. 'So this was the reason you made the move? Meier's Sacrifice?'

Jeffrey stared at Kenny for a long moment.

'You killed my dad when he stepped out of line,' he said. 'You tried to take my empire before I even built it. And you think I give a shit about *chess moves?* I only put that on the door to distract you from Benny disappearing.'

'But the move,' Kenny was struggling here. 'Surely you knew what you intended to do—'

'Man, I just took your piece,' Jeffrey said, picking the gun up again. 'I didn't care what happened next. I wasn't gonna *play* another move. Except for this.'

And, this explained, Jeffrey Tsang fired two bullets into his uncle, watching dispassionately as he slumped to the floor.

'You screw me? You're next,' he muttered at Maurice.

'You forget,' Maurice walked over, taking the gun from Jeffrey and wiping it down with his handkerchief. 'This isn't about screwing anyone over. This is about creating a scene, a moment. Something we can build the war on, before bringing peace back—'

Blam.

Maurice had spun as he spoke, firing point-blank at Kayas Ashad, catching him between the eyes as the hooded man, already dead, his eyes staring into nothing as a trickle of blood fell between them collapsed to the ground as if someone cut his strings.

Now, crouching down, he placed the gun in the late Kenneth Tsang's hand.

'They fought, Kenny was shot, but in his last moments, he grabbed the gun and killed his attacker,' he said, moving Kenny's arm to show a final angle. Then, leaning over, he used Kenny's dead finger to fire twice more.

'After a couple of missed shots,' he explained. 'Ones that also give him gunpowder residue on his hands. And his nephew, poor Jeffrey, held by the evil Johnny and his sidekick Kayas, could get free.'

He applauded Jeffrey as if it was the end of a performance.

'So that's Johnny and Kenny off the board of directors,' Anita smiled. 'Nicky said that Max won't be a problem; all he wants these days is his meds and a comfy chair. That just leaves Janelle and Maurice as the original board members, both of whom can vote on the proposal for new members.'

There was a motion to the side, and a muscular, blonde-haired woman brought into the room a struggling Janelle.

'One of yours?' Maurice asked.

'Johnny's,' Anita smiled. 'Thought it might be nice for Janelle to have some female company at the end.'

She looked over at the blind matriarch.

'You understand, right?' she asked mockingly. 'You vote against us, I kill your beautiful daughter.'

Silently, Janelle simply nodded.

'Right then,' Maurice smiled. 'I call this meeting to order.'

'Just so I know,' a voice spoke from the shadows. 'What point do we get to any other business?'

The group spun around as Declan walked into the room, followed by Doctor Marcos and Ellie Reckless. As Doctor Marcos crouched beside Kenneth, checking for a pulse, Declan grinned.

'I mean, I'm guessing you're voting to change the board,' he said. 'You have the votes, even Nicky doesn't have to come and get his fingers dirty.'

He looked at Maurice.

'He has you for that, doesn't he?' he asked lightly.

'Lies and fallacies,' Maurice snapped. 'He just wants to split us, make us distrust each other.'

'We've always distrusted each other,' Anita stated, pulling her ivory-handled gun out and training it on the new arrivals. Declan held his hands up in a peaceful gesture, smiling as he did so.

'I'm just here to tell you it's over,' he said. 'As we speak, my colleagues are rounding up your accessories, and we'll have you all under lock and key within a few hours.'

He pointed at the gun.

'So you might as well drop the weapon, *Jackie*,' he finished.

Anita Taborsky did nothing of the kind, instead laughing as she looked over at Janelle Delcourt.

'Did you know about this?' she snapped. 'Was this you?'

'Would you blame her?' Declan walked into the centre of the group now. 'After all, you're the one who turned her own daughter against her.'

'Is Molly okay?' Janelle asked, her voice only a whisper.

'She's being picked up as well,' Declan replied.

'This is bullshit,' Jeffrey Tsang muttered from the wall. 'The guy knows nothing. Let's just kill him and move on. There ain't nobody outside.'

'You could,' Maurice added, stroking his chin as he considered the horrific option, 'but, we need to know if he's bluffing. I, for one, don't want to walk out into a police wagon.'

Declan gave the group a moment to consider this before continuing.

'Tell you what,' he offered. 'Let me do you a deal. I'll tell you what I know, and what I've deduced so far, and if I'm wrong? Then we can decide how to proceed. But—' and with this he lowered his voice, bringing the group in, '—if I'm right? Then you'd better drop that gun because I'm done playing.'

Anita considered this, nodding to the others.

'Well, go on then,' she muttered. 'Amaze us all.'

'First off, let me congratulate you,' Declan slowly clapped his hands as he turned in a slow circle. 'You really did a good job here. And there was every chance you could have gotten away with it. Until you didn't.'

'What gave it away?' Maurice asked, glaring at Jeffrey as he *tutted* loudly. 'I mean, hypothetically?'

'There's no hypothetical here,' Declan said. 'But even though the motive is simple, the story starts a long time ago, back when Johnny and Jackie were teenagers. The Krays were gone, the gangs were disbanded, and they saw an opportunity, thanks to their elder sister.'

He nodded at Anita.

'You guided them to their first bite of the cherry, didn't you?' he asked. 'Showed them what they could do if they really put their minds to it.'

Anita smiled, performing a mocking bow.

'By the early eighties, Jackie and Johnny are in their twenties and have carved up East London for their own. Mama Delcourt's own mama is running the Seven Sisters, Paddy Simpson is settled after replacing the Richardsons south of the Thames, and the Turk controls West London. Anita sees a Russian gangster, Sergei Taborsky, against the wishes of her brothers, marrying him and leaving the Lucas clan forever,' Declan continued. 'But then it all went wrong, didn't it?'

'Alright, sure, it wasn't a secret,' Anita replied. 'Jackie couldn't bear it. He set up an ambush, attacking and killing Sergei. I thought I was next, so I threw myself on the mercy of the Seven Sisters. Mama Delcourt senior, she gave me protection, and I stayed loyal from then on.'

Declan glanced down at Doctor Marcos; she was staunching the wounds on Kenneth Tsang, and Declan wondered for a moment whether he was still alive, before continuing.

'At this point, Jackie was really losing it,' he started once more. 'It was bad for business. Johnny was the *Tommy Shelby* to his older brother's *Arthur*. The brains who couldn't get the plan into his brother's thick head. The only solution was for him to go.'

Declan shook his head.

'But it didn't work out, did it?'

'No, because he had to pretend Jackie was still around. And, after a while, *Jackie* became real,' Ellie added. 'Guilt, madness, whatever you want to call it. He knew the 'Twins' were scarier than just him.'

'But Jackie was gone,' Declan continued. 'Killed in a Bogotá prison twenty-odd years ago.'

There was silence at this.

'And now we jump,' Declan carried on now, aware he had their attention still. 'Now we're up to modern day—well, a year or so back. And Moses Delcourt decides he wants to take over the North London gangs. However, because he's not a *sister*, he plans a coup instead. One that ends with him in prison, and Mama Delcourt blinded. Now, she knew she was going to be deposed soon; after all, a blind leader only seems to work when they're a ninja or has enhanced senses, according to films and books. Mama Delcourt had neither. What she had was a daughter too young to take over, a daughter that she didn't want to see involved in this world anymore, and a family friend who'd moved in to look after her.'

He turned to Anita.

'But you weren't there to look after her, were you?' he asked with a smile on his face, already knowing the answer. 'You were there to keep her close by, make sure you were inseparable. The queen maker, there to find your moment to take out the old ruler, and replace them yourself.'

'I never wanted the throne of the Seven Sisters,' Anita laughed. 'I could have run the East End if I wanted power.'

'Then why did you do it?' Declan asked, frowning—but then his eyes widened in realisation.

'Molly,' he said.

JESS WATCHED OUT OF THE BACK OF THE VAN, CROUCHING BY the window as Molly snacked on a chocolate bar.

'I don't think they saw us,' she said.

Molly, still eating, nodded.

'Good,' she replied with a half-full mouth. 'I didn't want to be found right now, anyway.'

Jess looked back at the teenager. For someone hiding for her life, she seemed very calm.

'What's the chocolate?' she asked cautiously.

Molly went to reply, but then stopped herself.

'It's a Hershey's,' she eventually replied, realising she'd said too much.

'And you found it in the glove compartment?'

'Yeah.'

Jess leaned back against the wall of the van.

'So the one chocolate you really love just happens to be in here, in the van you found open,' she mused. 'Tell me it's not milk chocolate with almonds.'

Molly stopped eating, placing the bar quietly to the side.

'You played me,' Jess muttered, rising. 'You led me right here. Why?'

'Because I needed this,' Molly said, her hand rising, a gun in it. 'You brought a cop. I said not to do that. I had to wait for her to piss off before I could sort you out.'

Jess almost laughed.

'It's always the daughters that I have problems with,' she muttered as she sat back on the painters' cloths.

'So, did you decide to groom Molly, or did Molly groom *you?*' Declan asked Anita. 'Because, according to my daughter, she seems pretty capable.'

'A bit of both,' Anita replied.

Declan nodded.

'So let's see, you groomed her for the role from an early age, and when Moses was arrested, she blamed her mum for it. Doesn't help she saw the oil painting of the two of them every day. After that, it was easy for you to reel her in.'

Anita didn't reply, staring coldly at Declan.

'But why?' Janelle exploded. 'What did I ever do to you?'

'Nothing,' Anita replied bluntly. 'But you were always a tool to be used. I wanted more than your throne.'

'You wanted London,' Declan stated. 'You wanted what Maurice promised you. The wrong Lucas was getting all the *Shand* money. *You* should have been getting it.'

'Why shouldn't I?' Anita looked over at Maurice, who nodded softly, agreeing. Seeing this, Declan continued.

'You knew as the eldest Lucas you could take over everything. There was just one problem with that. Johnny.'

'He was still powerful, and his men were loyal,' Anita nodded. 'I couldn't beat him as Anita Lucas, the long-forgotten sister. I'd spent too many years opposite him. But I could beat him as his brother. I could use my *own* Jackie to fix my wrongs.'

She looked around the room.

'And then I realised we could *all* use Jackie to do that,' she said. 'Just like Jackie did all *this*, too.'

Declan looked around.

'Jackie killed Kayas?' he asked.

'Oh no,' Anita smiled. 'That was you.'

29

GUNPLAY

DECLAN WEIGHED HIS WORDS CAREFULLY.

'I don't have a gun,' he said splaying his arms out.

'She doesn't need a gun,' Doctor Marcos said, looking up. 'She just needs the story.'

'And the story's the reason we're all here,' Declan said as he watched Anita. 'All of you wanted what you believed was yours. Jeffrey here had an uncle he hated; one who killed his father, and another that wanted his nightclub, one of the few things he'd created on his own. Jackie Lucas was a way to do this, to finish his family rivals without gaining the wrath of the Wo Shing Wo Triad. All he had to do was aim them at Johnny.'

He continued around the room.

'Molly wanted to be queen, but knew you wouldn't allow it,' he said to Janelle. 'Anita wanted her brother to lose his position, and wanted someone she could mould as the new head of the Seven Sisters. Jackie Lucas provided both options. But Jackie was dead—or maybe not.'

Ellie smiled, kneeling beside Doctor Marcos as she assisted the faintly groaning Kenneth Tsang.

'Luckily for you, he wasn't,' she added. 'There was never an official certificate from La Moreno. And Johnny keeping 'the Twins' alive meant that *you* could easily bring Jackie to life. It also helped that, as the sister, you had similar features. Add prosthetics, a wig and a known companion in the late Mickey Trackies, and nobody would doubt you. But his men might.'

Declan walked over to Maurice now.

'What you needed was someone in the know, someone everyone knew of, even if they thought he was a joke, to validate the existence of Jackie Lucas. And here was Maurice once more, always looking for a way to make more money.'

He leant in.

'Tell me,' he half-whispered. 'Did you piss yourself deliberately, or use some sort of device?'

'You sell the moment,' Maurice replied with a surprising hint of pride. 'I convinced Jeffrey to fill the club with Instagram influencers and TikTok names. People constantly looking for things to take photos of and live stream. By the time I faced 'Jackie', a couple were filming.'

He sniffed.

'When they realised that Maurice Hamilton, one-time associate of the Krays, had pissed himself with fear at this new arrival, then they all started filming. We were trending on Twitter by the time she fired the first bullet.'

'No offence, but I don't think most of them knew your name,' Declan gave an apologetic look as he replied. 'But nice touch. And why kill David Banner?'

'Because he was being a bitch,' Jeffery hissed. 'He'd told

his sister to keep away from me. Started mouthing off, saying I wasn't man enough for her.'

'But it wasn't just that, was it?' Declan frowned, shaking his head. 'No, he learned about your plan to get revenge on your uncles, didn't he? Maybe he tried to use it as leverage against you.'

Declan considered the scene, running it through his mind once more.

'You needed a sacrifice, and picked him to be killed.'

He looked back at Anita.

'When you placed the gun in the wound, you did it to give a physical image for the people filming,' he said. 'And then the second shot killed him; not just to sacrifice him, but to show intent, prove that anyone could die here. But mainly, it was to reach the third, blank round, for when you 'shot' Jeffrey, wasn't it?'

'You seem to know everything,' Anita hissed.

Declan nodded, glancing now at Jeffrey.

'Pretty much,' he smiled. 'We guessed about a pint of blood in a bag that was cut open when the gun was held nearby. That way you could spurt it out. Am I close?'

Jeffrey didn't reply, simply nodding.

'I'm guessing Benny was already dead by then,' Declan paced around the room once more. 'The club was closed at six that day, and Mickey was the one with the keys. You spent hours on him, went to the club, faked your abduction, and then returned.'

Jeffrey paused, but then reluctantly nodded again, as Anita hissed at him to stop.

'Uncle Benny was my task,' he admitted, ignoring her. 'All I had to do was make sure he was unrecognisable. Our contacts would do the rest, make sure you found it. The problem was, it wasn't supposed to be found until morning. The timelines didn't match with the midnight discovery, and it made Jackie's appearance in Oxford Street a little confusing.'

'When did you get Cheryl involved?' Doctor Marcos now asked. 'And is she dead?'

'No, she's in the back room, tied up and compliant. Never know when you'll need a patsy,' Anita replied, giving up any pretence now. 'She was an East End girl. Nicky hired her to run security, but she stayed in people's places, drinking their expensive bottles and pretending she was one of them.'

She glanced behind her, back at the storeroom door.

'She was found out, but before they fired her, we decided to use this on her. I gave her a way to live the lifestyle she wanted, and in return, she slept with Johnny. She'd had a thing for him since she was a teenager. She didn't know she was setting him up for murder though, and by the time she worked it out, it was too late and she had to stay the course, or lose everything.'

'Tell me about the meeting with Janelle at the health club,' Declan moved on. 'Why?'

'We wanted to spread disinformation,' Anita shrugged. 'Janelle didn't realise I was even in the car, Molly said only Maurice was with them. And mummy here believed everything her daughter said.'

'So you dressed as Jackie, drove Janelle to a Nicky Simpson health club and pretended to be a financial advisor?'

'I only needed the optics,' Anita replied. 'I didn't care what Janelle wanted to talk about. I wanted Nicky to see us on his CCTV. I wanted people to believe we were all working together.'

'And the photo?'

'That was Molly's idea,' Anita spoke proudly. 'We knew that eventually people would work out that I wasn't Johnny's *Mister Hyde* personality, and you would release Johnny. But if we made it look like they were working together before this, then we could continue to smudge the lines long enough to keep the war going.'

'So you placed the photo of the two of you in the office, and made sure Molly gave us the photo of you in the club, logo carefully placed in the background,' Declan nodded. 'Clever. Didn't work, but clever.'

'Didn't need to work forever,' Maurice, tired of standing, walked over to a bar chair and sat down. 'Can we wrap this up? I'm getting bored.'

'I'm guessing Mickey Trackies was collateral damage?' Declan interrupted before Anita could do anything. 'The first casualty in the war?'

'Yes,' Maurice said, and for the first time Declan heard remorse in his voice. 'He was told to lie low for a few days, but he couldn't help himself. Within an hour of his arrival, everyone in Whitechapel knew he was there. And the moment he climbed out of his hole, someone took a shot.'

'We heard from witnesses, that Mickey knew his killer,' Declan looked back at Jeffrey. 'This was you, back from the dead, which would have really thrown him, as Mickey thought your death was real.'

Jeffrey looked to the ceiling.

'He was surprised, yeah,' he replied. 'I thought it'd be better for me to do it, as I had an alibi, being dead and all that.'

'So Nicky Simpson wasn't involved?'

With no answer to his question forthcoming, Declan walked to the window, staring out.

'Jackie Lucas abducts Jeffrey Tsang and kills his uncle Benny. Kenneth Tsang starts a war with the East End, with both Kenneth and Johnny Lucas likely wiping each other out. Then, when the dust settles, Mama Delcourt, or more likely Molly, learns where Jeffrey is, frees him and returns him to his family. Now, with no uncles to tell him what to do, Jeffrey takes over the west of London, Anita returns to Globe Town, perhaps with Maurice guiding her, to take over the firm and Molly moves into her mother's role, ending the war, and letting the house prices build back up just in time for a healthy profit to be made. How am I doing?'

'Close,' Maurice smiled. 'As CEO, I could bring them into the company, so we could replace the dearly departed. I was just the conduit for change.'

'Oh, no need to be bashful,' Declan smiled now, and for the first time since he arrived there, he gave off a definite sense of foreboding. 'You'd gain a lot once the dust settled. And your boss comes in and hoovers up the remains.'

There was a moment of confusion as the others in the room looked around at each other.

'Didn't he tell you?' Declan asked. 'Maurice has been working for Nicky Simpson. Well, he started with Max, his dad, but he's been really pulling his weight recently.'

Anita's eyes widened as she realised what Declan was implicating.

'Simpson wanted you to fight each other, to go to war,' Declan straightened. 'He wasn't helping you, he was fattening you up. Killing off your soldiers so that when he came in, you wouldn't be able to stop him. Allowing you to place him on this board without him ever having to set foot near you, with his own puppet at the helm. The Richardsons finally getting one over on the Krays.'

'You traitor,' Janelle hissed. 'If I could see you, I'd kill you.'

'Look, he's just saying anything to play for time!' Maurice pleaded. 'Don't listen to his lies! Let's just get on with it and move on!'

Anita waved the gun at Doctor Marcos and Ellie, motioning for them to rise.

'Well done,' she said. 'But you won't be telling anyone. By now, Molly has your daughter at gunpoint, and is waiting for our call. A little backup plan, you see, in case you tried to ruin our game. If she receives it? Jess—it is Jess, isn't it?—goes free. You will have killed Kenneth and Kayas, and your two friends over there and, overcome by guilt, taken your own life... but your child would live.'

'And if I don't?' Declan's voice was soft.

'Then she kills your daughter very slowly,' Maurice rose from the bar stool. 'She learned well from her mother.'

The room was silent as the people in it waited for Declan's response.

'Yeah,' he said, shaking his head as he spoke. 'That's not gonna happen. You see, Molly may have learned from Janelle there, but Jess? She learned from *me*. So come on then, let's take a vote. Let's see how it goes, before the world ends.'

Maurice and Anita looked at each other in confusion.

'Why bother?' Anita eventually asked. 'Maurice and Janelle will vote to change the board. Johnny is dead, and Max is abstaining. Even if Kenneth votes against us, he loses by a margin of two to one.'

'And if Janelle goes against you?' Ellie asked.

'She knows better than to,' Anita smiled. 'She puts Molly on the board, I'll let her stay as ruler until Molly comes of age. Sure, she's a surrogate, a puppet, but what other work is the blind bitch going to find?'

Declan nodded.

'And if it's a tie?'

'I'd be remarkably impressed to see that,' Maurice laughed. 'You have a ouija board?'

'No, we have this,' Ellie rose now, phone out, screen facing Maurice and Anita. On it was the smiling face of Johnny Lucas, live by video call.

'Hi everyone,' he grinned. 'Yeah, you might have shot your bolt a little too soon, sis. Looks like I'm not dead after all. And, if that's the case, and Kenny's still breathing, thank you so much. Because you've taken a war and created peace, because if he's your enemy and I'm your enemy…' he let the phrase tail off.

'I vote to remove Maurice Hamilton from the board of directors,' he said.

'I do… too…' Kenneth Tsang feebly whispered.

Maurice cursed.

'I say nay,' Anita replied, looking at Janelle's handler, passing the woman her gun. 'If she goes against us, shoot her. Before she makes it permanent.'

'Looks like it's up to you,' Declan said to Janelle. 'No matter what happens, you've lost Molly. She's gone down a dark path, and you might not get her back.'

'I'm sorry she took your girl,' Janelle replied. 'I truly am.'

'Just get on with it so we can end this,' Maurice sighed. 'I'm hungry.'

'I—I vote to remove Maurice Hamilton,' Janelle hissed. 'And with Max abstaining, that makes it three votes to one, you prick.'

'This is bullshit!' Maurice exclaimed. 'It means nothing!'

Anita looked back at the handler.

'She made her move, now end her,' she ordered angrily. The blonde handler, however, simply smiled, aiming the gun now at Anita.

'I don't work for you, bitch,' she said with a shrug. 'I work for her.'

As Anita looked across the room, she realised that Ellie Reckless was now smiling.

'This is Tinker Jones,' she said. 'She's my—well, let's call her my driver.'

'It's over,' Declan said as Ellie disconnected the call. 'The police are outside, there's no escape for any of you. Don't make it harder for yourselves.'

'Your daughter's dead,' Anita hissed. 'Molly will kill her as revenge. They've been in a van together, waiting for help that'll never come. A van I set up, and one with a revolver for her to use. A first kill, to place her on the right path.'

'Yeah, I'm not sure about that,' Declan shrugged, a slight hit of a smile on his lips. 'I have to say, though—bad parenting. Seriously. But you see, she was with Anjli Kapoor. And there's not a better copper, a more astute copper in the entire force. Even if my daughter didn't see through this, Anjli would have.'

He relaxed, leaning against a pillar, as in the distance the sound of sirens, many sirens, could be heard. To the side, he saw Ellie Reckless take the gun from Kenneth's hand, now aiming it at Jeffrey.

'Call her, see what she says,' he added. 'I'll wait.'

Molly hadn't taken her eye off Jess since the gun appeared five minutes earlier. Jess, for her part, had simply relaxed into the pile of cloths.

'You'll be my first,' Molly explained. 'The daughter of the copper who took my brother, who took my mother's sight.'

'First? Your brother, from what I hear, was a grade A douche,' Jess replied casually. 'And second, your mother couldn't even kill herself, so I'm guessing you won't be able to do this.'

She smiled.

'Also, if you wanted me dead, you would have done it. I reckon you're keeping me on ice until something happens. Maybe until someone turns up?'

'Shut up,' Molly said.

'Do you have any of your chocolate?' Jess held a hand out. 'Dying woman's request?'

'You need to take this more seriously!' Molly snapped, almost petulantly. 'I could kill you!'

'You won't kill me,' Jess shook her head. 'Anita won't let you. She doesn't want a traumatised teenager, she needs someone to walk into the darkness slowly. You're probably waiting for someone to get us.'

As if called to existence by this, there was a knock on the door.

'Miss Delcourt,' a male voice spoke. 'I've been sent to bring you to your mother. She needs persuasion.'

'Who sent you?' Molly shouted out, gun now aimed at the door.

'Anita Lucas,' the voice said. 'The queen of the East End.'

'Tell me something only she would know.'

'She was in the car with you when you drove to Battersea,'

the voice said. 'She sat in front of you, but she was in disguise.'

With a triumphant smile at Jess, Molly opened the back doors to the van—

To stare at a squad of officers, a man in a three-piece tweed suit at the front.

'Hi,' he said, holding up a warrant card. 'DC Fitzwarren, City police. Put the gun down, please.'

Molly stumbled back into the van, the fear of being caught obvious on her face—but Jess, now with the extendable baton out, clipped down hard on her wrist, shattering the bone, the gun dropping to the floor as Molly screamed out in pain. As she struggled to get away from Jess, pinning her down, Jess leant close, whispering in her ear.

'Anjli showed me a text,' she breathed. 'She knew you were aiming us here. She guessed you were bait. I was told to keep you occupied until we worked out what was going on.'

She nodded at Anjli, standing to the side.

'Looks like we worked out what was going on.'

'Bitch—get off me—'

'You weren't even a threat,' Jess finished, leaning back as De'Geer moved in now, grabbing Molly and cuffing her. 'They'll eat you up in juvenile detention.'

Anjli came in now, hugging her.

'You okay?' she asked, visually checking her over. 'She didn't hurt you?'

'I'm good,' Jess said as she climbed out of the van. 'Dad?'

'They contacted Johnny Lucas while he was calming his men down,' Anjli replied. 'I think they're sorted.'

Among the other police officers was a very stressed looking DCI Farrow, who ran forwards now.

'I'm so sorry,' he said, grabbing her hand. 'I shouldn't have let you go with your father. I'll tell your mother—'

'Nothing,' Jess replied coldly. 'Henry, this wasn't on my dad, this was on me. I'll keep quiet if you do, okay?'

Farrow smiled and nodded.

'You're definitely a Walsh,' he said, looking up in confusion. 'Can anyone else hear a phone going off?'

EPILOGUE

WITH HER WEAPON GONE, THE PHONE UNANSWERED AND WITH guns now aimed at her, the fight finally left Anita Lucas, and she slumped to the ground, her head hanging low.

'All these years,' she hissed. 'All to fail.'

Maurice and Jeffrey stood sullenly to the side as, with Kenneth stable, Doctor Marcos went into the side room and brought out a sobbing and tied Cheryl Jenkins, her makeup smudged and stained with tears. As the police finally arrived, Declan handcuffed Anita himself, allowing her to be led out as he walked over to the fallen, dead form of Kayas Ashad.

'Bloody idiot,' he mumbled. 'Your taste in leaders was always shite.'

Kenneth Tsang was being placed onto a gurney by paramedics, Doctor Marcos at his side, and Declan again wondered what that mysterious past she had with the Tsangs was, before deciding he probably didn't want to know. And, walking out into the fresh air, he was rewarded by a call from Jess, telling him everything was okay, Johnny Lucas had stopped a war and Molly was in custody, although she may have broken her wrist in her attempted escape. Anjli had also come onto the phone, explaining that *some old guy in an ascot tie* had gone mental at the other looters, holding them back until Johnny, Anjli, and the police returned.

'You've got a good team,' Ellie said as she walked out, Tinker by her side.

'So have you,' Declan replied. 'I think your guy Ramsey saved my daughter's life.'

'So then you owe me a favour,' Ellie smiled. 'I'll add it to the two Johnny Lucas owes me.'

'Listen,' Declan started, and from the tone Ellie could see he was serious. 'I don't know what happened with you and Bryan Noyce, and I don't know how you'll clear your name, but know this. Whatever you need, whenever you need it, I'll be there for you. Okay?'

'Silly rabbit,' Ellie *boop*ed Declan's nose. 'That's what a favour *is*.'

And, with Tinker taking the keys and settling into the driver's seat, Ellie Reckless climbed into her car, nodded at Declan and drove off.

'He got away with it,' Doctor Marcos said as she walked over. 'Nicky Simpson. Didn't turn up, can't be nailed on any of this, and in the process he removed some major players on his chessboard.'

Declan looked at the people being placed in cars; Anita Lucas, Jeffrey Tsang and Maurice Hamilton were going the way of Moses Delcourt; none of them would be on the streets again for a very long time. And nothing would change; Kenny Tsang would run the west, as before, Janelle Delcourt the north, as before, Johnny Lucas the east, as before and Nicky Simpson the south.

As before.

'At least the Tsangs and the Lucas clan might get something out of this,' he suggested. Doctor Marcos stifled a laugh.

'You think?' she exclaimed. 'There's still Mickey Trackie's death, and a Chinese casino's arson to negotiate. This war might go on for years.'

Declan shrugged noncommittally.

'I live in hope,' he replied.

'That's what I love about you, Declan,' Doctor Marcos slid an arm through his as they walked away from the crime scene. 'Your undying, naïve optimism.'

AFTER TWO WEEKS, JESS RETURNED HOME TO HER MUM, WHO was eager to show her daughter the new engagement ring she now wore on her finger, complete with the whole story of how it came out of the blue, she hadn't pegged Henry to have such good taste in rings, and how she was lucky to have a man like this—with an apology to Declan for saying such a thing in front of him. Declan smiled in return, gave the requisite number of impressed *oohs* and *aahs* at it, promised he was totally alright with this, and that he completely approved of Henry Farrow, before making his excuses and returning to the Command Unit. With the case now solved, and the job now not to arrest the perpetrators, but to make sure they stayed arrested, the last few days had been filled with unending paperwork.

And, for a change, Declan was happy with that.

On her last day, Jess had been given an honorary unit mug, and told she could work a case with them any time, although Declan did point out that staying in the Unit building, and never being allowed out again was a deal breaker from now on. Billy pointed out that once more, he'd found himself at the other end of a gun, but nobody gave him any sympathy, because he'd kind of brought it on himself.

Cheryl Jenkins and Janelle Delcourt gave detailed statements, but they did the latter in secret, while she officially returned to her duties as Mama Delcourt, matriarch of the Seven Sisters. Although Declan could see now a weariness in her demeanour that wasn't there before, a shame, almost, that even with everything she gave them, her children still came out worse than she could ever have feared.

Cheryl, meanwhile, apologised to Johnny, explaining why she'd been forced to do this. Surprisingly, he accepted her apology and took her back, his legal firm covering her defence. Declan hoped that this was actual love, rather than a need to have her released, so she could be taken somewhere and made to disappear quietly. Declan agreed to monitor the situation, just in case.

Nicky Simpson kept building his empire, making his YouTube videos and raising his subscriber numbers.

'I CAN'T BELIEVE IT'S THE END OF AUGUST,' MONROE SAID AS they walked through Meath Park, in Globe Town. 'Soon the leaves will come down. And then the bloody bairns will start knocking down conkers from the trees, and those spiky buggers will land on our heads.'

'I don't think kids play with conkers anymore,' Declan replied. 'I think it's all Switches and Consoles and suchlike.'

'That's it, Walsh, kill my dreams you blasted doomsayer,' Monroe nodded over to a corner of the park, where a small gathering of people stood. Among them was Anjli, and she smiled, giving a little wave.

'The little wave was for you, in case you didn't guess it,' Monroe smiled. 'You guys doing okay?'

'Yeah,' Declan watched Anjli return to the gathering, a small smile on his lips. 'We're taking it easy, getting to know each other. With Jess gone, although it's weird not having her around, it's better. We don't have to be on our best behaviour.'

'Aye, that can be a bugger.'

'And you and Doctor Marcos?'

'Aye, we're surviving,' Monroe kicked a stone. 'She's spent a lot of time with Kenneth Tsang while he's recuperated, and that's been a strain, time wise, but we're strong, laddie. You never know, I might even ask you to come with me, pick out a ring.'

Declan laughed.

'The day that happens, I'll—'

He stopped.

'You're serious?'

Monroe shrugged.

'Let's just get through this, aye?' He replied. 'Where's Billy, anyway?'

'On a date with his Colombian friend.'

'Again?' Monroe sighed. 'Poor De'Geer. Prettiest man in the Unit, and all us ugly ones get the girls.'

'I think he's fine with that,' Declan said as they walked up to the crowd, Declan moving next to Anjli.

At the front was Johnny Lucas, a whisky in his hand. He was sober, but he'd obviously been talking for a while. Behind him, on the rose garden, was a plaque; on it read *MICHAEL 'THE FIST' KENT*.

'I let him down,' Johnny was saying. 'I let him down, and

he died because of me. Because of my sister. Because of Jackie.'

There was a faint murmuring to this. Declan noted DCI Esposito and DS McAlroy on the other side of the group; they were there for the same reason Declan was, to show a willingness to continue a relationship with the crime lord, but only if it was along their terms.

Esposito had almost lost his job, when it came out he'd faked Johnny's death with the help of Ellie Reckless, but Bullman had convinced Bradbury to claim credit, saying it was an inter-Unit sting operation, and that Esposito and his team had gone beyond duty to save many lives.

They'd even pinned a medal on him. Or given him a glass paperweight, one of the two. And Declan had once more wondered what the relationship that Bullman had with Bradbury truly was.

'So today, we bury two people,' Johnny said. 'The memory of Mickey, and the memory of Jackie. No more will the Twins rule. Now I will lead. A community leader with a wealth of knowledge and a firm belief in justice and social reform, I announce my candidacy for the role of MP for Bethnal Green and Bow, at the upcoming By-Election.'

As the surrounding crowd started applauding, Declan glanced at Anjli.

'Did you know this?' he asked, half in shock. Anjli's equally shocked expression gave all the answers he needed.

'Great,' Declan sighed, staring up at the late-August sky. 'Another bloody politician.'

DI Walsh and the team of the *Last Chance Saloon* will return in their next thriller

STALKING THE RIPPER

Released 10th July 2022

Order Now at Amazon:

http://mybook.to/stalkingtheripper

Ellie Reckless and her team
will return in their debut thriller

PAINT
— THE —
DEAD

Released 29th May 2022

Order Now at Amazon:
http://mybook.to/paintthedead

or read on for a sneak preview…

ROOFTOP VIEW

TO SOME PEOPLE, THE SKYLINE OF THE CITY OF LONDON AT night was like a cluster of sparkling jewels, each shining brightly as they boasted their existence out to the world; each a window, an office still lit up, people still working, going about their lives, and unaware, for the moment, of the world outside. Some windows might even have people staring out at their *own* skylines, but with the lights on, they were more likely to be checking their own reflections in the full-length mirrors that the windows became after the sunset.

For Ellie Reckless, the skyline was something she'd looked at every day. It was an old friend, although tonight, it seemed to have had a bit of a *falling out* with her.

'As fun as this is and all that, can we move on?' she asked politely, a hint of tiredness in her voice. 'I've got a dinner date.'

Ellie was in her mid-to-late-thirties, her dark brown, almost-black hair shoulder length and curly, with the look of a style that had started the day in a bunch, but at some point had just given up the whole idea. She was wearing a cheap navy suit, and a pastel open-necked and collared blouse, both of which were badly clashing with the grey *Converse* trainers she wore on her feet. They weren't the Chuck Taylor 'high top' style that was still popular; they were the 'ox' style of low ankle trainers, favoured by Ellie purely because it meant she could kick them off when she got home, and didn't have to fiddle drunkenly with the laces before collapsing into her bed.

Not that she was expecting to be doing that tonight, she thought to herself as she played a smile for the audience. *Right now she'd be happy if she managed a hospital bed rather than the morgue.*

Her audience comprised what could only be described as a bag of muscles that had squashed into a tight-fitting grey suit, with a shaven, flushed head plonked on top; this was Josh, and he was the one who had a gun aimed at her. Ellie, however, knew that although Josh was the one with the weapon, he wasn't the one that was going to be a problem.

The problem was the runt of a man that was currently leaning against an air conditioning unit, watching her with the weakest attempt of a *sneer*.

Walker.

A skinny, balding, middle-aged *dickhead* in a shiny three-piece suit, obviously bought off the peg from one of those super-cheap market shops that claimed to be *Italian menswear*, Walker was a man who believed that he was *better* than his station in life.

'Oh, you do, do you?' he asked mockingly, the slight sneer now resting comfortably on his lips. 'That's a shame, because Josh here was gonna shoot you in the face.'

Ellie tutted, shaking her head.

'Christ, how did I find myself in the middle of a bloody amateur hour?' she asked herself, perhaps a little too loudly.

'You have a problem with being shot in the face?' Walker enquired, a little surprised by the response.

Ellie shrugged.

'It's just stupid, that's all,' she replied. 'I mean, we're on a rooftop. Why don't you just throw me off? That way, you don't have to explain the bullet when forensics finds it, and you can just claim that I fell.'

Walker looked at Josh, who didn't look back, eyes and weapon still trained on Ellie as she continued.

'I'm guessing you're both pretty bad at this, because maybe you've not had much experience before?' she asked, looking at Josh. 'Am I right?'

Josh shrugged noncommittally at this, a motion that irritated Walker immensely. But before he could reply, he realised Ellie was looking at him now, a smile forming on her lips.

'Look, Mister Walker, I get why you're pissed at me,' she said calmly. 'I came to steal your Lamborghini.'

'Damn right I got a problem with you about that,' Walker hissed.

Ellie held a hand up to stop him.

'But, you see, I'm doing this on behalf of my client, Big Slim, who *you* stole the Lamborghini from.'

It was Walker's turn to shrug now.

'If he's got a problem with that, then he should go to the police,' he replied.

Ellie nodded, as if agreeing.

'But then he'd have to explain to them how he got it in the first place,' she stated calmly, still watching Walker, even though Josh was the one with the gun. 'And we both know that's not gonna happen.'

Walker considered Ellie for a long moment, as if measuring her up.

'You know, I've heard of you,' he eventually said. 'Ellie Reckless, the bitch that works for favours.'

'Sometimes,' Ellie replied calmly.

'Working for cash is better,' Walker offered.

'Depends on the favour,' Ellie smiled again.

Walker moved closer to Ellie now, a quick movement that encroached on her personal space, forcing her to step backwards, moving closer to the edge of the building.

'You might make the suits shit themselves, but you don't mean nothing to me,' he hissed. 'You're nothing but a corrupt ex-cop, and we got tons of them on the books.'

Ellie bristled at this.

'I'm not corrupt,' she whispered.

Walker laughed at her answer.

'Of course you are,' he mocked. 'Nobody gets kicked off the force for being a Girl Scout, *ex-* Detective Inspector Reckless.'

He smiled.

'As I said, I've heard of you.'

'If you had, you'd know that I quit the force,' Ellie's back was against the edge of the building now.

'Jumped before you were pushed, more like,' Walker replied. 'Still, you've made a big splash in what, under a year since you lost your job? Lot of favours owed to you in that time, so I hear.'

He spat to the ground.

'Like that'll mean anything.'

'Your point?' Ellie frowned at this. In response, Walker chuckled.

'You ask a criminal to owe you, to repay this favour… do you honestly think they'll actually *do* it? That Big Slim will give you something you ask for, once his Lambo is back in his garage?' Walker laughed. 'Christ, no. Why would they?'

'Because they know if they don't, I'll burn a bigger favour to remove them,' Ellie's voice was cold and dead. 'I've done it before, and people know it. And as much as they probably want to screw me over—and yes, I know there's no *honour among thieves*—they're too scared of what would happen if they *refuse*.'

She shrugged.

'Also, they *want* me on their side,' she added. 'I can do things, find things, solve problems better than any of their other guys, and my favours are usually cheaper in the long run.'

Walker considered this for a moment, before smiling widely, as if looking like a brilliant idea had suddenly come into his head.

'Josh, mate. Don't waste a bullet. Throw Miss Reckless over the edge, will you?'

Josh, placing away the gun carefully, started towards Ellie, who raised up her hands.

'Wait!' she protested. 'Don't I get a last phone call at least?'

Josh stopped, looking at Walker.

'Calling the cops?' Walker asked.

Ellie spat to the side.

'Please,' she scoffed. 'They'd want tickets to watch. You can toss me off the building in a moment, but don't insult me.'

Walker watched Ellie now, as if trying to work out whether this was some kind of plan. Then, relenting, he stepped back, motioning for Ellie to pull out her phone.

'You call anyone I don't like, or try anything stupid...' he muttered, leaving the ending empty, the warning obvious. Ellie flashed him a grin as a reply, moving through her contacts list.

'We're not up here by chance, are we?' she asked. 'I mean, you have offices in the building, right?'

'So what?' Walker looked at Josh now, confused.

Ellie tapped a contact, letting it dial.

'I was just confirming that you distributed for Johnny Lucas,' she replied.

Walker didn't like the way this conversation was going.

'And what if I do?'

Ellie held up a finger to silence him as her call connected.

'Johnny? It's Ellie,' she said into the mouthpiece. 'Ellie Reckless. Sorry to call so late.'

She held a hand over the mouthpiece as she looked at Walker.

'I think he was asleep,' she whispered. 'He's not happy. Maybe it's Jackie, he's a miserable bastard at the best of times. Nah, that personality's gone now, hasn't he?'

'Wait,' Walker looked nervous now. 'You're calling Johnny Lucas?'

But Ellie had already returned to the phone.

'Those favours you owe me?' she asked conversationally. 'When I saved your arse recently? I'm calling one in. You know a "Walker" that works for you?'

She stopped, listening, looking back at the now scared, weary-looking man.

'He asks what's your first name?'

'Bill,' Walker replied automatically.

Ellie gave a cheerful thumbs up.

'Bill, or maybe William,' she said into the phone. 'Yeah, that's the one. Terrible shiny suits.'

As she continued, she looked directly at Walker.

'I want him removed from your organisation,' she said. 'No, I don't care how, I just want it done immediately. Do that, and you only owe me *one* favour.'

A moment later, she looked down at the phone as the call disconnected, before looking back at Walker, an almost apologetic expression on her face, as if she'd heard something bad, and didn't know how to explain it.

'He didn't even argue,' she said. 'That's how little you matter to him.'

'What did you just do?' Walker spat, his face pale now.

Ellie moved away from the wall as Josh, realising what was happening already pulled out his gun in preparation, Walker now the one stepping back as she encroached on *his* space.

'I'm the cop for criminals, the one that takes cases for favours,' Ellie replied softly. 'You already know that. But the thing is, these favours? They're set before I take on the case. If I work for a favour, then that favour can be called in at any *time*, about any *thing*, and at any *size*. If it's within your remit, you *have* to do it. And as I've already said, you *don't* want to see what happens if you refuse. You understand?'

Nervously, Walker licked his lips as he nodded.

'Basically, if you take the deal, then you pretty much have something big and bad you need sorted. And your boss, Mister Lucas? A little while back, he had something big and bad that he needed, well, to be sorted. You may have heard of it. And I did it for a favour.'

Walker was continuing to back away; he'd heard the rumours of how Johnny Lucas had stopped a recent gangland coup on his territory, and had also heard whispers of Reckless' involvement, but Ellie hadn't finished just yet.

'Now I take these cases, because I want these favours. I'm banking them, you see, chits from the biggest and most brutal out there. I have a plan for them, too. But sometimes? Sometimes you just need to burn one to remove an irritation.'

She looked over at Josh now.

'There'll be a job opportunity opening up soon, mate. Might want to check for a text.'

Josh nodded, pulling out his phone, watching it intently.

'What are you doing?' Walker wailed to his bodyguard, still not understanding the situation he was now in.

'He's wondering if he'll be the one that gives you the severance package,' Ellie replied. 'The one thing he *won't* be doing is tossing me off this building, because he doesn't yet know what other favours I have set up, ones that go into action after my death, aimed at whoever kills me.'

Walker was hopping from foot to foot now, nervous, angry, almost hysterical. Reaching into his jacket, he pulled out his own gun; a chrome-plated Glock 19.

'I'll give you bloody severance—' he started, but he didn't finish the sentence, as before he could fully extend the gun, Ellie had moved in, now within his reach, grabbing the wrist that held the Glock and twisting, pocketing the Glock into her own jacket as it fell from his pain-filled hand to the sound of a yelp from Walker as she twisted harder, snapping something loudly within the wrist, punctuated by a louder scream.

'Wrong move,' she hissed as, still holding onto the now-broken wrist, she used the momentum to spin Walker around, slamming his head hard into the side of the metal air conditioning unit.

As Walker staggered back, blood streaming from his nose, Ellie grabbed him once more, pulling out a car remote from his pocket before sending him stumbling towards Josh, crumpling to the floor in front of his onetime bodyguard, now staring down at him as if unsure what to do.

'He's all yours, mate,' Ellie said with a weary smile, already walking off towards the rooftop door, while Josh glanced at his phone, still waiting for a message.

'I'll get you for this, Reckless!' Walker, for the moment still untouched by his bodyguard, shouted out angrily.

At the door, Ellie looked back and grinned.

'Good for you. Always stay positive,' she encouraged, before leaving the two men alone on the roof.

THE BUILDING WAS PART OF A HALF-BUILT SCIENCE PARK JUST south of the Thames, to the right of North Greenwich and the O2 Arena. And although those two areas were a hive of tourist activity, this area still felt like the *old* London that the new buildings had tried to replace. As Ellie left the dark brick building and walked across the car park, she could almost hear the theme tune of the Eighties movie *The Long Good Friday* playing, and expected to see Bob Hoskins turn up in his "flash mo-tarr".

Instead, ahead of her was an army-green 1992 Land Rover Defender, complete with khaki material roof and spare wheel on the bonnet, parked up next to a hideous yellow Lamborghini. In front of it, leaning against the bonnet and in her own olive-coloured German Army coat and blue jeans, her curly blonde hair pulled back into a better ponytail than Ellie had managed, currently poking out from under a grey *New York Mets* baseball cap, was a woman, a wide grin on her face.

'Took your time,' she said mockingly.

Ellie smiled. Tinker Jones would have finished this repo job in a matter of moments, and wouldn't have blown a favour on it, Ellie was sure. But, at the same time, Tinker Jones would have racked up a body count that would have had every police force in the district looking for her.

'Here, do something with this,' Ellie said as she approached, passing Tinker the shiny Glock that she'd taken from Walker. 'You know I hate the bloody things.'

She stopped, grabbing Tinker's arm where, around her sleeve, were the telltale signs of blood.

'What's this?' she asked. 'You were only supposed to drive me here, not kick off a fight.'

Tinker shrugged.

'I didn't start it,' she explained. 'Some "locals" wanted me to leave.'

'You should be more careful,' Ellie admonished.

Tinker laughed.

'What about you?' she asked. 'I noted you didn't call me in.'

'Didn't want the body count,' Ellie shrugged.

As if accepting this answer, Tinker nodded to the car.

'You get them?'

Ellie pulled out the remote, waggling it at Tinker.

'Want to take it back to Big Slim?' she asked with a slight smile.

'Christ no,' Tinker laughed. 'I wouldn't be seen dead in that bloody thing.'

Ellie sighed.

'I'll do it then,' she replied. 'Take off for the night and I'll see you tomorrow.'

'Grab some dinner first?' Tinker suggested. 'There's a great street van by the Greenwich Yacht Club. We could leave a kebab in the boot of the lambo, see how long Slim takes to realise.'

Ellie shook her head, glancing at her watch.

'No time,' she replied. 'I want an early night because I've got brunch with the ex tomorrow. Although you're welcome to come along to that, if you want?'

'Brunch with Nathan?' Tinker shuddered. 'That's not a meal, that's an execution squad. I'll pass.'

Ellie nodded, fully understanding what Tinker meant. Which was a shame, because if Tinker had gone, then Nathan might have been on better behaviour.

Who was she kidding? Nathan was always going to be a prick.

'Although I never thought you'd be a brunch kind of person,' Tinker smiled.

'Tomorrow, Caesar's, noon,' Ellie ignored the jibe, pressing a button on the remote and watching one of the Lamborghini doors open slowly.

'We could move it to the *Ritz*?' Tinker suggested innocently. 'We could have little sandwiches with the crusts cut off. I mean, it sounds like you're into that sort of thing now. I hear *Claridges* does an amazing lunch deal.'

In the distance, from the top of a building, they heard a gunshot.

'That sounds ominous,' Tinker whispered, reaching into her jacket instinctively. 'How did you get out again?'

Ellie looked up at the building.

'Burned a favour,' she said. 'Had Walker fired.'

'Did you mean *literally?*' Tinker raised an eyebrow as Ellie shook her head.

'Josh the bodyguard? He's not dumb,' she replied, climbing into the car. 'If he wanted him dead, he could have thrown him off the edge and saved a bullet.'

'And how would he know that?' Tinker climbed up into the Defender's driver's seat.

'Because I told him,' Ellie finished as she closed the driver's door, revved the Lamborghini engine, and sped off into the night.

ACKNOWLEDGEMENTS

When you write a series of books, you find that there are a ton of people out there who help you, sometimes without even realising, and so I wanted to do a little acknowledgement to some of them.

There are people I need to thank, and they know who they are. People who patiently gave advice when I started this back in 2020, the people on various Facebook groups who encouraged me when I didn't know if I could even do this, the designers who gave advice on cover design and on book formatting, all the way to my friends and family, who saw what I was doing not as mad folly, but as something good, including my brother Chris Lee, who I truly believe could make a fortune as a post-retirement copy editor, if not a solid writing career of his own, and Jacqueline Beard MBE, who has copyedited all eleven books so far (including the prequel), as well as my other book, *The Lionheart Curse,* line by line for me, and deserves *way more* than our agreed fee.

Also, I couldn't have done this without my growing army of ARC readers who not only show me where I falter, but also raise awareness of me in the social media world, ensuring that other people learn of my books.

But mainly, I tip my hat and thank you. *The reader.* Who, ten books ago took a chance on an unknown author in a pile of

Kindle books, and thought you'd give them a go, and who has carried on this far with them.

I write Declan Walsh for you. He (and his team) solves crimes for you. And with luck, he'll keep on solving them for a very long time.

Jack Gatland / Tony Lee,
London, April 2022

ABOUT THE AUTHOR

Jack Gatland is the pen name of *#1 New York Times Bestselling Author* Tony Lee, who has been writing in all media for thirty-five years, including comics, graphic novels, middle grade books, audio drama, TV and film for *DC Comics, Marvel, BBC, ITV, Random House, Penguin USA, Hachette* and a ton of other publishers and broadcasters.

These have included licenses such as ***Doctor Who, Spider Man, X-Men, Star Trek, Battlestar Galactica, MacGyver,*** BBC's ***Doctors, Wallace and Gromit*** and ***Shrek***, as well as work created with musicians such as ***Ozzy Osbourne, Joe Satriani, Beartooth*** and ***Megadeth.***

As Tony, he's toured the world talking to reluctant readers with his 'Change The Channel' school tours, and lectures on screenwriting and comic scripting for *Raindance* in London.

An introvert West Londoner by heart, he lives with his wife Tracy and dog Fosco, just outside London.

Locations In The Book

The locations and items I use in my books are real, if altered slightly for dramatic intent. Here's some more information about a few of them...

Tsang City doesn't exist, but the area does; and the BBC Television Centre does now hold restaurants, bars and the West London *White City House.*

The Boxing Club near Meath Gardens in which the brutal instigating murder occurs doesn't exist, and neither do the Twins - but the location used is the current **Globe Town Social Club**, within **Green Lens Studios**, a community centre formerly known as Eastbourne House, that I would pass occasionally in my 20s.

Chinatown, the pedestrianised area north of Shaftesbury Ave exists, and has done for decades now. However, as mentioned in the novel, Chinatown was once based in Limehouse, before moving more central.

The real Chinatown, however is very much a tourist spot, and every February hosts an amazing *Chinese New Year* festival.

The Cirque Apartments don't exist, but are loosely based on the *Circus Apartments* in Canary Wharf. The jetty outside the apartments does however lead to a ferry that crosses the Thames to Rotherhithe, however, and in particular the *Doubletree By Hilton* Hotel. I gained the idea for this scene back in November 2021 when, as a guest of a *Star Trek* convention at the Excel, we stayed here.

In addition, **The Blacksmith's Arms** was first recorded on census in 1793 as *The Smiths* (as it was originally named until 1825), and is located at 129 Rotherhithe Street.

For my American readers, a small piece of trivia; if you ever visit the pub, travel around half a mile north, along the south bank, because there you'll find the remains of the jetty where the *Mayflower* docked, taking on board 65 passengers before sailing to Plymouth on July 1620, preparing for their voyage to America. The Captain of the vessel, Christopher Jones, is buried at nearby St. Mary's church.

The Old Bank of England pub is real, and the description and the history written in the book explain more than I could here, although one thing I don't mention, which is currently (as of writing) true is that in their 'sun garden' is a double decker bus that you can drink in!

Finally, **Simpsons On The Strand** is indeed the restaurant used in *Sherlock Holmes*, and everything I mention in the book is true. At the time of writing, however, it's currently closed, but the website claims it'll reopen later in 2022. Whether it'll be the same as before, we don't know.

If you're interested in seeing what the *real* locations look like, I post 'behind the scenes' location images on my Instagram feed. This will continue through all the books, and I suggest you follow it.

In fact, feel free to follow me on all my social media by clicking on the links below. Over time these can be places where we can engage, discuss Declan and put the world to rights.

www.jackgatland.com
www.hoodemanmedia.com

Subscribe to my Readers List:
www.subscribepage.com/jackgatland

www.facebook.com/jackgatlandbooks
www.twitter.com/jackgatlandbook
ww.instagram.com/jackgatland

Want more books by Jack Gatland? Turn the page...